The Vicar of Tours

Honoré de Balzac

Translated by Katharine Prescott Wormeley

DEDICATION

To David, Sculptor:

The permanence of the work on which I inscribe your name —twice made illustrious in this century—is very problematical; whereas you have graven mine in bronze which survives nations —if only in their coins. The day may come when numismatists, discovering amid the ashes of Paris existences perpetuated by you, will wonder at the number of heads crowned in your atelier and endeavour to find in them new dynasties.

To you, this divine privilege; to me, gratitude.

De Balzac.

The Vicar of Tours

I

Early in the autumn of 1826 the Abbe Birotteau, the principal personage of this history, was overtaken by a shower of rain as he returned home from a friend's house, where he had been passing the evening. He therefore crossed, as quickly as his corpulence would allow, the deserted little square called "The Cloister," which lies directly behind the chancel of the cathedral of Saint-Gatien at Tours.

The Abbe Birotteau, a short little man, apoplectic in constitution and about sixty years old, had already gone through several attacks of gout. Now, among the petty miseries of human life the one for which the worthy priest felt the deepest aversion was the sudden sprinkling of his shoes, adorned with silver buckles, and the wetting of their soles. Notwithstanding the woollen socks in which at all seasons he enveloped his feet with the extreme care that ecclesiastics take of themselves, he was apt at such times to get them a little damp, and the next day gout was sure to give him certain infallible proofs of constancy. Nevertheless, as the pavement of the Cloister was likely to be dry, and as the abbe had won three francs ten sous in his rubber with Madame de Listomere, he bore the rain resignedly from the middle of the place de l'Archeveche, where it began to come down in earnest. Besides, he was fondling his chimera,—a desire already twelve years old, the desire of a priest, a desire formed anew every evening and now, apparently, very near accomplishment; in short, he had wrapped himself so completely in the fur cape of a canon that he did not feel the inclemency of the weather. During the evening several of the company who habitually gathered at Madame de Listomere's had almost guaranteed to him his nomination to the office of canon (then vacant in the metropolitan Chapter of Saint-Gatien), assuring him that no one deserved such promotion as he, whose rights, long overlooked, were indisputable.

If he had lost the rubber, if he had heard that his rival, the Abbe Poirel, was named canon, the worthy man would have thought the rain extremely chilling; he might even have thought ill of life. But it so chanced that he was in one of those rare moments when happy inward sensations make a man oblivious of discomfort. In hastening his steps he obeyed a more mechanical impulse, and truth (so essential in a history of manners and morals) compels us to say that he was thinking of neither rain nor gout.

In former days there was in the Cloister, on the side towards the Grand'Rue, a cluster of houses forming a Close and belonging to the cathedral, where several of the dignitaries of the Chapter lived. After the confiscation of ecclesiastical property the town had turned the passage through this close into a narrow street, called the Rue de la Psalette, by which pedestrians passed from the Cloister to the Grand'Rue. The name of this street, proves clearly enough that the precentor and his pupils and those connected with the choir formerly lived there. The other side, the left side, of the street is occupied by a single house, the walls of which are overshadowed by the buttresses of Saint-Gatien, which have their base in the narrow little garden of the house, leaving it doubtful whether the cathedral was built before or after this venerable dwelling. An archaeologist examining the arabesques, the shape of the windows, the arch of the door, the whole exterior of the house, now mellow with age, would see at once that it had always been a part of the magnificent edifice with which it is blended.

An antiquary (had there been one at Tours,—one of the least literary towns in all France) would even discover, where the narrow street enters the Cloister, several vestiges of an old arcade, which formerly made a portico to these ecclesiastical dwellings, and was, no doubt, harmonious in style with the general character of the architecture.

The house of which we speak, standing on the north side of the cathedral, was always in the shadow thrown by that vast edifice, on which time had cast its dingy mantle, marked its furrows, and shed its chill humidity, its lichen, mosses, and rank herbs. The darkened dwelling was wrapped in silence, broken only by the bells, by the chanting of the offices heard through the windows of the church, by the call of the jackdaws nesting in the belfries. The region is a desert of stones, a solitude with a character of its own, an arid spot, which could only be inhabited by beings who had either attained to absolute nullity, or were gifted with some abnormal strength of soul. The house in question had always been occupied by abbes, and it belonged to an old maid named Mademoiselle Gamard. Though the property had been bought from the national domain under the Reign of Terror by the father of Mademoiselle Gamard, no one objected under the Restoration to the old maid's retaining it, because she took priests to board and was very devout; it may be that religious persons gave her credit for the intention of leaving the property to the Chapter.

The Abbe Birotteau was making his way to this house, where he had lived for the last two years. His apartment had been (as was now the canonry) an object of envy and his "hoc erat in votis" for a dozen years. To be Mademoiselle Gamard's boarder and to become a canon were the two great desires of his life; in fact they do present accurately the ambition of a priest, who, considering himself on the highroad to eternity, can wish for nothing in this world but good lodging, good food, clean garments, shoes with silver buckles, a sufficiency of things for the needs of the animal, and a canonry to satisfy self-love, that inexpressible sentiment which follows us, they say, into the presence of God,—for there are grades among the saints. But the covetous desire for the apartment which the Abbe Birotteau was now inhabiting (a very harmless desire in the eyes of worldly people) had been to the abbe nothing less than a passion, a passion full of obstacles, and, like more guilty passions, full of hopes, pleasures, and remorse.

The interior arrangements of the house did not allow Mademoiselle Gamard to take more than two lodgers. Now, for about twelve years before the day when Birotteau went to live with her she had undertaken to keep in health and contentment two priests; namely, Monsieur l'Abbe Troubert and Monsieur l'Abbe Chapeloud. The Abbe Troubert still lived. The Abbe Chapeloud was dead; and Birotteau had stepped into his place.

The late Abbe Chapeloud, in life a canon of Saint-Gatien, had been an intimate friend of the Abbe Birotteau. Every time that the latter paid a visit to the canon he had constantly admired the apartment, the furniture and the library. Out of this admiration grew the desire to possess these beautiful things. It had been impossible for the Abbe Birotteau to stifle this desire; though it often made him suffer terribly when he reflected that the death of his best friend could alone satisfy his secret covetousness, which increased as time went on. The Abbe Chapeloud and his friend Birotteau were not rich. Both were sons of peasants; and their slender savings had been spent in the mere costs of living during the disastrous years of the Revolution. When Napoleon restored the Catholic worship the Abbe Chapeloud was appointed canon of the cathedral and Birotteau was made vicar of it. Chapeloud then went to board with Mademoiselle Gamard. When Birotteau first came to visit his friend, he thought the arrangement of the rooms excellent, but he noticed nothing more. The outset of this concupiscence of chattels was very like that of a true passion, which often begins, in a young man, with cold admiration for a woman whom he ends in loving forever.

The apartment, reached by a stone staircase, was on the side of the house that faced south. The Abbe Troubert occupied the ground-floor, and Mademoiselle Gamard the first floor of the main building, looking on the street. When Chapeloud took possession of his rooms they were bare of furniture, and the ceilings were blackened with smoke. The stone mantelpieces, which were very badly cut, had never been painted. At first, the only furniture the poor canon could put in was a bed, a table, a few chairs, and the books he possessed. The apartment was like a beautiful woman in rags. But two or three years later, an old lady having left the Abbe Chapeloud two thousand francs, he spent that sum on the purchase of an oak bookcase, the relic of a chateau pulled down by the Bande Noire, the carving of which deserved the admiration of all artists. The abbe made the purchase less because it was very cheap than because the dimensions of the bookcase exactly fitted the space it was to fill in his gallery. His savings enabled him to renovate the whole gallery, which up to this time had been neglected and shabby. The floor was carefully waxed, the ceiling whitened, the wood-work painted to resemble the grain and knots of oak. A long table in ebony and two cabinets by Boulle completed the decoration, and gave to this gallery a certain air that was full of character. In the course of two years the liberality of devout persons, and legacies, though small ones, from pious penitents, filled the shelves of the bookcase, till then half empty. Moreover, Chapeloud's uncle, an old Oratorian, had left him his collection in folio of the Fathers of the Church, and several other important works that were precious to a priest.

Birotteau, more and more surprised by the successive improvements of the gallery, once so bare, came by degrees to a condition of involuntary envy. He wished he could possess that apartment, so thoroughly in keeping with the gravity of ecclestiastical life. The passion increased from day to day. Working, sometimes for days together, in this retreat, the vicar could appreciate the silence and the peace that reigned there. During the following year the Abbe Chapeloud turned a small room into an oratory, which his pious friends took pleasure in beautifying. Still later, another lady gave the canon a set of furniture for his bedroom, the covering of which she had embroidered under the eyes of the worthy man without his ever suspecting its destination. The bedroom then had the same effect upon the vicar that the gallery had long had; it dazzled him. Lastly, about three years before the Abbe Chapeloud's death, he completed the comfort of his apartment by decorating the salon. Though the furniture was plainly covered in red Utrecht velvet, it fascinated Birotteau. From the day when the canon's friend first laid eyes on the red damask curtains, the mahogany furniture, the Aubusson carpet which adorned the vast room, then lately painted, his envy of Chapeloud's apartment became a monomania hidden within his breast. To live there, to sleep in that bed with the silk curtains where the canon slept, to have all Chapeloud's comforts about him, would be, Birotteau felt, complete happiness; he saw nothing beyond it. All the envy, all the ambition which the things of this world give birth to in the hearts of other men concentrated themelves for Birotteau in the deep and secret longing he felt for an apartment like that which the Abbe Chapeloud had created for himself. When his friend fell ill he went to him out of true affection; but all the same, when he first heard of his illness, and when he sat by his bed to keep him company, there arose in the depths of his consciousness, in spite of himself, a crowd of thoughts the simple formula of which was always, "If Chapeloud dies I can have this apartment." And yet— Birotteau having an excellent heart, contracted ideas, and a limited mind—he did not go so far as to think of means by which to make his friend bequeath to him the library and the furniture.

The Abbe Chapeloud, an amiable, indulgent egoist, fathomed his friend's desires—not a difficult thing to do—and forgave them; which may seem less easy to a priest; but it must be remembered that the vicar, whose friendship was faithful, did not fail to take a daily walk with his friend along their usual path in the Mail de Tours, never once depriving him of an instant of the time devoted for over twenty years to that exercise. Birotteau, who regarded his secret wishes as crimes, would have been capable, out of contrition, of the utmost devotion to his friend. The latter paid his debt of gratitude for a friendship so ingenuously sincere by saying, a few days before his death, as the vicar sat by him reading the "Quotidienne" aloud: "This time you will certainly get the apartment. I feel it is all over with me now."

Accordingly, it was found that the Abbe Chapeloud had left his library and all his furniture to his friend Birotteau. The possession of these things, so keenly desired, and the prospect of being taken to board by Mademoiselle Gamard, certainly did allay the grief which

Birotteau felt at the death of his friend the canon. He might not have been willing to resuscitate him; but he mourned him. For several days he was like Gargantus, who, when his wife died in giving birth to Pantagruel, did not know whether to rejoice at the birth of a son or grieve at having buried his good Babette, and therefore cheated himself by rejoicing at the death of his wife, and deploring the advent of Pantagruel.

The Abbe Birotteau spent the first days of his mourning in verifying the books in *his* library, in making use of *his* furniture, in examining the whole of his inheritance, saying in a tone which, unfortunately, was not noted at the time, "Poor Chapeloud!" His joy and his grief so completely absorbed him that he felt no pain when he found that the office of canon, in which the late Chapeloud had hoped his friend Birotteau might succeed him, was given to another. Mademoiselle Gamard having cheerfully agreed to take the vicar to board, the latter was thenceforth a participator in all those felicities of material comfort of which the deceased canon had been wont to boast.

Incalculable they were! According to the Abbe Chapeloud none of the priests who inhabited the city of Tours, not even the archbishop, had ever been the object of such minute and delicate attentions as those bestowed by Mademoiselle Gamard on her two lodgers. The first words the canon said to his friend when they met for their walk on the Mail referred usually to the succulent dinner he had just eaten; and it was a very rare thing if during the walks of each week he did not say at least fourteen times, "That excellent spinster certainly has a vocation for serving ecclesiastics."

"Just think," the canon would say to Birotteau, "that for twelve consecutive years nothing has ever been amiss,—linen in perfect order, bands, albs, surplices; I find everything in its place, always in sufficient quantity, and smelling of orris-root. My furniture is rubbed and kept so bright that I don't know when I have seen any dust — did you ever see a speck of it in my rooms? Then the firewood is so well selected. The least little things are excellent. In fact, Mademoiselle Gamard keeps an incessant watch over my wants. I can't remember having rung twice for anything—no matter what— in ten years. That's what I call living! I never have to look for a single thing, not even my slippers. Always a good fire, always a good dinner. Once the bellows annoyed me, the nozzle was choked up; but I only mentioned it once, and the next day Mademoiselle gave me a very pretty pair, also those nice tongs you see me mend the fire with."

For all answer Birotteau would say, "Smelling of orris-root!" That "smelling of orris-root" always affected him. The canon's remarks revealed ideal joys to the poor vicar, whose bands and albs were the plague of his life, for he was totally devoid of method and often forgot to order his dinner. Therefore, if he saw Mademoiselle Gamard at Saint-Gatien while saying mass or taking round the plate, he never failed to give her a kindly and benevolent look,—such a look as Saint Teresa might have cast to heaven.

Though the comforts which all creatures desire, and for which he had so often longed, thus fell to his share, the Abbe Birotteau, like the rest of the world, found it difficult, even for a priest, to live without something to hanker for. Consequently, for the last eighteen months he had replaced his two satisfied passions by an ardent longing for a canonry. The title of Canon had become to him very much what a peerage is to a plebeian minister. The prospect of an appointment, hopes of which had just been held out to him at Madame de Listomere's, so completely turned his head that he did not observe until he reached his own door that he had left his umbrella behind him. Perhaps, even then, if the rain were not falling in torrents he might not have missed it, so absorbed was he in the pleasure of going over and over in his mind what had been said to him on the subject of his promotion by the company at Madame de Listomere's,—an old lady with whom he spent every Wednesday evening.

The vicar rang loudly, as if to let the servant know she was not to keep him waiting. Then he stood close to the door to avoid, if he could, getting showered; but the drip from the roof fell precisely on the toes of his shoes, and the wind blew gusts of rain into his face that were much like a shower-bath. Having calculated the time necesary for the woman to leave the kitchen and pull the string of the outer door, he rang again, this time in a manner that resulted in a very significant peal of the bell.

"They can't be out," he said to himself, not hearing any movement on the premises.

Again he rang, producing a sound that echoed sharply through the house and was taken up and repeated by all the echoes of the

7

cathedral, so that no one could avoid waking up at the remonstrating racket. Accordingly, in a few moments, he heard, not without some pleasure in his wrath, the wooden shoes of the servant-woman clacking along the paved path which led to the outer door. But even then the discomforts of the gouty old gentleman were not so quickly over as he hoped. Instead of pulling the string, Marianne was obliged to turn the lock of the door with its heavy key, and pull back all the bolts.

"Why did you let me ring three times in such weather?" said the vicar.

"But, monsieur, don't you see the door was locked? We have all been in bed ever so long; it struck a quarter to eleven some time ago. Mademoiselle must have thought you were in."

"You saw me go out, yourself. Besides, Mademoiselle knows very well I always go to Madame de Listomere's on Wednesday evening."

"I only did as Mademoiselle told me, monsieur."

These words struck the vicar a blow, which he felt the more because his late revery had made him completely happy. He said nothing and followed Marianne towards the kitchen to get his candlestick, which he supposed had been left there as usual. But instead of entering the kitchen Marianne went on to his own apartments, and there the vicar beheld his candlestick on a table close to the door of the red salon, in a sort of antechamber formed by the landing of the staircase, which the late canon had inclosed with a glass partition. Mute with amazement, he entered his bedroom hastily, found no fire, and called to Marianne, who had not had time to get downstairs.

"You have not lighted the fire!" he said.

"Beg pardon, Monsieur l'abbe, I did," she said; "it must have gone out."

Birotteau looked again at the hearth, and felt convinced that the fire had been out since morning.

"I must dry my feet," he said. "Make the fire."

Marianne obeyed with the haste of a person who wants to get back to her night's rest. While looking about him for his slippers, which were not in the middle of his bedside carpet as usual, the abbe took mental notes of the state of Marianne's dress, which convinced him that she had not got out of bed to open the door as she said she had. He then recollected that for the last two weeks he had been deprived of various little attentions which for eighteen months had made life sweet to him. Now, as the nature of narrow minds induces them to study trifles, Birotteau plunged suddenly into deep meditation on these four circumstances, imperceptible in their meaning to others, but to him indicative of four catastrophes. The total loss of his happiness was evidently foreshadowed in the neglect to place his slipppers, in Marianne's falsehood about the fire, in the unusual removal of his candlestick to the table of the antechamber, and in the evident intention to keep him waiting in the rain.

When the fire was burning on the hearth, and the lamp was lighted, and Marianne had departed without saying, as usual, "Does Monsieur want anything more?" the Abbe Birotteau let himself fall gently into the wide and handsome easy-chair of his late friend; but there was something mournful in the movement with which he dropped upon it. The good soul was crushed by a presentiment of coming calamity. His eyes roved successively to the handsome tall clock, the bureau, curtains, chairs, carpets, to the stately bed, the basin of holy-water, the crucifix, to a Virgin by Valentin, a Christ by Lebrun,—in short, to all the accessories of this cherished room, while his face expressed the anguish of the tenderest farewell that a lover ever took of his first mistress, or an old man of his lately planted trees. The vicar had just perceived, somewhat late it is true, the signs of a dumb persecution instituted against him for the last three months by Mademoiselle Gamard, whose evil intentions would doubtless have been fathomed much sooner by a more intelligent man. Old maids have a special talent for accentuating the words and actions which their dislikes suggest to them. They scratch like cats. They not only wound but they take pleasure in wounding, and in making their victim see that he is wounded. A man of the world would never have allowed himself to be scratched twice; the good abbe, on the contrary, had taken several blows from those sharp claws before he could be brought to believe in any evil intention.

But when he did perceive it, he set to work, with the inquisitorial sagacity which priests acquire by directing consciences and burrowing into the nothings of the confessional, to establish, as though it were a matter of religious controversy, the following proposition: "Admitting that Mademoiselle Gamard did not remember it was Madame de Listomere's evening, and that Marianne did think I was home, and did really forget to make my fire, it is impossible, inasmuch as I myself took down my candlestick this morning, that Mademoiselle Gamard, seeing it in her salon, could have supposed I had gone to bed. Ergo, Mademoiselle Gamard intended that I should stand out in the rain, and, by carrying my candlestick upstairs, she meant to make me understand it. What does it all mean?" he said aloud, roused by the gravity of these circumstances, and rising as he spoke to take off his damp clothes, get into his dressing-gown, and do up his head for the night. Then he returned from the bed to the fireplace, gesticulating, and launching forth in various tones the following sentences, all of which ended in a high falsetto key, like notes of interjection:

"What the deuce have I done to her? Why is she angry with me?. Marianne did *not* forget my fire! Mademoiselle told her not to light it! I must be a child if I can't see, from the tone and manner she has been taking to me, that I've done something to displease her. Nothing like it ever happened to Chapeloud! I can't live in the midst of such torments as—At my age—"

He went to bed hoping that the morrow might enlighten him on the causes of the dislike which threatened to destroy forever the happiness he had now enjoyed two years after wishing for it so long. Alas! the secret reasons for the inimical feelings Mademoiselle Gamard bore to the luckless abbe were fated to remain eternally unknown to him,—not that they were difficult to fathom, but simply because he lacked the good faith and candor by which great souls and scoundrels look within and judge themselves. A man of genius or a trickster says to himself, "I did wrong." Self-interest and native talent are the only infallible and lucid guides. Now the Abbe Birotteau, whose goodness amounted to stupidity, whose knowledge was only, as it were, plastered on him by dint of study, who had no experience whatever of the world and its ways, who lived between the mass and the confessional, chiefly occupied in dealing the most trivial matters of conscience in his capacity of confessor to all the schools in town and to a few noble souls who rightly appreciated him,—the Abbe Birotteau must be regarded as a great child, to whom most of the practices of social life were utterly unknown. And yet, the natural selfishness of all human beings, reinforced by the selfishness peculiar to the priesthood and that of the narrow life of the provinces had insensibly, and unknown to himself, developed within him. If any one had felt enough interest in the good man to probe his spirit and prove to him that in the numerous petty details of his life and in the minute duties of his daily existence he was essentially lacking in the self-sacrifice he professed, he would have punished and mortified himself in good faith. But those whom we offend by such unconscious selfishness pay little heed to our real innocence; what they want is vengeance, and they take it. Thus it happened that Birotteau, weak brother that he was, was made to undergo the decrees of that great distributive Justice which goes about compelling the world to execute its judgments,—called by ninnies "the misfortunes of life."

There was this difference between the late Chapeloud and the vicar, —one was a shrewd and clever egoist, the other a simple-minded and clumsy one. When the canon went to board with Mademoiselle Gamard he knew exactly how to judge of his landlady's character. The confessional had taught him to understand the bitterness that the sense of being kept outside the social pale puts into the heart of an old maid; he therefore calculated his own treatment of Mademoiselle Gamard very wisely. She was then about thirty-eight years old, and still retained a few pretensions, which, in well-behaved persons of her condition, change, rather later, into strong personal self-esteem. The canon saw plainly that to live comfortably with his landlady he must pay her invariably the same attentions and be more infallible than the pope himself. To compass this result, he allowed no points of contact between himself and her except those that politeness demanded, and those which necessarily exist between two persons living under the same roof. Thus, though he and the Abbe Troubert took their regular three meals a day, he avoided the family breakfast by inducing Mademoiselle Gamard to send his coffee to his own room. He also avoided the annoyance of supper by taking tea in the houses of friends with whom he spent his evenings. In this way he seldom saw his landlady except at dinner; but he always came down to that meal a few minutes in advance of the hour. During this visit of courtesy, as it may be called, he talked to her, for the twelve years he had lived under her roof, on nearly the same topics, receiving from her the same answers. How she had slept, her breakfast, the trivial domestic events, her looks, her health, the weather, the time the church services had lasted, the incidents of the mass, the health of such or such a priest,—these were the subjects of their daily conversation. During dinner he invariably paid her certain indirect compliments; the fish had an excellent flavor; the seasoning of a sauce was delicious; Mademoiselle Gamard's capacities and virtues as mistress of a household were great. He was sure of flattering the old maid's vanity by praising the skill with which she made or prepared her preserves and pickles and pates and other gastronomical inventions. To cap all, the wily canon never left his landlady's yellow salon after dinner without remarking that there was no house in Tours where he could get such good coffee as that he had just imbibed.

Thanks to this thorough understanding of Mademoiselle Gamard's character, and to the science of existence which he had put in practice for the last twelve years, no matter of discussion on the internal arrangements of the household had ever come up between them. The Abbe Chapeloud had taken note of the spinster's angles, asperities, and crabbedness, and had so arranged his avoidance of her that he obtained without the least difficulty all the concessions that were necessary to the happiness and tranquility of his life. The result was that Mademoiselle Gamard frequently remarked to her friends and acquaintances that the Abbe Chapeloud was a very amiable man, extremely easy to live with, and a fine mind.

As to her other lodger, the Abbe Troubert, she said absolutely nothing about him. Completely involved in the round of her life, like a satellite in the orbit of a planet, Troubert was to her a sort of intermediary creature between the individuals of the human species and those of the canine species; he was classed in her heart next, but directly before, the place intended for friends but now occupied by a fat and wheezy pug which she tenderly loved. She ruled Troubert completely, and the intermingling of their interests was so obvious that many persons of her social sphere believed that the Abbe Troubert had designs on the old maid's property, and was binding her to him unawares with infinite patience, and really directing her while he seemed to be obeying without ever letting her percieve in him the slightest wish on his part to govern her.

When the Abbe Chapeloud died, the old maid, who desired a lodger with quiet ways, naturally thought of the vicar. Before the canon's will was made known she had meditated offering his rooms to the Abbe Troubert, who was not very comfortable on the ground-floor. But when the Abbe Birotteau, on receiving his legacy, came to settle in writing the terms of his board she saw he was so in love with the apartment, for which he might now admit his long cherished desires, that she dared not propose the exchange, and accordingly sacrificed her sentiments of friendship to the demands of self-interest. But in order to console her beloved canon, Mademoiselle took up the large white Chateau-Renaud bricks that made the floors of his apartment and replaced them by wooden floors laid in "point de Hongrie." She also rebuilt a smoky chimney.

For twelve years the Abbe Birotteau had seen his friend Chapeloud in that house without ever giving a thought to the motive of the canon's extreme circumspection in his relations to Mademoiselle Gamard. When he came himself to live with that saintly woman he was in the condition of a lover on the point of being made happy. Even if he had not been by nature purblind of intellect, his eyes were too dazzled by his new happiness to allow him to judge of the landlady, or to reflect on the limits which he ought to impose on their daily intercourse. Mademoiselle Gamard, seen from afar and through the prism of those material felicities which the vicar dreamed of enjoying in her house, seemed to him a perfect being, a faultless Christian, essentially charitable, the woman of the Gospel, the wise virgin, adorned by all those humble and modest virtues which shed celestial fragrance upon life.

So, with the enthusiasm of one who attains an object long desired, with the candor of a child, and the blundering foolishness of an old man utterly without worldly experience, he fell into the life of Mademoiselle Gamard precisely as a fly is caught in a spider's web. The first day that he went to dine and sleep at the house he was detained in the salon after dinner, partly to make his landlady's acquaintance, but chiefly by that inexplicable embarrassment which often assails timid people and makes them fear to seem impolite by breaking off a conversation in order to take leave. Consequently he remained there the whole evening. Then a friend of his, a certain Mademoiselle Salomon de Villenoix, came to see him, and this gave Mademoiselle Gamard the happiness of forming a card-table; so that when the vicar went to bed he felt that he had passed a very agreeable evening. Knowing Mademoiselle Gamard and the Abbe Troubert but slightly, he saw only the superficial aspects of their characters; few persons bare their defects at once, they generally take on a becoming veneer.

The worthy abbe was thus led to suggest to himself the charming plan of devoting all his evenings to Mademoiselle Gamard, instead of spending them, as Chapeloud had done, elsewhere. The old maid had for years been possessed by a desire which grew stronger day by day. This desire, often formed by old persons and even by pretty women, had become in Mademoiselle Gamard's soul as ardent a longing as that of Birotteau for Chapeloud's apartment; and it was strengthened by all those feelings of pride, egotism, envy, and vanity which pre-exist in the breasts of worldly people.

This history is of all time; it suffices to widen slightly the narrow circle in which these personages are about to act to find the coefficient reasons of events which take place in the very highest spheres of social life.

Mademoiselle Gamard spent her evenings by rotation in six or eight different houses. Whether it was that she disliked being obliged to go out to seek society, and considered that at her age she had a right to expect some return; or that her pride was wounded at receiving no company in her house; or that her self-love craved the compliments she saw her various hostesses receive, — certain it is that her whole ambition was to make her salon a centre towards which a given number of persons should nightly make their way with pleasure. One morning as she left Saint-Gatien, after Birotteau and his friend Mademoiselle Salomon had spent a few evenings with her and with the faithful and patient Troubert, she said to certain of her good friends whom she met at the church door, and whose slave she had hitherto considered herself, that those who wished to see her could certainly come once a week to her house, where she had friends enough to make a card-table; she could not leave the Abbe Birotteau; Mademoiselle Salomon had not missed a single evening that week; she was devoted to friends; and—et cetera, et cetera. Her speech was all the more humbly haughty and softly persuasive because Mademoiselle Salomon de Villenoix belonged to the most aristocatic society in Tours. For though Mademoiselle Salomon came to Mademoiselle Gamard's house solely out of friendship for the vicar, the old maid triumphed in receiving her, and saw that, thanks to Birotteau, she was on the point of succeeding in her great desire to form a circle as numerous and as agreeable as those of Madame de Listomere, Mademoiselle Merlin de la Blottiere, and other devout ladies who were in the habit of receiving the pious and ecclesiastical society of Tours.

But alas! the abbe Birotteau himself caused this cherished hope to miscarry. Now if those persons who in the course of their lives have attained to the enjoyment of a long desired happiness and have therefore comprehended the joy of the vicar when he stepped into

Chapeloud's vacant place, they will also have gained some faint idea of Mademoiselle Gamard's distress at the overthrow of her favorite plan.

After accepting his happiness in the old maid's salon for six months with tolerable patience, Birotteau deserted the house of an evening, carrying with him Mademoiselle Salomon. In spite of her utmost efforts the ambitious Gamard had recruited barely six visitors, whose faithful attendance was more than problematical; and boston could not be played night after night unless at least four persons were present. The defection of her two principal guests obliged her therefore to make suitable apologies and return to her evening visiting among former friends; for old maids find their own company so distasteful that they prefer to seek the doubtful pleasures of society.

The cause of this desertion is plain enough. Although the vicar was one of those to whom heaven is hereafter to belong in virtue of the decree "Blessed are the poor in spirit," he could not, like some fools, endure the annoyance that other fools caused him. Persons without minds are like weeds that delight in good earth; they want to be amused by others, all the more because they are dull within. The incarnation of ennui to which they are victims, joined to the need they feel of getting a divorce from themselves, produces that passion for moving about, for being somewhere else than where they are, which distinguishes their species,—and also that of all beings devoid of sensitiveness, and those who have missed their destiny, or who suffer by their own fault.

Without really fathoming the vacuity and emptiness of Mademoiselle Gamard's mind, or stating to himself the pettiness of her ideas, the poor abbe perceived, unfortunately too late, the defects which she shared with all old maids, and those which were peculiar to herself. The bad points of others show out so strongly against the good that they usually strike our eyes before they wound us. This moral phenomenon might, at a pinch, be made to excuse the tendency we all have, more or less, to gossip. It is so natural, socially speaking, to laugh at the failings of others that we ought to forgive the ridicule our own absurdities excite, and be annoyed only by calumny. But in this instance the eyes of the good vicar never reached the optical range which enables men of the world to see and evade their neighbours' rough points. Before he could be brought to perceive the faults of his landlady he was forced to undergo the warning which Nature gives to all her creatures—pain.

Old maids who have never yielded in their habits of life or in their characters to other lives and other characters, as the fate of woman exacts, have, as a general thing, a mania for making others give way to them. In Mademoiselle Gamard this sentiment had degenerated into despotism, but a despotism that could only exercise itself on little things. For instance (among a hundred other examples), the basket of counters placed on the card-table for the Abbe Birotteau was to stand exactly where she placed it; and the abbe annoyed her terribly by moving it, which he did nearly every evening. How is this sensitiveness stupidly spent on nothings to be accounted for? what is the object of it? No one could have told in this case; Mademoiselle Gamard herself knew no reason for it. The vicar, though a sheep by nature, did not like, any more than other sheep, to feel the crook too often, especially when it bristled with spikes. Not seeking to explain to himself the patience of the Abbe Troubert, Birotteau simply withdrew from the happiness which Mademoiselle Gamard believed that she seasoned to his liking,—for she regarded happiness as a thing to be made, like her preserves. But the luckless abbe made the break in a clumsy way, the natural way of his own naive character, and it was not carried out without much nagging and sharp-shooting, which the Abbe Birotteau endeavored to bear as if he did not feel them.

By the end of the first year of his sojourn under Mademoiselle Gamard's roof the vicar had resumed his former habits; spending two evenings a week with Madame de Listomere, three with Mademoiselle Salomon, and the other two with Mademoiselle Merlin de la Blottiere. These ladies belonged to the aristocratic circles of Tourainean society, to which Mademoiselle Gamard was not admitted. Therefore the abbe's abandonment was the more insulting, because it made her feel her want of social value; all choice implies contempt for the thing rejected.

"Monsieur Birotteau does not find us agreeable enough," said the Abbe Troubert to Mademoiselle Gamard's friends when she was forced to tell them that her "evenings" must be given up. "He is a man of the world, and a good liver! He wants fashion, luxury, witty conversation, and the scandals of the town."

These words of course obliged Mademoiselle Gamard to defend herself at Birotteau's expense.

"He is not much a man of the world," she said. "If it had not been for the Abbe Chapeloud he would never have been received at Madame de Listomere's. Oh, what didn't I lose in losing the Abbe Chapeloud! Such an amiable man, and so easy to live with! In twelve whole years I never had the slightest difficulty or disagreement with him."

Presented thus, the innocent abbe was considered by this bourgeois society, which secretly hated the aristocratic society, as a man essentially exacting and hard to get along with. For a week Mademoiselle Gamard enjoyed the pleasure of being pitied by friends who, without really thinking one word of what they said, kept repeating to her: "How *could* he have turned against you?—so kind and gentle as you are!" or, "Console yourself, dear Mademoiselle Gamard, you are so well known that—" et cetera.

Nevertheless, these friends, enchanted to escape one evening a week in the Cloister, the darkest, dreariest, and most out of the way corner in Tours, blessed the poor vicar in their hearts.

Between persons who are perpetually in each other's company dislike or love increases daily; every moment brings reasons to love or hate each other more and more. The Abbe Birotteau soon became intolerable to Mademoiselle Gamard. Eighteen months after she had taken him to board, and at the moment when the worthy man was mistaking the silence of hatred for the peacefulness of content, and applauding himself for having, as he said, "managed matters so well with the old maid," he was really the object of an underhand persecution and a vengeance deliberately planned. The four marked circumstances of the locked door, the forgotten slippers, the lack of fire, and the removal of the candlestick, were the first signs that revealed to him a terrible enmity, the final consequences of which were destined not to strike him until the time came when they were irreparable.

As he went to bed the worthy vicar worked his brains—quite uselessly, for he was soon at the end of them—to explain to himself the extraordinarily discourteous conduct of Mademoiselle Gamard. The fact was that, having all along acted logically in obeying the natural laws of his own egotism, it was impossible that he should now perceive his own faults towards his landlady.

Though the great things of life are simple to understand and easy to express, the littlenesses require a vast number of details to explain them. The foregoing events, which may be called a sort of prologue to this bourgeois drama, in which we shall find passions as violent as those excited by great interests, required this long introduction; and it would have been difficult for any faithful historian to shorten the account of these minute developments.

II

The next morning, on awaking, Birotteau thought so much of his prospective canonry that he forgot the four circumstances in which he had seen, the night before, such threatening prognostics of a future full of misery. The vicar was not a man to get up without a fire. He rang to let Marianne know that he was awake and that she must come to him; then he remained, as his habit was, absorbed in somnolent musings. The servant's custom was to make the fire and gently draw him from his half sleep by the murmured sound of her movements,—a sort of music which he loved. Twenty minutes passed and Marianne had not appeared. The vicar, now half a canon, was about to ring again, when he let go the bell-pull, hearing a man's step on the staircase. In a minute more the Abbe Troubert, after discreetly knocking at the door, obeyed Birotteau's invitation and entered the room. This visit, which the two abbe's usually paid each other once a month, was no surprise to the vicar. The canon at once exclaimed when he saw that Marianne had not made the fire of his quasi-colleague. He opened the window and called to her harshly, telling her to come at once to the abbe; then, turning round to his ecclesiastical brother, he said, "If Mademoiselle knew that you had no fire she would scold Marianne."

After this speech he inquired about Birotteau's health, and asked in a gentle voice if he had had any recent news that gave him hopes of his canonry. The vicar explained the steps he had taken, and told, naively, the names of the persons with whom Madam de Listomere was using her influence, quite unaware that Troubert had never forgiven that lady for not admitting him—the Abbe Troubert, twice proposed by the bishop as vicar-general!—to her house.

It would be impossible to find two figures which presented so many contrasts to each other as those of the two abbes. Troubert, tall and lean, was yellow and bilious, while the vicar was what we call, familiarly, plump. Birotteau's face, round and ruddy, proclaimed a kindly nature barren of ideas, while that of the Abbe Troubert, long and ploughed by many wrinkles, took on at times an expression of sarcasm, or else of contempt; but it was necessary to watch him very closely before those sentiments could be detected. The canon's habitual condition was perfect calmness, and his eyelids were usually lowered over his orange-colored eyes, which could, however, give clear and piercing glances when he liked. Reddish hair added to the gloomy effect of this countenance, which was always obscured by the veil which deep meditation drew across its features. Many persons at first sight thought him absorbed in high and earnest ambitions; but those who claimed to know him better denied that impression, insisting that he was only stupidly dull under Mademoiselle Gamard's despotism, or else worn out by too much fasting. He seldom spoke, and never laughed. When it did so happen that he felt agreeably moved, a feeble smile would flicker on his lips and lose itself in the wrinkles of his face.

Birotteau, on the other hand, was all expansion, all frankness; he loved good things and was amused by trifles with the simplicity of a man who knew no spite or malice. The Abbe Troubert roused, at first sight, an involuntary feeling of fear, while the vicar's presence brought a kindly smile to the lips of all who looked at him. When the tall canon marched with solemn step through the naves and cloisters of Saint-Gatien, his head bowed, his eye stern, respect followed him; that bent face was in harmony with the yellowing arches of the cathedral; the folds of his cassock fell in monumental lines that were worthy of statuary. The good vicar, on the contrary, perambulated about with no gravity at all. He trotted and ambled and seemed at times to roll himself along. But with all this there was one point of resemblance between the two men. For, precisely as Troubert's ambitious air, which made him feared, had contributed probably to keep him down to the insignificant position of a mere canon, so the character and ways of Birotteau marked him out as perpetually the vicar of the cathedral and nothing higher.

Yet the Abbe Troubert, now fifty years of age, had entirely removed, partly by the circumspection of his conduct and the apparent lack of all ambitions, and partly by his saintly life, the fears which his suspected ability and his powerful presence had roused in the minds of his superiors. His health having seriously failed him during the last year, it seemed probable that he would soon be raised to the office of vicar-general of the archbishopric. His competitors themselves desired the appointment, so that their own plans might have time to mature during the few remaining days which a malady, now become chronic, might allow him. Far from offering the same hopes to rivals, Birotteau's triple chin showed to all who wanted his coveted canonry an evidence of the soundest health; even his gout seemed to them, in accordance with the proverb, an assurance of longevity.

The Abbe Chapeloud, a man of great good sense, whose amiability had made the leaders of the diocese and the members of the best society in Tours seek his company, had steadily opposed, though secretly and with much judgment, the elevation of the Abbe Troubert. He had even adroitly managed to prevent his access to the salons of the best society. Nevertheless, during Chapeloud's lifetime Troubert treated him invariably with great respect, and showed him on all occasions the utmost deference. This constant submission did not, however, change the opinion of the late canon, who said to Birotteau during the last walk they took together: "Distrust that lean stick of a Troubert, —Sixtus the Fifth reduced to the limits of a bishopric!"

Such was the friend, the abiding guest of Mademoiselle Gamard, who now came, the morning after the old maid had, as it were, declared war against the poor vicar, to pay his brother a visit and show him marks of friendship.

"You must excuse Marianne," said the canon, as the woman entered. "I suppose she went first to my rooms. They are very damp, and I coughed all night. You are most healthily situated here," he added, looking up at the cornice.

"Yes; I am lodged like a canon," replied Birotteau.

"And I like a vicar," said the other, humbly.

"But you will soon be settled in the archbishop's palace," said the kindly vicar, who wanted everybody to be happy.

"Yes, or in the cemetery, but God's will be done!" and Troubert raised his eyes to heaven resignedly. "I came," he said, "to ask you to lend me the 'Register of Bishops.' You are the only man in Tours I know who has a copy."

"Take it out of my library," replied Birotteau, reminded by the canon's words of the greatest happiness of his life.

The canon passed into the library and stayed there while the vicar dressed. Presently the breakfast bell rang, and the gouty vicar reflected that if it had not been for Troubert's visit he would have had no fire to dress by. "He's a kind man," thought he.

The two priests went downstairs together, each armed with a huge folio which they laid on one of the side tables in the dining-room.

"What's all that?" asked Mademoiselle Gamard, in a sharp voice, addressing Birotteau. "I hope you are not going to litter up my dining-room with your old books!"

"They are books I wanted," replied the Abbe Troubert. "Monsieur Birotteau has been kind enough to lend them to me."

"I might have guessed it," she said, with a contemptuous smile. "Monsieur Birotteau doesn't often read books of that size."

"How are you, mademoiselle?" said the vicar, in a mellifluous voice.

"Not very well," she replied, shortly. "You woke me up last night out of my first sleep, and I was wakeful for the rest of the night." Then, sitting down, she added, "Gentlemen, the milk is getting cold."

Stupefied at being so ill-naturedly received by his landlady, from whom he half expected an apology, and yet alarmed, like all timid people at the prospect of a discussion, especially if it relates to themselves, the poor vicar took his seat in silence. Then, observing in Mademoiselle Gamard's face the visible signs of ill-humour, he was goaded into a struggle between his reason, which told him that he ought not to submit to such discourtesy from a landlady, and his natural character, which prompted him to avoid a quarrel.

Torn by this inward misery, Birotteau fell to examining attentively the broad green lines painted on the oilcloth which, from custom immemorial, Mademoiselle Gamard left on the table at breakfast-time, without regard to the ragged edges or the various scars displayed on its surface. The priests sat opposite to each other in cane-seated arm-chairs on either side of the square table, the head of which was taken by the landlady, who seemed to dominate the whole from a high chair raised on casters, filled with cushions, and standing very near to the dining-room stove. This room and the salon were on the ground-floor beneath the salon and bedroom of the Abbe Birotteau.

When the vicar had received his cup of coffee, duly sugared, from Mademoiselle Gamard, he felt chilled to the bone at the grim silence in which he was forced to proceed with the usually gay function of breakfast. He dared not look at Troubert's dried-up features, nor at the threatening visage of the old maid; and he therefore turned, to keep himself in countenance, to the plethoric pug which was lying on a cushion near the stove,—a position that victim of obesity seldom quitted, having a little plate of dainties always at his left side, and a bowl of fresh water at his right.

"Well, my pretty," said the vicar, "are you waiting for your coffee?"

The personage thus addressed, one of the most important in the household, though the least troublesome inasmuch as he had ceased to bark and left the talking to his mistress, turned his little eyes, sunk in rolls of fat, upon Birotteau. Then he closed them peevishly. To explain the misery of the poor vicar it should be said that being endowed by nature with an empty and sonorous loquacity, like the resounding of a football, he was in the habit of asserting, without any medical reason to back him, that speech favored digestion. Mademoiselle Gamard, who believed in this hygienic doctrine, had not as yet refrained, in spite of their coolness, from talking at meals; though, for the last few mornings, the vicar had been forced to strain his mind to find beguiling topics on which to loosen her tongue. If the narrow limits of this history permitted us to report even one of the conversations which often brought a bitter and sarcastic smile to the lips of the Abbe Troubert, it would offer a finished picture of the Boeotian life of the provinces. The singular revelations of the Abbe Birotteau and Mademoiselle Gamard relating to their personal opinions on politics, religion, and literature would delight observing minds. It would be highly entertaining to transcribe the reasons on which they mutually doubted the death of Napoleon in 1820, or the conjectures by which they mutually believed that the Dauphin was living,—rescued from the Temple in the hollow of a huge log of wood. Who could have helped laughing to hear them assert and prove, by reasons evidently their own, that the King of France alone imposed the taxes, that the Chambers were convoked to destroy the clergy, that thirteen hundred thousand persons had perished on the scaffold during the Revolution? They frequently discussed the press, without either of them having the faintest idea of what that modern engine really was. Monsieur Birotteau listened with acceptance to Mademoiselle Gamard when she told him that a man who ate an egg every morning would die in a year, and that facts proved it; that a roll of light bread eaten without drinking for several days together would cure sciatica; that all the workmen who assisted in pulling down the Abbey Saint-Martin had died in six months; that a certain prefect, under orders from Bonaparte, had done his best to damage the towers of Saint-Gatien, —with a hundred other absurd tales.

But on this occasion poor Birotteau felt he was tongue-tied, and he resigned himself to eat a meal without engaging in conversation. After a while, however, the thought crossed his mind that silence was dangerous for his digestion, and he boldly remarked, "This coffee is excellent."

That act of courage was completely wasted. Then, after looking at the scrap of sky visible above the garden between the two buttresses of Saint-Gatien, the vicar again summoned nerve to say, "It will be finer weather to-day than it was yesterday."

At that remark Mademoiselle Gamard cast her most gracious look on the Abbe Troubert, and immediately turned her eyes with terrible severity on Birotteau, who fortunately by that time was looking on his plate.

No creature of the feminine gender was ever more capable of presenting to the mind the elegaic nature of an old maid than Mademoiselle Sophie Gamard. In order to describe a being whose character gives a momentous interest to the petty events of the present drama and to the anterior lives of the actors in it, it may be useful to give a summary of the ideas which find expression in the being of an Old Maid,—remembering always that the habits of life form the soul, and the soul forms the physical presence.

Though all things in society as well as in the universe are said to have a purpose, there do exist here below certain beings whose purpose and utility seem inexplicable. Moral philosophy and political economy both condemn the individual who consumes without producing; who fills a place on the earth but does not shed upon it either good or evil, —for evil is sometimes good the meaning of which is not at once made manifest. It is seldom that old maids of their own motion enter the ranks of these unproductive beings. Now, if the consciousness of work done gives to the workers a sense of satisfaction which helps them to support life, the certainty of being a useless burden must, one would think, produce a contrary effect, and fill the minds of such fruitless beings with the same contempt for themselves which they inspire in others. This harsh social reprobation is one of the causes which contribute to fill the souls of old maids with the distress that appears in their faces. Prejudice, in which there is truth, does cast, throughout the world but especially in France, a great stigma on the woman with whom no man has been willing to share the blessings or endure the ills of life. Now, there comes to all unmarried women a period when the world, be it right or wrong, condemns them on the fact of this contempt, this rejection. If they are ugly, the goodness of their characters ought to have compensated for their natural imperfections; if, on the contrary, they are handsome, that fact argues that their misfortune has some serious cause. It is impossible to say which of the two classes is most deserving of rejection. If, on the other hand, their celibacy is deliberate, if it proceeds from a desire for independence, neither men nor mothers will forgive their disloyalty to womanly devotion, evidenced in their refusal to feed those passions which render their sex so affecting. To renounce the pangs of womanhood is to abjure its poetry and cease to merit the consolations to which mothers have inalienable rights.

Moreover, the generous sentiments, the exquisite qualities of a woman will not develop unless by constant exercise. By remaining unmarried, a creature of the female sex becomes void of meaning; selfish and cold, she creates repulsion. This implacable judgment of the world is unfortunately too just to leave old maids in ignorance of its causes. Such ideas shoot up in their hearts as naturally as the effects of their saddened lives appear upon their features. Consequently they wither, because the constant expression of happiness which blooms on the faces of other women and gives so soft a grace to their movements has never existed for them. They grow sharp and peevish because all human beings who miss their vocation are unhappy; they suffer, and suffering gives birth to the bitterness of ill-will. In fact, before an old maid blames herself for her isolation she blames others, and there is but one step between reproach and the desire for revenge.

But more than this, the ill grace and want of charm noticeable in these women are the necessary result of their lives. Never having felt a desire to please, elegance and the refinements of good taste are foreign to them. They see only themselves in themselves. This instinct brings them, unconsciously, to choose the things that are most convenient to themselves, at the sacrifice of those which might be more agreeable to others. Without rendering account to their own minds of the difference between themselves and other women, they end by feeling that difference and suffering under it. Jealousy is an indelible sentiment in the female breast. An old maid's soul is jealous and yet void; for she knows but one side—the miserable side —of the only passion men will allow (because it flatters them) to women. Thus thwarted in all their hopes, forced to deny themselves the natural development of their natures, old maids endure an inward torment to which they never grow accustomed. It is hard at any age, above all for a woman, to see a feeling of repulsion on the faces of others, when her true destiny is to move all hearts about her to emotions of grace and love. One result of this inward trouble is that an old maid's glance is always oblique, less from modesty than from fear and shame. Such beings never forgive society for their false position because they never forgive themselves for it.

Now it is impossible for a woman who is perpetually at war with herself and living in contradiction to her true life, to leave others in peace or refrain from envying their happines. The whole range of these sad truths could be read in the dulled gray eyes of Mademoiselle Gamard; the dark circles that surrounded those eyes told of the inward conflicts of her solitary life. All the wrinkles on her face were in straight lines. The structure of her forehead and cheeks was rigid and prominent. She allowed, with apparent indifference, certain scattered hairs, once brown, to grow upon her chin. Her thin lips scarcely covered teeth that were too long, though still quite white. Her complexion was dark, and her hair, originally black, had turned gray from frightful headaches,—a misfortune which obliged her to wear a false front. Not knowing how to put it on so as to conceal the junction between the real and the false, there were often little gaps between the border of her cap and the black string with which this semi-wig (always badly curled) was fastened to her head. Her gown, silk in summer, merino in winter, and always brown in color, was invariably rather tight for her angular figure and thin arms. Her collar, limp and bent, exposed too much the red skin of a neck which was ribbed like an oak-leaf in winter seen in the light. Her origin explains to some extent the defects of her conformation. She was the daughter of a wood-merchant, a peasant, who had risen from the ranks. She might have been plump at eighteen, but no trace remained of the fair complexion and pretty color of which she was wont to boast. The tones of her flesh had taken the pallid tints so often seen in "devotes." Her aquiline nose was the feature that chiefly proclaimed the despotism of her nature, and the flat shape of her forehead the narrowness of her mind. Her movements had an odd abruptness which precluded all grace; the mere motion with which she twitched her handkerchief from her bag and blew her nose with a loud noise would have shown her character and habits to a keen observer. Being rather tall, she held herself very erect, and justified the remark of a naturalist who once explained the peculiar gait of old maids by declaring that their joints were consolidating. When she walked her movements were not equally distributed over her whole person, as they are in other women, producing those graceful undulations which are so attractive. She moved, so to speak, in a single block, seeming to advance at each step like the statue of the Commendatore. When she felt in good humour she was apt, like other old maids, to tell of the chances she had had to marry, and of her fortunate discovery in time of the want of means of her lovers,—proving, unconsciously, that her worldly judgment was better than her heart.

This typical figure of the genus Old Maid was well framed by the grotesque designs, representing Turkish landscapes, on a varnished paper which decorated the walls of the dining-room. Mademoiselle Gamard usually sat in this room, which boasted of two pier tables and a barometer. Before the chair of each abbe was a little cushion covered with worsted work, the colors of which were faded. The salon in which she received company was worthy of its mistress. It will be visible to the eye at once when we state that it went by the name of the "yellow salon." The curtains were yellow, the furniture and walls yellow; on the mantelpiece, surmounted by a mirror in a gilt frame, the candlesticks and a clock all of crystal struck the eye with sharp brilliancy. As to the private apartment of Mademoiselle Gamard, no one had ever been permitted to look into it. Conjecture alone suggested that it was full of odds and ends, worn-out furniture, and bits of stuff and pieces dear to the hearts of all old maids.

Such was the woman destined to exert a vast influence on the last years of the Abbe Birotteau.

For want of exercising in nature's own way the activity bestowed upon women, and yet impelled to spend it in some way or other, Mademoiselle Gamard had acquired the habit of using it in petty intrigues, provincial cabals, and those self-seeking schemes which occupy, sooner or later, the lives of all old maids. Birotteau, unhappily, had developed in Sophie Gamard the only sentiments which it was possible for that poor creature to feel,—those of hatred; a passion hitherto latent under the calmness and monotony of provincial life, but which was now to become the more intense because it was spent on petty things and in the midst of a narrow sphere. Birotteau was one of those beings who are predestined to suffer because, being unable to see things, they cannot avoid them; to them the worst happens.

"Yes, it will be a fine day," replied the canon, after a pause, apparently issuing from a revery and wishing to conform to the rules of politeness.

Birotteau, frightened at the length of time which had elapsed between the question and the answer,—for he had, for the first time in his life, taken his coffee without uttering a word,—now left the dining-room where his heart was squeezed as if in a vise. Feeling that the coffee lay heavy on his stomach, he went to walk in a sad mood among the narrow, box-edged garden paths which outlined a star in the little garden. As he turned after making the first round, he saw Mademoiselle Gamard and the Abbe Troubert standing stock-still and silent on the threshold of the door,—he with his arms folded and motionless like a statue on a tomb; she leaning against the blind door. Both seemed to be gazing at him and counting his steps. Nothing is so embarrassing to a creature naturally timid as to feel itself the object of a close examination, and if that is made by the eyes of hatred, the sort of suffering it causes is changed into intolerable martyrdom.

Presently Birotteau fancied he was preventing Mademoiselle Gamard and the abbe from walking in the narrow path. That idea, inspired equally by fear and kindness, became so strong that he left the garden and went to the church, thinking no longer of his canonry, so absorbed was he by the disheartening tyranny of the old maid. Luckily for him he happened to find much to do at Saint-Gatien,—several funerals, a marriage, and two baptisms. Thus employed he forgot his griefs. When his stomach told him that dinner was ready he drew out his watch and saw, not without alarm, that it was some minutes after four. Being well aware of Mademoiselle Gamard's punctuality, he hurried back to the house.

He saw at once on passing the kitchen door that the first course had been removed. When he reached the dining-room the old maid said, with a tone of voice in which were mingled sour rebuke and joy at being able to blame him:—

"It is half-past four, Monsieur Birotteau. You know we are not to wait for you."

The vicar looked at the clock in the dining-room, and saw at once, by the way the gauze which protected it from dust had been moved, that his landlady had opened the face of the dial and set the hands in advance of the clock of the cathedral. He could make no remark. Had he uttered his suspicion it would only have caused and apparently justified one of those fierce and eloquent expositions to which Mademoiselle Gamard, like other women of her class, knew very well how to give vent in particular cases. The thousand and one annoyances which a servant will sometimes make her master bear, or a woman her husband, were instinctively divined by Mademoiselle Gamard and used upon Birotteau. The way in which she delighted in plotting against the poor vicar's domestic comfort bore all the marks of what we must call a profoundly malignant genius. Yet she so managed that she was never, so far as eye could see, in the wrong.

III

Eight days after the date on which this history began, the new arrangements of the household and the relations which grew up between the Abbe Birotteau and Mademoiselle Gamard revealed to the former the existence of a plot which had been hatching for the last six months.

As long as the old maid exercised her vengeance in an underhand way, and the vicar was able to shut his eyes to it and refuse to believe in her malevolent intentions, the moral effect upon him was slight. But since the affair of the candlestick and the altered clock, Birotteau would doubt no longer that he was under an eye of hatred turned fully upon him. From that moment he fell into despair, seeing everywhere the skinny, clawlike fingers of Mademoiselle Gamard ready to hook into his heart. The old maid, happy in a sentiment as fruitful of emotions as that of vengeance, enjoyed circling and swooping above the vicar as a bird of prey hovers and swoops above a field-mouse before pouncing down upon it and devouring it. She had long since laid a plan which the poor dumbfounded priest was quite incapable of imagining, and which she now proceeded to unfold with that genius for little things often shown by solitary persons, whose souls, incapable of feeling the grandeur of true piety, fling themselves into the details of outward devotion.

The petty nature of his troubles prevented Birotteau, always effusive and liking to be pitied and consoled, from enjoying the soothing pleasure of taking his friends into his confidence,—a last but cruel aggravation of his misery. The little amount of tact which he derived from his timidity made him fear to seem ridiculous in concerning himself with such pettiness. And yet those petty things made up the sum of his existence,—that cherished existence, full of busyness about nothings, and of nothingness in its business; a colorless barren life in which strong feelings were misfortunes, and the absence of emotion happiness. The poor priest's paradise was changed, in a moment, into hell. His sufferings became intolerable. The terror he felt at the prospect of a discussion with Mademoiselle Gamard increased day by day; the secret distress which blighted his life began to injure his health. One morning, as he put on his mottled blue stockings, he noticed a marked dimunition in the circumference of his calves. Horrified by so cruel and undeniable a symptom, he resolved to make an effort and appeal to the Abbe Troubert, requesting him to intervene, officially, between Mademoiselle Gamard and himself.

When he found himself in presence of the imposing canon, who, in order to receive his visitor in a bare and cheerless room, had hastily quitted a study full of papers, where he worked incessantly, and where no one was ever admitted, the vicar felt half ashamed at speaking of Mademoiselle Gamard's provocations to a man who appeared to be so gravely occupied. But after going through the agony of the mental deliberations which all humble, undecided, and feeble persons endure about things of even no importance, he decided, not without much swelling and beating of the heart, to explain his position to the Abbe Troubert.

The canon listened in a cold, grave manner, trying, but in vain, to repress an occasional smile which to more intelligent eyes than those of the vicar might have betrayed the emotions of a secret satisfaction. A flame seemed to dart from his eyelids when Birotteau pictured with the eloquence of genuine feeling the constant bitterness he was made to swallow; but Troubert laid his hand above those lids with a gesture very common to thinkers, maintaining the dignified demeanor which was usual with him. When the vicar had ceased to speak he would indeed have been puzzled had he sought on Troubert's face, marbled with yellow blotches even more yellow than his usually bilious skin, for any trace of the feelings he must have excited in that mysterious priest.

After a moment's silence the canon made one of those answers which required long study before their meaning could be thoroughly perceived, though later they proved to reflecting persons the astonishing depths of his spirit and the power of his mind. He simply crushed Birotteau by telling him that "these things amazed him all the more because he should never have suspected their existence were it not for his brother's confession. He attributed such stupidity on his part to the gravity of his occupations, his labors, the absorption in which his mind was held by certain elevated thoughts which prevented his taking due notice of the petty details of life." He made the vicar observe, but without appearing to censure the conduct of a man whose age and connections deserved all respect, that "in former days, recluses thought little about their food and lodging in the solitude of their retreats, where they were lost in holy contemplations," and that "in our days, priests could make a retreat for themselves in the solitude of their own hearts." Then, reverting to Birotteau's affairs, he added that "such disagreements were a novelty to him. For twelve years nothing of the kind had occurred between Mademoiselle Gamard and the venerable Abbe Chapeloud. As for himself, he might, no doubt, be an arbitrator between the vicar and their landlady, because his friendship for that person had never gone beyond the limits imposed by the Church on her faithful servants; but if so, justice demanded that he should hear both sides. He certainly saw no change in Mademoiselle Gamard, who seemed to him the same as ever; he had always submitted to a few of her caprices, knowing that the excellent woman was kindness and gentleness itself; the slight fluctuations of her temper should be attributed, he thought, to sufferings caused by a pulmonary affection, of which she said little, resigning herself to bear them in a truly Christian spirit." He ended by assuring the vicar that "if he stayed a few years longer in Mademoiselle Gamard's house he would learn to understand her better and acknowledge the real value of her excellent nature."

Birotteau left the room confounded. In the direful necessity of consulting no one, he now judged Mademoiselle Gamard as he would himself, and the poor man fancied that if he left her house for a few days he might extinguish, for want of fuel, the dislike the old maid felt for him. He accordingly resolved to spend, as he formerly did, a week or so at a country-house where Madame de Listomere passed her autumns, a season when the sky is usually pure and tender in Touraine. Poor man! in so doing he did the thing that was most desired by his terrible enemy, whose plans could only have been brought to nought by the resistant patience of a monk. But the vicar, unable to divine them, not understanding even his own affairs, was doomed to fall, like a lamb, at the butcher's first blow.

Madame de Listomere's country-place, situated on the embankment which lies between Tours and the heights of Saint-Georges, with a southern exposure and surrounded by rocks, combined the charms of the country with the pleasures of the town. It took but ten minutes from the bridge of Tours to reach the house, which was called the "Alouette," —a great advantage in a region where no one will put himself out for anything whatsoever, not even to seek a pleasure.

The Abbe Birotteau had been about ten days at the Alouette, when, one morning while he was breakfasting, the porter came to say that Monsieur Caron desired to speak with him. Monsieur Caron was

Mademoiselle Gamard's laywer, and had charge of her affairs. Birotteau, not remembering this, and unable to think of any matter of litigation between himself and others, left the table to see the lawyer in a stage of great agitation. He found him modestly seated on the balustrade of a terrace.

"Your intention of ceasing to reside in Mademoiselle Gamard's house being made evident—" began the man of business.

"Eh! monsieur," cried the Abbe Birotteau, interrupting him, "I have not the slightest intention of leaving it."

"Nevertheless, monsieur," replied the lawyer, "you must have had some agreement in the matter with Mademoiselle, for she has sent me to ask how long you intend to remain in the country. The event of a long absence was not foreseen in the agreement, and may lead to a contest. Now, Mademoiselle Gamard understanding that your board—"

"Monsieur," said Birotteau, amazed, and again interrupting the lawyer, "I did not suppose it necessary to employ, as it were, legal means to—"

"Mademoiselle Gamard, who is anxious to avoid all dispute," said Monsieur Caron, "has sent me to come to an understanding with you."

"Well, if you will have the goodness to return to-morrow," said the abbe, "I shall then have taken advice in the matter."

The quill-driver withdrew. The poor vicar, frightened at the persistence with which Mademoiselle Gamard pursued him, returned to the dining-room with his face so convulsed that everybody cried out when they saw him: "What *is* the matter, Monsieur Birotteau?"

The abbe, in despair, sat down without a word, so crushed was he by the vague presence of approaching disaster. But after breakfast, when his friends gathered round him before a comfortable fire, Birotteau naively related the history of his troubles. His hearers, who were beginning to weary of the monotony of a country-house, were keenly interested in a plot so thoroughly in keeping with the life of the provinces. They all took sides with the abbe against the old maid.

34

"Don't you see, my dear friend," said Madame de Listomere, "that the Abbe Troubert wants your apartment?"

Here the historian ought to sketch this lady; but it occurs to him that even those who are ignorant of Sterne's system of "cognomology," cannot pronounce the three words "Madame de Listomere" without picturing her to themselves as noble and dignified, softening the sternness of rigid devotion by the gracious elegance and the courteous manners of the old monarchical regime; kind, but a little stiff; slightly nasal in voice; allowing herself the perusal of "La Nouvelle Heloise"; and still wearing her own hair.

"The Abbe Birotteau must not yield to that old vixen," cried Monsieur de Listomere, a lieutenant in the navy who was spending a furlough with his aunt. "If the vicar has pluck and will follow my suggestions he will soon recover his tranquillity."

All present began to analyze the conduct of Mademoiselle Gamard with the keen perceptions which characterize provincials, to whom no one can deny the talent of knowing how to lay bare the most secret motives of human actions.

"You don't see the whole thing yet," said an old landowner who knew the region well. "There is something serious behind all this which I can't yet make out. The Abbe Troubert is too deep to be fathomed at once. Our dear Birotteau is at the beginning of his troubles. Besides, would he be left in peace and comfort even if he did give up his lodging to Troubert? I doubt it. If Caron came here to tell you that you intended to leave Mademoiselle Gamard," he added, turning to the bewildered priest, "no doubt Mademoiselle Gamard's intention is to turn you out. Therefore you will have to go, whether you like it or not. Her sort of people play a sure game, they risk nothing."

This old gentleman, Monsieur de Bourbonne, could sum up and estimate provincial ideas as correctly as Voltaire summarized the spirit of his times. He was thin and tall, and chose to exhibit in the matter of clothes the quiet indifference of a landowner whose territorial value is quoted in the department. His face, tanned by the Touraine sun, was less intellectual than shrewd. Accustomed to weigh his words and measure his actions, he concealed a profound vigilance behind a misleading appearance of simplicity. A very slight observation of him sufficed to show that, like a Norman peasant, he invariably held the upper hand in business matters. He was an authority on wine-making, the leading science of Touraine. He had managed to extend the meadow lands of his domain by taking in a part of the alluvial soil of the Loire without getting into difficulties with the State. This clever proceeding gave him the reputation of a man of talent. If Monsieur de Bourbonne's conversation pleased you and you were to ask who he was of a Tourainean, "Ho! a sly old fox!" would be the answer of those who were envious of him—and they were many. In Touraine, as in many of the provinces, jealousy is the root of language.

Monsieur de Bourbonne's remark occasioned a momentary silence, during which the persons who composed the little party seemed to be reflecting. Meanwhile Mademoiselle Salomon de Villenoix was announced. She came from Tours in the hope of being useful to the poor abbe, and the news she brought completely changed the aspect of the affair. As she entered, every one except Monsieur de Bourbonne was urging Birotteau to hold his own against Troubert and Gamard, under the auspices of the aristocractic society of the place, which would certainly stand by him.

"The vicar-general, to whom the appointments to office are entrusted, is very ill," said Mademoiselle Salomon, "and the archbishop has delegated his powers to the Abbe Troubert provisionally. The canonry will, of course, depend wholly upon him. Now last evening, at Mademoiselle de la Blottiere's the Abbe Poirel talked about the annoyances which the Abbe Birotteau had inflicted on Mademoiselle Gamard, as though he were trying to cast all the blame on our good abbe. 'The Abbe Birotteau,' he said, 'is a man to whom the Abbe Chapeloud was absolutely necessary, and since the death of that venerable man, he has shown'—and then came suggestions, calumnies! you understand?"

"Troubert will be made vicar-general," said Monsieur de Bourbonne, sententiously.

"Come!" cried Madame de Listomere, turning to Birotteau, "which do you prefer, to be made a canon, or continue to live with Mademoiselle Gamard?"

"To be a canon!" cried the whole company.

"Well, then," resumed Madame de Listomere, "you must let the Abbe Troubert and Mademoiselle Gamard have things their own way. By sending Caron here they mean to let you know indirectly that if you consent to leave the house you shall be made canon,—one good turn deserves another."

Every one present applauded Madame de Listomere's sagacity, except her nephew the Baron de Listomere, who remarked in a comic tone to Monsieur de Bourbonne, "I would like to have seen a fight between the Gamard and the Birotteau."

But, unhappily for the vicar, forces were not equal between these persons of the best society and the old maid supported by the Abbe Troubert. The time soon came when the struggle developed openly, went on increasing, and finally assumed immense proportions. By the advice of Madame de Listomere and most of her friends, who were now eagerly enlisted in a matter which threw such excitement into their vapid provincial lives, a servant was sent to bring back Monsieur Caron. The lawyer returned with surprising celerity, which alarmed no one but Monsieur de Bourbonne.

"Let us postpone all decision until we are better informed," was the advice of that Fabius in a dressing-gown, whose prudent reflections revealed to him the meaning of these moves on the Tourainean chess-board. He tried to enlighten Birotteau on the dangers of his position; but the wisdom of the old "sly-boots" did not serve the passions of the moment, and he obtained but little attention.

The conference between the lawyer and Birotteau was short. The vicar came back quite terrified.

"He wants me to sign a paper stating my relinquishment of domicile."

"That's formidable language!" said the naval lieutenant.

"What does it mean?" asked Madame de Listomere.

"Merely that the abbe must declare in writing his intention of leaving Mademoiselle Gamard's house," said Monsieur de Bourbonne, taking a pinch of snuff.

"Is that all?" said Madame de Listomere. "Then sign it at once," she added, turning to Birotteau. "If you positively decide to leave her house, there can be no harm in declaring that such is your will."

Birotteau's will!

"That is true," said Monsieur de Bourbonne, closing his snuff-box with a gesture the significance of which it is impossible to render, for it was a language in itself. "But writing is always dangerous," he added, putting his snuff-box on the mantelpiece with an air and manner that alarmed the vicar.

Birotteau was so bewildered by the upsetting of all his ideas, by the rapidity of events which found him defenceless, by the ease with which his friends were settling the most cherished matters of his solitary life, that he remained silent and motionless as if moonstruck, thinking of nothing, though listening and striving to understand the meaning of the rapid sentences the assembled company addressed to him. He took the paper Monsieur Caron had given him and read it, as if he were giving his mind to the lawyer's document, but the act was merely mechanical. He signed the paper, by which he declared that he left Mademoiselle Gamard's house of his own wish and will, and that he had been fed and lodged while there according to the terms originally agreed upon. When the vicar had signed the document, Monsieur Caron took it and asked where his client was to send the things left by the abbe in her house and belonging to him. Birotteau replied that they could be sent to Madame de Listomere's,—that lady making him a sign that she would receive him, never doubting that he would soon be a canon. Monsieur de Bourbonne asked to see the paper, the deed of relinquishment, which the abbe had just signed. Monsieur Caron gave it to him.

"How is this?" he said to the vicar after reading it. "It appears that written documents already exist between you and Mademoiselle Gamard. Where are they? and what do they stipulate?"

"The deed is in my library," replied Birotteau.

"Do you know the tenor of it?" said Monsieur de Bourbonne to the lawyer.

"No, monsieur," said Caron, stretching out his hand to regain the fatal document.

"Ha!" thought the old man; "you know, my good friend, what that deed contains, but you are not paid to tell us," and he returned the paper to the lawyer.

"Where can I put my things?" cried Birotteau; "my books, my beautiful book-shelves, and pictures, my red furniture, and all my treasures?"

The helpless despair of the poor man thus torn up as it were by the roots was so artless, it showed so plainly the purity of his ways and his ignorance of the things of life, that Madame de Listomere and Mademoiselle de Salomon talked to him and consoled him in the tone which mothers take when they promise a plaything to their children.

"Don't fret about such trifles," they said. "We will find you some place less cold and dismal than Mademoiselle Gamard's gloomy house. If we can't find anything you like, one or other of us will take you to live with us. Come, let's play a game of backgammon. To-morrow you can go and see the Abbe Troubert and ask him to push your claims to the canonry, and you'll see how cordially he will receive you."

Feeble folk are as easily reassured as they are frightened. So the poor abbe, dazzled at the prospect of living with Madame de Listomere, forgot the destruction, now completed, of the happiness he had so long desired, and so delightfully enjoyed. But at night before going to sleep, the distress of a man to whom the fuss of moving and the breaking up of all his habits was like the end of the world, came upon him, and he racked his brains to imagine how he could ever find such a good place for his book-case as the gallery in the old maid's house. Fancying he saw his books scattered about, his furniture defaced, his regular life turned topsy-turvy, he asked himself for the thousandth time why the first year spent in Mademoiselle Gamard's house had been so sweet, the second so cruel. His troubles were a pit in which his reason floundered. The canonry seemed to him small compensation for so much misery, and he compared his life to a stocking in which a single dropped stitch resulted in destroying the whole fabric. Mademoiselle Salomon remained to him. But, alas, in losing his old illusions the poor priest dared not trust in any later friendship.

In the "citta dolente" of spinsterhood we often meet, especially in France, with women whose lives are a sacrifice nobly and daily offered to noble sentiments. Some remain proudly faithful to a heart which death tore from them; martyrs of love, they learn the secrets of womanhood only though their souls. Others obey some family pride (which in our days, and to our shame, decreases steadily); these devote themselves to the welfare of a brother, or to orphan nephews; they are mothers while remaining virgins. Such old maids attain to the highest heroism of their sex by consecrating all feminine feelings to the help of sorrow. They idealize womanhood by renouncing the rewards of woman's destiny, accepting its pains. They live surrounded by the splendour of their devotion, and men respectfully bow the head before their faded features. Mademoiselle de Sombreuil was neither wife nor maid; she was and ever will be a living poem. Mademoiselle Salomon de Villenoix belonged to the race of these heroic beings. Her devotion was religiously sublime, inasmuch as it won her no glory after being, for years, a daily agony. Beautiful and young, she loved and was beloved; her lover lost his reason. For five years she gave herself, with love's devotion, to the mere mechanical well-being of that unhappy man, whose madness she so penetrated that she never believed him mad. She was simple in manner, frank in speech, and her pallid face was not lacking in strength and character, though its features were regular. She never spoke of the events of her life. But at times a sudden quiver passed over her as she listened to the story of some sad or dreadful incident, thus betraying the emotions that great sufferings had developed within her. She had come to live at Tours after losing the companion of her life; but she was not appreciated there at her true value and was thought to be merely an amiable woman. She did much good, and attached herself, by preference, to feeble beings. For that reason the poor vicar had naturally inspired her with a deep interest.

Mademoiselle de Villenoix, who returned to Tours the next morning, took Birotteau with her and set him down on the quay of the cathedral leaving him to make his own way to the Cloister, where he was bent on going, to save at least the canonry and to superintend the removal of his furniture. He rang, not without violent palpitations of the heart, at the door of the house whither, for fourteen years, he had come daily, and where he had lived blissfully, and from which he was now exiled forever, after dreaming that he should die there in peace like his friend Chapeloud. Marianne was surprised at the vicar's visit. He told her that he had come to see the

Abbe Troubert, and turned towards the ground-floor apartment where the canon lived; but Marianne called to him:—

"Not there, monsieur le vicaire; the Abbe Troubert is in your old apartment."

These words gave the vicar a frightful shock. He was forced to comprehend both Troubert's character and the depths of the revenge so slowly brought about when he found the canon settled in Chapeloud's library, seated in Chapeloud's handsome armchair, sleeping, no doubt, in Chapeloud's bed, and disinheriting at last the friend of Chapeloud, the man who, for so many years, had confined him to Mademoiselle Gamard's house, by preventing his advancement in the church, and closing the best salons in Tours against him. By what magic wand had the present transformation taken place? Surely these things belonged to Birotteau? And yet, observing the sardonic air with which Troubert glanced at that bookcase, the poor abbe knew that the future vicar-general felt certain of possessing the spoils of those he had so bitterly hated,— Chapeloud as an enemy, and Birotteau, in and through whom Chapeloud still thwarted him. Ideas rose in the heart of the poor man at the sight, and plunged him into a sort of vision. He stood motionless, as though fascinated by Troubert's eyes which fixed themselves upon him.

"I do not suppose, monsieur," said Birotteau at last, "that you intend to deprive me of the things that belong to me. Mademoiselle may have been impatient to give you better lodgings, but she ought to have been sufficiently just to give me time to pack my books and remove my furniture."

"Monsieur," said the Abbe Troubert, coldly, not permitting any sign of emotion to appear on his face, "Mademoiselle Gamard told me yesterday of your departure, the cause of which is still unknown to me. If she installed me here at once, it was from necessity. The Abbe Poirel has taken my apartment. I do not know if the furniture and things that are in these rooms belong to you or to Mademoiselle; but if they are yours, you know her scrupulous honesty; the sanctity of her life is the guarantee of her rectitude. As for me, you are well aware of my simple modes of living. I have slept for fifteen years in a bare room without complaining of the dampness,—which, eventually will have caused my death. Nevertheless, if you wish to return to this apartment I will cede it to you willingly."

After hearing these terrible words, Birotteau forgot the canonry and ran downstairs as quickly as a young man to find Mademoiselle Gamard. He met her at the foot of the staircase, on the broad, tiled landing which united the two wings of the house.

"Mademoiselle," he said, bowing to her without paying any attention to the bitter and derisive smile that was on her lips, nor to the extraordinary flame in her eyes which made them lucent as a tiger's, "I cannot understand how it is that you have not waited until I removed my furniture before—"

"What!" she said, interrupting him, "is it possible that your things have not been left at Madame de Listomere's?"

"But my furniture?"

"Haven't you read your deed?" said the old maid, in a tone which would have to be rendered in music before the shades of meaning that hatred is able to put into the accent of every word could be fully shown.

Mademoiselle Gamard seemed to rise in stature, her eyes shone, her face expanded, her whole person quivered with pleasure. The Abbe Troubert opened a window to get a better light on the folio volume he was reading. Birotteau stood as if a thunderbolt had stricken him. Mademoiselle Gamard made his ears hum when she enunciated in a voice as clear as a cornet the following sentence:—

"Was it not agreed that if you left my house your furniture should belong to me, to indemnify me for the difference in the price of board paid by you and that paid by the late venerable Abbe Chapeloud? Now, as the Abbe Poirel has just been appointed canon—"

Hearing the last words Birotteau made a feeble bow as if to take leave of the old maid, and left the house precipitately. He was afraid if he stayed longer that he should break down utterly, and give too great a triumph to his implacable enemies. Walking like a dunken man he at last reached Madame de Listomere's house, where he found in one of the lower rooms his linen, his clothing, and all his papers packed in a trunk. When he eyes fell on these few remnants of his possessions the unhappy priest sat down and hid his face in his hands to conceal his tears from the sight of others. The Abbe

Poirel was canon! He, Birotteau, had neither home, nor means, nor furniture!

Fortunately Mademoiselle Salomon happened to drive past the house, and the porter, who saw and comprehended the despair of the poor abbe, made a sign to the coachman. After exchanging a few words with Mademoiselle Salomon the porter persuaded the vicar to let himself be placed, half dead as he was, in the carriage of his faithful friend, to whom he was unable to speak connectedly. Mademoiselle Salomon, alarmed at the momentary derangement of a head that was always feeble, took him back at once to the Alouette, believing that this beginning of mental alienation was an effect produced by the sudden news of Abbe Poirel's nomination. She knew nothing, of course, of the fatal agreement made by the abbe with Mademoiselle Gamard, for the excellent reason that he did not know of it himself; and because it is in the nature of things that the comical is often mingled with the pathetic, the singular replies of the poor abbe made her smile.

"Chapeloud was right," he said; "he is a monster!"

"Who?" she asked.

"Chapeloud. He has taken all."

"You mean Poirel?"

"No, Troubert."

At last they reached the Alouette, where the priest's friends gave him such tender care that towards evening he grew calmer and was able to give them an account of what had happened during the morning.

The phlegmatic old fox asked to see the deed which, on thinking the matter over, seemed to him to contain the solution of the enigma. Birotteau drew the fatal stamped paper from his pocket and gave it to Monsieur de Bourbonne, who read it rapidly and soon came upon the following clause:—

"Whereas a difference exists of eight hundred francs yearly between the price of board paid by the late Abbe Chapeloud and that at which the said Sophie Gamard agrees to take into her house, on the above-named stipulated condition, the said Francois Birotteau; and whereas it is understood that the undersigned Francois Birotteau is not able for some years to pay the full price charged to the other boarders of Mademoiselle Gamard, more especially the Abbe Troubert; the said Birotteau does hereby engage, in consideration of certain sums of money advanced by the undersigned Sophie Gamard, to leave her, as indemnity, all the household property of which he may die possessed, or to transfer the same to her should he, for any reason whatever or at any time, voluntarily give up the apartment now leased to him, and thus derive no further profit from the above-named engagements made by Mademoiselle Gamard for his benefit—"

"Confound her! what an agreement!" cried the old gentleman. "The said Sophie Gamard is armed with claws."

Poor Birotteau never imagined in his childish brain that anything could ever separate him from that house where he expected to live and die with Mademoiselle Gamard. He had no remembrance whatever of that clause, the terms of which he had not discussed, for they had seemed quite just to him at a time when, in his great anxiety to enter the old maid's house, he would readily have signed any and all legal documents she had offered him. His simplicity was so guileless and Mademoiselle Gamard's conduct so atrocious, the fate of the poor old man seemed so deplorable, and his natural helplessness made him so touching, that in the first glow of her indignation Madame de Listomere exclaimed: "I made you put your signature to that document which has ruined you; I am bound to give you back the happiness of which I have deprived you."

"But," remarked Monsieur de Bourbonne, "that deed constitutes a fraud; there may be ground for a lawsuit."

"Then Birotteau shall go to the law. If he loses at Tours he may win at Orleans; if he loses at Orleans, he'll win in Paris," cried the Baron de Listomere.

"But if he does go to law," continued Monsieur de Bourbonne, coldly, "I should advise him to resign his vicariat."

"We will consult lawyers," said Madame de Listomere, "and go to law if law is best. But this affair is so disgraceful for Mademoiselle

Gamard, and is likely to be so injurious to the Abbe Troubert, that I think we can compromise."

After mature deliberation all present promised their assistance to the Abbe Birotteau in the struggle which was now inevitable between the poor priest and his antagonists and all their adherents. A true presentiment, an infallible provincial instinct, led them to couple the names of Gamard and Troubert. But none of the persons assembled on this occasion in Madame de Listomere's salon, except the old fox, had any real idea of the nature and importance of such a struggle. Monsieur de Bourbonne took the poor abbe aside into a corner of the room.

"Of the fourteen persons now present," he said, in a low voice, "not one will stand by you a fortnight hence. If the time comes when you need some one to support you you may find that I am the only person in Tours bold enough to take up your defence; for I know the provinces and men and things, and, better still, I know self-interests. But these friends of yours, though full of the best intentions, are leading you astray into a bad path, from which you won't be able to extricate yourself. Take my advice; if you want to live in peace, resign the vicariat of Saint-Gatien and leave Tours. Don't say where you are going, but find some distant parish where Troubert cannot get hold of you."

"Leave Tours!" exclaimed the vicar, with indescribable terror.

To him it was a kind of death; the tearing up of all the roots by which he held to life. Celibates substitute habits for feelings; and when to that moral system, which makes them pass through life instead of really living it, is added a feeble character, external things assume an extraordinary power over them. Birotteau was like certain vegetables; transplant them, and you stop their ripening. Just as a tree needs daily the same sustenance, and must always send its roots into the same soil, so Birotteau needed to trot about Saint-Gatien, and amble along the Mail where he took his daily walk, and saunter through the streets, and visit the three salons where, night after night, he played his whist or his backgammon.

"Ah! I did not think of it!" replied Monsieur de Bourbonne, gazing at the priest with a sort of pity.

All Tours was soon aware that Madame la Baronne de Listomere, widow of a lieutenant-general, had invited the Abbe Birotteau, vicar of Saint-Gatien, to stay at her house. That act, which many persons questioned, presented the matter sharply and divided the town into parties, especially after Mademoiselle Salomon spoke openly of a fraud and a lawsuit. With the subtle vanity which is common to old maids, and the fanatic self-love which characterizes them, Mademoiselle Gamard was deeply wounded by the course taken by Madame de Listomere. The baroness was a woman of high rank, elegant in her habits and ways, whose good taste, courteous manners, and true piety could not be gainsaid. By receivng Birotteau as her guest she gave a formal denial to all Mademoiselle Gamard's assertions, and indirectly censured her conduct by maintaining the vicar's cause against his former landlady.

It is necessary for the full understanding of this history to explain how the natural discernment and spirit of analysis which old women bring to bear on the actions of others gave power to Mademoiselle Gamard, and what were the resources on her side. Accompanied by the taciturn Abbe Troubert she made a round of evening visits to five or six houses, at each of which she met a circle of a dozen or more persons, united by kindred tastes and the same general situation in life. Among them were one or two men who were influenced by the gossip and prejudices of their servants; five or six old maids who spent their time in sifting the words and scrutinizing the actions of their neighbours and others in the class below them; besides these, there were several old women who busied themselves in retailing scandal, keeping an exact account of each person's fortune, striving to control or influence the actions of others, prognosticating marriages, and blaming the conduct of friends as sharply as that of enemies. These persons, spread about the town like the capillary fibres of a plant, sucked in, with the thirst of a leaf for the dew, the news and the secrets of each household, and transmitted them mechanically to the Abbe Troubert, as the leaves convey to the branch the moisture they absorb.

Accordingly, during every evening of the week, these good devotees, excited by that need of emotion which exists in all of us, rendered an exact account of the current condition of the town with a sagacity worthy of the Council of Ten, and were, in fact, a species of police, armed with the unerring gift of spying bestowed by passions. When they had divined the secret meaning of some event their vanity led them to appropriate to themselves the wisdom of their sanhedrim, and set the tone to the gossip of their respective spheres. This idle but ever busy fraternity, invisible, yet seeing all things, dumb, but perpetually talking, possessed an influence which its nonentity seemed to render harmless, though it was in fact terrible in its effects when it concerned itself with serious interests. For a long time nothing had entered the sphere of these existences so serious and so momentous to each one of them as the struggle of Birotteau, supported by Madame de Listomere, against Mademoiselle Gamard and the Abbe Troubert. The three salons of Madame de Listomere and the Demoiselles Merlin de la Blottiere and de Villenoix being considered as enemies by all the salons which Mademoiselle Gamard frequented, there was at the bottom of the quarrel a class sentiment with all its jealousies. It was the old Roman struggle of people and senate in a molehill, a tempest in a teacup, as Montesquieu remarked when speaking of the Republic of San Marino, whose public offices are filled by the day only,—despotic power being easily seized by any citizen.

But this tempest, petty as it seems, did develop in the souls of these persons as many passions as would have been called forth by the highest social interests. It is a mistake to think that none but souls concerned in mighty projects, which stir their lives and set them foaming, find time too fleeting. The hours of the Abbe Troubert fled by as eagerly, laden with thoughts as anxious, harassed by despairs and hopes as deep as the cruellest hours of the gambler, the lover, or the statesman. God alone is in the secret of the energy we expend upon our occult triumphs over man, over things, over ourselves. Though we know not always whither we are going we know well what the journey costs us. If it be permissible for the historian to turn aside for a moment from the drama he is narrating and ask his readers to cast a glance upon the lives of these old maids and abbes, and seek the cause of the evil which vitiates them at their source, we may find it demonstrated that man must experience certain passions before he can develop within him those virtues which give grandeur to life by widening his sphere and checking the selfishness which is inherent in every created being.

Madame de Listomere returned to town without being aware that for the previous week her friends had felt obliged to refute a rumour (at which she would have laughed had she known if it) that her affection for her nephew had an almost criminal motive. She took Birotteau to her lawyer, who did not regard the case as an easy one. The vicar's friends, inspired by the belief that justice was certain in so good a cause, or inclined to procrastinate in a matter which did not concern them personally, had put off bringing the suit until they returned to Tours. Consequently the friends of Mademoiselle Gamard had taken the initiative, and told the affair wherever they could to the injury of Birotteau. The lawyer, whose practice was exclusively among the most devout church people, amazed Madame de Listomere by advising her not to embark on such a suit; he ended the consultation by saying that "he himself would not be able to undertake it, for, according to the terms of the deed, Mademoiselle Gamard had the law on her side, and in equity, that is to say outside of strict legal justice, the Abbe Birotteau would undoubtedly seem to the judges as well as to all respectable laymen to have derogated from the peaceable, conciliatory, and mild character hitherto attributed to him; that Mademoiselle Gamard, known to be a kindly woman and easy to live with, had put Birotteau under obligations to her by lending him the money he needed to pay the legacy duties on Chapeloud's bequest without taking from him a receipt; that Birotteau was not of an age or character to sign a deed without knowing what it contained or understanding the importance of it; that in leaving Mademoiselle Gamard's house at the end of two years, when his friend Chapeloud had lived there twelve and Troubert fifteen, he must have had some purpose known to himself only; and that the lawsuit, if undertaken, would strike the public as an act of ingratitude;" and so forth. Letting Birotteau go before them to the staircase, the lawyer detained Madame de Listomere a moment to entreat her, if she valued her own peace of mind, not to involve herself in the matter.

But that evening the poor vicar, suffering the torments of a man under sentence of death who awaits in the condemned cell at Bicetre the result of his appeal for mercy, could not refrain from telling his assembled friends the result of his visit to the lawyer.

"I don't know a single pettifogger in Tours," said Monsieur de Bourbonne, "except that Radical lawyer, who would be willing to take the case, — unless for the purpose of losing it; I don't advise you to undertake it."

"Then it is infamous!" cried the navel lieutenant. "I myself will take the abbe to the Radical—"

"Go at night," said Monsieur de Bourbonne, interrupting him.

"Why?"

"I have just learned that the Abbe Troubert is appointed vicar-general in place of the other man, who died yesterday."

"I don't care a fig for the Abbe Troubert."

Unfortunately the Baron de Listomere (a man thirty-six years of age) did not see the sign Monsieur de Bourbonne made him to be cautious in what he said, motioning as he did so to a friend of Troubert, a councillor of the Prefecture, who was present. The lieutenant therefore continued:—

"If the Abbe Troubert is a scoundrel—"

"Oh," said Monsieur de Bourbonne, cutting him short, "why bring Monsieur Troubert into a matter which doesn't concern him?"

"Not concern him?" cried the baron; "isn't he enjoying the use of the Abbe Birotteau's household property? I remember that when I called on the Abbe Chapeloud I noticed two valuable pictures. Say that they are worth ten thousand francs; do you suppose that Monsieur Birotteau meant to give ten thousand francs for living two years with that Gamard woman,—not to speak of the library and furniture, which are worth as much more?"

The Abbe Birotteau opened his eyes at hearing he had once possessed so enormous a fortune.

The baron, getting warmer than ever, went on to say: "By Jove! there's that Monsieur Salmon, formerly an expert at the Museum in Paris; he is down here on a visit to his mother-in-law. I'll go and see him this very evening with the Abbe Birotteau and ask him to look at those pictures and estimate their value. From there I'll take the abbe to the lawyer."

Two days after this conversation the suit was begun. This employment of the Liberal laywer did harm to the vicar's cause. Those who were opposed to the government, and all who were known to dislike the priests, or religion (two things quite distinct which many persons confound), got hold of the affair and the whole town talked of it. The Museum expert estimated the Virgin of Valentin and the Christ of Lebrun, two paintings of great beauty, at eleven thousand francs. As to the bookshelves and the gothic furniture, the taste for such things was increasing so rapidly in Paris that their immediate value was at least twelve thousand. In short, the appraisal of the whole property by the expert reached the sum of over thirty-six thousand francs. Now it was very evident that Birotteau never intended to give Mademoiselle Gamard such an enormous sum of money for the small amount he might owe her under the terms of the deed; therefore he had, legally speaking, equitable grounds on which to demand an amendment of the agreement; if this were denied, Mademoiselle Gamard was plainly guilty of intentional fraud. The Radical lawyer accordingly began the affair by serving a writ on Mademoiselle Gamard. Though very harsh in language, this document, strengthened by citations of precedents and supported by certain clauses in the Code, was a masterpiece of legal argument, and so evidently just in its condemnation of the old maid that thirty or forty copies were made and maliciously distributed through the town.

IV

A few days after this commencement of hostilities between Birotteau and the old maid, the Baron de Listomere, who expected to be included as captain of a corvette in a coming promotion lately announced by the minister of the Navy, received a letter from one of his friends warning him that there was some intention of putting him on the retired list. Greatly astonished by this information he started for Paris immediately, and went at once to the minister, who seemed to be amazed himself, and even laughed at the baron's fears. The next day, however, in spite of the minister's assurance, Monsieur de Listomere made inquiries in the different offices. By an indiscretion (often practised by heads of departments in favor of their friends) one of the secretaries showed him a document confirming the fatal news, which was only waiting the signature of the director, who was ill, to be submitted to the minister.

The Baron de Listomere went immediately to an uncle of his, a deputy, who could see the minister of the Navy at the chamber without loss of time, and begged him to find out the real intentions of his Excellency in a matter which threatened the loss of his whole future. He waited in his uncle's carriage with the utmost anxiety for the end of the session. His uncle came out before the Chamber rose, and said to him at once as they drove away: "Why the devil have you meddled in a priest's quarrel? The minister began by telling me you had put yourself at the head of the Radicals in Tours; that your political opinions were objectionable; you were not following in the lines of the government,—with other remarks as much involved as if he were addressing the Chamber. On that I said to him, 'Nonsense; let us come to the point.' The end was that his Excellency told me frankly you were in bad odor with the diocese. In short, I made a few inquiries among my colleagues, and I find that you have been talking slightingly of a certan Abbe Troubert, the vicar-general, but a very important personage in the province, where he represents the Jesuits. I have made myself responsible to the minister for your future conduct. My good nephew, if you want to make your way be careful not to excite ecclesiastical enmities. Go at once to Tours and try to make your peace with that devil of a vicar-general; remember that such priests are men with whom we absolutely *must* live in harmony. Good heavens! when we are all striving and working to re-establish religion it is actually stupid, in a lieutenant who wants to be made a captain, to affront the priests. If you don't make up matters with that Abbe Troubert you needn't count on me; I shall abandon you. The minister of ecclesiastical affairs told me just now that Troubert was certain to be made bishop before long; if he takes a dislike to our family he could hinder me from being included in the next batch of peers. Don't you understand?"

These words explained to the naval officer the nature of Troubert's secret occupations, about which Birotteau often remarked in his silly way: "I can't think what he does with himself,—sitting up all night."

The canon's position in the midst of his female senate, converted so adroitly into provincial detectives, and his personal capacity, had induced the Congregation of Jesus to select him out of all the ecclesiastics in the town, as the secret proconsul of Touraine. Archbishop, general, prefect, all men, great and small, were under his occult dominion. The Baron de Listomere decided at once on his course.

"I shall take care," he said to his uncle, "not to get another round shot below my water-line."

Three days after this diplomatic conference between the uncle and nephew, the latter, returning hurriedly in a post-chaise, informed his aunt, the very night of his arrival, of the dangers the family were running if they peristed in supporting that "fool of a Birotteau." The baron had detained Monsieur de Bourbonne as the old gentleman was taking his hat and cane after the usual rubber of whist. The clear-sightedness of that sly old fox seemed indispensable for an understanding of the reefs among which the Listomere family suddenly found themselves; and perhaps the action of taking his hat and cane was only a ruse to have it whispered in his ear: "Stay after the others; we want to talk to you."

The baron's sudden return, his apparent satisfaction, which was quite out of keeping with a harrassed look that occasionally crossed his face, informed Monsieur de Bourbonne vaguely that the lieutenant had met with some check in his crusade against Gamard and Troubert. He showed no surprise when the baron revealed the secret power of the Jesuit vicar-general.

"I knew that," he said.

"Then why," cried the baroness, "did you not warn us?"

"Madame," he said, sharply, "forget that I was aware of the invisible influence of that priest, and I will forget that you knew it equally well. If we do not keep this secret now we shall be thought his accomplices, and shall be more feared and hated than we are. Do as I do; pretend to be duped; but look carefully where you set your feet. I did warn you sufficiently, but you would not understand me, and I did not choose to compromise myself."

"What must we do now?" said the baron.

The abandonment of Birotteau was not even made a question; it was a first condition tactily accepted by the three deliberators.

"To beat a retreat with the honors of war has always been the triumph of the ablest generals," replied Monsieur de Bourbonne. "Bow to Troubert, and if his hatred is less strong than his vanity you will make him your ally; but if you bow too low he will walk over you rough-shod; make believe that you intend to leave the service, and you'll escape him, Monsieur le baron. Send away Birotteau, madame, and you will set things right with Mademoiselle Gamard. Ask the Abbe Troubert, when you meet him at the archbishop's, if he can play whist. He will say yes. Then invite him to your salon, where he wants to be received; he'll be sure to come. You are a woman, and you can certainly win a priest to your interests. When the baron is promoted, his uncle peer of France, and Troubert a bishop, you can make Birotteau a canon if you choose. Meantime yield,—but yield gracefully, all the while with a slight menace. Your family can give Troubert quite as much support as he can give you. You'll understand each other perfectly on that score. As for you, sailor, carry your deep-sea line about you."

"Poor Birotteau?" said the baroness.

"Oh, get rid of him at once," replied the old man, as he rose to take leave. "If some clever Radical lays hold of that empty head of his, he may cause you much trouble. After all, the court would certainly give a verdict in his favour, and Troubert must fear that. He may forgive you for beginning the struggle, but if they were defeated he would be implacable. I have said my say."

He snapped his snuff-box, put on his overshoes, and departed.

The next day after breakfast the baroness took the vicar aside and said to him, not without visible embarrassment:—

"My dear Monsieur Birotteau, you will think what I am about to ask of you very unjust and very inconsistent; but it is necessary, both for you and for us, that your lawsuit with Mademoiselle Gamard be withdrawn by resigning your claims, and also that you should leave my house."

As he heard these words the poor abbe turned pale.

"I am," she continued, "the innocent cause of your misfortunes, and, moreover, if it had not been for my nephew you would never have begun this lawsuit, which has now turned to your injury and to ours. But listen to me."

She told him succinctly the immense ramifications of the affair, and explained the serious nature of its consequences. Her own meditations during the night had told her something of the probable antecedents of Troubert's life; she was able, without misleading Birotteau, to show him the net so ably woven round him by revenge, and to make him see the power and great capacity of his enemy, whose hatred to Chapeloud, under whom he had been forced to crouch for a dozen years, now found vent in seizing Chapeloud's property and in persecuting Chapeloud in the person of his friend. The harmless Birotteau clasped his hands as if to pray, and wept with distress at the sight of human horrors that his own pure soul was incapable of suspecting. As frightened as though he had suddenly found himself at the edge of a precipice, he listened, with fixed, moist eyes in which there was no expression, to the revelations of his friend, who ended by saying: "I know the wrong I do in abandoning your cause; but, my dear abbe, family duties must be considered before those of friendship. Yield, as I do, to this storm, and I will prove to you my gratitude. I am not talking of your worldly interests, for those I take charge of. You shall be made free of all such anxieties for the rest of your life. By means of Monsieur de Bourbonne, who will know how to save appearances, I shall arrange matters so that you shall lack nothing. My friend, grant me the right to abandon you. I shall ever be your friend, though forced to conform to the axioms of the world. You must decide."

The poor, bewildered abbe cried aloud: "Chapeloud was right when he said that if Troubert could drag him by the feet out of his grave he would do it! He sleeps in Chapeloud's bed!"

"There is no use in lamenting," said Madame de Listomere, "and we have little time now left to us. How will you decide?"

Birotteau was too good and kind not to obey in a great crisis the unreflecting impulse of the moment. Besides, his life was already in the agony of what to him was death. He said, with a despairing look at his protectress which cut her to the heart, "I trust myself to you—I am but the stubble of the streets."

He used the Tourainean word "bourrier" which has no other meaning than a "bit of straw." But there are pretty little straws, yellow, polished, and shining, the delight of children, whereas the bourrier is straw discolored, muddy, sodden in the puddles, whirled by the tempest, crushed under feet of men.

"But, madame, I cannot let the Abbe Troubert keep Chapeloud's portrait. It was painted for me, it belongs to me; obtain that for me, and I will give up all the rest."

"Well," said Madame de Listomere. "I will go myself to Mademoiselle Gamard." The words were said in a tone which plainly showed the immense effort the Baronne de Listomere was making in lowering herself to flatter the pride of the old maid. "I will see what can be done," she said; "I hardly dare hope anything. Go and consult Monsieur de Bourbonne; ask him to put your renunciation into proper form, and bring me the paper. I will see the archbishop, and with his help we may be able to stop the matter here."

Birotteau left the house dismayed. Troubert assumed in his eyes the dimensions of an Egyptian pyramid. The hands of that man were in Paris, his elbows in the Cloister of Saint-Gatien.

"He!" said the victim to himself, "He to prevent the Baron de Listomere from becoming peer of France!—and, perhaps, 'by the help of the archbishop we may be able to stop the matter here'!"

In presence of such great interests Birotteau felt he was a mere worm; he judged himself harshly.

The news of Birotteau's removal from Madame de Listomere's house seemed all the more amazing because the reason of it was wholly impenetrable. Madame de Listomere said that her nephew was intending to marry and leave the navy, and she wanted the vicar's apartment to enlarge her own. Birotteau's relinquishment was still unknown. The advice of Monsieur de Bourbonne was followed. Whenever the two facts reached the ears of the vicar-general his self-love was certain to be gratified by the assurance they gave that even if the Listomere family did not capitulate they would at least remain neutral and tacitly recognize the occult power of the Congregation,— to reconize it was, in fact, to submit to it. But the lawsuit was still sub judice; his opponents yielded and threatened at the same time.

The Listomeres had thus taken precisely the same attitude as the vicar-general himself; they held themselves aloof, and yet were able to direct others. But just at this crisis an event occurred which complicated the plans laid by Monsieur de Bourbonne and the Listomeres to quiet the Gamard and Troubert party, and made them more difficult to carry out.

Mademoiselle Gamard took cold one evening in coming out of the cathedral; the next day she was confined to her bed, and soon after became dangerously ill. The whole town rang with pity and false commiseration: "Mademoiselle Gamard's sensitive nature has not been able to bear the scandal of this lawsuit. In spite of the justice of her cause she was likely to die of grief. Birotteau has killed his benefactress." Such were the speeches poured through the capillary tubes of the great female conclave, and taken up and repeated by the whole town of Tours.

Madame de Listomere went the day after Mademoiselle Gamard took cold to pay the promised visit, and she had the mortification of that act without obtaining any benefit from it, for the old maid was too ill to see her. She then asked politely to speak to the vicar-general.

Gratified, no doubt, to receive in Chapeloud's library, at the corner of the fireplace above which hung the two contested pictures, the woman who had hitheto ignored him, Troubert kept the baroness waiting a moment before he consented to admit her. No courtier and no diplomatist ever put into a discussion of their personal interests or into the management of some great national negotiation more shrewdness, dissimulation, and ability than the baroness and the priest displayed when they met face to face for the struggle.

Like the seconds or sponsors who in the Middle Age armed the champion, and strengthened his valor by useful counsel until he entered the lists, so the sly old fox had said to the baroness at the last moment: "Don't forget your cue. You are a mediator, and not an interested party. Troubert also is a mediator. Weigh your words; study the inflection of the man's voice. If he strokes his chin you have got him."

Some sketchers are fond of caricaturing the contrast often observable between "what is said" and "what is thought" by the speaker. To catch the full meaning of the duel of words which now took place between the priest and the lady, it is necessary to unveil the thoughts that each hid from the other under spoken sentences of apparent insignificance. Madame de Listomere began by expressing the regret she had felt at Birotteau's lawsuit; and then went on to speak of her desire to settle the matter to the satisfaction of both parties.

"The harm is done, madame," said the priest, in a grave voice. "The pious and excellent Mademoiselle Gamard is dying." ("I don't care a fig for the old thing," thought he, "but I mean to put her death on your shoulders and harass your conscience if you are such a fool as to listen to it.")

"On hearing of her illness," replied the baroness, "I entreated Monsieur Birotteau to relinquish his claims; I have brought the document, intending to give it to that excellent woman." ("I see what you mean, you wily scoundrel," thought she, "but we are safe now from your calumnies. If you take this document you'll cut your own fingers by admitting you are an accomplice.")

There was silence for a moment.

"Mademoiselle Gamard's temporal affairs do not concern me," said the priest at last, lowering the large lids over his eagle eyes to veil his emotions. ("Ho! ho!" thought he, "you can't compromise me. Thank God, those damned lawyers won't dare to plead any cause that could smirch me. What do these Listomeres expect to get by crouching in this way?")

"Monsieur," replied the baroness, "Monsieur Birotteau's affairs are no more mine than those of Mademoiselle Gamard are yours; but, unfortunately, religion is injured by such a quarrel, and I come to you as a mediator—just as I myself am seeking to make peace." ("We are not decieving each other, Monsieur Troubert," thought she. "Don't you feel the sarcasm of that answer?")

"Injury to religion, madame!" exclaimed the vicar-general. "Religion is too lofty for the actions of men to injure." ("My religion is I," thought he.) "God makes no mistake in His judgments, madame; I recognize no tribunal but His."

"Then, monsieur," she replied, "let us endeavor to bring the judgments of men into harmony with the judgments of God." ("Yes, indeed, your religion is you.")

The Abbe Troubert suddenly changed his tone.

"Your nephew has been to Paris, I believe." ("You found out about me there," thought he; "you know now that I can crush you, you who dared to slight me, and you have come to capitulate.")

"Yes, monsieur; thank you for the interest you take in him. He returns to-night; the minister, who is very considerate of us, sent for him; he does not want Monsieur de Listomere to leave the service." ("Jesuit, you can't crush us," thought she. "I understand your civility.")

A moment's silence.

"I did not think my nephew's conduct in this affair quite the thing," she added; "but naval men must be excused; they know nothing of law." ("Come, we had better make peace," thought she; "we sha'n't gain anything by battling in this way.")

A slight smile wandered over the priests face and was lost in its wrinkles.

"He has done us the service of getting a proper estimate on the value of those paintings," he said, looking up at the pictures. "They will be a noble ornament to the chapel of the Virgin." ("You shot a sarcasm at me," thought he, "and there's another in return; we are quits, madame.")

"If you intend to give them to Saint-Gatien, allow me to offer frames that will be more suitable and worthy of the place, and of the works themselves." ("I wish I could force you to betray that you have taken Birotteau's things for your own," thought she.)

"They do not belong to me," said the priest, on his guard.

"Here is the deed of relinquishment," said Madame de Listomere; "it ends all discussion, and makes them over to Mademoiselle Gamard." She laid the document on the table. ("See the confidence I place in you," thought she.) "It is worthy of you, monsieur," she added, "worthy of your noble character, to reconcile two Christians,— though at present I am not especially concerned for Monsieur Birotteau—"

"He is living in your house," said Troubert, interrupting her.

"No, monsieur, he is no longer there." ("That peerage and my nephew's promotion force me to do base things," thought she.)

The priest remained impassible, but his calm exterior was an indication of violent emotion. Monsieur Bourbonne alone had fathomed the secret of that apparent tranquillity. The priest had triumphed!

"Why did you take upon yourself to bring that relinquishment," he asked, with a feeling analogous to that which impels a woman to fish for compliments.

"I could not avoid a feeling of compassion. Birotteau, whose feeble nature must be well known to you, entreated me to see Madaemoiselle Gamard and to obtain as the price of his renunciation—"

The priest frowned.

"of rights upheld by distinguished lawyers, the portrait of—"

Troubert looked fixedly at Madame de Listomere.

"the portrait of Chapeloud," she said, continuing: "I leave you to judge of his claim." ("You will be certain to lose your case if we go to law, and you know it," thought she.)

The tone of her voice as she said the words "distinguished lawyers" showed the priest that she knew very well both the strength and weakness of the enemy. She made her talent so plain to this connoisseur emeritus in the course of a conversation which lasted a long time in the tone here given, that Troubert finally went down to Mademoiselle Gamard to obtain her answer to Birotteau's request for the portrait.

He soon returned.

"Madame," he said, "I bring you the words of a dying woman. 'The Abbe Chapeloud was so true a friend to me,' she said, 'that I cannot consent to part with his picture.' As for me," added Troubert, "if it were mine I would not yield it. My feelings to my late friend were so faithful that I should feel my right to his portrait was above that of others."

"Well, there's no need to quarrel over a bad picture." ("I care as little about it as you do," thought she.) "Keep it, and I will have a copy made of it. I take some credit to myself for having averted this deplorable lawsuit; and I have gained, personally, the pleasure of your acquaintance. I hear you have a great talent for whist. You will forgive a woman for curiosity," she said, smiling. "If you will come and play at my house sometimes you cannot doubt your welcome."

Troubert stroked his chin. ("Caught! Bourbonne was right!" thought she; "he has his quantum of vanity!")

It was true. The vicar-general was feeling the delightful sensation which Mirabeau was unable to subdue when in the days of his power he found gates opening to his carriage which were barred to him in earlier days.

"Madame," he replied, "my avocations prevent my going much into society; but for you, what will not a man do?" ("The old maid is going to die; I'll get a footing at the Listomere's, and serve them if they serve me," thought he. "It is better to have them for friends than enemies.")

Madame de Listomere went home, hoping that the archbishop would complete the work of peace so auspiciously begun. But Birotteau was fated to gain nothing by his relinquishment. Mademoiselle Gamard died the next day. No one felt surprised when her will was opened to find that she had left everything to the Abbe Troubert. Her fortune was appraised at three hundred thousand francs. The vicar-general sent to Madame de Listomere two notes of invitation for the services and for the funeral procession of his friend; one for herself and one for her nephew.

"We must go," she said.

"It can't be helped," said Monsieur de Bourbonne. "It is a test to which Troubert puts you. Baron, you must go to the cemetery," he added, turning to the lieutenant, who, unluckily for him, had not left Tours.

The services took place, and were performed with unusual ecclesiastical magnificence. Only one person wept, and that was Birotteau, who, kneeling in a side chapel and seen by none, believed himself guilty of the death and prayed sincerely for the soul of the deceased, bitterly deploring that he was not able to obtain her forgiveness before she died.

The Abbe Troubert followed the body of his friend to the grave; at the verge of which he delivered a discourse in which, thanks to his eloquence, the narrow life the old maid had lived was enlarged to monumental proportions. Those present took particular note of the following words in the peroration: —

"This life of days devoted to God and to His religion, a life adorned with noble actions silently performed, and with modest and hidden virtues, was crushed by a sorrow which we might call undeserved if we could forget, here at the verge of this grave, that our afflictions are sent by God. The numerous friends of this saintly woman, knowing the innocence and nobility of her soul, foresaw that she would issue safely from her trials in spite of the accusations which blasted her life. It may be that Providence has called her to the bosom of God to withdraw her from those trials. Happy they who can rest here below in the peace of their own hearts as Sophie now is resting in her robe of innocence among the blest."

"When he had ended his pompous discourse," said Monsieur de Bourbonne, after relating the incidents of the internment to Madame de Listomere when whist was over, the doors shut, and they were alone with the baron, "this Louis XI. in a cassock—imagine him if you can!—gave a last flourish to the sprinkler and aspersed the coffin with holy water." Monsieur de Bourbonne picked up the tongs and imitated the priest's gesture so satirically that the baron and his aunt could not help laughing. "Not until then," continued the old gentleman, "did he contradict himself. Up to that time his behavior had been perfect; but it was no doubt impossible for him to put the old maid, whom he despised so heartily and hated almost as much as he hated Chapeloud, out of sight forever without allowing his joy to appear in that last gesture."

The next day Mademoiselle Salomon came to breakfast with Madame de Listomere, chiefly to say, with deep emotion: "Our poor Abbe Birotteau has just received a frightful blow, which shows the most determined hatred. He is appointed curate of Saint-Symphorien."

Saint-Symphorien is a suburb of Tours lying beyond the bridge. That bridge, one of the finest monuments of French architecture, is nineteen hundred feet long, and the two open squares which surround each end are precisely alike.

"Don't you see the misery of it?" she said, after a pause, amazed at the coldness with which Madame de Listomere received the news. "It is just as if the abbe were a hundred miles from Tours, from his friends, from everything! It is a frightful exile, and all the more cruel because he is kept within sight of the town where he can hardly ever come. Since his troubles he walks very feebly, yet he will have to walk three miles to see his old friends. He has taken to his bed, just now, with fever. The parsonage at Saint-Symphorien is very cold and damp, and the parish is too poor to repair it. The poor old man will be buried in a living tomb. Oh, it is an infamous plot!"

To end this history it will suffice to relate a few events in a simple way, and to give one last picture of its chief personages.

Five months later the vicar-general was made Bishop of Troyes; and Madame de Listomere was dead, leaving an annuity of fifteen hundred francs to the Abbe Birotteau. The day on which the dispositions in her will were made known Monseigneur Hyacinthe, Bishop of Troyes, was on the point of leaving Tours to reside in his diocese, but he delayed his departure on receiving the news. Furious at being foiled by a woman to whom he had lately given his countenance while she had been secretly holding the hand of a man whom he regarded as his enemy, Troubert again threatened the baron's future career, and put in jeopardy the peerage of his uncle. He made in the salon of the archbishop, and before an assembled party, one of those priestly speeches which are big with vengeance and soft with honied mildness. The Baron de Listomere went the next day to see this implacable enemy, who must have imposed sundry hard conditions on him, for the baron's subsequent conduct showed the most entire submission to the will of the terrible Jesuit.

The new bishop made over Mademoiselle Gamard's house by deed of gift to the Chapter of the cathedral; he gave Chapeloud's books and bookcases to the seminary; he presented the two disputed pictures to the Chapel of the Virgin; but he kept Chapeloud's portrait. No one knew how to explain this almost total renunciation of Mademoiselle Gamard's bequest. Monsieur de Bourbonne supposed that the bishop had secretly kept moneys that were invested, so as to support his rank with dignity in Paris, where of course he would take his seat on the Bishops' bench in the Upper Chamber. It was not until the night before Monseigneur Troubert's departure from Tours that the sly old fox unearthed the hidden reason of this strange action, the deathblow given by the most persistent vengeance to the feeblest of victims. Madame de Listomere's legacy to Birotteau was contested by the Baron de Listomere under a pretence of undue influence!

A few days after the case was brought the baron was promoted to the rank of captain. As a measure of ecclesiastical discipline, the curate of Saint-Symphorien was suspended. His superiors judged him guilty. The murderer of Sophie Gamard was also a swindler. If Monseigneur Troubert had kept Mademoiselle Gamard's property he would have found it difficult to make the ecclestiastical authorities censure Birotteau.

At the moment when Monseigneur Hyacinthe, Bishop of Troyes, drove along the quay Saint-Symphorien in a post-chaise on his way to Paris poor Birotteau had been placed in an armchair in the sun on a terrace above the road. The unhappy priest, smitten by the archbishop, was pale and haggard. Grief, stamped on every feature, distorted the face that was once so mildly gay. Illness had dimmed his eyes, formerly brightened by the pleasures of good living and devoid of serious ideas, with a veil which simulated thought. It was but the skeleton of the old Birotteau who had rolled only one year earlier so vacuous but so content along the Cloister. The bishop cast one look of pity and contempt upon his victim; then he consented to forget him, and went his way.

There is no doubt that Troubert would have been in other times a Hildebrand or an Alexander the Sixth. In these days the Church is no longer a political power, and does not absorb the whole strength of her solitaries. Celibacy, however, presents the inherent vice of concentating the faculties of man upon a single passion, egotism, which renders celibates either useless or mischievous. We live at a period when the defect of governments is to make Man for Society rather than Society for Man. There is a perpetual struggle going on between the Individual and the Social system which insists on using him, while he is endeavoring to use it to his own profit; whereas, in former days, man, really more free, was also more loyal to the public weal. The round in which men struggle in these days has been insensibly widened; the soul which can grasp it as a whole will ever be a magnificent exception; for, as a general thing, in morals as in physics, impulsion loses in intensity what it gains in extension. Society can not be based on exceptions. Man in the first instance was purely and simply, father; his heart beat warmly, concentrated in the one ray of Family. Later, he lived for a clan, or a small community; hence the great historical devotions of Greece and Rome. After that he was a man of caste or of a religion, to maintain the greatness of which he often proved himself sublime; but by that time the field of his interests became enlarged by many intellectual regions. In our day, his life is attached to that of a vast country; sooner or later his family will be, it is predicted, the entire universe.

Will this moral cosmopolitanism, the hope of Christian Rome, prove to be only a sublime error? It is so natural to believe in the realization of a noble vision, in the Brotherhood of Man. But, alas! the human machine does not have such divine proportions. Souls that are vast enough to grasp a range of feelings bestowed on great men only will never belong to either fathers of families or simple citizens. Some physiologists have thought that as the brain enlarges the heart narrows; but they are mistaken. The apparent egotism of men who bear a science, a nation, a code of laws in their bosom is the noblest of passions; it is, as one may say, the maternity of the masses; to give birth to new peoples, to produce new ideas they must unite within their mighty brains the breasts of woman and the force of God. The history of such men as Innocent the Third and Peter the Great, and all great leaders of their age and nation will show, if need be, in the highest spheres the same vast thought of which Troubert was made the representative in the quiet depths of the Cloister of Saint-Gatien.

ADDENDUM

The following personages appear in other stories of the Human Comedy.

Birotteau, Abbe Francois
  The Lily of the Valley
  Cesar Birotteau

Bourbonne, De
  Madame Firmiani

Listomere, Baronne de
  Cesar Birotteau
  The Muse of the Department

Troubert, Abbe Hyacinthe
  The Member for Arcis

Villenoix, Pauline Salomon de
  Louis Lambert
  A Seaside Tragedy

Printed in the United Kingdom
by Lightning Source UK Ltd.
118273UK00001B/283

NEARHOPE

JOHN REGAN

DEDICATION

To my wife, Vicky, with love. My biggest fan and harshest critic. Without which, I would never have finished this book.

ACKNOWLEDGEMENTS

It goes without saying that to produce anything worthwhile requires help from others. Writing a book such as this is aided and abetted by numerous people. Some of whom subtly assist and others profoundly. My thanks go to anyone who, however small, contributed to this novel. However, my principal appreciation is to the people who purchased and read my first seven books: The Hanging Tree, Persistence of Vision, The Romanov Relic, The Space Between Our Tears, The Fallen leaves, The Lindisfarne Liturgy and The Whitby Wailers. Your support is greatly appreciated. Many thanks go to fellow author Deborah Barwick for her invaluable support and help in making this book possible. Finally, to anyone who is reading this book. I hope you find it enjoyable, and any feedback is always appreciated.

August 2022.

DISCLAIMER

Many of the places mentioned in this book exist. However, the author has used poetic license to maintain an engaging narrative. Therefore, no guarantee of accuracy in some respects should be expected. The characters depicted, however, are wholly fictional. Therefore, any similarity to persons living or dead is accidental.

THE BEGINNING

FELIX – 'You're not going Leyburn way, are you?' a voice called out. A man approached me from across the filling station forecourt. About thirty with dark hair – his thick army coat collar pulled up high to keep out the biting December evening wind.

Staring into his green eyes, I was momentarily held fast. 'Leyburn? Yes.'

He stepped closer and smiled. 'I don't suppose there's any chance of a lift?'

'To Leyburn?' I asked.

'Close to it.'

I could have declined, I suppose. I could have made up some excuse. Giving a lift to a stranger was not the sort of thing I would usually do, but those eyes drew me in and swept aside, with ease, any protestations I had.

I smiled back. 'Jump in,' I said as I got into my car.

As he climbed in beside me, he offered his hand. 'James,' he said.

I shook it firmly. 'Felix. Felix Halshaw.'

He smiled again and nodded as if he already knew who I was but didn't offer up his surname, then he turned and looked out of the car windscreen. 'I'm heading for a place called Nearhope,' he said

I steered the car from the filling station onto the road and glanced at him. 'Nearhope? I've never heard of it.'

'It's on the way to Leyburn.'

This puzzled me as I'd lived around Leyburn all my life but had never encountered a place called Nearhope. After considering this for a moment, I glanced at him again, but any chance of further conversation evaporated as my companion rested his head against the window, closed his eyes and promptly fell asleep.

Except for my passenger's low sleep-full murmurings, we travelled on in silence until a worrisome red light appeared on the dashboard. I allowed the car to drift into a convenient layby just before the engine spluttered and stopped.

James opened his eyes and stretched. 'We're here.'

'There's something up with the car,' I said as I reached into the glove box and pulled out the owner's manual, optimistically hoping I could diagnose the problem.

He placed his hand on the book and fixed me with those eyes. 'You won't need that.'

Viewing him suspiciously, I asked why not?

He opened the door, stepped out into the night and stretched again. 'Because the dead don't drive.'

Stranded in the middle of nowhere late at night with someone I'd only just met, why wasn't I scared? Why wasn't I terrified? But I wasn't. Something in the way he spoke, his words, wore the patina of honesty. I can't explain any better than that. I believed what he said, so I jumped out of the car, followed him, and took hold of his arm. 'Where are you going?' I asked. 'I'll phone the AA. They'll send someone out to fix it.'

He smiled. 'Nearhope. I'm going to Nearhope.'

I glanced about. 'We're in the middle of nowhere,' I protested. 'The nearest village—'

He looked away from me and nodded towards a signpost on the corner of a side road. It said *Nearhope 1 mile*. I stepped closer to better examine the sign. 'I've never seen that turn-off before,' I said. 'I don't understand. I know this area well, and I've never seen that sign or road. So what the hell is going on?' I said and faced my companion.

James laughed. 'Just because you don't see something doesn't mean it's not there.'

I shook my head. 'What are you talking about? A road can't be there one minute and not there … And what did you mean back in the car about the dead not driving?'

He strolled back to the vehicle and pointed inside. I wandered across, bent to see inside, and jumped back in horror. 'What on earth …?'

'Those chest pains you've been having,' he said. 'The ones you haven't told anyone about …?'

I rubbed a hand across my chest. The dull ache that had been there for days was gone. 'But how …?'

'Heart attack,' he said. 'You were lucky not to crash the car.'

I couldn't remember any pain before pulling over, so I bent low again and viewed the driver once more. It was me, all right. My face frozen in a grimace, my eyes locked in a sightless stare. 'I'm dreaming,' I whispered. 'I must be.' I closed my eyes and shook my head. The body, or rather me, was still there, and so was the side road and signpost. Slumping against the vehicle, I attempted to gather my thoughts. 'This is not happening …' I said.

James placed a hand on my shoulder. 'You should come with me, Felix.'

Staring into his eyes again, I faltered. 'I can't just …' I rubbed my chin. 'This isn't happening. I'm dreaming. I'm undoubtedly having one of those vivid lucid dreams I've read about.'

He walked towards the side road. 'It's not a dream. I can assure you of that. You need to come with me. There's nothing for you here, Felix.' He paused and looked around. 'This is a place for the living.'

I hurried across to him and stopped close by. 'Am I a ghost? Have you come to take me to …?' The words dried up. It seemed absurd.

He shook his head. 'No. You are what is left of a person when their corporeal body dies.'

'Where will I go? Where are you taking me?' I asked.

'To Nearhope.'

'But … This Nearhope … Why? Why would I go there?'

He smiled. 'All in good time. Give me your hand.'

I glanced at the car once more and then faced him. 'I'm not sure.' Backing away, I looked at his hand. 'This is crazy.'

'I know it's confusing,' he said. 'I understand your reluctance, but it is what it is. There is nothing for you here. Your time in this place is over.' He smiled again and held his hand outstretched, waiting for me to grasp it. 'Take it. It does not hurt.'

I allowed myself a final look at the car and my body inside, then clasped his hand.

From a blackness so dark no light could penetrate, I stepped forth and surveyed the room I found myself in – a dilapidated church.

I looked at James. 'Where did I go when I took your hand?'

He sighed. 'It's difficult to explain.' He considered my words for a few seconds. 'I conjoined with you,' he said.

'Conjoined? What does that mean?'

'Conjoining allows me to carry your entity within my own.'

'Why did we have to conjoin?'

'I have to tread carefully in Nearhope and its surrounding area. Daytime is fine, but at night … they could find me, and conjoining with you gives me enough of a disguise.'

'Who could find you?'

Slumping onto an old pew, he swatted away my inquiry. 'Too many questions,' he said. 'I'm tired. I travelled a great distance to find you. Tomorrow.' He yawned. 'Tomorrow, I will answer your questions.'

'Find me?' I said. 'What do you mean by that?'

James lowered his head onto his rucksack and closed his eyes. Clearly, any questions would have to wait. I felt irritated and confused but held onto my words.

Something else struck me when I looked around at the ramshackle building that creaked with age. The church appeared to have aged in the minutes I'd been cognizant – the walls and fittings older, crumbling and rustier than before. A hole in the ceiling, which I would have sworn was not there previously, now gave a glimpse of the full moon outside.

James appeared to read my thoughts and opened an eye. 'It isn't always like this,' he said. 'In the daytime, it's beautiful.'

'What's happening to it?'

'It dies at night. Falls into ruin and crumbles into decay. It is its fate.'

I scoffed. 'Buildings don't die.'

James altered his position, trying to get comfortable. 'Things happen differently in Nearhope,' he said. 'You will find that out.'

'James,' I said. 'I have so many questions. Why am I here? Why am I in this place?'

He yawned. 'In the morning, I will be refreshed. I'll tell you everything you need to know, but now ...' He closed his eyes again. 'I must sleep.'

'What will I do? Sleep too?'

'If you can.' He sat up and appraised me through weary eyes. 'Don't go outside, though. There are things outside ...' He dropped his head back down as tiredness swept him up in its arms, and within seconds, he was asleep.

I wandered over to the entrance and peered through a crack in the door and into the gloom outside. A graveyard wrapped itself around the church with headstones of great age scattered in every direction. Something briefly appeared within my peripheral vision, a fox, perhaps? As my eyes adjusted to the darkness, I saw further movement as their forms became more distinct. Although they moved on all fours, they weren't quadruped at all. However, whatever they were, they appeared more human than animal. As if sensing my presence, one stopped and turned its head, staring at me with sunken eyes lost in the sockets of a gaunt face. Its mouth contorted into a horrible grimace. As its eyes bared down on me, it raised an emaciated hand and, within it, gripped tightly, a bone, or what was left of it. I gasped and stepped backwards away from the door without taking my eyes off them until they scuttled away. Hurrying along the aisle, I joined James on the pew. I was pleased I wasn't alone in a place such as this.

THE CHURCH

FELIX – Trying to shift the tiredness that still clouded me, I opened my eyes and rubbed them. James stood at the far end of the church, staring up at a huge painting of Jesus on the cross. I climbed to my feet and surveyed the room. As James had said, it was indeed beautiful, but how could it be so different from the previous night? A smell drifted into my nostrils – beeswax – as if the pews had been polished by some unseen hand. Shielding my eyes from the sunlight that erupted through the massive stained-glass window, showering the church in a myriad of colours, I paused to view the beauty of my surroundings.

'I told you it was beautiful,' he said without moving from his position.

Stepping forward, I joined him at the altar. 'None of this can be real. How can a ruin …' I said, sweeping my arm around in a wide arc, '… become this?'

He turned to face me with tear-laden eyes. 'Nearhope is no ordinary place. It exists on the boundary between good and evil, acting as a buffer between the two.' And, as if regretting what he had said, he patted me on the shoulder. 'You may see many things in the coming days that will test your belief in what is real and what is not. You will have to accept the evidence of your eyes.'

'Last night you said you would explain. You told me—'

'Are you hungry?' he said and grinned. 'I'm famished.' From his rucksack, he handed me a bottle of water. 'The Slaughtered Man makes a fine breakfast.'

'The Slaughtered Man?'

'The pub in the village. We'll eat, and then I will tell you all you need to know.'

'Very well,' I said sternly, 'but I won't be put off forever.'

James stared at the painting again. 'You're not a believer. I can sense it.'

It was a statement rather than a question. 'No,' I said. 'I was brought up as a Catholic, but I'm no longer a believer.'

'Faith is important. In the days ahead, it will be your best weapon.' He looked at me and smiled. 'Nourishment,' he said and strode off with me following in his wake.

'Last night,' I said, through captured breaths as I struggled to keep up with him. 'I spotted something in the churchyard. A ... creature.'

He paused. 'Carrion,' he said and resumed his relentless march.

'Carrion?'

He stopped again. 'They feed on the dead.'

'Are they dangerous?'

'Not really. There are much more dangerous ...' his words barely a whisper.

I shook my head. 'These creatures ... Why?'

'They have their place in Nearhope. They were once human like you. A long time ago. But they're lost now. A punishment for ... Still ...' He smiled again. 'They serve a purpose, I suppose. Like the animals in your world that feed on the dead. Crows, foxes and the little creatures that dispose of them. Without which, you would be knee-deep in corpses.'

'Do a lot of people die in Nearhope?'

He took in a lungful of air. 'Nearhope is on the edge of a battleground, and wherever there is conflict, deaths ensue.' With that, he strode on again.

The walk was a pleasant one. The lane into the village meandered down along a hedge-lined road and through the most breathtaking countryside I'd ever encountered. The beauty of the flowers and shrubs was utterly captivating – like nothing I'd ever seen. Animals were abundant – rabbits and squirrels danced across our path as we continued, and birds of all sizes and colours darted from hedgerow to field and back again. I was astounded at the variety and the number of trees stretching out into the distance as far as the eye could see. As if the best springtime elements had been stitched together into one glorious and wondrous tapestry.

James slowed as we reached a large stone signpost with NEARHOPE carved into it and abruptly stopped. 'I must tell you, Felix, not to be taken in by what you see. Appearances can easily fool.'

'But back there, you said—'

He smiled. 'I will instruct you. You must listen and do as I ask. I alone am the one you should trust.' His green eyes bore down on me and swept aside my protestations.

I nodded my understanding and trained my gaze along the road. People milled about, seemingly oblivious to us. The style of dress was unusual – it wasn't entirely modern, but it wasn't old-fashioned either. Unique was the word that sprung to mind.

We carried on past shops – butcher, baker, post office, ironmonger, chemist, and many more. Nearhope was like a small, quaint village, almost, but not quite, quintessentially English but lacking something that made it appear odd.

We reached the pub, and I gazed up at the sign swaying gently in the breeze – a picture of a man lying dead on some battlefield. The Somme, perhaps?

James placed a hand on my shoulder. 'Will a full English do you?' he said.

'I'm ravenous.' I hadn't noticed my appetite on the walk into the village, but now my stomach ached with the familiar pain one experiences when you haven't eaten for a long time. I followed him inside and sat opposite my companion.

A burly, red-faced man looked up from behind the bar and placed several bottles on the countertop. 'Martha,' he shouted, 'we have customers.'

A door swung open to the right of the bar, and a woman emerged. 'Morning, gents,' she said, wiping her flour-covered hands across her apron. 'What will it be?'

James fixed her with those green eyes of his. 'Two cooked breakfasts, please.' She nodded and returned to the kitchen.

'James,' I said. 'How can I be hungry if I'm dead?'

He sat back in his chair. 'There are places beyond life. Places beyond death. These places …' He tapped his chin with his index finger. 'Can appear as real as the life you knew.' He smiled. 'It does not do to dwell on such matters. On the contrary, acceptance of this is for the best. After all, even in your world, things you accept as real are not as they are.' He tapped his head. 'Your brain conjures up a sense of reality. Isn't that so?'

'Well, yes, I suppose. Of course, as a man of science, I understand what you are saying, but …?'

'Well then, Felix, you must accept the evidence of your senses unless I instruct you otherwise.'

I had many more questions, but James looked away in his imitable style, non-verbally informing me that the conversation, or at least this part, was at an end.

I had to admit that the meal was superb. I rarely ate a large breakfast – some fruit or toast usually sufficed – but the wonderfully prepared fare was most welcome.

James leant back in his chair and smiled. 'Nice?'

'It was,' I said and wiped my mouth with the napkin. I studied my companion as he sipped his tea. 'You must understand,' I said, 'it's been a puzzling time since we met.'

'I realise that.'

'It's just …' I paused, searching for the appropriate words. 'My head is filled with questions.' I patted my jacket pocket, pulled out a small pad I always carried, plucked a pen from my pocket, and opened the book. 'You don't mind if I make some notes, do you?'

James held up a hand. 'It's difficult for me to explain everything. Words are not always the ideal way to get something across. They can be clumsy, cumbersome.'

'It's the lecturer in me,' I said. 'I'm always taking down notes.' I leant in closer as the landlord appraised us, not even attempting to disguise the fact he was looking across. 'Tell me about Nearhope. Why does it look like an English village, and why have we come here? Why did you bring me? What is to become of me?' I glanced over James's shoulder at the landlord, who was still looking at us.

James leant closer. 'Ignore him. He's unimportant.' He clasped his hands together and rested them against his chin. 'Nearhope,' he began, 'as I told you in the church, Nearhope is a place which sits between good and evil. A hinterland, you might say. As I explained earlier, do not believe everything you see.' I nodded, and he continued as I took notes. 'The people who inhabit this place are lost. They don't know they're dead. They don't even know who they were previously.'

I paused in my scribblings. 'I'm dead, and I know who I am?'

'You're different. I sought you out and brought you here.'

'Why?'

He drained his cup. 'I've been here before. You are my ticket to areas of Nearhope, and beyond, that I need to travel to. My presence mustn't be known about unless I wish it.'

'Nearhope and beyond?'

He waved a dismissive hand. 'Later. I will explain what lies beyond Nearhope later.'

'Why me, though? There must be a reason you chose me?'

He shrugged. 'I can't answer that yet. There was a trail, a sense of you, which I followed. I don't know why you were chosen. Your face and the knowledge of where I would find you arrived like any other thought.'

I glanced across at the landlord, now joined by his wife, and then back to James. 'How can they not know they are dead?'

'You didn't.'

I rubbed at the bristles on my chin. He had a point. I didn't.

'Check the pulse in your neck.'

I did as he instructed and frowned. 'I have a pulse. It beats as it always has.'

'Is the beating real or not?' he said somewhat enigmatically.

'Well, it feels real to me.'

'Maybe it's just an illusion.'

11

'I suppose, but …'

'The people in Nearhope live a perilous existence,' he said. 'Their …' He glanced away as if looking for the right words. '… soul is the prize.'

I scoffed. 'Soul. Oh, come on, James. You don't expect—?'

'What you believe is up to you. But, unfortunately, reality has a habit of forcing acceptance on people.'

'If the soul is the prize,' I said, 'who is battling for them?'

'I think you already know that.'

We both looked at the door as it burst open, and a man carrying a rifle entered. He strode across to the bar and slammed his weapon on the counter.

'What's up?' the landlord asked.

He grunted. 'Two large whiskies.'

The landlord pushed a glass under the optic and placed it in front of the man before repeating the process.

He downed the contents of the first glass and snatched up the second. 'Molly's missing.'

The landlord's eyes widened. 'George's girl?'

He nodded and tipped the second drink into his mouth, swallowing it with a grimace. 'We're getting a search party together. George is rounding them up.'

The landlady leant forward. 'When did she go—?'

'Last night, at about eight o'clock.'

She glanced at her husband. 'What on earth was she doing outside at that time?' she said.

The man rubbed his face. 'Some daft argument at home.'

'She shouldn't be out at night,' the landlord said. 'Everyone knows how dangerous it is.'

He pushed the empty glasses towards the landlord. 'Don't you think I know that? Another whisky.' He tossed some coins onto the bar. 'One more, and I'm going.'

The landlord pulled off his apron and laid it across the bar. 'Keep your money.' He pushed it back across the counter and glanced at his wife. 'Look after the place. I'm going with them.'

She took hold of his arm. 'Are you sure?' she whispered. 'You know how—?'

'Just do as I say, Martha.' His wife nodded, filled another glass and handed it to the man.

I leant in closer and nudged James. 'Should we help?'

James shook his head. 'It's none of our business.'

'But a girl's missing,' I said. 'She could—?'

'She's lost. If she was out last night, she's lost.' He stood and fished inside his trouser pocket.

I followed him towards the bar. Grasping hold of his arm, I halted his progress. 'How can you be so certain?'

James sighed. A long world-weary sigh. 'I just know. The creatures you saw last night … Eventually, she will become like them.' He continued over to the bar and stopped. 'Have you any rooms?' he asked.

The landlady focused her attention on him as the man with the gun eyed him up and down. 'Yes,' she said. 'Two rooms, is it?'

'Yes. How much do I owe you for the breakfasts?'

'I'll put it on your room,' she said.

The man sipped his whisky as he continued to stare at James. 'Don't I know you? Your face seems familiar.'

James turned to him. 'I don't see how. I've never been to Nearhope in my life.'

The man picked up his glass again, furrowed his brow and looked at the landlady. 'Tell Oliver to meet us in the town square.' He downed his drink in one. 'Gentlemen,' he said and hastened through the door.

'How long are we staying?' I asked, looking down at James stretched out on his bed.

He yawned. 'I'm not sure. But a bed for the night is better than sleeping on a pew at the church.'

I agreed with him on that. While James slept, I retired to my own room and lay down. The events of the previous day still puzzled me. I suppose one would think them dreamlike, but I can assure you it didn't feel that way. Everything about Nearhope appeared genuine. The town, buildings, and people all possessed a solidity that screamed reality. I made further notes before placing my book back inside my jacket.

My attention was drawn to a commotion outside. I wandered over to the window and, lifting the net curtain, peered out. A group of people gathered, some carrying guns, others makeshift weapons. Reminiscent of one of those movies I watched as a child – Frankenstein or The Werewolf – where the townsfolk search for the monster that has committed some horrific act. I don't know why that thought came to me. It just did. One of the group – an imposing bruiser of a man – addressed the crowd and barked what I took to be instructions before they headed along the road and out of sight. I returned to my bed and resumed my position.

Why did James think searching for the girl was a waste of time? And what did he mean by *lost*? Not dead, lost. He said she would become one of those creatures. Why and how? I resolved to get to the bottom of Nearhope when he woke – I would not put up with his obfuscation any longer. I closed my eyes and thought of Jenny, my wife. Ten years had passed since she'd died. The thoughts of her had a habit of appearing when I was worried or concerned about something, arriving unwanted and unwelcome, returning me to that fateful day. I closed my eyes and tried to push the memories aside, hoping, rather foolishly, that their visit would be a brief one. Shifting onto my side, I winced at the sting of anguish that washed over me – the utter feeling of desolation. The guilt, the impotence, and a plethora of other well-known emotions hectored me like playground bullies until they ultimately got their wish, and I drowned in a sea of tears.

THE REAL JAMES

FELIX – On waking, I felt the presence of James sitting opposite me in an armchair.

'You've been asleep a long time,' he said.

'How long?'

'Four hours.'

I sat up in bed and, planting my feet on the floor, stood. 'I know what they mean when people say, *I slept like the dead.*'

He smiled. 'I guess so. We have to hurry. It's afternoon, and we need to make tracks.'

I rubbed my eyes. 'Where?'

'All in good time.'

I paused, considering my response with my arms folded. 'I'm not going anywhere until you tell me everything.'

James laughed. 'Everything is a lot.' I slumped back onto the bed, mentally biting my tongue. Clearly, he sensed my annoyance. He sighed. 'What do you want to know?'

'Why have you brought me here?'

'I told you,' he said. 'I needed you to get to where I'm going.'

I stood again. 'But why me?'

'I told you that—'

'You're lying,' I said. 'I can tell.'

'We have to go to the other side of Nearhope.' He wandered across to the window and looked out. 'All will become clear then.'

'No,' I said firmly. 'I won't go. You drag me to this place and expect me to do your bidding. Well, I won't have it.'

'There are things—'

I huffed. 'There are things? I'm not a bloody child. Good God, man.'

'Please don't take his name in vain,' he said, 'and I'm not a man.'

'What are you, then? What are you if you're not a man?'

15

He grunted. 'You wouldn't understand. You can't comprehend.'

'How the hell do you know? How dare you assume—'

'Felix, calm down.'

'Why should I? For all I know, you could be tricking me. Using me for your own nefarious deeds.'

He strode towards the door. 'I'll meet you downstairs.'

'No, you bloody well don't,' I said and took hold of his arm.

I fell from a place of safety to a place of torment. The images that assaulted my mind came thick and fast. A lifetime – James's lifetime – cascaded and washed over me in a torrent of torture and misery. I saw it all in the moment I held onto his arm. The corruption, the pain, the anguish in graphic detail as it bludgeoned its way into my consciousness and crushed my soul in one swift onslaught. The blood-curdling screams of agony from countless individuals assaulted my senses. Skin flayed from bodies, eyes gouged from their sockets, limbs severed, and others ripped from their owners. Pitiful people burnt alive, others crushed, smashed and bloodied beyond recognition. And the smell – few of my senses were spared the worst of it all – pervaded and seeped into every pore of my being. A lifetime of suffering and obscenity laid bare before my eyes. But not like a film or an image. As if I was there. As if partaking and, on some occasions, perpetrating these acts. I dropped to the floor as my legs gave way and curled into a ball. I recognised the place I'd seen. It had a name feared the world over. Hell.

James lifted me into a seated position and propped me against the wall. I wiped the tears from my eyes and stared at him. I couldn't speak. The images had stolen my voice.

'I'm sorry,' he said. 'You weren't meant to see that. You caught me unawares.'

'I–I–I saw it. I saw that place. It truly exists.'

James squatted, clasped his hands together in a prayer-like stance, and held them over his mouth. 'Yes.'

'And you,' I said. 'You're a Demon?'

'I am.'

Tears rolled down my cheeks unabated. 'The things you have done. The things you have seen.' I covered my mouth with a hand, ran for the bathroom, and dropped to my knees just in time as my breakfast was heaved from my stomach and deposited into the toilet.

I emerged ten minutes later and sat on the bed. 'Sorry about that.'

'Now you know.'

'If you're a Demon, what are you doing here?'

He sat next to me. 'You know how evolution works?' I nodded. 'You also know why there are so many different species in your world?'

'Yes, I know that. Over time slight variations to creatures make for the complexity of life.'

'I was a Demon. As you saw, Demons are awful creatures. Demons carry out terrible things.'

'Yes, I saw that too.'

'Don't ask me how, but almost imperceptibly, I changed from who I was to who I am.'

'When did this happen?'

'The time in your world is different. In my world, time doesn't exist, not as you know it. But if I hazarded a guess, I'd say thousands of years ago using your understanding.'

'Are there more like you?' I asked. 'More that have changed?'

'There are. As you can imagine, in my world, they are not welcome. They are feared.'

'I see. And Nearhope?'

'Nearhope is a place where souls I have saved reside.'

'Why do you bring them here?'

He sighed. 'I can't answer that. I'm just … I know it's what I must do. I have to save the tormented. They don't belong in that place.'

'Who tells you to do this?'

'I think we both know who.'

I stood and walked over to the window and stared outside. Nearhope looked different from the springtime scene which greeted us on our arrival. It now appeared later in the year, as if in the middle of summer. I turned to face James. 'It looks different.'

He joined me at the window. 'Different? How?'

'It was spring when we arrived this morning. Now it's—'

'Ah, yes,' he said. 'I'd almost forgotten. It's summer.'

'Yes.'

'Do you remember the night we arrived and how cold it was?'

'Yes. Like winter.'

'Like winter. Later today, as the evening approaches, you will notice more changes.'

'Autumn?'

'Yes.'

'This is all so strange.'

'Nearhope is a strange place in many ways, but over time you don't notice anymore.'

I thought for a moment about what James had said earlier and gathered my thoughts before I spoke. 'If someone tells you to save these people, how do … How do you know who to save?'

'I am compelled. Their image appears, and I know I must bring them here.'

'The girl who went missing. What has happened to her?'

'She will be lost again.'

'Lost?'

He nodded. 'She is lost for good. There are no second chances.'

'But if you've saved her once, can you not save her again?'

'I know that I mustn't. Don't ask me how I know, I just do. There are no words. It's as if a seed is planted and grows until I have the notion. It's a bit like not understanding, and then …'

'And you know you mustn't save someone you have already saved?'

He placed a hand on my shoulder, and I flinched, remembering our earlier touch. 'That's it exactly.' He tapped his head. 'It's inside here. The knowledge that once they are taken back, there is no return. It's as if they were given one more chance, and when that chance is squandered …'

'Why Nearhope, though? Why bring them here?'

He looked out of the window again. 'It's better than where they have come from. Unfortunately, they have no true home, so Nearhope will have to do.'

'Yes, I can see that, but it seems such a futile endeavour. If you are going to save them, surely there is a place the opposite of …' I don't know why, but I could not bring myself to utter the words. It seemed wrong to speak their names.

James continued to stare down. 'The people you see here …' He nodded outside at the people merrily going about their business. 'Are not who they seem.'

I studied him, trying to divine his thoughts. He appeared to be struggling with the words. 'I'm not sure I understand,' I said.

'The people in Nearhope are here because of what they did in your world.'

'They did wrong?'

He half-smiled. 'We're not talking about trivialities. The people in Nearhope.' He pointed towards the average-looking inhabitants below. 'Have done terrible things. Almost unforgivable things. But Christ offers them forgiveness. They are forbidden from entering the Almighty's realm, so he has created this place for them.'

'But surely, Nearhope isn't large enough to accommodate them all?'

'There are other places like Nearhope which are beyond my scope. My realm is Nearhope. I do what I must. I do what I can.'

'Why do you think you are commanded to bring them here?'

'Maybe …' He shrugged. 'Maybe they have served their sentence. Maybe it's believed that they have suffered enough for their crimes. Forgiveness is *His* alone. I do not judge. No one is beyond redemption.'

'Yes,' I said. 'I can see how that might seem.'

He hurried towards the door. 'We must go. We don't want to be out in the open late at night.'

'James,' I said. He stopped and turned to face me, his face betraying him. He knew what I would ask. 'When I touched your arm, amongst …'

I gulped and shuddered as I remembered the images. 'There was something else. I recognised Jenny.'

He closed his eyes briefly and then looked directly at me. 'Some people do not deserve to be there but somehow slip through the net.'

I brought a hand up to cover my mouth. 'She's there, in that dreadful place? My Jenny?'

'That's why I brought you here. We're going to get Jenny out and bring her to Nearhope.'

BENJI

FELIX – James and I walked away from the pub and out of town. Our feet crunched along the path covered in red and gold leaves still floating down from lofty trees above, creating a carpet of autumnal colour. And like all the countryside surrounding Nearhope, it appeared to go on forever. I pulled my heavy coat around my neck as the wind shivered through the trees.

I had been silent since the revelation and didn't know what to say. If words existed to describe my inner thoughts, they were beyond me. I tried not to think of Jenny or, indeed, Benji. No good could come from dwelling on it, only a place of sadness and darkness.

The happy years, for there were happy years before their deaths, were now tainted. The memories of our good times resided in a place I no longer wished to visit. I asked James why she was there in that place of filth, decay, corruption, and utter desolation. He shrugged and repeated what he'd told me in my room. I wavered in asking him about my son. I feared what he would say, but James smiled and assured me that Benji was not there, that he was not dammed, like his mother, to live in eternal purgatory. I somehow managed to hang on to my tears until James had gone downstairs.

We walked on, but the memories from my past would not be quieted. As I knew they would, they arrived and carried me forcibly to a place I did not want to go. My mind drifted back to ten years before.

The day dawned like any other day – unremarkable and mundane. I had a couple of meetings, one in the morning and the other late afternoon. I couldn't tell you what they were about, unimportant as they now appear, as my mind has expunged them. Sitting in my office and about to leave for home, Jenny phoned.

'Felix,' she said, her voice vastly different from her usual calm, assured self. 'Benji's missing.'

It was Wednesday and Jenny's turn to collect him from school. She'd been working on a new vaccine, lost track of time, and when she arrived at the school, there was no sign of him. I asked her all the usual questions – had another parent taken him home with their child? Was he with friends? But gradually, reality chipped away at hope. As hours became days and days turned into weeks, it eventually dawns on you that you will probably not see your son alive again. Jenny blamed herself, and I watched as my gorgeous, funny, intelligent wife slipped inexorably into despair. She thought I blamed her, and I'm ashamed to admit that in my darkest hours, I did. If only she'd been there to pick him up. If only … It's incredible the hours you spend mulling over the events. Unbelievable how all-consuming it becomes. How things you loved to do together, food and drink you once enjoyed, the visits to shows and events, the activities you adored and how all of it, every aspect and facet that made up your life, are swept away and crushed in the tidal wave of loss.

Loss is not a unique experience, and it turned out that the abduction of a child was not as rare as I imagined. We attended meetings with other parents who, over ten years, had, like us, a child who disappeared. They were all boys, and the police clearly thought them linked. The children had gone missing after school, like Benji. There were times when what was happening to us seemed like one long nightmare and didn't appear to wear the clothes of reality. Having your child abducted happened to other people, not us. It happened to parents who didn't bother with their children, who didn't look after them properly. That's what you think. But the parents I met were just like us. They loved their boys. They adored and worshipped their children and, like us, were utterly bereft at their loss.

Would it be better never to find out what happened to them? Would it be better not to know of their suffering? Or, to use that awful phrase, *did we want closure*? The choice was not ours to make.

The television sprung into life as I sat and watched the news. I reached for the remote and increased the volume when I recognised the detective dealing with Benji's abduction. They had pursued a suspect after some information came to light regarding his vehicle. A car crash had killed the two occupants outright. The police searched the house they lived in, but, in a less guarded moment, the detective admitted he was confident it was connected to the disappearance of young boys going back over a decade.

When you think the blackest time you have ever lived through couldn't get any blacker, life has a habit of disabusing you of that notion. William Arthur Franklyn – a forty-five-year-old man, father of a sixteen-year-old girl – was the perpetrator. They found traces of the boys and footage on a computer that catalogued his crimes and what he did to them inside his house. His daughter, only a mere child when the first boy was taken, assisted him. This twisted pair planned and executed each abduction to perfection. We waited for news of where he'd hidden the bodies, and that wasn't long in coming. In the back garden of his property lay the final resting place of six children. Benji was the third recovered. DNA identified our son, and the closure I mentioned earlier was ours. The funeral, tears, and media frenzy went on and on for an interminable time.

I devoured every bit of information I could about Franklyn and his daughter. What turns people into monsters? His neighbours and former friends came forward and spoke of someone who seemed ordinary. On the face of it, he was someone who appeared to be a single parent trying his best to bring up his daughter. We were spared a trial by their deaths, something that may well have ultimately crushed me. I blame myself for what happened to Jenny. Grief is an individual journey endured on one's own. I never noticed how far she'd slipped down into her personal abyss.

On the anniversary of the loss of Benji, she'd taken a handful of tablets and run a warm bath, downed a bottle of wine, and, the inquest would say later, slipped beneath the water and drowned. The pills probably would not have killed her if discovered earlier. Another funeral, another long, black road I had to travel and slowly, painfully so, I stitched the remnants of my life back together. From a previously unknown place, I found the resolve and strength to not give up.

You never forget those people who are taken. You carry them inside. The memories sit in a dark and dismal place where you hope and pray they will stay. But of course, they won't. They arrive when you least expect them. A maelstrom of loss and despair takes you back to square one, and this is your burden, which you must put up with until you, too, die. Losing Benji was horrible, but my cross may have been easier to bear if I still had Jenny. At times I hated her for leaving me alone to grieve and taking the easy way out. How stupid was I to think that? But feelings manifest out of nowhere, and we need to deal with them. These phantoms of sadness appear and disappear, at will, and forever haunt. You have to fight, though, or you may find yourself slipping towards your end. Jenny must have been so sad, so unbelievably grief-stricken, that the dawning of a new day was too much to contemplate. It isn't an easy way out. It's a realisation that you cannot go on anymore. Fighting and resistance are so futile that there is no other choice.

I carried on with a mixture of stubbornness and strategy. Avoiding the places we used to go together, I altered almost everything associated with the three of us. I ate different food and drank an alternative wine. I rarely went out and even shunned people I knew would remind me of Jenny and Benji. I Ignored birthdays and anniversaries. As much as I wanted to remember them, I also tried to erase them from my life. I desperately wanted to once again experience a new day that wasn't tainted by the emptiness and sadness of bereavement. A chance to judge my life by what it was now, not what it once was.

James and I continued in silence, with these thoughts hanging heavy in my mind.

THE FACE OF EVIL

James halted, took in a lungful of air and continued.

'You've been quiet.' I said.

'You were lost in your thoughts.' He stopped again. 'They were not pleasant?'

I lowered my head. 'No.'

'We'll stop up ahead,' he said. 'I'll need to scout the area.'

'Are we close?'

'Half a mile or so.'

We walked on for a few more moments before stopping near a dense group of trees. He crouched, picked up a handful of soil and leaves, and sniffed them. 'One of my brethren passed this way.'

'A Demon?' James nodded. I shuddered. The image of what one looked like still burnt brightly in my mind.

'It was some time ago.' He looked around. 'Over here,' he said, pointing to a small opening beneath a wizened old tree. 'You wait in there. I've often rested inside there myself. I won't be too long.'

'You will come back for me?'

He smiled and placed a hand on my shoulder. 'Of course. But keep out of sight.'

I watched as James slowly picked his way through the undergrowth in the ever-dying light. Then I climbed beneath the tree and inside the surprisingly roomy opening. I have no idea how much time had passed as my watch, I'd discovered, did not work anymore. I didn't know if it was broken or if this place caused it to cease working. Then I heard it. Hardly a noise at first, but then a little louder. A voice, a girl's voice. I climbed from my redoubt and strained to hear. 'Help me,' she said. 'Please help me.'

What should I do? I was torn. It had to be the missing girl from the village. Using the plaintive cries of the girl to guide me, I inched my way closer. The daylight was almost gone, and, like a vast blanket of black, the darkness wrapped itself around me and everything else. Her shouts had faded to a whimper as I spotted her up ahead. Something was fastened to her foot, tightly gripping her ankle, and as I edged ever nearer, I realised what held her fast. With its jagged-toothed jaws biting deeply into bloodied flesh, a mantrap tethered her to the ground. I hurried across, but as she rotated her head, I caught sight of her face. I recoiled as a lightning bolt of recognition hit me, and as I watched, she changed from the familiar to something hideous.

The eyes, now bright red, burrowed into me. I took a step backwards, unable to pull my gaze away from this aberration. The creature – for that's what it had become – made some unearthly guttural noise that shook me to my core. I edged away as it bared its teeth – discoloured, rapier-sharp teeth that grew from shrunken gums. I knew what was coming. The creature sprang forward, and as I backed further away, I stumbled and fell. The pain was unbearable as it grasped the lower part of my leg and pressed talon-like nails deep into my calf. I screamed in agony, and more with desperation than design, kicked out, catching the head of the beast. It hung onto its prey with those nails pressing further into my flesh as blood oozed through my trousers and dropped onto the floor. I kicked again and then again. The creature, seemingly dazed, loosened the vice-like grip, and I pulled my legs away from those ghastly weapons and edged my way backwards. The beast, blood now coating those horrible teeth from the blows I delivered, growled as spittle dripped sickeningly from its mouth. It prepared to launch again, but as I backed away from this Demon, I felt the rough bark of a tree behind me, and terror rooted me to the spot. Gazing wide-eyed, I was helpless to save myself as it sprang, those torturous claws ready to wreak more injury, but it stopped mid-air and fell to the earth, its reach half a metre short.

The Demon growled and pulled on the chain anchoring the mantrap to the ground. It held firm, the creature's efforts to get to me, its quarry, thwarted by the metal fetter. Briefly, relief washed over me, but as I watched, it crawled back closer to where it was fastened, allowing some slackness in the chain. Contorting its body until bent double at the waist, it began chewing through its leg above the jaws of the mantrap. I gagged at the sound of ripping flesh and the crunch of teeth against bone. It turned and looked at me, bits of flesh and bone expelled from its mouth in one bloody mass. Still seated on the ground, I edged around the tree and waited as it finally severed the foot from the leg and launched itself again. I threw my arms up in a futile attempt at self-preservation and closed my eyes in anticipation of its coup de gras.

I heard a thud and then a whimper as the creature was thrown to one side. James stood nearby with a large piece of a branch hanging from his hands, gazing at me through eyes which blazed red, even redder than the creatures. And then, a crunching, grinding noise, as two small nubs appeared on his forehead. These grew in length, forcing their way upwards until they reached about five inches high. The horns resembled a ram's as they twisted and curled above him. He strode towards the stricken Demon lying on the floor, but it scurried away from him, climbing clumsily upright, hobbling on its one good foot and the bloody stump before disappearing deep into the trees.

'Sicarius,' it taunted. 'Sicarius.' The voice faded into nothingness as it moved further away.

I glanced towards the mantrap, which held the foot between the teeth. Then the stink hit me. My sense of smell, dormant during the attack, now allowed the putrid stench to assault and assail my nostrils. I watched as the foot decayed in front of me. First, the flesh rotted until it fell from the bone and leeched into the earth below. Then the bone disintegrated into an ever-growing pile of powder and quickly followed it. I retched. The miasma of putrescent decay hung heavy around me, and then, as I thought the smell could not get any worse, it vanished.

James joined me near the tree and knelt. His features were back to normal save for his eyes which briefly glowed red before returning to a striking viridescence. 'Are you ok?' he said.

I groaned and tentatively probed my injury. 'My leg ...'

He opened his backpack, took out a small bottle, and, pulling my trouser up to expose the wound, tipped clear liquid onto my leg. I grimaced – the pain, though terrible, wasn't as bad as that inflicted by the creature. He hooked an arm beneath my shoulder and assisted me to my feet. Placing my foot on the floor, I slowly applied my body weight. It wasn't perfect, but I could walk.

'We have to get away from here,' he said. 'There may be more.'

'The creature feared you. It was terrified when it saw your face.'

'Even here, there is a hierarchy. It's one of the lower order.'

'Who is Sicarius?' I asked.

'Someone from the past. We must go now.'

'How did it get trapped?' I said, following him.

'The people from Nearhope set the traps,' he said over his shoulder. 'They place them in the daytime, hoping to ensnare one.'

We travelled on, my leg improving with every footfall. 'James?' I said. He glanced at me. 'The girl?'

I stopped. 'Yes, the girl. It was Molly Franklyn. Her father murdered my boy.'

'I know,' he said.

'You know? Yet you brought them to Nearhope? Liberated them from their place of torture?'

'Yes. I was compelled to do so.'

I scoffed. 'Compelled? William Franklyn murdered my son. He murdered at least five other sons. He tortured and murdered them, and Molly Franklyn assisted him. She watched and laughed as he ...' my words dried up to nothing.

'I know all this, Felix. I understand—'

'You understand nothing. Whatever was being inflicted on those two, they deserved it. You don't care about what they did, do you?'

'You've seen into my mind. You know what I have done, what I have witnessed.'

I shook my head and walked on. James quickly caught up with me. 'I have no choice,' he said. 'I don't decide.'

'Who does?' I said. 'Who *compels* you? Whose beck and call are you at? God? Well, if it is, he's not *my* bloody God.'

James took hold of my face between his hands and looked deep into my eyes. 'I'm sorry that I don't have the answers you seek. I'm sorry you saw that back there. I'm just a small part in ... I have to do it.'

My anger, under his gaze, evaporated. 'I'm sorry,' I said.

'We're nearly there.' He nodded forward. 'Just over that hill. I need you to be strong, Felix. There must be other reasons you're here. Not just Jenny.' He tapped his head. 'When the time is right, he will let me know.' I lowered my head. 'Maybe,' he continued, 'maybe he wanted you to see her.' He shrugged unconvincingly.

I shook my head. 'I don't know. I really don't. And Molly Franklyn? What will happen to her?'

He paused before answering, 'As I told you earlier. She was given a second chance which she squandered. The Demon inside her will slowly devour her soul. It will search for another when this is complete, leaving only a husk behind.' He paused again. 'The creatures you saw outside the church ... That is her destiny,' he said. He lowered his eyes, a sadness clouding them. Then he turned away from me and surveyed the hill. Clearly, our conversation was at an end. I looked upwards too, but not at the slope, at the moon – full and glowing, but with a tinge of red etched across it. I stood transfixed.

'When we reach the top, I want to do something,' he said, breaking my almost hypnotic stare.

'What?'

'Can you remember when we travelled into Nearhope?'

I nodded. 'A blackness where light could not penetrate.'

James placed a hand on my shoulder. 'I had to lock you out. But you and I have come far, Felix.' I indicated that I understood, and he continued. 'The creature who attacked you may have alerted someone to my presence.'

'Who?'

James lowered his eyes and winced as if remembering something harrowing. 'Asmodeus,' he barely whispered, as if uttering his name was forbidden.

'Asmodeus?' I repeated. But as his name stumbled from my lips, a searing pain erupted in my leg from where the creature injured me. I dropped to my knees and then onto my side. I was sure I could feel fingers clawing, pressing, tearing at the wound. James took hold of me, and the pain eased and dissipated as he held me in his arms. 'What was that?' I said.

'We are close to his realm. The creature back there may have a close bond to him.'

I struggled to my feet, the pain now nothing more than an echo. 'If you knew it would recognise you, why didn't you kill it?'

'It's my kin,' he said. 'Let's not dwell on that now. We need to disguise ourselves. I will do as I did before,' he said, 'however, you will be aware this time.'

'I see. I sense a but …'

He frowned. 'This is not as easy for me to do. I find it exhausting.' He paused and searched for words. 'It's like trying to hold a door shut while others push from the opposite side.'

'Ok. Is there anything I can do to help?'

'If I weaken or falter, tread carefully,' he said. 'You have seen inside here.' With this, he tapped his head with a finger. 'There are things, worse things, you would not want to encounter.'

I understood. I had no desire to stare into the face of Hades again.

James held out a hand. 'Ready?'

'Ready,' I said and took hold of it. For a few seconds, I said nothing. I say said, but when I spoke, it wasn't words. It was thoughts. I viewed my hand and examined it, familiarising myself with my new surroundings. It was James's eyes I looked through.

'Everything all right?' his voice drifted from somewhere and landed in my consciousness.

'Yes,' I responded. My words created and given birth within me floated gently free.

'We must move on.'

DARK NEARHOPE

FELIX – We ascended the hill at a pace surprising to my middle-aged mind. Strangely reminiscent of being much younger, much fitter, but the heavy breaths I could hear were not mine – they belonged to James and the effort and toil to climb the hill was his alone.

We reached the top. I don't know what I expected to find there, but pausing, we scanned the land. The road wound its way down towards the houses below. It looked just like Nearhope, but then again, it didn't. I can't explain it better than that. It was Nearhope, but it wasn't Nearhope. I don't have any other experience with which to draw. The road, the town up ahead, was the absolute image of Nearhope but also wholly unlike it.

We walked on with feet that skimmed across the ground. James focused our gaze up ahead, barely glancing left or right. I could hear creatures nearby – not the cute furry animals back at Nearhope, but noisy, chattering, scurrying, unfamiliar creatures. The type that hides in the shadows in your worst nightmares.

We reached a stone sign similar to the one at Nearhope but crumbling and cracked with barely readable letters. A dark, almost black vine of a type I had never seen before wrapped itself around the sign, appearing, as silly as it sounds, to be choking the life from it. A smell drifted into my mind that I can only describe as an odour of putrid vegetables left to rot in the fields. We passed shops, the windows cracked and filthy, their signs hanging forlornly from gallows brackets.

We stopped fifty metres from the pub as the door came crashing open, and a man stumbled out. Blood dripped from his arm, which hung loosely by his side. He passed us and glanced over his shoulder towards the pub as another man emerged and hurried after him, carrying a large axe which he juggled from hand to hand. The injured man stumbled and fell onto his back as his attacker reached him.

'Please,' he pleaded and held up a defensive hand. The axe crashed and smashed into the arm between his wrist and elbow. The man screamed. I would never have imagined the sound he made had I not witnessed it. The noise appeared to emanate from his soul. His arm snapped but hung on grimly to the rest of his body, barely held there by flesh and sinew. A jet of red liquid fountained from the gaping wound and onto the road with every pump of the victim's heart. His assailant struck again, catching the man on his knee, as bone yielded quickly to the onslaught of metal, then one blow followed another. I gave up counting as the weapon continued to smash and pulverise his body until it barely resembled a man. And then, with one final sickening blow, the axeman brought it down onto his victim's head. The blade sunk deep between the lifeless eyes of the twitching body. The attacker turned, briefly narrowed his eyes at us, and then wandered off as if merely taking an evening stroll.

'Sorry I had to show you that,' James said. The words drifted into my mind from his.

'It was horrific.' I caught my breath. *'You knew it would happen?'*

'His sentence for mortal sins.'

'He killed someone like this?' I asked.

'His wife.'

I took stock but said nothing.

'You feel sorry for him?' James said.

'Yes.'

'What about his wife?' he said.

'Well ... of course. I ... Yes, it must have been terrible.'

'You must understand where we are, Felix, and what we are up against.'

He allowed the words to permeate, and, pushing the door open, we entered the pub. The lighting inside was dim. Lighted candles placed around the room, in different locations, licked hopelessly at the forbidding darkness in an effort to illuminate the gloom. The bar was like the pub back in Nearhope, but then again, it differed so much. A thought entered my head – it was a negative of a photo. James, or rather we – my vantage point dictated by where he looked – surveyed the room. Only a handful of people occupied it, scattered about. They glanced towards us and then lowered their heads as if trying to appear invisible – a palpable fear emanating from every corner. Our conjoined form strode to the bar and hopped onto a stool at one end of the counter. The massive man behind the bar, he must have been six-foot-eight, looked up and wandered across. He stared at us with his dark eyes, then picked up a glass and jerked his head backwards in a non-verbal question.

'A beer with a double vodka in it,' James said.

The man briefly smiled. 'Long time ...' he whispered. 'I didn't recognise you.'

'It's been a while,' James said softly, 'and I'm with someone.'

He nodded knowingly. 'That will be why. Has he a name? Your friend?'

'Felix.'

The giant held out his equally giant hand and swallowed James's in his. 'Felix.'

'I need a favour, Khar?'

'Anything.' he said.

'I have a mission. I'm in search of someone.'

The big man smiled. 'Of course you are. Do you have a name?'

'Jennifer Halshaw. Jenny.'

I snatched at a breath. The mention of her name in this place was somehow wrong.

'It'll take time,' Khar said.

James nodded. 'I realise that.' He took a gulp of his drink. It wasn't unpleasant, but certainly, not the lovely glass of red I would have preferred. 'I need to rest,' he continued. 'You know how exhausting doing this can be.'

Khar plucked a key from a board behind him. 'Room two on the second floor,' he said and placed the key on the bar.

'Thanks.'

'Have you eaten?' Khar said.

'Not for a while.'

'I'll send some food up,' he said and disappeared into the back.

'How do you know Khar?' I asked through thought.

'You make alliances,' James said. *'You help people, and they help you. For the greater cause.'*

'Unusual name, Khar?'

'Kharon,' James said.

'Is he a ... is he like you?'

'Khar is a cross. A crossbreed. His mother was human, his father, a Demon.' James downed his drink, picked up the key and headed up a flight of stairs. We stepped into a dimly lit bedroom with an open fire in one corner, and James paused. I stepped free from him, or rather, James released his hold.

'Ok?' he said.

I nodded. 'Are we safe here?'

'Perfectly.' Someone tapped on the door, and James hurried to open it. Outside, on the floor, lay a wooden tray with the food Khar promised. James returned and offered me one of the plates from the tray, which I thankfully accepted.

'We'll be fine here,' he said. 'As long as we conjoin when in public.'

'Won't they be suspicious of a stranger?'

'We come and go. My world is a huge place. My own face, which you saw back at the wood, might be recognised, but ours will not.'

James placed his half-eaten plate of food onto a small table and lay on one of the two beds. Within moments, my companion's peaceful sleep sound filled the air.

After eating the tasty, yet simple fare, I rested on the bed and tried to sleep. Something, I suspected, would prove a difficult task.

Benji and I walked into the room, and we paused. 'I'll give you twenty seconds start,' I said, 'and then I'm coming after you.'

He laughed, his eyes wide with excitement, and then he was off. 'Eleven, twelve, thirteen,' I said. His fading giggles disappeared as he got further away from me. 'Sixteen, seventeen,' I continued. 'Nineteen, twenty. I'm coming.' A corridor, a room, I wandered slowly, smiling as I crept forward, trying not to make a noise. A floorboard creaked beneath me, begrudging the weight it now bore. Another door, a clown's face picked out in bright colours. I smiled to myself again as I pushed it open and stared into his room, replete with toys. The unmade bed to the left, a desk and chair to the right, and at the end, a wardrobe – the door an inch or two open. 'You'll have to do better than that,' I whispered. 'It's always the same place.' I reached for the handle and silently curled my fingers around it. *One, two, three,* I said in my head and pulled it open. I frowned. It was empty. 'Well, well,' I said, 'not so daft, after all.' That floorboard creaked again, and still smiling, I slowly turned around. He stood there, my Benji, his eyes blood-red, two small horns rising and twisting from his head, his long razor-like teeth set in a sickly grin.

'I've come for you, Daddy,' he said raspingly. 'Mummy's waiting.' I backed away, and as he stepped closer, I caught sight of the axe in his hands as he juggled it from one hand to the other. Then, as my back found the solid wall behind, he launched himself at me …

I sat upright in bed and gasped for air, the image as he bore down on me full of hatred. Rubbing my eyes, I stared at James.

'I was about to wake you,' he said.

I cupped my hands over my face and sucked in air as the image from my dream slowly dissolved into nothingness.

'This place,' he said. 'It brings bad dreams. Nightmares have a life, an existence of their own. They seek you out as you sleep.' He walked over and patted me on the shoulder. 'Come. We must go.'

I stood and stretched. My body ached with a weariness never experienced. James peered outside, and I walked across over to him. 'Shouldn't we wait until morning?'

He smiled. 'There is no morning here.' He held out his hand. 'Ready?' I nodded and took hold of it.

Khar raised his head as we entered the bar. 'Breakfast is on the table,' he said.

James grunted, and we found a seat.

'Tea?' Khar said.

'Yes. Milk and three sugars.' I shuddered. I drank coffee, mainly, but black and unsweetened when I did have the occasional tea.

Khar placed a cup on the table and filled it. 'The legion is here,' he said.

James scooped three spoonsful of sugar into his tea and stirred thoughtfully. 'Have you heard anything?' James said grumpily.

Khar rolled his eyes. 'About the legion? Give me a chance. You only arrived last night.' Khar laughed. 'Ignore him, Felix. James was never an early riser.'

'When will you have some news?' James said.

'I'll send Celestine when I have something.'

I sensed James's face crumpling into a smile. 'How is she?'

'She's well.' Khar tossed the cloth he'd used to wipe the bar over his shoulder. 'Are you staying here long?'

James slurped his sickly-tasting tea. 'I can't. We're travelling back to Nearhope. Tell Celestine she can find me at the pub.'

He nodded. 'I will. Come and see me before you go.'

James grunted and carried on eating his breakfast.

'Who's Celestine?' I asked.

He paused with a piece of bacon in mid-air. *'A friend.'*

'Is she a ...' It was odd how even thinking about what these creatures were, was so difficult.

'She's a Demon hybrid,' he said.

'Like Khar?'

'Not quite. Khar is half human and half Demon. Celestine's mother is half human, and her father is a Demon. Many variations exist in this world.'

'I see. Is she like you?'

'She follows the same path as me. There are many of us from different denominations. We must remain clandestine, though. It would not do if we were discovered.'

'You're a sort of underground?'

'If you like. We do it because we feel it's the right thing to do. But, as I told you, we follow a higher power. We have no choice. It's who we are. But there are those in this realm and beyond who fear us. Fear what we do. They would seek to destroy us given a chance.'

'And the Legion?'

'He commands them. They are his elite. They travel this realm and seek out the new and ...' His voice trailed off.

'Those that are condemned?'

'Your description is quite simple, childlike even, but yes, that's what it amounts to.'

Choosing my words with care, I persisted. *'Aren't you frightened that this Legion may discover you?'*

'Of course, but if I am taken, so be it.'

'Because this higher power has willed it?'

James drained his cup. *'He has no sway over this realm. I could give you a history lesson on how this all began, but it does not matter now. There is a power struggle. There always has been and always will be. Good and evil are just words humans use to describe what they know little about.'*

'I'm sorry,' I said. *'I didn't mean to offend you.'*

'You didn't. It's this place. It calls and hectors me. My defensive carapace is under constant attack. Forgive my rudeness, Felix.'

I stepped back from our thoughts. His need for quietness was palpable.

James held out his hand to Khar. 'Thanks for the hospitality,' he said.

Khar smiled. 'Anytime. You should hear from Celestine in a day or two.'

I glanced into the mirror behind the bar. Khar partially obscured James, but his face was visible. What a bizarre visage greeted me. Though clearly a Demon, James's face bore traces of something else, something human. Me. The image I viewed in the mirror was an amalgamation of the two of us. I smiled inwardly. I then became aware that Khar and James had stopped talking.

'Everything all right, Felix?' Khar asked.

'Fine,' I, or rather James, answered. We exited the pub into a bitterly cold night. It was strange to me, as I was experiencing this vicariously. A commotion to our left caught James's attention, and he turned.

Four figures – human-looking – stared up at the window of a house. A head appeared through the gap and grinned. 'I've found one of them,' he said.

A second head appeared – the person held tightly by the first man. A brief struggle followed before the poor victim was pushed through the gap and plummeted. A sickening thud followed as the body smashed into the ground. The three men below jeered and kicked the prone body of this unfortunate individual. He did not move.

'See if there are any more?' one of the men below said and brought his boot down heavily onto the head of their prey. He laughed as he wiped his blood-covered boot on the victim's clothing before giving the body a final kick.

The door to the property opened, and two more men emerged, holding on to a woman tightly. One of the men outside stepped forward and grabbed her by the throat. 'You know the penalty for harbouring Janus.' He nodded towards what was left of the man. 'You're going to the furnace.' He gripped tighter as the woman fought for breath. 'But not before we have some enjoyment. Bring the rest of the family.'

'There's a youngster,' one of the men holding the woman said. 'What shall I do with it?'

'Bring it too. Our animals need to be fed.' He roared with laughter, and James hurried off down the street.

'Who are they?' I asked.

'The Legion.'

'And the people?'

'The one they killed is Janus. They are cursed and despised. It's against justice to harbour them.'

'What will happen to the people?'

James sighed wearily. 'You don't want to know,' he said.

'But surely these people are Demons like the rest of you?'

'I shouldn't have to remind you of human history. How people who are like you have been despised and victimised. Why should this world be any different?'

I conceded this point, and our journey was quiet until we separated again.

CELESTINE

FELIX – The return journey to Nearhope was uneventful. The heaviness that dogged me – which I hadn't noticed until we got further away from that place – lifted.

While James slept, I took an opportunity to familiarise myself with the town. It was an unsettling place, and the thought that the people who inhabited it had perpetrated such appalling things worried me. Yet, they seemed like anyone from my world. That was the most disturbing thing, their ordinariness. As I wandered, I watched spring turn into summer in a matter of hours. I smiled as I thought about how people in Britain often note that we can have all four seasons in one day – Nearhope truly did. I thought about James's calling and his liberation of the eternally damned. Then I thought about Jenny, my Jenny, and how she must be suffering in that dark place we'd left. I returned to the pub as the green leaves on the trees became tinged with orange, red and gold. The apples and pears on the branches swelled, ripened, and then fell before the chill which accompanied the night in this place dusted the trees with white icing.

James stretched and yawned as he opened the door to his room. He smiled. 'You must be hungry?'

I was indeed hungry. Ravenous, actually. We settled in the pub and enjoyed a hearty meal and several beers. I marvelled at how The Slaughtered Man resembled many a country pub I had frequented before I came to this place. Nearby, the fire in the grate burnt low, and we lapsed into a companionable silence when the door burst open. A small, hooded figure entered, shook the snow from their coat, and strode to the bar. The hood was pulled down, revealing a woman with close-cropped hair.

'A large whisky,' she said to the landlord, who pushed a glass under the optic and half-filled it.

'Put that on my room,' James said.

The woman leant against the bar and smiled. 'Just because you buy someone a drink doesn't give you any rights,' she said.

James stood and wandered over to her. 'Of course not.' A few seconds passed before the pair let out a roar and embraced.

'Uneventful journey?' James said to her.

'Pretty much.'

He led her across to our table. 'This is Felix.'

She held out a hand and shook mine. 'Celestine,' she said. Then, removing her coat, tossed it over a chair and sat opposite us. Celestine had spiked, punk-like hair and reddish-brown, almost mahogany eyes, which, like James's, captivated me.

'You have news?' James said.

Her mouth creased into a frown. 'It's not good. I've located the woman.'

James glanced at me. 'Felix's wife.'

'Ah,' she said. 'Sorry about that, Felix.' She knitted her brow and slightly lowered her gaze.

I shrugged. 'You weren't to know.'

Celestine, regaining her former confidence, leant in close. 'She was taken to the citadel.'

I looked at James, his face clouded with concern as he rubbed his chin. 'I see. I hoped she would be at one of the ...' His voice faded.

'The citadel?' I said. 'Where ... What is the citadel?'

James sighed. 'It's the inner sanctum. The most heavily guarded and widest feared.' He leant closer still to Celestine. 'Do we have anyone there who would aid us? The citadel will not be easy to breach.'

She sat upright and glanced at me. 'No offence, Felix,' she said, 'but entering the citadel would be madness. It could jeopardise our whole organisation. I've discussed it with—'

'Will you help?' James said tersely.

'Why is Felix's wife so important?' she said.

'I don't know at this moment.'

Celestine looked upwards and sighed. 'James,' she said, 'we can't just act on a whim. What if you're discovered? Your knowledge—'

'It came to me in a vision.' James briefly closed his eyes as if deep in thought and then blinked them open. 'He has decreed it. He told me to find Felix and bring him here. He has never failed us before.'

Celestine sipped her drink and sucked in a deep breath. 'If you're sure? There may be a way.'

'I am sure. He would not ask this of me ... of us, if it wasn't important.' James's eyes darted between Celestine and me. 'I sense that this is the beginning.'

'Beginning of what?' she said.

He held up his hand and grasped at thin air. 'It's just out of reach. But of great importance.'

She stood abruptly and swallowed the rest of her drink. 'I'll see what I can do, but I can't promise I can get you in and out of there unharmed.'

James nodded again, and we stood. As I shook hands with Celestine, I caught sight of her reflection in the mirror. The woman's features were now replaced with a demonic face. I pulled my eyes away and sat as James and Celestine embraced before she was gone. He returned to his seat and rubbed his chin again.

'What are you thinking?' I asked. 'Can you get Jenny out of the citadel?'

He smiled unconvincingly at me. 'We can try. That's all we can do.'

We all know how time drags when we wait for something to happen, which is how it was in Nearhope. Days crawled past with a monotony never felt before. Nevertheless, I continued to study James as we endured our tedious and strangely tiring existence.

We ventured into the pub for something to eat when a strange event occurred. The people who came and went in the pub seemed so ordinary, as I've said, that it was easy to forget that they'd committed terrible crimes. But as a man walked in and settled himself at the bar, I stared at him. People who have had loved ones murdered wouldn't expect to come face to face with their killer – certainly not across a bar from them. But here I was in this world, less than four metres from William Franklyn. I studied him as anger welled up in me. A rage I hitherto thought impossible to feel. I stood and set myself to confront this monster when James took hold of my arm.

'He won't remember,' he said.

I glared at James. 'Why?'

'I don't know. But going over there to do ...' He allowed the words to fade.

'Why should he have the luxury of forgetting what he did?' I said through undisguised anger. 'Why shouldn't he be haunted by his crimes?'

James gently pulled me back into my seat. 'I can't answer that. What I do know, what I fervently believe is ...' He looked at me apologetically. '...that forgiveness is the most powerful emotion we have in our possession. It's without equal. You should always remember that.'

'I could never forgive him. How could I? I was robbed of my future, and so were my wife and son.'

'He will have suffered,' James said. 'At the hands of my kin, he will have suffered.'

Tears gently fell from my eyes, and I fought to say the words as my lips quivered with emotion. 'I wasn't there to watch him suffer. I wasn't there to witness his pain.'

James knitted his brow. 'If you had been, would that have made things better?' He placed a hand on my chest. 'Would it have removed the ache from here?'

I wiped away my tears with the sleeve of my shirt and shrugged. 'Maybe.'

James shook his head. 'It wouldn't. When I gained compassion, it crept through me until, like a beacon, it blazed and blinded me with brilliance. I could do nothing to assuage the pain within. Every molecule inside screamed at me like a countless number of accusers. I concealed it from my brethren. Had they found out …' Tears appeared but didn't drop from his eyes. 'The pain inside me was without end. I almost …' He forced a smile and slowly shook his head. 'From a pit of darkness I climbed and slowly my life gained meaning. He called to me and showed me the way.'

Distracted from my own grief, I studied him. 'How did you know you weren't the only one who felt that way?'

'I saw the same thing in others. A look in their eyes that I recognised. When you're not the only one, the burden is not yours to carry alone.'

I looked back towards Franklyn. His head lowered as he sipped his drink.

'He has lost his daughter,' James said. 'He grieves for her as anyone else would.'

'Your faith,' I said. 'Your faith in …?'

James placed a hand on his chest. 'It's like salve to my wound. It will never take the pain away, but it makes it bearable.'

'What happened to Franklyn back there in that dark place?'

'You saw what was inflicted on the man in the street. The one killed with the axe?' I nodded. 'My kin,' he continued, 'are particularly good at enacting suitable punishments. *That inflicted by thee shall be inflicted on thee.*'

I looked to Franklyn again as the merest trace of sympathy tiptoed inside me.

On my daily walk around Nearhope, with the glorious spring sunshine that welcomed me, I perused the shops as if the most natural thing to do. I chatted pleasantly with shopkeepers and customers as one would do in any town. The realisation that these individuals committed heinous crimes hardly occurred to me. James and I enjoyed our usual hearty breakfast before he retired to his room for a customary nap while I stretched my legs.

As I re-entered the pub, I met Franklyn on his way out. His face drawn and haggard.

'Sorry,' he mumbled as we very nearly collided.

I took hold of his arm. 'I'm sorry about your daughter,' I found myself saying.

He lowered his reddened eyes. 'I don't know what possessed her to go so far from the village at night.' He shook his head. 'We don't even have a body to bury.'

I shrugged. What could I say? Why was I even speaking to this man? But James's words about forgiveness resonated with me. I patted him on the shoulder as he left.

'It's a grand day out there,' the landlord said as I entered.

I smiled. 'It is. Every day in Nearhope is a grand day,' I said under my breath.

'Pint?' he asked.

I hopped up onto a stool. 'Why not.' Paying for drinks was never a problem in Nearhope. James suggested that I put a hand in my pocket when I asked him how he paid for things – this I did and discovered money there. Strange, but no stranger than everything else.

He nodded towards the door where Franklyn left. 'He'll never recover from it,' the landlord said as he poured my drink. He shook his head slowly, placed my glass down and wiped the counter with a cloth. 'Never.'

'What do you think happened to her?' I asked, pushing a few coins his way.

He paused his wiping. 'Not sure. Nothing good, though.'

'But she can't just have disappeared.'

'There are beasts out there in the woods,' he said, eyes wide and staring. 'Savage beasts. The people of Nearhope know the score. Don't venture past Mossy Hill after dusk. My parents used to drum that into me.'

'What sort of beasts?'

The landlord rubbed his unruly beard. 'Bears, wolves, lions and the like.'

'I see.'

He leant in closer. 'We put traps out to catch the buggers.'

I took a long, thoughtful drink of my beer. 'Have you caught many?'

He laced his hands and lay them across his ample girth. 'We have. But not enough.'

'Have they ever come into the village?'

The landlord laughed. 'I've never known any in my lifetime, although,' he said, 'they're cunning creatures. They like to stalk and kill. I don't think they'd have the nerve to venture into Nearhope. But, if they did ...' He fixed me with a terrifying glare.

I wondered what he'd done in my world. 'How long have you lived here?' I said.

'All my life. Man and boy. My mother and father before me, and their parents too. There isn't any place like Nearhope.'

'No,' I said quietly. 'Have you ever ventured beyond Nearhope?'

He looked at me as if I'd grown two heads. 'Ventured where?'

'Up the hill.'

The landlord frowned. 'Now, why would I do that? There's nothing beyond.' The door opened, and another customer entered. 'Now then, Tom,' he said to the new arrival. 'What will it be? The usual?'

I drained my glass, nodded at the landlord and Tom, and then headed upstairs. My hand found the door handle when I paused. The unmistakable sound of voices emanating from James's room caught my attention, so I knocked.

'Come in,' James shouted. He stood with Celestine.

'Hello,' I said to her.

She smiled. 'How are you, Felix?'

'I'm well.' I looked at James and then back to Celestine. 'You have news?'

She glanced at James and then back to me. 'I do. It won't be easy getting her out.'

'Jenny,' I said. 'She's called Jenny.'

'Sorry, Felix. Jenny. She's in the deepest part of the citadel.'

I looked at James and shrugged. 'And that's not good?'

He shook his head. 'I know the place. It's heavily guarded.'

'How do you know it?' I asked.

'I spent a long time there.'

'I should go,' Celestine said. 'My absence may be noted if I stay too long.'

James held up his hand with what looked like a piece of paper clutched within it. 'Thanks for this,' he said to Celestine.

She held out her hand. 'Felix,' she said.

I thanked her, and then she left.

James dropped onto the bed. 'Celestine has given me a couple of names. People who are sympathetic to our cause.' He fixed me with a stare. 'I won't lie, Felix. This will not be easy.'

'But we can get her out?'

'Hopefully.'

I slumped down next to him. 'When?'

He sighed. 'I see no reason to delay. Gather your things, and we'll head off.'

I paused at the door. 'I spoke to the landlord earlier.' I searched for the right words. 'He said there are beasts in the woods. Not Demons.'

James smiled. 'The people here don't see Demons. A Demon to them may be a wolf or bear. It's better this way.'

'How come Celestine can come and go if other Demons can't.'

'She's part human, as I told you. That gives her access to Nearhope. But, to the townspeople, she is just another person.'

I asked him about the land beyond the church, the way we came in and why the landlord knew nothing of it.

'There is nothing up the hill,' James said. 'They do not see the church. The people of Nearhope know nothing more than their town, and they know to avoid the woods at night. They are like innocent children.' He looked away in that manner of his. Our conversation was clearly over.

An odd thing to say, I thought as I returned to my room. But lots of stuff in Nearhope was odd. I collected the few items I'd acquired since my arrival and pushed them into my rucksack.

James sat in a corner staring out of the window and into the street as I entered the bar. I sat opposite him and tapped his arm to gain his attention.

'I'm ready when you are,' I said.

He stood. 'Very well.' James addressed the landlord. 'Thanks for the hospitality.'

'You gents off, are you?'

James nodded. 'I've left payment with your wife.'

'Well,' he said, 'anytime you need a bed for the night …'

I joined James and stepped outside. The warm summer sun beat down on the inhabitants of this strange place as James and I briefly exchanged glances and then set off.

THE REALM OF ASMODEUS

FELIX – We walked un-conjoined through late summer and autumn until we found ourselves in winter, where the frost-coated trees glistened beneath the ever-present full moon. We marched on, leaving Nearhope in our wake as we traced the same journey made days earlier until we came across a clearing. James stopped as if trying to remember the way.

'Is everything all right?' I asked as I moved next to him, as he stood close to what looked like a venerable oak tree.

'I'm just trying to get my bearings.'

'Where is it we're going?'

'We have a contact to meet,' he said before striding off with me trailing behind. 'I think this is the right way,' he said over his shoulder as I struggled to keep up. Finally, he stopped and indicated for me to do the same. We edged back into the thicker undergrowth and crouched behind a huge tree.

'What is it?' I whispered.

'Sentinels.'

I frowned. 'What's a—?'

James brought a finger to his lips, indicating he wanted silence. I complied, the pounding of my heart reverberated throughout my body as I looked around, but I couldn't see anything. James appeared to have his sight fixed ahead. Then I spotted someone within the trees, and then a second.

James glanced at me. 'The sentinels are hunting Janus.'

I followed his gaze as he looked away from the two forms ahead. Four men crept into view – they were huge, and each carried some sort of weapon. Stopping in the clearing, they surveyed the terrain.

'They definitely came this way,' one of them said.

We watched as the first one of the Janus bolted and then the other.

One of the sentinels released something from his hand, which flew through the air and wrapped around the first Janus's leg. She crashed to the ground. Her male companion briefly halted but resumed his flight after seeing the other sentinels bearing down on him. Two of the sentinels followed while the other two grabbed the female. She struggled fruitlessly as the two massive brutes punched and kicked her until her movements ceased and all that remained were her low groans. One sentinel pulled a rope he was carrying over his shoulder free and threw one end over a tree branch.

I looked on in horror and nudged James. 'Can't we help? They're going to kill her,' I whispered.

James shook his head. 'We cannot afford to risk being discovered.'

'But—?'

James took hold of my hand, and I was gone. Subsumed within him, I was powerless to do anything as a blood-curdling scream from not far away pierced the night. The male Janus, I suspected.

By now, the sentinels had secured one end of the rope over the tree and the other around their victim's neck. I wanted to look away, but I couldn't. My sight was not my own, my vision fixed with James's. They tugged on the rope – her small frame pulled closer to the tree until her body slammed into the trunk. The men continued to pull and hoisted the woman upwards until she hung two feet from the ground, writhing like some grotesque marionette at the mercy of its puppet master.

One sentinel stepped forward and pulled a large knife from his belt. Then, cutting and removing her clothing until she was naked, he swiftly drew the knife from just below her navel to the middle of her breasts. Her face turned purple. Her tongue, almost black, protruded from her mouth. I watched on in a sea of disgust as the woman's innards were ripped from her torso and allowed to fall to the ground until they formed a bloody pile in front of her. Then the assailant reached into the cavity of her body and cut out the heart. Far removed from suffering, the woman swung gently in the cold breeze as the two sentinels shared and greedily devoured their prize.

James looked to his left as the other sentinels returned, their mouths covered in blood.

'Did you get him?' asked one of the woman's murderers.

He grinned and held up the head of the second Janus. 'We did.'

He nodded to the hanging corpse. 'Take her head too. That makes seven this week.'

Laughter filled the air as they carried out the woman's decapitation and then disappeared from where they'd come.

I fell back onto the floor as James released his hold on me. 'I had to do that,' he said. 'I was terrified you would give us away.'

I rubbed my face in an effort to shake the image of what happened from my head, but it stubbornly remained. 'Those poor people,' I said. 'Why did you make me watch?'

James grabbed me by the arm and shook me. 'Where we are going, Felix, we will see more. The citadel is an awful place. You must be strong. You need to be prepared.'

'This place is Hell,' I said.

James stood, pulling me to my feet. 'This is just the outskirts of Hell. Whatever you've heard about it, whatever you may have seen in drawings, does not do it justice.'

'Jenny's in there. Jenny is in that dreadful place.'

He nodded. 'That's why we have to get her out.'

'What happens if they capture me?' I asked.

James patted my shoulder in his now familiar way of placating me. 'I won't let that happen.' He pointed into the distance. 'We have to hurry. The person we are meeting will not wait forever.'

I followed in his wake once more, past the woman's bloodied, headless corpse and into the ever-increasing darkness of the wood. We climbed a steep slope, and on reaching the top, we paused. In front of us stood a building I might have mistaken for a church if it wasn't for the awful miasma surrounding it. The windows were pitted with grime. The door – a vast expanse of wood – with two large black handles and a face of a Demon on each, in the middle of it. We entered this horrid place and waited.

James leant forward, peered through a gap in the door and outside into the darkness – darkness my eyes struggled to penetrate.

'Keep quiet,' he whispered.

The two of us edged away and further into the gloom. Then, finally, the door was slowly pushed open, and a figure entered.

'James?' a voice said.

James moved nearer. 'Headron?'

A match was struck and offered to a lamp, illuminating the small area where we stood. The figure, holding the light, held out his other hand. 'Nice to meet you,' he said.

James briskly shook it and turned to me. 'This is Felix.'

I stared at the man – for that is what he looked like to me – as he nodded. 'Felix,' he said before turning his attention back to James. 'I have what you need.' The man fumbled inside his coat with his free hand and pulled out an oblong, metal object about the size of a playing card. I leant closer and stared at the image embossed into it – a hideous Demon with claw-like feet. Above the image's right shoulder was a bull's head, and above and to the left, a ram. To the lower left of the Demon rose a serpent with an animal's head. A lion or tiger, perhaps?

'And this will gain me access?' James said. He turned the object over, revealing a star with six jagged points.

'It's the most up-to-date seal.'

James pushed his fingers through the small, braided loop hung from one end. 'I don't feel anything.'

Headron sighed. 'It's a replica.'

James rubbed a hand across his face in a gesture I took to be frustration. 'What if they take hold of it?'

Headron shrugged. 'Getting the real thing is difficult. Losses are informed of straight away. One of our best men has fashioned it. The onus will be on you to avoid contact with others.'

James glanced at me and thrust it into his pocket. 'It will have to do.'

Headron nodded. 'One more thing,' he said.

'Yes?'

'He is in the citadel. He will recognise you if he—'

James placed a hand on my shoulder. 'Together, the difference should be enough.'

Headron nodded again. 'Felix,' he said, 'nice to meet you.' We shook hands, and he turned back to James. 'Good luck,' he said. The pair embraced, and then he was gone.

James forced a smile. 'I sense you have questions?'

'Who is this *he* you talked about?' I asked.

'Asmodeus,' James said. 'He is rarely at the citadel. So he must have a reason for going there.'

'What?'

James shrugged. 'I don't know.'

'Headron indicated that this *Asmodeus* could recognise you.'

James sat on a nearby piece of fallen masonry. 'I feel a history lesson is in order.'

I sat next to him. 'I agree.'

'There are seven realms,' he began, 'ruled over by a Demon Prince, each covering a deadly sin.'

'You mean such as envy and gluttony?'

James cupped his hands together. 'Yes. Asmodeus is lust. The titles are just names and have long since lost their significance.'

'I see.'

'The realms are closely governed by each prince. His people ensure that total control is maintained. The other princes are envious of each other and jealously guard their birthright. They only answer to *He who reigns supreme.*'

'Were you in Asmodeus's close circle?'

'I was his dextral. His right-hand and most important lieutenant.'

'Surely he will recognise you?' I said.

'As you know, my appearance is changed when you and I conjoin. Masked even. He should not recognise me.'

'If he does?'

James closed his eyes briefly. 'We should not dwell on that.'

'If these realms are so closely guarded, won't they be suspicious of a stranger?'

He held up the seal. 'The seals are fashioned a long way from here and give credence to whoever holds them. Their importance is significant.'

'What did you mean by not feeling anything when you hold it?'

'The seal is cursed by *He who reigns supreme*. When you hold one, you can feel his power.'

'If it's a forgery, will they know?'

'Only if it's handled by them. I must ensure it is not.'

'You mention *He who reigns supreme* as if you admire him. But you claim to be working for a higher power.'

James laughed. 'I'm not sure about admire. It was what it was. Who I was. But now it is not so. I am on a different side.'

'The side of … right?'

James shrugged. 'I cannot answer that. I must do what I'm compelled to do.'

'But whoever compels you now is the most important?' I said.

'I hope so. I have lost a great deal.'

'Will he help us?'

'This place is beyond his reach. Here, we are alone.'

THE CITADEL

FELIX – Onwards, we marched through the ever-thickening forest, through trees which appeared to grow everywhere – ugly and unattractive. Unlike trees back home, their branches were contorted and misshapen, curled and twisted like a corkscrew, as if every inch they put onto their size was tortured from the trunk it grew. They creaked and groaned in an almost human-like way, and I was thankful that James accompanied me, as they didn't seem to bother him. This was not a place to wander into alone.

Eventually, we found ourselves at the top of a slight incline and away from the denseness of the forest. A wide river flowed past below us.

'We have to cross,' James said.

I glanced back at the river and then at James. 'How? I'm a poor swimmer.'

'I would not ask you to swim. The river will swallow any that enter.'

I followed him as he made his way down, paused at the edge, and then crept along the water's length. 'This way,' he said. I meekly followed until he stopped. 'Help me,' James commanded.

Together we removed branches until we revealed a boat. James took hold of my arm. 'Remember this place,' he said. 'If anything should happen to me, you will need the boat to cross the Acheron.'

'Acheron?' I said.

'The river. There are five. They converge at a place where *He* reigns supreme. We need to cross it to make our way to the citadel.'

James and I pulled the boat towards the water's edge and, clambering aboard, pushed it away from the bank. He pulled out two oars from beneath the front of the boat and commenced his rowing. As the vessel glided almost silently across the water, I looked down into the inky blackness of the liquid. Something stirred, and James paused his rowing as I lowered my head.

'Be careful, Felix,' he said. 'There are things down there you would not want to meet.'

I sat up straight and shuffled towards the centre as he recommenced his rowing. We reached the other side, climbed out, pulled the boat free of the water, and covered it with vegetation before ascending the bank to the top. A small crumbling building lay just in front of us.

'Remember this ruin,' he said. 'It will guide you to where the boat is hidden.'

I nodded my understanding. 'What is the building?' I asked.

'There was once a ferryman, and the boat was his. He was condemned to carry souls across the river for eternity. He would throw them into the river if they could not pay.'

'That sounds like the legend of the river Styx.'

'There are many parts of legends that have a patina of truth, but many that do not.'

'What happened to the man?' I said.

'You met him. Kharon. He runs the pub in Dark Nearhope.'

As the landscape changed, the trees stopped abruptly at the top of the rise. We walked through a marshy area with dark green, almost black vegetation covering the ground. The smell was nauseating, like mountains of rotten cabbages, only much worse. Littered about, seemingly everywhere, bones – human bones, or at least that's what they appeared to be. I put a hand to my nose to gain a little protection from the putrid stench. Skulls and various other bones, in different states of decomposition, appeared to carpet the terrain as far as I could see. And amongst them, black scuttling creatures, the size of my fist, feasted on the remains of the long-dead.

'You will become accustomed to the smell,' James said, clearly sensing my disgust.

'Who are they?'

'The remnants of a great battle,' he said.

'Your people?'

James paused. 'My people and others from another realm.'

We walked on, carefully avoiding standing on what remained of one of these unfortunate beings. I don't know how long we walked through this unforgiving horror, but it seemed like days. Eventually, we came to another clearing with blackened tree stumps everywhere, as if some long-ago conflagration had razed them to the ground.

James stopped and took off his backpack. 'From this point on, we must conjoin.' I removed my own bag and handed it to James, and he secreted them both beneath some rocks. He held out his hand, and I stepped inside and behind those eyes. We carried on down a slope that twisted and turned beneath us, and then something else drifted into our nostrils – a smell of burning. I somehow knew it was the smell of burning flesh.

And then it came into view. An enormous wall disappeared into the distance. The surface was constructed in a red-coloured stone. Within the wall – about a hundred or so metres away – loomed an entrance with an arch decorated in symbols and demonic carvings. James halted, gazing upon this grand entrance as if summoning his courage and then carried on. As we entered, I could hear the screams of the tortured, blood-curdling, deafening screams like nothing I could ever imagine. I wanted to run. I wanted to put my hands over my ears to drown out the relentless barrage of noise, but my senses were not my own, and with a mixture of horror and curiosity, I endured them.

Someone stepped in front of James, barring his way. 'Who are you?' he said, looking us up and down. The man was huge, at least six feet seven or eight.

James pulled the seal from his pocket and held it up. 'Nefluous,' he said.

The man scrutinized the seal, and as he read the inscription on it, he lowered his head. 'I'm sorry,' he said. 'I did not mean any disrespect.'

James waved a dismissive hand. 'I have travelled far. I need to eat and rest.'

'Of course,' the man said. 'This way.'

We followed him through this hell, past buildings where the screams had emanated, before reaching another entrance. The torturous sounds faded as we passed through and further from them.

He stopped. 'Perhaps you would like a tour?'

James shook his head. 'Maybe later,' he said. 'I'm exhausted.'

'As you like,' he said and pointed to a door. 'Everything you need is in here.'

'The prince?' James said. 'He is here?'

'Yes. He is at the castle.'

James pushed open the door, paused briefly before entering and closed the door behind us. He surveyed the room. An ornately carved wooden chair sat in one corner. A small kitchen area lay to our left, and a room with a single bed to the right.

'So far, so good,' he said to me.

We gazed at the images on the walls. Depictions of torment and torture filled the space – horrific and disturbing images. Scenes that seemed to have a malevolence of their own wormed their way into my psyche and squatted there, corrupting everything. Thoughts I did not wish to have, hectored and pilloried me, pushing any decent thoughts, anything pleasant, to the far reaches of my mind. Any happy memories appeared stranded on an island I could not get to, so inwardly, I closed my eyes against this horror.

James bolted the door and released his grip on me. He put a finger to his lips. 'We must be quiet.'

I nodded. I am not sure I would have been able to speak had I wished.

'Are you hungry?' he asked. I shook my head, unsure if I would ever be hungry again. My stomach groaned at the thought of food.

'A drink, perhaps?' he said.

'A little water.'

James filled a goblet and handed it to me. 'We will look around tomorrow.'

'The screams?' I said.

James lowered his eyes. 'The tormented. There is no release for them. Eternity is their punishment.'

'Why is Jenny here? Why is she in this terrible place?'

James sat in the chair and laced his fingers. '… I don't know. You shouldn't dwell on such things.' He nodded towards the bedroom. 'Get some sleep. I'll make do with this chair.'

I sensed he was holding something back. Something he wasn't telling me. 'I'm not sure I can sleep.'

'Try,' he said and leant back in the chair. 'We have much to do.'

Try as I might, my sleep was fitful. Unlike anything I'd ever endured, nightmares and terrors assailed me, conjuring images and dreams that will live with me until my final days.

It appeared James's sleep was not as troubled as mine. I sat on the bed and watched him wake from his slumber.

He rubbed his eyes and stretched before climbing to his feet. 'How did you sleep?' he said.

'Poorly,' I replied.

'I understand. I, too, experienced those nightmares when I first started to change. After time, they halted. It's not the sleeping I fear now, but the times I'm awake.'

'What are we going to do today?'

James fixed me with a stare. 'We must go through the charade of being shown around the citadel. It will be expected. And then …' He appeared to be stealing himself before continuing, '… we must go to the castle.'

'Where *he* is?' I said.

'Where *he* is,' he echoed. 'As far as he knows, I'm from another realm with which he has an alliance. He will expect it.'

An ache rose inside my chest. 'What will happen?'

'You must be strong.' He stepped nearer and placed a hand on my shoulder. 'What you will encounter today will test your faith to the limit. I know you said you did not believe, but it will be your only protection from this point on.'

'I'm not sure I have that belief,' I said.

'When the time comes, you will have. He would not have chosen you otherwise.'

Conjoined, we were escorted around the citadel by one of the guards. The scenes encountered were worse than anything witnessed since arriving in this hideous land. James was right. His kin were indeed inventive. The tortures and torments enacted on these wretched souls were horrendous, reminding me somewhat of the medieval times I'd read about. But what made this much worse was the thought that having endured horrifying punishments once, the victims would have endured them again and again. The tour culminated in a visit to the furnaces reserved for the poor Janus. Beaten and battered, one by one, they were fed into the huge openings to be incinerated by the flames while still alive. Each victim witnessed what would happen to them as they watched their brethren slowly consumed. And lying nearby, an enormous pile of ashes – raked from the furnaces. I felt sick to my stomach. Men, women and children systematically transformed from living, breathing individuals into ashes and smoke. And the smell – a sickly aroma that will haunt me forever, clung to every fibre of my psyche.

Eventually, and thankfully, it ended, and we were led away from this place and back to our room. James relinquished his grip on me, and I fled into the bathroom to throw up. Some time passed before I was well enough to climb to my feet and join him.

'I'm sorry,' he said.

I slumped into the chair. 'Don't make me go back there. I would rather you leave me in the darkness I endured when I first met you.'

'I'm unable to do that too often because it's exhausting,' he said. 'However, I see no reason why you should have to endure again what you did today.'

'Good.' I rubbed my face. 'We didn't see Jenny. That's something, I suppose.'

'She must be at the castle,' he said.

'We have to go there, then.'

'Yes, we do.' He sighed. 'But first, I must meet with Asmodeus. He will expect me to pass on good wishes from Belphegor.'

'Belphegor?' I said.

'He is the Prince of the realm my seal is supposed to be from. He and Asmodeus are the closest of allies.' James held up a small card. 'This was pushed under the door while you were in the bathroom. There is a feast in my honour tonight.' James lay back on the bed with his hands behind his head. 'For now, I must sleep. I will need all my strength to conjoin with you this evening.'

THE CASTLE

FELIX – James slept for a couple of hours. I, on the other hand, had gone over the day's events. I didn't want to, but it's difficult to think of anything else when witnessing such atrocities.

Eventually, James woke and readied himself. Dressing in an ornate uniform that I'd not seen before – I presumed provided for him by our hosts – and seemingly satisfied by his appearance, he turned to face me. 'I don't know what to expect tonight,' he said. 'I must attempt to convince them that I am from Belphegor's realm.'

'Will you be able to do that?'

'They will hopefully take me at my word. It would take them a couple of days to confirm who I am, and by then, we should be on our way.'

'With Jenny?' I said.

'Yes, with Jenny.'

'Won't they wonder what you're doing here?'

James stroked his chin. 'I'm sure they will, but I am hoping to come up with a plausible story.'

I raised my eyebrows. 'Which is?'

'Belphegor's realm borders another prince's realm. This prince is called Sathanas, and he and Asmodeus are long-time enemies. Sathanas is one of the most powerful of the princes. Alone, Asmodeus would not dare to attack him. I will confabulate a story that Belphegor is open to an alliance, and I'm hoping Asmodeus will believe this.'

'Only hoping?'

'The princes are arrogant. They only seek to please *He who reigns supreme*.'

'What does *He* think of them fighting?' I said.

James smiled ruefully. '*He* encourages it. *He* believes that the princes will only remain powerful through their constant battling. If they mistrust one another, they are unlikely to challenge him.'

I shook my head. 'It all seems so ludicrous. Surely they would be stronger if they all joined forces.'

James stepped closer. 'You would not want that. If it ever happened, they could challenge not only your world but the Almighty's. It was a close-run thing when they were cast from the Almighty's realm. For good …' he paused before continuing, '… for your idea of good to prevail, you must hope this never happens. Humans are not liked or admired in the Prince's realms. They would almost be as low as the Janus, and you've seen their fate.'

I shuddered. 'Yes. I see. It's in humanity's interest to ensure that the princes continue their disagreements?'

'Indeed,' he said. He straightened his uniform and looked me in the eyes. 'Ready?'

I nodded and took hold of his proffered hand.

We waited a few more minutes before someone knocked on the door.

A uniformed man stood outside. 'Sir,' he said. 'I'm Braxas. The prince's dextral. I have come to escort you to the great hall.' James nodded and followed the man. Then, mercifully, we headed away from the citadel and along a winding path that led to the enormous castle which dominated the landscape. It stretched upwards majestically with high turrets and an immense serpentine wall wrapped around it. The stonework mirrored that of the citadel – a deep red. Not what the brick-red houses back home are made of, but a dark, almost blood-coloured red. It lent an air of impressiveness and a feeling of seeing something unlike any other. Yet, despite this, it appeared to possess a life of its own, as if the building was watching us. I may have been awe-struck in a different setting, but the situation I found myself in easily swept aside any admiration for the edifice.

Entering the building via a substantial wooden drawbridge lowered across the wide moat of jet-black water, we marched until Braxas halted outside a wooden door.

'I'll announce you,' he said.

A few minutes passed until the door opened, and we were ushered inside. A gargantuan table dominated the centre of the room. The paintings adorning the walls depicted the usual scenes of torture I had almost become accustomed to. At the end of the room sat a roaring fire crouched ominously beneath a chimney breast stretching up to the ceiling.

We strode purposefully inside and towards a throne-like chair at the table's far end.

The occupant stood, a small and unprepossessing individual, no more than five and a half feet. Even from the distance we were from him, he appeared to have a pronounced stoop.

We continued towards him and stopped about eight feet away. At this close distance, he was even less impressive. And yet, there was something about him that emanated malevolence. I looked, or rather we looked, into the jet-black depths of his eyes, and I shuddered.

We bowed and dropped to one knee. 'It's a pleasure to meet you.'

Asmodeus held out his hand. A large ring with mythical creatures adorning it wrapped around one of his fingers. 'You are welcome in my realm.'

A small kiss was planted onto his outstretched hand, and we stood. 'Nefluous, sir. I am Belphegor's dextral.'

Asmodeus smiled and pointed for us to sit. 'His dextral? I am indeed honoured.'

We sat. 'I have a message from my prince. For your ears alone.'

Asmodeus eased himself into his chair. 'I trust Braxas implicitly.'

'I understand that, sir, but Belphegor was quite adamant.'

Asmodeus scrutinised us then looked to his dextral. 'Leave us. I'll summon you if I need you.'

'As you wish,' Braxas said. He glanced at us before exiting and closing the door quietly behind him.

Asmodeus sat upright. 'Go on,' he said and took a sip of his drink.

'For some time, Belphegor has been troubled by Sathanas.'

Asmodeus frowned. 'I wasn't aware of this.'

'Sathanas coverts our realm. He is trying to curry favour with *He who reigns supreme*. Belphegor is of the opinion that with an alliance between you and him, Sathanas could be defeated. If he were, our three realms would be feared by the others. We could then exert our influence over them.'

The corner of Asmodeus's mouth lifted into a smirk. 'I see.' He stood and made his way across to the fireplace. 'Belphegor is sure about this?'

'Yes. He feels that if things continue, Sathanas will invade our realm and if that happens …'

Asmodeus spun around. 'Mine will follow?'

'Exactly.'

Asmodeus re-joined us at the table. 'I have much to think about.'

'He wants it to remain between the two of you for the time being.'

'My troops are loyal.'

I felt James's unease as we shuffled in the seat. 'He asked me to remind you of Sicarius.'

Asmodeus scowled and spat on the floor. 'He was a mistake. I stupidly allowed a human into my inner circle. I alone gave him a chance. Eternal damnation was all that awaited him, and look at how he repaid me.' Asmodeus gripped the arms of his chair and growled. 'Once a traitor, always a traitor.'

'Have you caught him yet?'

The prince drummed the arm of his chair. 'Not yet, but I will. His torture will be unique and endured for eternity.'

'The phage that stalks your realm?'

Asmodeus smiled. 'It's genetic. I have secured a human female. She's versed in such matters, and we hope to stop and even reverse the transformations.'

I sensed the worry in James. I don't know how I knew, but I just did. What Asmodeus said perturbed him.

'Good news, indeed. Belphegor will be pleased to hear this.'

Asmodeus pulled a cord next to his chair. 'Enough of business. You have given me much to think about. I will let you have my answer tomorrow. But, for now, we will have a feast.'

The doors to the room swung open, and two dozen people entered. As Asmodeus thoughtfully rubbed his chin, they each took their place at the table.

The rest of the evening went by in a blur. Dish after dish was put before us, and drinks flowed lavishly. I must admit that some of the food presented was new to me. Some resembled items from home, but others were nothing like anything I had experienced. It would have been like dinner parties I'd attended throughout my life was it not for the meal's conclusion. Two poor wretches were hauled into the room, stripped naked, tortured, and killed in front of us before having the hearts ripped from their bodies. The organ was offered to Asmodeus, who had it chopped into smaller pieces and then presented it to the more important guests, including James.

It was utterly revolting, but luckily James ate only a tiny amount, sensing my repugnance. Instead, managing to secrete the bulk of it inside his pocket. We were about to leave when a uniformed man whispered something into our host's ear.

'Bring him in,' Asmodeus said.

To our horror, the Demon who attacked me in the woods was brought forth.

He obsequiously threw himself on the floor at Asmodeus's feet. 'My prince,' he said. 'Thank you for seeing me. I am your humble—'

Asmodeus looked upwards and rolled his eyes. 'Yes, yes, what is it?' he demanded. 'Can't you see I have guests? This had better be good, or you may find yourself on my menu.'

The Demon lowered his head. 'I can only apologise for my intrusion. I did not intend—'

'Yes, yes,' Asmodeus repeated, waving a hand for him to continue.

'I saw him.'

Asmodeus glowered. 'Who?'

'Sicarius.'

Asmodeus sprang to his feet and grabbed the one-footed interloper around the neck. 'Where?'

'In the woods outside the forbidden town. He was with a human.'

Asmodeus growled and glared at his men. 'Find him.' He brought his fist down hard on the table. 'Find him now,' he said and stormed out.

After this, the guests disappeared, and we searched for our host before returning to our room. Asmodeus stood with two guards, and as we neared, he was obviously berating them.

'Remind the woman why she's here. She's stalling. I want the antidote. I will not lose any more to Sicarius and his followers.'

'Everything all right?' James said.

Asmodeus spun around. 'Yes, yes. Nothing I can't handle.'

'Of course. I didn't mean to imply anything.'

Asmodeus glowered at his men. 'Go,' he said, and they hurried off.

'Thank you for a wonderful evening,' James said.

Asmodeus faced us again. 'That thing we discussed …'

'Yes?'

'Tell Belphegor that the answer is yes.' He smiled, nodded at us politely, and then strode off.

'Were they talking about Jenny?' I asked silently from inside James's mind.

'Maybe,' he said, and we headed out of the castle and back towards the citadel. Quickly closing the distance between ourselves and the two guards, we stealthily followed them into a building and took up a vantage point where we could see and hear them. Despite our conjoined form, my heart appeared to pound in my chest as we spotted her. *'Jenny.'* I said. He didn't need to answer. Jenny sat looking down at the floor as two men towered over her.

'Asmodeus is unhappy with your progress,' one of the men said.

'I'm doing my best,' she said. 'It's difficult.'

The first man looked at his friend. 'What do you think?' he asked.

The second man sneered. 'She's stalling.'

She looked up. 'I'm not, I swear.'

The second man scoffed. 'She swears.'

We crept closer and stood in the shadows, away from anyone passing but within clear earshot of Jenny and the two men.

'We warned you what would happen,' the first man said.

'Please,' she said. 'I'm trying my best.'

The second man stood with his hands on his hips and legs astride. 'Maybe we should remind her what it's like?'

'No, please,' she said. 'I'll try harder.'

The two men took hold of her and, dragging the struggling Jenny, pulled her towards another door.

'We've got to help,' I screamed inside James's head.

'*We can't intervene,*' James said.

'*Those bastards are going to harm her. Take me to her.*'

James resisted as I mentally assailed him.

'*Felix,*' he said. '*You must stop.*'

I couldn't. Through the open door, we could see the two men. They were forcing something over Jenny's mouth, and she was struggling less. Clearly, whatever they'd done, subdued her in some way. I screamed at James and mentally kicked and pushed against the doors of his mind, but he held firm. By now, it began to dawn on me what was happening. The men filled a bath and lowered my wife into it. She continued to struggle but could not battle against either the men or the substance they'd given her. We watched as she thrashed about and was pulled by her legs, slowly slipping below the surface. She sputtered and fought for her life as water cascaded over the side of the bath while the men laughed at her feeble resistance. James looked away to spare me from witnessing more of this spectacle, but I felt his resolve weaken. He implored me to stop, but I wouldn't. I couldn't. Incessantly, I continued my mental attack. Finally, a door in his mind cracked, and I could see it as if it was in front of me. I pushed and kicked harder, but it held. I felt his anguish as words were uttered. '*No, not that door.*'

And then it burst open. My final assault smashed the door from its hinges, and a scene met me. A familiar one, but one from a different perspective than I had previously known. I watched as it unfolded before me, and mentally dropping to my knees, I fell down a bottomless well and into a sea of despair.

JENNY

FELIX – Opening an eye, I glanced across at James. 'How did I get here?'

'I managed to get us back. I had enough energy left to get you here. I thought I was going to lose you. My hold on you hung by a thread.'

'Why didn't you tell me?'

'It wasn't your fault, Felix. Loss does strange things to people.'

I turned away from him to face the wall. Thankfully, he did not try to placate me further.

It was my fault. A conversation years ago with a friend of mine had been overheard by my wife. I didn't even know Jenny was in the house. She'd left to visit her mother in the morning, and I knew nothing of her return. I spoke with my friend, and he'd tried to comfort me about the loss of Benji. Foolishly, in my grief-stricken state, I'd confided in him that I blamed Jenny for Benji's death. Unbeknown to me, she overheard the conversation. I hadn't meant it. It was a stupid thing to say, but sometimes we say ridiculous things. It wasn't meant as a judgement. I was to blame for Jenny taking her own life. I was to blame for sending her to this hell. James, weakened by my assault, could not keep this secret hidden from me. The only reason she'd been forsaken, the only reason she'd been condemned to purgatory, was because the one person she loved and trusted could not forgive her. Forgiveness is everything, James said. Not just in words but in your heart. Only now did I understand the enormity of it.

Our conversation throughout the morning had been stilted, which suited me. I didn't want to discuss the previous night's events and prayed for this nightmare to end. We'd stayed in the room and conjoined only when someone came with food and drink. By mid-afternoon, I could stand it no more. The boredom was relentless.

'What are we going to do?' I said.

James looked up from his bed as I stood nearer. 'You must promise me,' he said. 'Promise me that you will not do what you did last night.'

'I'm sorry, but—'

James stood and placed a hand on my shoulder. 'I understand,' he said. 'I know how difficult this is for you. I carry a heavy burden myself, but had we been discovered … It would have meant disaster for us all. Me, you and Jenny.' He tapped his head. 'There are secrets in here that Asmodeus would love to get hold of. It's not just your life that I'm responsible for.'

'The others like you?' I said.

He nodded. 'There are people here and in your world that must be kept hidden from Asmodeus and his kind.'

I was puzzled. 'My world?'

'Your world is coveted not only by Asmodeus but also by *He who reigns supreme*. I have said too much. Shall we go and see Jenny?'

He held out his hand, and we conjoined.

We headed towards the same building as the night before and went inside. A guard stood outside Jenny's room.

He looked us up and down. 'Can I help you?' he said.

'Your prince said it would be all right for me to talk to the woman.'

'I've had no such order.'

We leant in closer. 'No one is beyond redemption,' James said.

The guard glanced left and right. 'No. He must follow his destiny.' The guard pulled a key from his pocket and opened the door. 'You don't have long,' he said. 'I will be relieved soon.'

James patted him on the shoulder and entered. The room was empty, but noise from an adjoining room alerted us to her presence. We followed the sound and found ourselves in a small laboratory.

She spun around as we entered. 'Yes?' she said.

'No one is beyond redemption,' James said.

Jenny smiled. 'They said you would come.'

'We haven't long. Your progress on the antidote?'

She slumped onto a nearby stool. 'I have it. I've had it for some time. I cannot put Asmodeus off for much longer.'

'I know. We will come for you tonight.'

'Do you think we can escape?' she said.

'Be ready tonight.' We moved towards the door and strained to hear the voices from outside.

'The new guard?' I said to James.

'I believe so.'

'What is it?' Jenny said.

'Another guard,' he said to her. 'I mustn't be discovered.'

Jenny ushered us to a cupboard. 'Hide in here. I'll distract him.'

Secreting ourselves in the cupboard, we shut the door and waited.

There was a crash from the laboratory.

The door opened, and the two guards entered. 'What's going on?' the new guard said.

'I'm sorry,' Jenny said. 'I knocked over some jars.'

We took our chance and crept from our hiding place. The new guard had his back to us as the guard, who had let us in, nodded for us to go. We didn't need any further invitation. Within seconds, we were outside in the corridor and making our way back to our room.

Once back there, James relinquished his grip on me. 'How are we going to get Jenny out?' I said.

James sat on the bed. 'We have allies. We can rely on the guard and a few others, but we'll need someone to conjoin with Jenny. Someone who won't arouse suspicion.'

'Do you know of someone?'

James frowned. 'Celestine said she will do it.'

'You seem unsure.'

He rubbed his chin. 'It's a great risk for her. She's known by some within the citadel, but it's a risk she's prepared to take.'

'If she's recognised?' I said.

'Hopefully she won't be. We're arranging a diversion.'

'Can she carry Jenny as you do me?'

James sighed. 'It's a difficult thing to do. I will have to give her some instruction, but I'm optimistic she can manage it.' I was about to speak again, but James held up a hand and lay down. 'I must rest,' he said. 'I need to be fully refreshed for tonight.'

I sat down in the chair and closed my eyes.

I jumped awake as something was pushed under the door. James still slept, so I roused him from his slumber and handed him the paper. He sat up and climbed out of bed before making his way over to the door. 'Give me your hand, Felix,' he said, and I did as I was told. He opened the door, and, conjoined, we stepped outside.

A group of soldiers gathered some fifty metres away. James halted a passing guard. 'What's happening?' he asked.

'The sentinels are going out on patrol,' the guard said. 'Sicarius has been spotted not far away.'

'I see.' James stepped back inside, closed the door and released me. 'The diversion I mentioned,' he said. 'My friends are drawing the sentinel away from here but won't have long before Jenny's absence is discovered. We have a much better chance if they are far away.'

I looked into those green eyes of his. 'I can't thank you enough for what you and your friends are doing.'

James placed a hand on my shoulder. 'I sense,' he said, placing a hand on his chest, 'that she's very important.'

I frowned. 'How …?'

James shrugged. 'I just know.'

I stood behind those eyes again as we headed from the room to Jenny's. James was ever watchful as we trod carefully across the courtyard and into the building. The same guard from earlier stood outside the door.

He looked around nervously. 'The sentinels have been gone for over an hour.'

'When will you be relieved by the new guard?' James asked.

'You have time to get clear of the citadel and maybe put a mile or two between you and here.'

'It will have to be enough time.'

The guard pulled a small club from inside his jacket. 'Here,' he said. 'It has to look convincing.' The guard turned. James took in a lungful of air and struck the guard at the base of the neck. He dropped to his knees and then tumbled forward onto his face. If he was playacting, he was convincing. James quickly located the keys in his pocket and opened the door.

Jenny spun around as we entered and stared. 'I was worried you wouldn't come.'

James looked about. 'Has Celestine not arrived?'

'No one has been here.'

He opened the door. The prostrate guard lay motionless to the side. James glanced along the corridor as Celestine came into the hall.

'Quickly in here,' he said. She followed, and he closed the door behind them. 'This is Jenny,' he said to Celestine. 'And this is Celestine. She will conjoin with you and get you out of the citadel.'

Jenny frowned. 'I don't understand.'

Celestine stepped forward. 'You will,' she said. She looked at us. 'I hope I can still do this.'

James instructed her as I listened from within for what seemed a long time but was probably only minutes.

Celestine stepped in front of Jenny. 'Ready?' she said, holding out her hand.

Jenny nodded and took hold of it. It was fascinating to view it as I'd grown accustomed to being on the other side. She disappeared, and the change in her and Celestine was immediate. Celestine stood there, but Jenny, her features I knew so well, were evident in the two women's amalgamation.

James moved towards the door. 'I'll check outside.' Seemingly satisfied that the coast was clear, he whispered, 'Ok, Celestine, let's go.'

ESCAPE FROM THE CITADEL

FELIX – Conjoined with our hosts, we made our way outside, headed through the citadel and towards the gate. Guards and soldiers appeared oblivious to us, save for the odd nod of acknowledgement. James was ambling rather than hurrying – I suspected he did not want to cause undue attention to us. We were now in sight of the gates when someone shouted. James spun around as Asmodeus's dextral approached.

'You're leaving?' Braxas said.

We halted. 'Yes. I have received news from Belphegor.' He nodded at Celestine. 'We have to return as soon as possible.'

Braxas appraised Celestine. 'Have we met before?'

'I don't think so,' she said.

His eyes lingered on her before he turned back to face us. 'Asmodeus would have liked to see you, I'm sure, but he's tied up at the moment.'

'With Sicarius?' James said.

Braxas lowered his brow. 'Yes. He has been spotted nearby. We hope to capture him soon.'

James put his hands behind his back and straightened himself further. 'Belphegor will be pleased to hear that. Sicarius has been troublesome for us too.'

'He has been fortunate so far.' Braxas sneered. 'Good fortune does not last forever.'

'Do you know the extent of his allies?'

Braxas narrowed his eyes. 'We will when we catch him.'

'Thank Asmodeus for his hospitality.'

'I will indeed, Nefluous.' He turned to Celestine. 'And it's nice to meet you …'

'Rubistine,' she said.

'Rubistine,' he repeated. Allowing the name to hang for a moment.

'Safe journey.' He nodded at us and marched off.

'I think he recognised me,' Celestine said.

We set off along with the Celestine and Jenny hybrid following. 'I don't think so,' James said. 'He would have stopped us if he had.'

'He knows my sister. I have met him several times.'

We carried on. 'All the more reason for us to hurry,' James said.

Reaching the gate, we stopped as a guard stepped out in front of us. 'Your seal,' he said.

'My what?' James said.

The guard lowered his head. 'I'm sorry, sir. My orders state that I must check the seals of all visitors.'

James grunted. 'I've been a guest of your prince. He will not be pleased when he hears of this.'

'I can only apologise, but …'

James pulled the seal from his pocket and held it up. 'There,' he said. 'Satisfied?'

'And your companion,' he said, facing Celestine.

I watched as, even to my mind, she nervously took it from her coat, but as she held it up, the seal slipped from her grasp and landed at the feet of the guard, and before she could recover it, he bent and plucked it from the earth and held it out to her. She quickly snatched it from him and deposited it back inside her coat. The guard paused.

'Is that everything?' James snapped. 'You've delayed us long enough.'

The guard briefly paused again. 'Yes,' he said, then opened the gate and stepped aside.

What happened next happened swiftly. It was a bizarre sensation to be involved in a physical confrontation when you were not the person grappling with another. The guard reached for his weapon, and James, seemingly anticipating his action, launched himself at him. The pair crashed to the ground, and I fell from James's grasp. I watched as the two of them wrestled for control until Celestine brought the event to an end. She snatched the weapon the guard had reached for and struck him across the back of his head. I lay stunned. This place was even worse without the protection and cover of James.

I looked on as Celestine and James bundled the guard inside the little hut to the side of the gate and raced to me. He grasped my hand and scooped me up, and once more, I found myself behind his eyes, albeit a little bewildered.

James and Celestine took off at an alarming pace away from the citadel. Onwards they careered through the terrain encountered on our way there. They paused for nothing, their footfalls quickening as a siren behind us sounded.

James took hold of Celestine as she appeared to falter. 'We're nearly at the wood,' he said. 'We can't slow down.'

She carried on as James held tightly onto her hand, pulling her behind him. We ran deeper into the wood, slaloming our way around trees and shrubs, then down a slope. James slipped as Celestine lost her footing too, and we barrelled our way down the incline until we abruptly stopped. Fortunately, our landing was soft as Jenny and I were ejected from our hosts. I took hold of James's arm, and Jenny grabbed Celestine, pulling the exhausted pair deep into the undergrowth.

I looked at them both slumped on the ground. 'You ok?' I said.

James nodded. 'We have to keep moving. They won't be far behind us.'

'You're exhausted,' I said.

He stood and pulled Celestine to her feet. 'Which way?'

Celestine glanced around as if trying to decipher where she was. 'That way.' She pointed to her right. 'I have a boat moored not far away.'

The pair took off, and I looked at the totally bewildered Jenny. I took hold of her hand and followed after them. 'Stay close to me,' I said. 'I'll look after you.'

The following hours were the most terrifying of my life. We heard and saw the sentinels looking for us on more than one occasion. I couldn't believe we went undiscovered, but somehow we did. Two massive brutes neared us on one occasion, only to move away as another in their party shouted to them. Eventually, they wandered off in a different direction, and we waited an interminable amount of time before moving on.

'I thought we were done for,' I said to James and Celestine. 'We were so lucky.'

Celestine stopped and looked at me. 'Luck had nothing to do with it. One of the sentinels is an ally of ours. Without him leading them away from us, we would be ...' Her words trailed off.

It didn't matter. I understood what she meant.

The journey to Nearhope took place in relative silence. Although we felt reasonably safe, James kept a watchful eye out for the sentinels. Once through the wood on the outskirts of Nearhope, we reached the gentle slope leading into the town. It was wonderful to see the early afternoon on reaching our destination with people merrily going about their business as the warm summer sun beat down.

James stopped outside the pub. 'Shall we?' he said.

I think I can speak for us all when I say that the thought of a pint of The slaughtered Man's fine ale and something to eat was a welcome distraction.

'Grab a table,' James said. 'I'll fetch us some drinks.'

Jenny glanced between Celestine and me. 'What will I do now?' she asked.

Celestine looked across at James and shrugged. 'I don't know. Only James can tell you that.'

I looked at him, deep in conversation with the landlord. Once the drinks were placed on the bar, he picked them up and made his way across to our table.

'Jenny was asking,' I said, pausing for Jenny to nod her approval, 'what will happen to her?'

James pushed my glass across to me. 'Up the street, there is an old apothecary. Perhaps,' he said, 'you might like to run the shop.'

She glanced at me and then back to James. 'I don't know anything about that particular art.'

'You had a laboratory in the citadel,' I said.

She frowned. 'The citadel?'

James tapped my arm. 'She doesn't remember,' he said.

I stared at Jenny, her eyes full of confusion. 'Jenny,' I said. 'Do you know who I am?'

She knitted her brow. 'I think you're called Felix?'

'That's right. Felix,' James said. 'We're your friends.'

She smiled at us. 'Yes. You're my friends.'

It was strange seeing the transformation in her. As James said, she remembered nothing of our life together and, thankfully, nothing of the citadel. However, fortunately, she still retained a glimmer of who we were.

Over the next few hours, the four of us chatted. Jenny enthusiastically questioned us about our lives. I thought it best to lie to her. Strange, but with each fabrication, her life in Nearhope was slowly woven together until she was subsumed into this peculiar place as if she'd always been here.

Jenny sat up straight. 'It's been lovely,' she said, 'but I must get along to my shop. I have much to do.'

We exited the pub into a fresh autumn breeze. The four of us strolled along the high street and stopped outside The Apothecary.

Jenny fumbled inside her pocket. 'I appear to have mislaid my keys.'

James held them up. 'I was wondering when you would realise they were missing.'

She tapped him playfully on the arm. 'James.' She lowered her eyebrows. 'Always the joker.' Unlocking the door, she pushed it open. 'Well,' she announced, 'it's been lovely seeing you all again. Stop by anytime.' She leant forward and hugged James and Celestine before turning to face me. 'Thank you, Felix,' she said.

I glanced at the other two. 'For what?'

Jenny placed a hand on her chin. 'I don't know. I just had the urge to say that. Strange.' She smiled, hugged me tightly, and gave me a peck on the cheek. 'Any time you're passing …' she said.

James turned to Celestine. 'What will you do?' he said.

She sighed. 'They'll be searching for me. I know of a place I can go to.'

'If I need to get in touch?' James said.

Celestine looked into the shop. 'I'll give Jenny a few days to settle, and then I'll leave word with her.'

James and I hugged Celestine. Then, like Jenny, she was gone.

'What about me?' I said. 'Will I stay here?'

He looked towards the church. 'No. Your place is not here.'

I didn't understand and said so.

He smiled. 'Follow me.'

We climbed the gentle slope towards the church but did not stop. Instead, we carried on and paused at the crest of the hill. 'Ready,' he said and held out a hand.

I was puzzled but took hold of it as if it was the most natural thing to do, and then the all-consuming darkness I remembered well enveloped me.

I groaned, clutched my chest as I struggled to breathe, and gulped greedily at the air from the mask attached to my mouth. I looked at the paramedic above me. 'Where am I?'

He took hold of my arm while still studying the instruments around him. 'You've had a heart attack, Felix. We're just taking you to the hospital.'

I took in this information but struggled to rationalise it. Finally, with my eyes now heavy, I reluctantly surrendered to sleep. I awoke in the hospital and spied James sitting on the chair opposite in my half-awake, half-asleep state. He rose, moved across to me and smiled.

'Hi, Felix,' he said.

'James,' is all I could muster. I took a deep breath. 'Was it all—?'

He placed a hand on my arm. 'You must rest.' James glanced towards the door and back to me. 'You will be needed again.'

'Needed?'

'He came to me last night,' James said. 'You must be ready when the time arrives. Humanity's future is at stake.'

'But …' I protested.

'You will know when the time has come.'

The door to my bedroom opened, and a nurse walked in. 'How are you feeling, Felix?'

'I was just talking to …' I turned to where James stood, but he was gone. So, I smiled at her. 'Nothing. I feel good.'

'Would you like some breakfast?' she said.

'Yes. I think that would be great.'

Gradually, over the course of the following days, I recovered further. I'd been fortunate that a passing motorist saw my car parked by the side of the road and stopped. He'd summoned an ambulance and probably saved my life. My friends Bill and Susan Carver and their daughter, Kate, were fantastic. Bill despatched a recovery vehicle to pick up the car and had it dropped off at my home. I told the three of them about my dream. Even after several days, it still burnt brightly. Kate was particularly intrigued – I suspected this was because of her profession as a psychiatrist. She'd provided a pen and pad to write down all I could remember. The need to do so seemed so important to me. A week later, I was allowed home and having taken on a housekeeper to assist me, life returned to its usual blandness. My scribblings, pages and pages, were deposited into the bottom of a drawer and forgotten about. Over time, the memory of Nearhope, the citadel, James and the events surrounding Jenny evaporated into nothing.

PART TWO

MARY

MARY, 2020 – I pulled the car up at a discreet distance and waited as a slow five minutes crawled by until he came out of the fire door at the back of the building. He paused to light up a cigarette before he drunkenly stumbled on. Looking to my left, I grabbed the knife from the passenger seat and gripped it tightly in my trembling hand. Easing myself from the car, I followed him. He stumbled again, placing a hand on top of a dustbin in a vain effort to support himself before crashing to the ground as the bin tipped over. I halted and watched as he groaned a little, then seemingly passed out.

My eyes fixed on the prone form of Charlie Creeney, looking for any sign of movement. I stood like that for what felt like an eternity with my hand involuntarily clasping the pendant hanging around my neck – a gift from Liam.

'Don't weaken,' I whispered. 'He deserves to die.'

Stepping closer, I looked down at his unconscious form as loud snores emanated from his half-open mouth. I stared at the knife in my hand and then at him. It would be so easy, I thought. No one could connect me to him. No one would ever know I did it. I lowered the blade to within inches of him – one quick thrust, and he would be gone.

A light appeared in my peripheral vision about twenty metres away. I watched on in ever-inquisitive fascination as the brightness grew, but I wasn't frightened. Quite the opposite. It appeared welcoming, and I stepped nearer as it continued to grow in intensity. Slowly, enveloped by the light, a feeling of unbelievable love consumed me, and inside the brightness, something formed. An entity. A shape of a man. He held out a hand to me, and, totally without fear, I took hold of it.

'This is not your destiny,' he said.

I woke inside my car, not behind the club, but outside my flat. It took a couple of moments for me to gather my thoughts. I glanced to my left and looked at the knife. Had I ...? I couldn't remember. Tentatively, I picked up my would-be weapon and examined it – it was clean, with no blood – maybe I'd wiped it on something. I opened my handbag and deposited it inside. The man I'd seen in the light ... Who was he? A notion arrived, but I ignored it. It was absurd. I shrugged and headed for my flat in a kind of daze.

The ringing of my mobile jolted me from my sleep. Bleary-eyed, I reached across to the bedside table and answered it.

'Yeah,' I croaked.

'Mary, it's Andy.'

I sat up and looked at the clock. 'What is it?'

'I know it hasn't been long after ... Liam,' he said, 'but you said if I had a story for you.'

Easing myself higher in bed, I rubbed the sleepiness from my eyes with my free hand. 'I'm listening.'

'Have a look on YouTube,' he said. 'Search for someone called *The Nazarian*.'

I rubbed my eyes again and yawned. 'The Nazarian?'

'Yeah. He's becoming quite the cause celebre.'

'Why?'

'He's making music videos. He plays all his own instruments and claims to write his own songs.'

'You want me to write a piece on the next Ed Sheeran? Give me a break. Give it to one of the trainees.'

'Mary,' he said, his voice tinged with a seriousness he rarely showed. 'Just humour me. No one knows who he is or where he lives. I've done a bit of checking myself. Nothing. He also dispenses advice to—'

I groaned loudly. 'Come off it, Andy. The Nazarian. He plays music and dispenses advice. He sounds like one of those religious nuts.'

'Just have a look,' he said. 'Then get back to me.'

'Yeah, yeah,' I said and hung up. I tossed the mobile onto the bedside table and lay back down.

Having failed to get back to sleep and cursing Andy for phoning, I climbed from my bed. Fifteen minutes later, showered and dressed, with a piece of toast in my mouth and a strong cup of coffee in my hand, I fired up my laptop.

'The Nazarian,' I muttered to myself. 'Bloody waste of time.' I waited for the videos to appear, and then several popped up, dating back a week. I pressed the oldest – a song called *The Better Part of You*. I leant nearer to the screen as the image of a man in a studio appeared. Vaguely familiar – white, mid-thirties with shoulder-length hair. I unmuted the computer and listened to him sing, and he could sing wonderfully. The song skipped along nicely, with a melody that instantly resonated with me. This surprised me because I could be quite critical of modern music. The pathetically simple tunes that seemed to populate the charts these days and the banal *cat sat on the mat* lyrics, but this was different. The song was good, but not just good. It was astonishing. I pressed the button below the video, and the lyrics appeared. Like poetry put to music, but unlike some songs where you know the writer has written a poem and then writes a melody around it. Although those songs can be good, you never shake the belief that they're a compromise, but this was nothing like that. The melody and lyrics melded in perfect synergy. Then, several smaller screens appeared around the main video, showing him playing all the instruments – the drums, keyboard, guitar and bass vied for position as the music continued. A guitar solo burst forth halfway through the song. The image of him playing this expanded to fill the screen, returning to him standing at the mic only when his singing resumed.

I listened until the end without taking an eye off the screen as I ate the toast and drank the coffee I'd prepared. Then, finally, it ended, and I smiled. For the first time in a long time, I smiled. Well, grinned, actually. The song lifted my spirits and exhilarated me. I fired up another video, then another and listened to all eight songs, one after the other. Each piece outmatched its predecessor in complexity and skill. When the final song ended, I picked up my mobile and called Andy.

It's funny how things prompt your memory. As I finished my second coffee, a Facebook picture appeared on my phone. A photo of Kate Carver, my long-time friend. Kate and I graduated from Newcastle University twenty years ago. She completed a degree in psychology, and I'd finished my degree in journalism. We shared accommodation in the halls of residence and then a house in Jesmond, becoming as close as sisters. We only lost this great bond after Kate met and married Iain, an Australian. Soon after, the pair emigrated down under, and we hadn't seen each other for years. Birthday and Christmas cards crossed continents, but the last time we'd been in the same room was when she came over for her cousin's wedding. I sighed – it's funny how you can allow the years to race past without contacting someone you laughed, cried and many other things with. A pang of guilt and a longing to speak with her sparked in me. So, I flicked through my contacts and found her name. My finger hovered over the call button as my phone rang, and I answered it. 'Hi, Andy,' I said. 'I'm on my way now.'

'Can we reschedule for this afternoon?' he said.

'Yeah. What's up?'

He sighed. 'Nothing much. I have a meeting regarding the possible

lockdown.'
'I groaned. 'Looks like it's going to happen.'
'They'll probably have us working from home.'
'Will it affect my story?' I asked.
'I don't think so. I'll know more later.'
'Ok,' I said. 'What time?'
'Same place, three o'clock.'

KATE

MARY – Pulling my phone from my handbag, I stared at an unfamiliar number. I paused, not wanting my now free morning interrupted by some cold call, but answered anyway.

'Hello,' I said, trying not to sound too friendly.

'Mary?' the voice on the other end asked.

'Yeah, who's this?'

'It's Kate.'

'Bloody hell, Kate,' I said. 'I was thinking of you earlier. I was about to ring. How are you?'

'I'm good. I'm back home, and you wouldn't have got through on my old number. I've got a new phone.'

'The one you're calling from?'

'Yeah.'

'So, you're back in Darlington? How long for?'

She paused on the other end. 'For good,' she said emphatically.

I considered my next words. 'Iain?'

'We've separated.'

'I see.'

'Listen, Mary,' she said. 'I'd love to meet up for a chat.'

'I'm free until three.'

'Can you come across here?' she said.

'No problem. Where?'

'Do you know a coffee shop in the centre called *The Quality Bean*?'

'No, but I should be able to find it.'

'I'll text you the postcode. Shall we say twelve?'

'Twelve's good,' I said and rang off. I smiled. Her ringing was one of those coincidences, I thought. Quickly saving her new number to my phone, I applied a little lipstick, grabbed my coat and keys and headed off.

As I entered the shop, I spotted her at a table in the corner. She hadn't aged, but her hair was much shorter, almost boyish. She stood, and we hugged as I reached the table.

'You look great,' I said genuinely.

'You too.'

'You're just being nice.'

She patted me on the arm and smiled. 'Well, I think you look bloody marvellous.'

I believed her. I could always tell when she was lying. 'Thanks,' I said and sat opposite her.

Kate caught the eye of a staff member, and we ordered our coffees. 'So,' she said, 'still looking for that scoop?'

'Yeah. It must be out there somewhere.' I said with a smile.

'And your love life? You'd just started going out with …?'

'Liam,' I said.

'You and he?' I shook my head. Kate narrowed her eyes. 'What's up?'

'Liam's dead.' I didn't know what else to say. I would have preferred to dodge the issue completely, but this was Kate. We rarely kept secrets from each other.

She reached across and took hold of my hand. 'I'm so sorry, Mary. Do you want to talk about it?'

Easing my hand from hers, I looked away. 'It's a long story,' I said. 'Perhaps another day.'

She nodded her understanding. 'Of course.'

The coffee arrived right on cue, for me, anyway. As they were laid before us, the topic of conversation evaporated. 'You and Iain?' I said.

'Separated.' She shrugged her shoulders. 'The marriage hasn't been working for a long time. He's already moved on.'

I nodded, studying her features. 'Does that bother you?'

'Not in the least. Good luck to him.' She smiled and sipped her coffee. 'Anyway,' she said, swiftly changing the subject. 'The reason I rang, apart from wanting to see you, of course, is to ask if you would be up for a story?'

'I'm starting one today,' I said. 'Do you remember Andy?'

'The sub-editor for—'

'Editor, now.'

'Yeah, I remember him.' She smiled. 'Is he still as handsome?'

I shrugged. 'I suppose.' Kate wasn't the first woman I'd known that found him attractive, but I never had.

'You'll have to re-introduce me to him.'

'This story?' I asked, brushing aside her appeal to my matchmaking skills.

Her eyes widened. 'Oh, yeah. Do you remember a friend of Mum and

Dad? Felix Halshaw?'

The name seemed familiar, but I couldn't place it. 'Remind me,' I said.

'He was a lecturer at Teesside University – History, I think. Well, twenty years ago, Felix was driving home from work when he suffered a heart attack on the Leyburn road.'

It came back to me. 'Ah! The guy with vivid dreams about demons and such like.'

Kate grinned. 'That's the one.'

'What about him?'

The smile fell from her face, and she fixed me with a stare. 'The hospital where I'm working admitted a man two days ago. He was ranting and raving, and we had to sedate him.'

I drummed my fingers on the table and comically rolled my eyes. 'Is there a point, Kate?'

'He was picked up in the exact spot where Felix had his heart attack.'

I shrugged. 'Coincidence.'

'He claimed a man called James took him to a place called ...'

'Nearhope,' I said. I'm not sure why I remembered the name, but I did.

'Yes,' Kate said. 'His story bears a striking similarity to Felix's.'

'Maybe he'd heard the story.'

'I've spoken to Felix, and he doesn't know him.'

I scoffed. 'Are you trying to say this place exists?'

'No. But two people having a similar experience over twenty years apart seems odd, don't you think?'

I didn't really. I thought it a coincidence, but something at the back of my mind nagged me. Something I couldn't put my finger on. 'I don't know. There has to be a rational explanation. Probably something quite mundane.'

She drained her cup. 'But I've piqued your interest. I can tell.'

I had to admit that she had, but I didn't want distracting from the story about The Nazarian. 'As I said, I've got this story Andy wants me to do.'

'What's that one about?'

'Have you heard of a guy on the internet who goes by the name of The Nazarian?' She shook her head. 'He's making quite an impact on YouTube.'

'Doing what?'

'He writes and performs his own songs.'

'I can't see how that will make a story.'

I smiled. 'Watch him.'

'The Nazarian,' she said. 'As in ...'

'Nazareth, I guess. The place where Jesus was born.'

'So, he's a religious nut?'

'Just watch him,' I said. 'You'll be impressed.'

'Ok.' She reached into her handbag and pulled out a Dictaphone. 'If I do, do me the favour of listening to this.'

I examined the machine. 'Jesus, Kate, a Dictaphone. Didn't the twenty-first century reach Oz? What's on it?'

She laughed. 'It's my interview with Reece Sadler.'

'The guy at your hospital?'

'Yes. Have a listen and tell me what you think. You can give me the Dictaphone back when we go up to Leyburn.'

I stared at her. 'Leyburn?'

'To meet with Felix.'

'Why are—?'

'Felix wanted to know why I was asking about Nearhope.'

'What did you say?'

She pulled a face. 'I managed to concoct some story, but I don't think he was convinced. I thought the two of us could go to his place and chat with him.'

'You could do that on your own, so why do you need me?'

'You're better at this than me,' she said. 'Plus, it'll be interesting.'

I wasn't convinced. The story Andy put me on seemed much more important. 'I'll tell you what,' I said. 'I'll have a listen to this.' I held up the Dictaphone. 'And then decide, but no promises.'

'Thanks.' She looked towards the waitress. 'Shall I get us another coffee?'

I checked my watch. 'It'll have to be quick. I'm meeting Andy.'

'If I didn't have to be back at work,' Kate said, 'I would have tagged along. 'Is he …?'

I rolled my eyes. 'Available?'

Kate nodded quickly. 'Yeah.'

'I think so. He split up with his girlfriend months back. But to be honest, I don't keep tabs on his love life.'

Kate winked. 'Maybe you could find out for me.'

'Maybe I could.'

Kate held up her hand to attract the attention of the waitress. I smiled. The years apart vanished into nothingness. As if Kate had always been in my life. Some people are like that. You don't see them for years, but when you do, you carry on as you always had, and I had to admit, I loved that.

ANDY

MARY – I pulled the car up outside the newspaper's offices and hurried into the building. I knocked on the door of Andy's office, who looked up from his desk and waved me inside.

'Have a seat,' he said. He stood and made his way across to the coffee pot in the corner and held it up. 'Coffee?'

'Of course,' I said.

He placed a cup in front of me and filled it. 'How are you?' he said, dropping onto his seat.

'Good.'

'Are you sure it's not too early after …?'

'Andy,' I said, 'I'm fine.' I took a large swig of my coffee and fixed him with a stare. 'Well?'

He smiled. 'Did you watch the videos?'

'I did.'

He folded his arms and sat back in his chair. 'What do you think?'

'He's brilliant. What do you know about him?'

Andy shrugged. 'Not a great deal.' He picked up a file and pushed it across the desk to me. 'One of the juniors checked his background. We didn't get much,'

'Someone must know him?'

'I know.' Andy said. 'No one gets that good without being noticed. His last video has 2.5 million views already.' He picked up a handful of newspapers and tossed them onto his desk. 'The tabloids are starting to pick up on it.'

I flicked through the headlines in the newspapers. *Who is The Nazarian?* screamed one. *Who is this musical genius?* said another. I looked at Andy. 'If the tabs are already covering this, is there any point in me—?'

He leant forward. 'I want you to interact with him.'

I frowned. 'Interact?'

'Yeah. You've seen the questions people ask him. He's acting like some musical agony aunt. So what I want you to do, Mary ...' He laced his hands together ... 'is get to know him.'

'They're talking about a lockdown.'

'I know, which is why we must act quickly,' he said.

'What the hell am I going to ask him?'

'Be creative, you've ...'

He stopped mid-sentence. 'You're suggesting I use Liam's murder?' I said. Andy looked sheepish as I glared at him. 'I don't believe it.'

'You don't know it was murder.'

I swatted the papers aside. 'Of course I know it was murder. Liam was investigating Creeney and was killed in a hit-and-run. I don't care that Creeney had an alibi. If he didn't kill Liam, one of his mates did.'

Andy held up his hands. 'I'm sorry. Listen, you know the score. We have to use every advantage we have. That's what journalism is all about.'

I stood and pointed at him. 'That's out of order, Andy. Is that the only reason you asked me to do this story?'

'Of course not. You're a bloody good journalist. Sit down, Mary.'

I was fuming. How the hell could he do this? 'Sod your story.' I said and fumbled for the door handle as he stepped towards me.

'I'm sorry, Mary. You're right. I was out of order.'

He put his arms around my shoulders, attempting to appease me. 'Get off me, you bastard,' I said.

He turned me around to face him. 'Forgive me. You know I loved Liam. He was my mate, too. You're not the only one who misses him.' Andy threw up his hands. 'Forget about the story. I'll get someone else to do it.'

My body trembled. The pain and loss I felt – that I'd managed to subdue until now – washed over me. My legs buckled, and Andy grasped me beneath my arms and led me back to the chair. Unable to prevent the torrent of tears that cascaded from me, I wrapped my arms protectively around my body. And then it subsided. My sobbing gradually dwindled to nothing.

Andy handed me a tissue. 'You ok? I didn't mean to upset you like this.'

Speaking still a little beyond me, I nodded. Then, someone tapped on the door, and I turned my head away in embarrassment.

'Yeah,' Andy said tetchily.

'Have you heard?' the female voice said.

'Heard what? I'm busy with Mary.'

'Oh,' she said. 'I didn't know Mary ...'

'Heard what?' Andy said, clearly irritated.

'Well … it's just …'

I turned and looked at the young woman standing there. Her eyes wide and fixed on me.

'What the hell is it, Megan?' Andy demanded of her.

'The news.' She glanced between Andy and me. 'Creeney.' Holding a piece of paper, Andy snatched it from her and read it.

'What about Creeney?' I asked.

Andy handed me the paper and studied me as I absorbed the information.

Man stabbed to death behind the back of nightclub identified as Charles Thomas Creeney of …

The rest of the words meant nothing. His life, suspected drug involvement, and extortion hardly registered as I dropped the paper onto Andy's desk.

'I'm sorry,' Megan said. 'I didn't know you were—'

'It's ok,' Andy said. 'Can you give us a minute?' She nodded and hurried from the room.

Staring at Andy, I blew out hard. 'When did it happen?' I said.

He picked up the piece of paper again. 'The police said sometime between eleven and midnight last night.'

The room closed in on me as my heart hammered inside my chest. 'I have to go.'

'Ok,' he said, not even attempting to persuade me otherwise.

Hurrying towards the door, I stopped at the threshold. 'I'll get back to you about the story.' I didn't even know why I said that to him.

'Don't worry about that,' he said.

'No,' I whispered. 'I want to.' With that, I left and raced from the building and into the sanctuary of my car. I wracked my brain. Had I killed him? I must have. I brought a hand to my mouth and gasped as the enormity of his murder crashed into me.

The journey home was on autopilot, and I went straight into the kitchen, pulled a bottle of wine from the rack, poured myself a large glass and downed it in one. A second bottle quickly followed the first, and maybe even a third, as the rest of the day sped by in a vino-induced blur.

THE NAZARIAN

MARY – The next day I woke up on the settee with what I can only describe as the worst hangover head I have ever had. Stumbling to my feet, I gingerly made my way into the bathroom and dropped to my knees, vomiting the contents of my stomach into the toilet bowl.

It took me most of the day to pull myself around, and it wasn't until late afternoon that I felt almost human again. Armed with a super-strong coffee, I fired up my laptop. Although part of me expected the police to show up any minute, I searched for the Nazarian and spotted a freshly posted video.

Another wonderful song filled the room as I closed my eyes and gently drifted between the lyrics and melody. The song was about forgiveness. The lyrics basically said you shouldn't beat yourself up for doing wrong. If you recognise what you have done and truly express remorse, that is enough. But what about what I'd done? Would I be forgiven for that? What if Creeney hadn't killed Liam? What if it was a tragic hit-and-run, as Andy said? But as I read the lyrics to the song, they seemed to resonate with me. I can't really explain my feelings at that moment, but it was as if something big, something huge, something beyond my comprehension, had forgiven me.

The song ended, and the singer looked into the camera. 'Thanks for listening to my latest song,' he said. His speaking voice just as tuneful as his singing. 'Don't forget to like my video and subscribe to my channel.' He smiled. A smile that appeared reserved for me – as if it was him and me on some video call.

'I have some messages for my loyal followers out there,' he said. One by one, I listened as he dispensed words of wisdom to people who messaged him – suicidal people, people losing hope, people on the very edge. Eventually, he put aside the last pieces of paper in his hand and stared down the camera lens again.

'One last message to someone who is hurting at this moment. Someone who fears that they may have done something terrible.' He smiled again. 'You have nothing to ask forgiveness for. Things are not always as they seem, Mary.'

My jaw dropped open as I held my breath. Was he talking about me? I laughed. You're not the only Mary in the world, I said to myself.

'Remember,' he continued, 'hope is never far away, Mary. Hope is always near.' He emphasised the words *hope* and *near*.

I jumped as the front doorbell chimed and leapt to my feet, but I couldn't resist one final glance at the screen as the video ended. I carefully opened the door, expecting the police to be there, but Kate stood outside.

She smiled. 'Hi. I managed to get away early and went to the newspaper office.' She frowned. 'Everything ok?'

I glanced up and down the road. 'Er ... yeah. Sorry,' I spluttered. 'I thought it was ...'

Kate narrowed her eyes. 'Thought it was who?'

I managed to snap out of my mental malaise and stepped back. 'Oh, nobody. Come in.'

She followed me through into the front room. 'Andy told me your address. He seemed a bit worried about you.'

'I'm fine,' I said but felt anything but. 'Can I get you a drink?'

'Coffee would be good.'

I nodded and hurried into the kitchen. Leaning against the worktop, I took deep breaths allowing myself to gain composure before making the coffee and returning to the living room.

'Did you listen to the Dictaphone?' she asked.

'Not yet, but I will.' I glanced towards my laptop. 'Can I show you something?' Kate nodded, and I turned the computer around to face her. 'Listen to this.'

'Is this the guy you were on about?'

'Yeah. Watch and pay particular attention to the end when he answers questions from subscribers.'

We sat in silence as he played and sang the song. Then listened as he answered questions and gave out advice. 'This bit,' I said as we reached the point where he'd mentioned me or what I took to be me. But the playback ended. I grabbed the computer and slid the bar back on the bottom of the screen. It wasn't there. The part I'd seen wasn't there.

'What's up?' Kate said.

'I ... I'm not sure. It was different the first time I heard it.'

'Different? How?'

'Well ...' I paused. Had I really seen it, or just imagined it? 'Nothing. I think I'm losing the plot.'

Kate threw back her head. 'So am I.' She pulled out her phone and held it up. 'I received a text from you.'

Puzzled, I shook my head. 'I haven't—'

'I know,' she said. 'I got a text and opened it.' She fixed me with a stare. 'It said. *Hope is always near.*'

'It said what?'

'Hope is always near.'

I grabbed the phone from her. 'Let me see.'

She took it back from me. 'It's not there.' She laughed. 'I must have imagined it. I'm cracking up too.'

I told Kate about what I had witnessed in the video and what The Nazarian said. We played the end of the video again, and there was still no message.

She sat back in her chair. 'What the hell's going on?'

'I don't know.' I drummed my fingers on the table. 'Can I ask you what made you get in touch with me yesterday after three years?'

'Nothing really ... except ...'

'Except?'

'I have a load of photos on the wall in one of the rooms back at mine. Pictures of places and people who are special to me. Family, holidays and such like. When I went in yesterday morning, one had fallen off the wall and smashed. Do you remember that photo I took of us two after we graduated?'

I took out my phone and retrieved the photo from my Facebook memories. 'This one?'

'That's it. That's the one which fell off the wall and smashed. I thought of you and felt compelled to phone.'

'Compelled?'

She nodded. 'That's the only way I can describe it.'

'The same picture came up on my Facebook memories earlier,' I said. 'Bit of a coincidence, don't you think?'

Kate screwed up her face. 'Not really. Photos come up on Facebook quite often, don't they?'

'On the anniversary it was posted.'

'There you go, then. It's—'

'Except it wasn't the anniversary of when I posted it.'

Kate scoffed. 'Are you sure?'

'Of course I'm sure. We didn't graduate in March.'

'Are you sure you didn't post at a later date?'

I shook my head. 'Positive.'

'You may have forgotten.'

I tapped the top of the computer. 'What about the text and video?'

'I don't know. It does seem strange.'

'It's as if someone is trying to get us together.'

Kate laughed. 'Like fate?'

'It does seem a little daft. But, on the other hand, I'm sure there's a perfectly rational explanation for it.'

'Anyway,' Kate said, 'the Dictaphone? Why not play it now. I'd be fascinated to know what you think.'

'Ok.' I retrieved the device from my bag and began playback.

'Interview with Dr Kate Carver and Reece Sadler,' it began. *'How are you, Reece?'*

'Fine,' replied a quiet voice.

'I'd like you to tell me what you remember.'

Reece sighed. 'I've explained all this.'

'I know you have, Reece, but could you explain again.'

'He took me to Nearhope.'

'Who did?' she said.

'James.'

'Can you tell me about James?'

'He's a ...' There was a long pause. '... a Demon.'

'A Demon?'

'I know it sounds stupid,' he said, 'but that's what he is.'

'I see. Where is this Nearhope?'

'Just off the Leyburn road.'

'I've checked the maps, Reece, and I can't find it.'

He scoffed. 'That's because it doesn't exist in our world ...'

We continued to listen as Reece recounted a fantastical tale about Nearhope and James. And beyond there, a dark place that sounded like the polar opposite of Nearhope. The Dictaphone ended, and Kate looked at me.

'Well?' she said.

'It sounds like the ravings of a madman,' I said. 'He mentioned Nearhope.'

Kate nodded. 'Like the video and my text.'

'But it's crazy. It has to be a coincidence.'

'I agree,' she said. 'However, it bears striking similarities to Felix's account.'

'Have you spoken to Felix again?'

'I've arranged to pop up and see him tomorrow. As I said, I'd really like you to come along.'

'Won't he think it strange, you bringing along a journo?'

'We'll concoct a story. We'll tell him you're recounting people's dreams and visions.'

'Sounds a bit thin,' I said, but I reasoned I could let Kate do the explaining. I stood. 'Why don't you stay the night? The truth is, I could do with a bit of company.'

She looked at me quizzically. 'Yeah, ok. I haven't any spare clothes, though.'

'Don't worry.' I smiled. 'You can borrow something of mine. We're about the same size.' She nodded her acquiescence. 'What about something a little stronger than coffee? Wine?'

'Yeah, why not. Just like old times.'

The evening passed solemnly. After consuming several wines, I bared my soul to Kate and told her about Liam. How he'd been knocked down in a hit and run, and the perpetrator never caught. I told her I suspected Creeney may have killed Liam or had him killed but couldn't prove it and that Creeney had been stabbed to death the previous night. For obvious reasons, I left out the fact that I'd been at the club when he came outside. I still wasn't totally sure that I'd been there. It now appeared as if I'd dreamt it. Maybe I had.

The following morning, we were both up early. After a light breakfast and the obligatory strong coffee, we set off to Leyburn. The conversation managed to somehow steer clear of Felix and the Nazarian. Instead, we spoke mainly of our past and what we'd got up to since our previous meeting.

Eventually, we reached Leyburn and stopped outside a large house set back from the road. Even at this time of the year, the garden was immaculately looked after – the trees and shrubs ready to burst forth in the early spring weather.

Kate looked at me. 'Ready?' she said.

'Yeah.'

'Let me do the talking initially, and then use your journalistic ability to tease out as much information as possible.'

'Ok,' I said. 'Lead on.'

We found ourselves in a large, ornate and slightly dated room, which Felix invited us into before disappearing to make drinks. I pulled out my mobile, notebook and pen.

Felix returned and placed a tray on the table between us. 'Help yourselves,' he said before sitting. 'So, what can I do for you two?'

'Mary and I,' she said and glanced at me, 'are trying to write a story about dreams and visions that people have had. I remembered you telling Mum and Dad about an experience you had some time ago.'

He thoughtfully filled his cup with tea and added milk before looking at the pair of us. 'Nearhope,' he said.

Kate threw another glance in my direction. 'Yes, Nearhope. Do you still remember?'

He glanced over the top of his spectacles as he sipped his tea before placing the cup down. 'I'd forgotten about it for a long time, then one morning, a couple of weeks ago, I woke, and there it was, back in my head, as if it all happened yesterday.'

I leant forward. 'Can you tell us about it?'

'Nearhope,' he began, 'is a strange place.'

'Is?' Kate said.

He smiled. 'It did feel so real. Even after all this time, the memories burn brightly. I wrote it down years ago, so I wouldn't forget, but I don't need to look back at the notes. I can let you have them if you like?'

I picked up my phone. 'That would be great. You don't mind if we record this?'

'Not at all,' he said.

I turned on the voice recorder and switched to journalist mode. 'Start from the beginning.'

'James,' he said. 'It all began when I met James ...'

MARTIN

MARCH 2020 – Martin awoke and allowed his senses to acclimatise before awkwardly climbing from his bed. A blood-covered t-shirt and jeans lay on the bathroom floor. Collecting a black sack from the kitchen and stuffing the items into it, he tied the bag and pushed it inside a second one. He gasped as he spotted a blood-smeared knife in the bottom of the sink. Tentatively he lifted it up by the handle, scrubbed it with a brush and sponge, then placed the knife back in the wooden block on the worktop and forced the brush and sponge inside the black sack along with the other items. Satisfied, he pulled on his coat, collected his guitar, and slung it over one shoulder. Then, carrying the sack, he headed for the door, grabbed his walking sticks in his free hand and left.

Martin limped along the road. The urge to urinate was now uppermost in his mind, and he looked around for a public toilet, but not knowing this part of town well, he wasn't confident of finding one. Then, spotting a pub, he pushed his guitar up higher and, using his two sticks to aid his progress, manoeuvred his twisted body across the road and inside the bar. The room was almost empty except for a man sitting on a barstool – his shoulder-length hair hung loosely behind his long coat. A portly man stood behind the bar, removed glasses from the dishwasher and placed them underneath the counter.

'Excuse me,' Martin said, looking towards the barman. 'I couldn't use your toilet, could I?'

The barman paused. 'The toilet's for customers, mate.'

'Oh, I see.'

'Let him use the loo,' the man on the stool said. 'Can't you see he has a disability?'

The barman sneered. 'The disabled toilet's broken.'

'I can use the other one,' Martin said.

'There you go,' the man on the stool said. He put his hand into his pocket and pulled out a note. 'I'll buy him a drink if that helps.'

The barman looked at the young man and nodded towards the gents. 'Yeah, go on then.' Martin thanked him and limped off.

The barman pulled two pints and placed them on the counter next to the banknote. As he moved to pick up the money, the man on the stool took hold of his arm. 'I think these drinks should be on you.'

The barman grimaced and tried to remove his arm. 'I … I …' he said. The grip on his arm now vice-like.

The long-haired man pulled him closer as the barman groaned and screwed up his face. 'Please,' he pleaded. 'I didn't mean any …'

He relinquished his grip on the barman as the toilet door swung open, and Martin returned. The barman stepped back and rubbed at his wrist.

Martin slowly made his way across to the man on the stool. 'Thanks,' he said.

'Have a seat.' He held out a hand. 'James. Well, that's what I will have to call myself for the time being. However, if you get to know me better, you can call me Asmodeus.'

'Asmodeus?' Martin said.

He increased his grip on Martin's hand. 'It will all become clear.'

Martin winced as a hot flash of pain shot up his arm. 'I'm Martin,' he whispered.

James released his hand and slid one of the pints across the bar. 'I got you one in, or rather our friendly barmen did.'

The barman nodded. 'Yeah, sorry about that. I didn't mean to offend you.'

'Thanks,' Martin said.

'I see you play an instrument.'

Martin slid the guitar from his back and leant it against the bar. 'Bass.'

'Bass, eh? Aren't we looking for a bassist, Eddie?' he said, looking at the barman.

'Yeah, we are.'

James nodded towards the pint. 'Have a drink.'

Martin frowned. 'I can't buy you one back. I'm on my way into town to sort my benefits out.'

'Why were you taking your guitar?'

Martin lowered his head. 'I was considering pawning it.'

'You won't have to now,' James said. 'Don't worry about the beer either. Now you're in our band …' He smiled. 'The beer's free.'

'I'm not sure I'll be good enough,' Martin said. 'My disability can—'

'Nonsense,' James said and fixed Martin with a stare. His eyes, a dark brown, almost black, bore down on Martin. 'What do you need those sticks for, anyway?'

Martin glanced across at Eddie and then back to James. 'I can't walk without them. I've got—'

James smiled. 'Of course you can.'

Martin picked up his pint and took a swig. 'I'd fall if I haven't anything to lean on.'

The smile fell from James's face as he glared at Martin. 'Throw them away.'

'I can't,' Martin said. 'I just can't.'

James gripped his arm. 'If this is going to work,' he said. 'You have to have faith in me. Now throw them away.'

Martin stared into those eyes. Eyes that drew him inside and locked him there. He stood transfixed, unable to move.

James leant closer. His eyes glowed red. 'Are you not listening? I said, throw them away.'

Martin looked at the two sticks in his hands and then at James. 'Where?'

James laughed and looked at the barman. 'What should we do with his sticks, Eddie?'

Eddie sniggered. 'Break them.'

'There you go,' James said. 'Eddie wants you to break them.'

Martin gulped. 'Ok.' He took hold of one of them and, placing it across the edge of the bar, bent the walking stick in half.

'And the other,' James said. 'Break the other.'

Martin repeated the process and tossed the second stick with the first on the floor. He looked at James as he hung onto the bar for support.

'Let go of the bar,' James whispered. 'You can't replace one crutch with another.'

'Please, I'll fall.'

James groaned. 'Just do as I tell you.' He moved his face closer to Martin. 'Just do as I say.'

Martin wiped the beads of sweat from his brow and stepped away from the counter. He didn't fall. Standing a metre from the bar, Martin looked down in amazement. 'I don't understand,' he said.

'I think there was nothing wrong with you,' James said. 'I think you're trying to rip off your government.' He laughed. 'He's one of those malingerers, Eddie.'

Martin walked a little and then spun around. 'It's a miracle.'

James jumped from his stool and walked across to him. 'When I ask you to do something in the future, what will you do?' he said, pushing his face closer again.

Martin edged away slightly. 'I'll do it.'

James grabbed his arm and pulled him nearer. 'Anything?'

Martin nodded. 'Anything.'

'I know what you did.'

Martin frowned. 'What I did?'

'The knife. The blood, I see it all. You can't hide anything from me.'

Martin glanced at the barman and back to James. 'How?'

James laughed. 'I knew as soon as you entered here. Your guilt is palpable.' James relinquished his grip. 'Don't worry, we won't say anything.' Martin took a large gulp from his pint.

James licked his lips. 'Did you enjoy killing him?'

'I don't know. He was a bully. He murdered someone I know. I'm not sure how I felt at the time.'

James's smile disappeared. 'Would you kill for me?'

Martin stared at his questioner as James locked his eyes on him. 'Yes.'

James smiled again. 'Good. I will hold you to that promise.'

The door opened and another man walked in. 'Ah, Cain,' James said. 'We have another person for our gang.'

Cain looked Martin up and down. 'He doesn't look up to much if you ask me.'

James patted Martin on the arm. 'This is Martin, and he'll do fine.'

Martin held out a hand. 'Nice to meet you.'

Cain ignored it. 'The club is ready for tonight.'

'Good. A little enjoyment before we get down to the real work.'

'Real work?' Martin said.

James drained his glass. 'We have much to do. You'll see. For now, it's on a strictly need-to-know basis.' He walked off. 'Show Martin where he'll be sleeping,' he said over his shoulder as he left.

FELIX'S STORY

MARY – Kate looked across at me. 'Wow,' she said. 'What a nightmare.'

Felix raised his eyebrows. 'It certainly was.' He stood. 'I'll make us another cup of tea, and then I'll tell you how we escaped from the citadel.'

I glanced at Kate and then back to Felix. 'There's more?'

'Oh, yes, there's more.' He smiled and then left the room.

'Are you going to mention Reece Sadler again?' I asked.

Kate slowly rubbed her chin. 'I don't think so. He said he didn't know him.'

'His story is amazing, though.'

Kate widened her eyes. 'Not to mention terrifying.'

'Maybe this is why some writers are so good at stories. Maybe they have this vivid imagination that most people don't possess.'

'Yeah.'

'It begs one question, though,' I said.

'What?'

'How is Reece Sadler's story so similar to Felix's?'

'What if Felix and Reece read the same story but have just forgotten?'

'I suppose,' I said. 'There's another possibility … That Felix knows Reece. You may well have to mention him.'

'Yes.'

'Leave it to me,' I said.

Felix returned and lay down the tray with fresh tea and biscuits. He sat and smiled at us both. 'So,' he said. 'Reece Sadler? The gentleman you asked me about on the phone?'

I glanced at Kate and then back to Felix. 'Reece?'

'I heard his name as I was coming back.' Felix clasped his hands together. 'Cards on the table, ladies. Why did you really come?'

'Reece is another person going to go into my book,' I said.

'I see.' He narrowed his eyes. 'Would it be rude of me to say I don't believe you?' Felix picked up my phone and smiled. The machine was still recording. 'Shall we listen to this?' he said.

'Look, Felix,' Kate said.

Felix held up a hand. 'Kate, it's only because I know your parents that I agreed to see you. But I don't take kindly to being treated as a fool.'

Kate lowered her head. 'Reece is one of my patients.' She glanced at me, then carried on. 'He was brought to the hospital a few days ago and had an incredible story.'

'About Nearhope?'

She furrowed her brow. 'Yes.'

'I've seen him,' Felix said. 'In my dreams. He appeared after you asked me about him.' He moved across to a dresser on the far side of the room. From one of the drawers, he plucked a piece of paper and handed it to Kate. 'Is this Reece?'

She studied the sketch. 'Yes. It looks like him.'

'Reece was in a dream of mine last week. He was with James. It has been such a long time since I dreamed of James. That's why I didn't believe your story. Too much of a coincidence.'

'What did you see?' I asked.

'I can't remember,' he said. 'It was vivid when I woke, but with each passing hour, it receded. Now I only retain a fleeting feeling. Something deep in here.' He tapped the side of his head.

'This James,' I said, 'he's a Demon?'

'He's more than that.' Felix stood, wandered over to the window and stared into the garden. 'I'd always believed Nearhope was no more than a fantasy. Now I know ...' He spun around to face us. 'Nearhope is real.'

Kate and I laughed. 'Felix,' Kate said. 'I think you're—'

'How do you explain Reece?' he said.

Kate stood and stared indignantly at him. 'How do we know you and Reece haven't concocted this story? How do we know ...' She looked at me as if looking for reassurance. '... that you and Reece haven't read a book in the past that planted this story in your head?'

Felix returned to his seat. 'I used to think I'd read about Nearhope in a book. I've searched the internet for years. You two try it. I've never come up with anything approaching my story.'

I placed a hand on Kate's as she was about to talk. 'You must admit,' I said, 'it does sound outlandish.'

'I can't explain any of this. I am a logical man and not one to go on flights of fancy. But I have always retained ...' He placed a hand on his chest. '... a belief that it was real. A feeling that I could not shake.'

'But there has to be a rational explanation,' I said.

Felix smiled. 'Who do you think The Nazarian is?'

Kate and I exchanged rapid glances. 'How ...?'

'I dreamed of him too,' Felix said. 'He needs our help.'

Kate frowned. 'Help? How can we help?'

'What did Reece say about James?' Felix said.

She paused and rubbed her chin again. 'He said he is lost. He claimed someone has captured him.' Opening her handbag, she pulled out a pad.

Felix shuddered. 'Asmodeus?' he said.

Kate looked up from the page as her jaw dropped open. 'Yes. But ...'

'He is the Demon Prince I told you about. I deliberately resisted saying his name. Even now, if I say his name out loud ...' He briefly closed his eyes. 'He rules over one of the Demon realms.'

I shook my head slowly. 'This is crazy.'

'I agree,' he said.

It was absurd. I couldn't believe that I was sitting here giving Felix's story any credence, but there was this small nagging doubt that we could be wrong. 'Finish your story, Felix. Tell us how you escaped from the citadel.'

Kate and I left Felix's late afternoon. We drove back to my house in silence until we stopped outside.

Kate turned off the ignition and looked at me. 'Well, what the hell did you make of that?'

I shrugged. I didn't really have any words. 'Bizarre,' is all I managed.

'Bizarre,' she said. 'Is that all you can say?'

'What do you want me to say?'

She gripped the steering wheel and stared out of the windscreen. 'It has to be a hoax.'

'But you've known Felix for a long time. Is he the type to do something like that?'

She shook her head. 'No. That's what's so ...'

'Bizarre?'

She turned to me and smiled. 'Yeah, ok. Bizarre.'

'His wife Jenny?' I said.

'What about her?'

'She's dead, right?'

Kate nodded. 'You gathered that from his story?'

'How did she end up there, in ...?'

'Hell,' Kate interjected.

'Yeah.'

Kate sighed. 'Felix and Jenny had a son. But, unfortunately, he was abducted and murdered by a guy called William Franklyn.'

'I remember him,' I said. 'Franklyn and his daughter murdered quite a number. I thought Felix's name sounded familiar.'

'His wife Jenny took her own life. I guess the loss of her son was too much to bear. I remember Mum and Dad being really cut up about it. But you know my parents, stoic is their middle name. They hardly ever mentioned it.'

'But that doesn't explain how she ended up there.'

Kate shrugged. 'Maybe she did something terrible during her life. Jenny was a geneticist. A brilliant one by all accounts.'

'I can't see how being a geneticist condemns you to a life in purgatory.'

'Taking your own life might,' she suggested. 'Maybe it's considered a terrible sin.'

'Possibly.'

Kate leant behind her and picked up the carrier bag. 'Felix said he wrote it all down. He said he only told us some of it. Maybe you should read his account first.'

'Are you sure?'

'I'll be honest, Mary. This is so much to take in.' She puffed out her cheeks. 'I'm going to interview Reece Sadler again. I'll subtly ask him about Felix.'

'You're still not convinced?'

'Are you?'

I laughed nervously. 'Let's just say I'm keeping an open mind.'

I climbed from the car and headed towards my house. Pausing briefly at the door, I waved at Kate as she drove away. I tossed the carrier onto the settee and poured myself a large glass of wine which I thought I richly deserved.

Halfway down the bottle, my phone sounded. 'Andy?' I said.

'Have you seen the news?'

'No. I've been busy all day.'

'The health secretary has informed the House of Commons that the country is going into lockdown.'

I took a sip of my wine. 'When?'

'The PM's making an announcement on Monday.'

'That's going to hamper my story about The Nazarian.'

'Maybe not,' he said. 'I've had a few people scanning the media for background on this guy.'

'And?'

'Zero. The BBC, Sky, Reuters and tabloids have nothing. Some of the papers have offered money to anyone who can identify him. If it wasn't for Covid, he'd be front-page everywhere.'

'What do you want me to do?'

'Listen,' he said. 'I know I upset you the other day, and I don't want you to use personal stuff, but can you build a relationship with him? Concoct some sad story.'

I groaned. 'Even sadder than my own?'

'Sorry, I didn't—'

'Forget it. I get the picture.'

'Some of the people who message him have dreadful lives. So if you're going to grab his attention, you'll have to stand out.'

'Ok,' I said. 'I'll have to use an alias.'

'Yeah, yeah, whatever you think.'

'Do you remember the guy I mentioned?'

'Which guy?' he said.

'The one with the bizarre story.'

'What about him?'

I paused. How was I going to explain this to Andy? 'Oh, nothing. It'll keep.'

'By the way, he's now up to five million views a video. His likes and channel subscriptions are off the scale too.'

'Did you watch his video from yesterday?' I asked, gently probing Andy. Wondering if he spotted the bit about me or what I thought to be me.

'Yeah. Of course.'

'Did you see the questions and answer bit at the end?'

'Yeah. Usual *Oh, my life is so shit* stuff.'

I took another swig of wine. 'Nothing unusual?'

'No, why do you ask?'

'Just some of the questions seemed—'

'It's old news anyway. What did you think of his latest video?'

'I haven't seen it.'

Andy groaned down the line. 'Come on, Mary. You have to keep ahead of the game. Great news stories don't hang around forever.'

'Ok, ok. I'll get onto it.' I hung up, drained my glass and then called Kate.

'What's up?' she said.

'Are you at home?'

'No. I'm in Morrisons at Morton Park getting some wine. Why?'

'When you've got that wine, bring it here.'

'Mary,' she said. 'I've got work in the morning, I—'

'He's made another video, and I want us to watch it together.'

'Can't you come over here?'

'I've had a glass of wine.'

She scoffed. 'You'll be fine with one glass.'

'It was quite a large one. I don't want to risk it.'

'Compromise, then. Jump in a taxi.'

'All right. But I'll meet you at Morrisons. Don't leave.'

KATE'S HOUSE

MARY – In less than half an hour, I reached the shop, met Kate with her wine, and travelled to her house.

'What did you get?' I said, peering inside the carrier.

'Merlot.'

I groaned. 'I prefer cab sav.'

'It's a good merlot and my favourite. Besides,' she said, 'I bought it for me, not you. If I'd known we were going to spend the evening together, I would have asked.'

I pulled a face. 'Andy rang.'

Kate shot me a worried glance. 'You didn't tell him about Reece and Felix, did you?'

'No,' I said. 'All he's concerned about is The Nazarian story. He wants me to invent a persona and sob story to build a rapport with The Nazarian.'

'How are you going to do that?'

'I'm not sure. It'll have to be good, or my comments will be lost in the words of the others.'

'Felix said, when we were at his ...' Kate pulled her car up at what I assumed was her house and fumbled for the carrier behind her.

'Felix said what?' I asked impatiently.

'*Who do you think The Nazarian is*? What do you suppose he meant by that?'

'I don't know. I've only just remembered that he said it. Why didn't we ask him what he meant?'

Kate shrugged. 'I don't know. It didn't seem that important at the time. Didn't he say he'd dreamed of The Nazarian?'

'That's right.' I picked up my large bag. 'I brought the story Felix gave us. If it is a story.'

'Come on. Let's see what this new video is like.'

With a glass of wine each, we positioned ourselves in front of the laptop and began to watch.

'You've got to admit,' Kate said, 'not only is he a great musician, but he's handsome too.'

'I've never really thought about it,' I said. 'But now you mention it ...'

Kate sipped her wine and slightly tilted her head. 'I don't normally find blondes attractive.'

I turned to face her. 'Blonde?' She nodded at the screen.

I looked back at the video. The Nazarian played and sang wonderfully, but one thing stood out. His hair was dark brown. 'He's not blonde.' I eyed Kate. Trying to decipher if she was winding me up.

She looked at me and frowned. 'He's blonde.'

I shook my head. 'He's got dark-brown hair.'

Kate's eyes darted between me and the screen. 'One or both of us needs to have our eyes tested.'

We turned back to the screen and watched as the song ended. '*Don't forget to like and subscribe*,' he said, then picked up a handful of paper and began his usual dispensing of advice. It seemed to go on forever. He was becoming increasingly popular with each new video, and his eyes bore down on me again. 'Hi, Mary,' he said in that utterly captivating voice of his. 'Thank you for going to see Felix. He will need your help. We need James too. Without him, Asmodeus will cause mayhem. It is your destiny.'

The playback finished, and I became acutely aware of Kate staring at me. 'Did you hear that?' I said, pointing at the screen.

She slowly shook her head. 'You were in a trance. You've just been staring at the screen. He finished ages ago.'

I stood up and looked at her. 'You didn't see it?'

'See what?'

'He spoke directly to me.' I pointed at the computer again. 'He mentioned Felix.'

Kate stood and took hold of my arm. 'Are you sure?'

'Yes. Of course I'm sure.'

'What did he say?' Her eyes widened in excitement.

'He thanked me for going to see Felix. He said Felix and James will need help.' I dropped onto the settee. 'He said ...' I swallowed a lump the size of a golf ball. For reasons I can't explain, I could hardly utter his name.

'He said what?' Kate encouraged me.

'He said As-mod-eus will cause mayhem.' I struggled to say.

Kate joined me on the chair. 'From Felix's story?' I nodded. 'Shit,' she said. 'Shit, shit, shit.'

I decided to stay at Kate's for the night. The thought of returning to my empty flat didn't seem that appealing, especially with everything happening. I needed company. I also needed Kate's help in deciphering this mystery. Kate showered, and then I did too. I padded down the stairs and into the front room, where she was finishing on the phone.

'Well,' she said, raising her eyebrows. 'That's interesting.'

I slumped down opposite her. Tiredness enveloped me. 'What?'

'I phoned around a few work colleagues and mates. I made discreet enquiries about our friend.' She nodded towards the computer. 'Trying to find out how they viewed him. His appearance, I mean.' I nodded that I understood her train of thought, and she continued. 'Everyone I spoke to has a different view about his appearance.'

'Hair colour, you mean?' I said.

'More than that. Ethnicity. A woman from work has a white dad and a black mum. She told me that the Nazarian is mixed race.'

'Wow,' was my unimaginative response.

She grinned. 'I think we can assume that different people have different views of him.'

'I suppose we could ask people of every colour and creed.'

'No need,' she said. 'I've been googling. It's common knowledge. The media think it's some trick, but no one has come up with a plausible explanation. One professor reckons it could be some collective delusion.'

'Have you any more wine?' I said. 'I think I need another drink.'

'There's some in the kitchen. I don't want any. I'll need a clear head tomorrow if I'm going to speak to Reece Sadler.'

I yawned. 'About you know who?'

She nodded. 'You look as though you need to get to bed.'

'Yeah. I think I do. I'll give the wine a swerve too.' I stood. 'Back bedroom, you said?'

'Back bedroom. The sheets are clean, and I've …'

Her words drifted out of earshot as I tramped my way upstairs.

I would like to say that I enjoyed a good night's sleep, but I can't. Fitful would best describe it, full of visions and dreams. The Nazarian was there with a child. Was it my child? I couldn't say. Felix and Reece appeared at one point. How could this be? I'd never met or even seen a photo of Reece, yet I knew it was him. There was also someone dark, someone terrifying, someone who I feared. Their face, though, just out of reach. The dreams and nightmares continued until I could no longer stand them and got up.

THE CORRUPTION OF MARTIN

Martin stared at himself in the mirror and grinned as he studied his image. With his pristine black suit set off by the dark-blue shirt and paisley tie – given to him by Asmodeus – he was the epitome of stylishness. He stood up straight and smiled at his image – his previous existence and body, spent in a slump that struggled to move in the way his brain wanted, but now he was upright, tall, muscular and handsome.

The door opened, and a young man walked in. 'Nice threads,' he said.

'Cheers,' Martin replied.

The man thrust out his hand. 'Thomas.'

Martin shook it firmly. 'Martin.'

Thomas nodded slowly. 'I know who you are,' he said as he stared at the frowning Martin.

'Is everything all right?' Martin said.

'Just a word of advice, mate,' he said. 'I was Asmodeus's first. I am his favourite.' He stepped closer to Martin. 'It would be good if you could remember that.'

Martin gulped and nodded. 'Of course.'

Thomas patted him on the cheek, stepped back and grinned. 'Good. The boss wants to see you.'

'I'll be along soon.'

Thomas sneered. 'Be as long as you like, but he hates being kept waiting.'

Martin allowed himself one final look in the mirror, then hurried after Thomas through the door, down a flight of steps and into another room. Music blared from a sound system controlled by a huge bear of a man who stood behind a deck with earphones held up to one ear.

Martin stared open-mouthed at the scene before him. The room pulsated with a sea of naked bodies, entwined and writhing in some or other sexual act. The colour rose from his neck to his cheeks, and he blinked slowly, unable to look away. Occasionally a strobe would pick out some previously unseen corner of the room, or a flash of light would briefly light the area surrounding him, revealing more copulating individuals. Someone appeared by his side and handed him a drink, but as he gulped at the liquid and the spirit slid down and warmed his throat, he never took his eyes off the graphic images playing out.

Asmodeus stepped from the shadows and joined him. 'Here's my new employee,' he said loudly. Some people in the room turned to face Martin as Asmodeus, palm outstretched, introduced him.

'You haven't even heard me play bass,' Martin shouted above the din.

Asmodeus brought his mouth close to Martin's ear. 'Yes, but the old one didn't cut the mustard and wasn't up to scratch. You can't be any worse.' He nodded to the corner of the room where a cage-like structure hung from the ceiling. Martin narrowed his eyes, trying to decipher the contents. Then as his eyesight adjusted to the dim lighting, the form became distinct. Inside lay a person, a man, naked and exposed. His bony hands clutched tightly to the bars of his cage.

Asmodeus patted Martin on his arm, rousing him from his reverie. 'I'm sure you'll do much better,' Asmodeus said. 'I'd hate to be disappointed a second time. You won't disappoint me, will you?'

Martin gulped and glanced back towards the cage. 'I'll try not to.'

'Good.' Asmodeus waved across to a group of people in the corner. 'Let's have some company for Martin. The young man needs someone to spend the evening with.'

Two women hurried across to them, and giggling, they took hold of one of Martin's arms each. 'We'll look after him,' said the blonde-haired one.

The brunette holding onto Martin's left arm kissed him on the cheek. 'We will,' she said.

Asmodeus smiled. 'Good.' He fixed those eyes on Martin. 'Enjoy yourself tonight, Martin. Tomorrow you'll have to earn your supper.' Martin watched as Asmodeus disappeared into the crowd of dancers before turning his attention to the women.

'Hi,' the blonde said, running her hand up and down his arm as the brunette placed her arm around his waist.

'I'm Martin,' he said, glancing between the scantily clad pair.

'Well, Martin,' the blonde said, 'why don't we find a seat.'

The two women tugged on his arms and steered him to a table across the room, past writhing bodies. More drinks were placed in front of them, and Martin snatched a tumbler and downed the contents in one.

One of the women pulled a small package from her jacket and placed it down. Then, opening the plastic bag, she poured the contents onto the table before lowering her head and sniffing up some of the contents. He watched on in fascination as the other woman did the same. 'Your turn,' she said.

He held up a hand. 'I'm not sure I should—'

She leant in closer. 'Asmodeus won't be happy. He likes his boys to let their hair down.'

Martin glanced at Asmodeus and then over to the cage before focusing on the powder. 'What is it?' he said.

The brunette put her hand beneath the table and slid it along the length of his thigh, stopping at his groin. 'Just something to help you relax.'

He gasped as the other woman's hand traced a similar route on his opposite leg. 'Don't be shy,' she said. 'You'll love it.'

Martin sniffed up the remaining powder and pinched his nostrils with his index finger and thumb to stop himself from sneezing. The effect was instant. He looked about as the figures scattered around the room became indistinct, and people on the dance floor merged into one homogeneous mass. One of the women kissed his ear as the other dropped to the floor and wrestled with the belt on his trousers, pulling his clothing down. Rising euphoria swept Martin up, and as his head lolled backwards, resting gently against the padded back of the seat, he closed his eyes. The pleasure continued its upward ascent. As both women ducked beneath the table, he groaned loudly, then drowned in an ocean of ecstasy.

Martin woke and rubbed his eyes. He lay in a bed but with no recollection of getting there. Two women, one on either side of him, dozed. He sat and gently climbed from the bed, found his way to the bathroom, and stared at his reflection in the mirror. He didn't look too bad and didn't feel too bad, either. Closing his eyes, he tried to remember the previous night. The drugs, the drink, of which there was plenty, and the women. His face glowed as he remembered what the three of them got up to. Would they have known it was his first time? So what if they did, he thought and smiled to himself. What a fantastic way to lose your virginity. Martin closed his eyes again and, grinning, slowly shook his head. When he re-opened them, he jumped back at the vision confronting him. He gasped as his heart pounded, and slowly, ever so slowly, he edged back in front of the mirror. His familiar features stared back. Martin brought a hand up to his mouth and laughed. 'Stupid twat,' he whispered as he turned away, pushing the demonic image he viewed in the mirror to the outskirts of his mind.

Martin sauntered into the dimly lit club, where two cleaners collected empties from the previous evening and placed them on the bar.

'There you are,' a voice said.

Martin spun around and viewed the man. He held out a hand, and Martin shook it. 'We didn't have a chance to meet the other day properly,' he said, looking Martin up and down. 'Cain.'

'Martin. The new bassist.'

Cain laughed. 'Yeah, bassist. I don't play an instrument, but I'm sure you're excellent.' Cain's smile fell from his face. 'Asmodeus wants to see us immediately.'

'Of course. I was—'

'Have you met Thomas?' Cain said.

'Yes. Yesterday.'

'Did he give you the *I'm his favourite* talk?' Martin nodded as Cain sneered. 'He is for now. This way,' Cain said.

Martin followed him across the dance floor, up a flight of steps and through a door. Cain paused outside another doorway and knocked before entering.

Asmodeus sat behind a massive wooden desk. The front ornately carved with images. 'Martin,' Asmodeus said and stood. 'How are you?'

Martin stared open-mouthed at the carvings on the desk. The images depicting scenes of torture – men skewered on stakes, others crucified. Some with their limbs cut off and held high by their torturers, but what continued to hold his vision as he studied the carvings was that they appeared to be moving. As if they had a life of their own.

'I see you're admiring my desk,' Asmodeus said, walking around where Martin stood.

Martin mentally shook himself and looked at Asmodeus. '... Yes ... It's very ...'

'Graphic?' Asmodeus said.

'Yes.'

Asmodeus pointed to a particularly gruesome image. 'I remember that scene well.' He grinned at Martin. 'The noise a person makes when limbs are wrenched from the body is quite unique. Only bettered ...' He winked at Cain, who smiled. '... by the sound they make when their skin is flayed from them.'

Martin brought a hand up to his mouth and gagged.

Asmodeus took a firm grip on his arm. 'You will have to toughen up in the coming weeks, Martin. I won't tolerate weakness. Do you understand?'

Martin swallowed a lump, pushing down the bile that reached his throat. 'I understand.'

Asmodeus patted him on the arm. 'Come with me.'

Martin followed Asmodeus and Cain as they strode purposefully from the office and down the stairs, but instead of entering the club, they carried on down a second flight and into the basement. The two men stopped and looked towards the man from the cage the previous night, chained to a wall. His limp body hung down, only prevented from falling by his fetters.

'This is Jacob,' Asmodeus said. He stepped forward and lifted the chin of his captive. The man groaned. Asmodeus turned to face Martin. 'He was so ungrateful,' Asmodeus said and turned back towards Jacob. 'When I met him, he couldn't see. Blind from birth. I gave him back his sight.' He turned once more to face Martin. 'Little did I know, but he was soiled by religion. Corrupt. A Christian.' Asmodeus's mouth twisted as he enunciated the words. 'A follower of The Nazarian.'

Cain spat on the floor. 'Filth,' he said.

'Christianity,' Asmodeus bellowed, 'is a massive lie. Look at the deaths in human history committed in his name. You don't believe that nonsense, do you?'

Martin shook his head. 'N-n-o.'

'Good.' Asmodeus threw open his arms. 'Where is his god now?' he said. Asmodeus took hold of Jacob's hair and shook him. 'Did he give you your sight? Did he allow you to see the world you live in?'

Jacob groaned and uttered a prayer.

Asmodeus laughed. 'Even now, he calls to his god. His saviour.' Asmodeus lowered his face towards Jacob's. 'Oh, where is he? Will he come and save you?' he said mockingly. 'What should we do?' he said to Martin.

Martin shook his head. 'I don't know.'

Asmodeus grabbed hold of Martin and pulled him closer. 'If he doesn't appreciate the gift I gave him,' he said, 'maybe I should take it back.' Asmodeus held out his other hand, and Cain handed him a knife. He grasped the blade and offered the dagger to Martin.

'Can you feel its power?' Asmodeus whispered into his ear. 'The handle is bone. Fashioned from the femur of John the Baptist. Have you heard of him?'

He nodded. 'Yes.'

Asmodeus laughed. 'What are you waiting for?'

Martin turned to face Asmodeus. 'What is it you want me to do?'

'Take back my gift.'

Martin's eyes darted between Asmodeus and Jacob. 'I-I-I can't,' he said.

Asmodeus plucked the knife from his grasp and sighed. 'You disappoint me.' He held the blade up, and Cain took it from him. 'Show him how it's done.'

Cain smirked and stepped forward as Asmodeus and Martin moved aside. Martin watched as Cain grabbed their victim's hair and pulled it back. 'Where is your god, now?' he said.

Martin wanted to escape this horror, but Asmodeus's hand grasped the back of his neck and held him tight. 'Watch,' he said. 'Watch and learn.'

Martin viewed the unfolding scene. His knees weakened, and he would have collapsed had it not been for Asmodeus's iron-clad grip on his neck. Asmodeus continued to whisper to him, promising him whatever he wanted while the screams from Jacob echoed around the room as first, one eyeball was carved from its socket, and then the other. Martin stood drinking in the continuing horror, and then it was over. As blood dripped from the sightless sockets, Jacob's head fell towards his chest.

Cain smiled and handed the eyeballs to Asmodeus. 'I think these are yours,' Cain said.

Asmodeus held out his palm and held them under Martin's face. 'As easy as that,' he said. 'Now,' Asmodeus said and ripped open Jacob's shirt, exposing his bare chest and stomach. 'I don't think Jacob's heart was in the job, do you?' Martin shook his head. 'Perhaps we should have that too,' he said as he tossed their victim's eyes aside. The sightless orbs bounced along the floor, leaving a bloody trail behind them before coming to a halt against the far wall.

Cain held out the knife, and Martin took it. 'When you're ready,' Asmodeus said.

Martin looked at the knife and then at Jacob, gulped in a large lungful of air and plunged in the blade. Jacob groaned, as Martin suppressing rising nausea, sliced Jacob open from his chest to his navel, reached inside his ribcage and cut out the heart. He turned to face the other two and held out the organ in his blood-covered hands.

Asmodeus grinned. 'Well done,' he said and snatched up the heart. He fixed Martin with a stare, and without looking away, he bit into the heart. Cain took it from him and did likewise before offering it to Martin.

Martin, trance-like, took it from him and lifted the remnants up to his mouth. Then, as the smell of blood reached his nostrils, he gagged.

'You must partake,' Asmodeus said. 'It will give you power.'

Martin closed his eyes and bit down mechanically on the lump of warm meat. His teeth struggled to bite through, but with a combination of biting and tearing, he pulled a piece free and swallowed it in one.

Asmodeus laughed. 'Well done. One more thing,' he said as he undid the cuff button on Martin's shirt and rolled up his sleeve. Asmodeus held out his right hand, a huge ring adorning the middle finger, and then began to mouth some indecipherable incantations. Martin watched as the ring glowed red and grimaced in pain as the red-hot piece of jewellery was pushed down onto his arm. The smell of scorched skin drifted up as Asmodeus removed his hand. On Martin's lower arm, an image of a Demon surrounded by mythical beings was now seared into his skin.

Asmodeus smiled at him and placed a hand on the side of his face. 'Everything you ever wanted is yours. Your greatest desires. Your long-sought-for dreams.'

Martin, tears pooling in the sides of his eyes, smiled back. Again, a feeling within the pit of his stomach rose, but not nausea this time, something different – a power, a potency he had never experienced before. It coursed through every atom of his body, and he gasped as it reached a crescendo then stopped. He smiled and looked at Asmodeus.

'See?' Asmodeus said. 'See how powerful he is?'

SICARIUS

Sicarius dropped to the floor and lay down his weapon as two others joined him and sat on either side.

'We've lost their trail,' one of them said.

Sicarius nodded slowly. 'We will rest here and set off in a few hours.'

'They may be heading towards the village,' the other said.

'They won't,' Sicarius said. 'They would not be welcome. They will be close by.' He lay his head down. 'We have come far and must rest.'

Sicarius opened his eyes. Something roused him from his slumber, but he was unsure what. He clambered to his feet and rubbed the tiredness from his eyes. There was a light in the distance. He narrowed his gaze and scrutinized it, then, glancing briefly at his sleeping comrades, he headed towards its source. As the light danced further into the trees, he strode onwards after it. Sicarius was mesmerised, but the light always kept a short distance from him. Finally, it stopped and grew to such a size it almost filled his vision. He frowned deeply as a sound, a voice, seemed to emanate from inside the light. A voice he recognised, a voice not heard for such a long time, beckoned him on. Then the light reduced to something the size of his hand and shot away from him. Sicarius gave chase, barrelling his way down the slope in pursuit of the light. Onto a street he ran, sprinting as fast as his legs would carry him. Not wanting to lose sight of it, he tripped and stumbled, almost regaining his balance until the weight of his body passed its centre of gravity, and he came to a crashing halt on the ground.

He looked up as voices drifted into his earshot. 'A wolf,' one of them shouted.

Sicarius sprung to his feet as a bullet whistled past him. He ran again as adrenalin coursed through his veins. Up an incline, he climbed as the voices were joined by more. He glanced over his shoulder at the baying mob, armed with weapons, less than a hundred metres away. A sharp pain shot through his arm, but he ignored it as gunshots filled the air. Knowing slowing or stopping would mean certain death, he ran towards a church, careering through the gate and across the graveyard. Skeletal creatures scuttled away into the darkness as he reached the huge door of the dilapidated building. He turned and briefly looked behind him while desperately searching for somewhere to hide, but as he looked back again, the men stopped outside the gate and appeared lost. They gazed around in all directions. How could they not see him? But they couldn't. He watched, entranced, as the men wandered off in different directions. Gulping in the air, he slid to the ground, allowing his breathing to reach normality. Sicarius rubbed his face and considered his options – how would he get back to his friends without walking through the town? Maybe he could wait until everyone was asleep? But unfamiliar with this place, he couldn't be sure they would not have guards. And why did they call him a wolf? He'd seen such creatures a long time ago.

He stood quickly as sound from inside the church caught his attention, and pushing his face against the wooden frame, he peered through a crack in the door. There it was – the light – hovering at the far end of the building as if waiting for him. He located the handle and pushed the door, which creaked and groaned with reluctance. Then, checking over his shoulder one last time and, sure there was no one else there, he entered and closed the door behind him. Sicarius paused before slowly making his way along the aisle towards the light. He stopped a few feet away and waited – for what, he knew not. The light grew in size once more, but this time, it glided towards him, shrouding Sicarius in its brilliance. He blinked, attempting to adjust to the blinding light that penetrated every molecule of his being. And then its brightness faded to a more tolerable level.

'Judas,' a voice said.

Sicarius narrowed his eyes. Such a long time had passed since he'd been called by that name. 'I ...'

'Judas, my friend.'

Sicarius put a hand to his mouth and dropped to his knees as realisation washed over him. 'My Lord,' he said.

A form stepped from the brightness – a face so familiar to him. Sicarius clasped his hands together and brought them up to his chin. 'I thought I was forsaken.' Tears rolled down his cheeks as he remembered what he'd done. 'Please forgive me.'

The man smiled. 'There is nothing to forgive,' he said. 'You did what you were always meant to.'

'But I gave you up. Had I known what they would do.'

The man briefly placed his hand on Sicarius's head. 'It was your destiny. I am the one who should be sorry. I could not save you from this place until now. You have more to do.'

'What more can you ask?' Sicarius said.

'There will come a time when you will be needed to save someone.'

'Who?'

'You will know when the time is right. Until then, you must seek out those like you. You will see the light within their eyes. Remember this, my friend – forgiveness is everything, and no one is beyond redemption.'

'But those at the citadel?' Sicarius said.

'They are not your true friends. They welcomed you into their fold for what you did. You must use their ignorance to our advantage.' He frowned. 'The months and years ahead will not be easy. You will gain your compassion and feel the pain of those in torture. This is the cross that you have to bear, but you must return to the citadel.'

'How will I get back there? The townspeople will—'

'You must trust me. They will not harm you.'

Sicarius watched as the light drifted away from him, shrinking in size until he could hardly see it. And then it was gone. A feeling swept over him that he hadn't known for such a long time, and it went by the name of loneliness. A deep, profound, bottomless loneliness.

He raced through the trees and towards the two comrades he had left sleeping. They turned to face him.

'Where have you been?' one of them said.

'You were sleeping. I thought I caught sight of our quarry.'

'And did you?' the other said.

Sicarius shook his head. 'No. I fear we have lost them for good. We will return to the citadel.'

The two men looked at each other. 'He will not be pleased if we come back empty-handed,' one said.

'I will explain,' Sicarius said. 'I alone will shoulder the blame.'

Asmodeus sat on the enormous, ornate chair as Sicarius made his way over to him and dropped to one knee. 'They escaped us, my prince. I am sorry I failed you.'

Asmodeus grasped the arms of the chair with his hands, his knuckles white. 'You are my best hunter, Sicarius. I was sure they would not evade you.'

'I'm sorry. They are clearly cunning.'

'Your comrades? Did they let you down?'

'No, sir. They performed well.'

'And yet you lost the Janus.'

He lowered his head. 'It's my fault alone. I accept responsibility. I am at your mercy.'

Asmodeus waved his hand in an upward gesture, and Sicarius stood. 'You are forgiven this indiscretion.' He stood and briefly turned away from Sicarius before facing him once more. 'However, I trust you will not fail again?'

'No, my prince,' Sicarius said.

Asmodeus nodded slowly. 'Very well, I will let this pass.'

The door to the room opened and someone entered. 'My prince. The sentinels have arrived back with the collaborator.'

Asmodeus grinned. 'Bring him here. I want to see him tortured. He killed two of my men. Balaam has promised me something unique.'

A large sentinel burst into the room, followed by two others who held on tightly to a battered and bloodied individual. The sentinel knelt in front of Asmodeus and offered his hand. 'This is the one, sir,' he said.

Asmodeus tapped Balaam's hand, moved to the stricken, semi-conscious individual, and kicked him. 'Harbouring and helping Janus is the most reprehensible of crimes. You will rue the day you helped those vermin.'

He lifted his head and stared at Asmodeus. 'Your reign is not absolute. It will end.' He briefly glanced at Sicarius before returning his gaze to Asmodeus. 'You are weak.'

Asmodeus laughed. 'Did you get his family too?' he said to Balaam. 'Yes, sir.'

'Good.' He looked at the bloodied victim on the ground and sneered. 'Give him something to make him fully conscious. I want him to witness everything we do to his brethren.' He looked at Balaam again. 'I want his torture to go on forever.'

Sicarius watched as they dragged him out and an odd sensation swept through him as he looked into the victim's eyes. Something he hadn't felt for a very long time – pity.

Months and years passed as Sicarius became increasingly aware of his past. Inside him, the horror of what he'd witnessed over decades, over centuries, tortured him. The memories he now harboured tormented and gripped like an ever-tightening noose around his neck until he could bear it no longer.

One morning, while the citadel was quiet, he made his way out of this hell and into Dark Nearhope. After witnessing the pain in their eyes, he managed to form alliances with a small band of demons like himself. Laying low for several weeks, he finally journeyed to Nearhope. Once there, he changed his name to James – a name he knew well from his past – and waited for instructions. These appeared from nowhere – a seed was planted in his mind, which grew into an idea until it formed into what he should do and who he should save from their pain and torment. This is how his life remained for years, drifting between the realm of darkness and Nearhope.

Then one morning, a thought appeared of what he should do. He packed a few things into his rucksack and headed away from Nearhope and along the road past the church. He turned and looked back down the hill at the village he'd helped populate with those he'd saved, bursting into springtime glory – a realm he'd known for so long. Finding himself across the road from a filling station, in a place so unfamiliar to him, a name and face drifted into his consciousness – Felix. This man's presence in Nearhope was somehow significant, and a woman, Jenny, Felix's wife before … he strained his senses … before, she was lost. It was vital, and he knew this. 'Yes.' He looked skywards. 'I understand what I must do.' His mental cloud lifted. He and Felix had to release Jenny from torture and take her to Nearhope – her presence there was critical.

A man exited the petrol station and approached his car.

'You're not going Leyburn way, are you?' James said.

The man turned to face him and frowned. 'Leyburn? Yes.'

FELIX AND REECE

MARY – After getting up and making myself a cup of tea, I went back to bed. This time I slept like the dead. If Kate entered the bedroom before she went to work, I couldn't say, but the house was empty by the time I dragged myself downstairs again. I yawned and read the note she had left. *Make yourself at home,* it said. *I'll see you tonight x.*

I made a light breakfast and downed two large cups of strong, black coffee. After placing the pots in the dishwasher, I got comfortable in the lounge, took out the huge slab of paperwork Felix had given us and the recordings I'd made, then set to work. He had told us how he and James found themselves in the citadel, so I located the appropriate page – titled, *The Escape from the citadel.* Then, with a mixture of excitement and trepidation, I read on …

Sitting back in my chair, I put down the last sheet of paper. The words, his words, were so vivid. Felix either had an unbelievable imagination or … I laughed at how preposterous it sounded … Nearhope and the citadel were real. They couldn't be, could they? Picking up my empty coffee cup, I went to make another drink. While the kettle boiled, someone entered through the front door, and I glanced at the clock. I'd been preoccupied all day and so absorbed that I hadn't noticed the time.

Kate bounded in and tossed her bag onto the kitchen table. 'Hi,' she said.

'I'm just making a coffee if you want one?'

She smiled. 'I'd rather have wine.'

Selecting a bottle from the rack, I held it aloft. 'Will this do?'

Kate kicked off her shoes. 'It will.'

I poured two glasses and handed her one. "I read through Felix's stuff. His writing is incredibly vivid.'

'Did he mention James?' she said.

'Yeah. James took him to Nearhope. From there, they travelled to a place called the—'

'Citadel,' she said and took a swig from her glass.

'Yes, the citadel. They escaped with Felix's wife, Jenny. According to Felix, she now resides in Nearhope.'

'Reece Sadler ...' she said enigmatically.

I sat opposite her. 'You interviewed him?'

'Reece believes that James was captured.'

'By whom?'

'Asmodeus.' Kate didn't appear to have the same problem saying his name as I did.

'I see.'

She let out an unconvincing laugh. 'Asmodeus.' She snatched up her handbag, fished inside, pulled out her Dictaphone and slid it across the table. 'It's all on here. Reece...' She paused, searching for the appropriate words. 'He seemed so lucid,' she continued, 'unlike the delusional patients I've met previously. He spoke so matter-of-factly. Like ...'

'Like he was telling the truth?' I said.

She narrowed her eyes at me, then frowned. 'Yes. But it can't be true, can it?'

I took a sip of wine. 'When we spoke to Felix, he sounded as if he was repeating a story. But when you read his account ... It appears as if he's recounting an event.'

'Yes, Reece seemed like that too.'

'This ...' I inhaled. 'Asmodeus?' I had no trouble saying his name this time. 'Who is he?'

'A Demon prince. Don't you remember Felix told us that?'

I didn't and laughed. 'A what?' Kate didn't laugh. She didn't even smile.

'That's what he said.' She rubbed the back of her neck to remove some stress or stiffness. 'I don't know, Mary,' she continued. 'I don't know what to think.'

'If this Asmodeus has James,' I found myself saying as if all this talk of Demons was normal, 'what does he think will happen to James?'

'Reece is convinced that Asmodeus will try to get out.'

I frowned. 'Get out? To where?'

'Here.' Kate bit her bottom lip. 'Reece is convinced Asmodeus can reach our world.'

'But how?'

'According to Reece ...' She looked upwards. 'I can't believe I'm saying this,' she said. 'Now that he has James's ...' She blew out hard. 'Now that he possesses his soul, he is no longer tethered to his own realm. With James's soul, he can pass from Nearhope into our world. Nearhope is a buffer between our world and …' Kate blew out again. 'Well, you get the picture.'

'Hell?' I offered. She nodded slowly. I took a sip. 'Where on earth do you begin with this, and how is this linked to the Nazarian?'

She shrugged. 'I don't know.' She drained her glass and pushed it across the table for a refill. 'I looked him up,' she said.

'Who? The Nazarian?'

'No. Asmodeus. He rules over one of the kingdoms of hell. There are several princes,' she went on, 'each covering a deadly sin. Asmodeus's deadly sin is lust.'

'Great,' I said. 'So, we're looking for a horny Demon?'

Kate smiled. 'I suppose.' She picked up the glass I'd replenished and took another large mouthful. 'I asked Reece if he knew the Nazarian.'

'And?'

'He doesn't.' She rubbed her eyes and yawned. 'What do we do?'

I shrugged. 'God knows.'

'Well …' she said. Fixing me with a stare. 'Let's hope he gets in touch soon.' She clicked her fingers. 'Have you checked YouTube?'

I hadn't. I'd been too engrossed in Felix's writing. 'No.'

She stood and retrieved her laptop, and within seconds she fired up the machine and located a new video. We watched as the usual music played out and the obligatory messages were read. Once this finished, the Nazarian looked straight down the camera at me, or that's how it appeared.

'Mary,' he began, 'the time is near when we must gather our forces. Judas is lost to us. He will not be able to withstand Asmodeus's onslaught forever. Without him, we cannot send Asmodeus back to his own realm. The Apostles must be guarded until their time comes. They are not yet aware of what is required. So, you must gather them.'

'How?'

'They will come to you when the time is right.'

'Judas? He is in the citadel?'

The Nazarian smiled reassuringly. 'Reece and Felix will be Kate's guide through Nearhope. There are others there who will assist you. If the Apostles fall, humanity will follow.'

The video ended, and I became aware of Kate eyeing me. 'Did you see any of that?' I asked.

She shook her head. 'The video ended, and you just zoned out. Then you were talking as if you were having a conversation with someone. I only got your side of it. You mentioned Judas.'

'Yes,' I said. 'I spoke to the Nazarian directly. He said Judas is lost to us.'

'Judas? … as in Judas Iscariot?'

'I think so.'

'Judas, who betrayed Jesus?'

'Again, I think so.'

'For thirty pieces of silver.'

I rolled my eyes. 'I know the story, Kate. I remember religious studies.' I rubbed my forehead as a small ache shot through my temple.

'Right,' Kate said. 'What else did he say?'

'He told me that I need to find the other Apostles.'

'Twelve,' Kate said. 'There were twelve Apostles.'

'Of which Judas was one. The Nazarian said that if the Apostles fall, so will humanity. We have to send Asmodeus back to his own realm.'

'Is James an Apostle?'

'I think …' I hesitated. 'I think James is Judas.'

Kate's mouth dropped open. 'James is Judas? Are you sure?'

I shrugged. 'I don't know for sure. It's just a feeling I have.'

She snatched up the empty wine bottle and stood. 'I need another drink.'

'He said something else,' I said.

She stopped at the doorway. 'What?'

'You have to go to Nearhope.'

'You're kidding. Christ, Mary.' She put a hand up to her mouth and, looking up, mouthed sorry. 'You've heard what Reece and Felix said about that place.'

'I know, but that's what he said. He said Felix and Reece would be your guides. He also told me there were others in Nearhope that would assist you.'

'How the hell are you … we … going to find these Apostles?'

I couldn't answer. The events of the previous days were ridiculous. I attempted to lighten the mood. 'Shall we google them?' I comically smiled at her. 'The phone book?'

Kate groaned and disappeared into the kitchen, returning moments later with two glasses of what looked like orange juice. I took one from her. 'We're on the soft drinks now, are we?'

'There's a good measure of vodka in there,' she said and sat opposite me. 'If Armageddon is on its way, I don't want to be anywhere near sober.'

I took a swig and grimaced. 'Bloody hell. You're not kidding.' I put down my glass. 'What did Reece tell you?'

'I told you,' she said. 'It's on the Dictaphone.'

'Just give me the potted highlights.'

Kate took a gulp of her drink, placed down the glass and began. 'He was taken to Nearhope by James to save his wife.'

Sensing my next question, Kate held up her hand and continued. 'Reece's wife was a geneticist. Quite a famous one, as it happens.

114

Reece is a botanist. Apparently, they were blissfully married until she was murdered.'

'Oh hell.'

'Someone she worked with became fixated with her, and after she made it clear she wanted nothing to do with him, he snapped and murdered her. He's inside for twenty-five years.'

'That's terrible. When and where did this happen?'

Kate thought for a moment. 'About five years ago. Somewhere in Kent. I can't remember the exact location.'

'Any kids?'

'No. As I said, it's on the Dictaphone.'

'There are similarities to Felix,' I said. 'His son was murdered, and his wife took her own life.'

Kate's phone sounded, and I took a large gulp of my drink. To be honest, I didn't think there was enough alcohol in the world to blot this nightmare out. I studied her, a deep frown etched on her face and followed the one-sided conversation.

'How long …?' she asked. 'I can't drive over ... I've had a bit to drink … I suppose you've phoned around family and …? I'll be there first thing in the morning.'

She hung up and looked at me. 'Reece has gone.'

'From the hospital?'

She nodded. 'It wasn't high security. So legally, we couldn't keep him there.'

'I wonder where he's gone?'

Kate rubbed her chin. 'He received a phone call before he left from someone called Felix.'

'Our Felix?'

'How many Felix's do you know?'

'Right. I wonder what was said?' Have you got his number?'

Kate searched through her contacts. 'What do I say?'

I took the phone from her just as he answered. 'Kate,' he said.

'It's Mary. You phoned Reece?'

'I did.'

I glanced at Kate, who lowered her head so she could follow the conversation. 'Can I ask what you talked about?'

'We have to go back,' he said. 'Reece and I.'

'To Nearhope?'

'Yes, to Nearhope. Reece is on his way there now. I'm not far away myself.'

'Felix,' I said in slow, measured tones, 'what are you planning to do?'

He said nothing for a few seconds. 'I think you already know.'

I looked at Kate again. 'He's hung up.'

Kate pushed the mobile into her back pocket. 'We can't drive. We've been drinking.'

'Get your keys,' I said. 'I'll drive. Losing my licence is the least of our worries.'

'Bloody hell, Mary,' Kate said as I careered along the road. 'You're going to get us killed driving like a lunatic.'

I glanced across at her. 'We must get there.'

'But what are you going to do when we do?'

I huffed. 'As I said, I don't know. But we need to speak to Felix and Reece.'

We exited the Bedale bypass road and headed onto the Leyburn road.

'How will we know where they are?' Kate said. 'We never got an exact location from them.'

I slowed as we entered a village. 'I don't know. I'm hoping we spot them. Leyburn isn't that far.'

We carried on in silence until, up ahead, we could see two parked cars. Coming to a halt behind them, we looked at each other and let out a deep breath before climbing from the car and creeping towards the first parked vehicle. It stood empty. We glanced at each other again and made our way to the second. I looked inside the driver's side. 'Is this Reece?' I said to Kate.

She lowered her face. 'Yes. He looks unconscious.'

I pulled open the door and placed my hand on Reece's neck as Kate walked around to the passenger side.

'No pulse,' I said to Kate as she opened the door. 'I think he's dead.'

Kate put two fingers on Felix's neck. 'He's got a very shallow pulse. He's barely alive. What the hell's happened?'

I nodded towards the dashboard. A syringe and two empty vials lay there. 'It looks as if they've taken something.'

Kate reached for the bottle. 'No!' I said. 'It's evidence.'

'For what?' Kate said. 'We have to phone an ambulance. They'll need to know what they've taken.'

'You're right. Phone 999.'

Kate pulled out her mobile and groaned. 'My phone's dead.'

'Dead?'

'Yes. I don't understand,' she said. 'It was almost fully charged when we left.' She shook the handset and then pushed it back into her pocket. 'Try your phone.'

I pulled the device from my jacket and stared at it. 'Mine's dead too.'

We exchanged glances. 'That can't be a coincidence,' Kate said. 'Help me get Felix out. We'll have to perform CPR on him and hope there's a passing motorist.'

I closed the driver's door and hurried around to Kate's side. We pulled the unconscious Felix from his seat and onto the ground. Kate felt for his pulse again. 'He's still alive,' she said.

I looked over my shoulder as a vehicle approached. 'Someone's coming,' I said and raced around the car and onto the road as Kate commenced CPR.

'It's a car,' I shouted and waved my hands for the vehicle to stop.

Kate blew a breath into Felix, then manoeuvred herself around to his side. 'Quickly, Mary,' she yelled.

I held up my hands as the car sped towards me. Then everything went black.

I stood and looked about, momentarily disorientated. About five feet from me lay Kate, and a man stood nearby frantically relaying details into his mobile. I edged closer and looked down at myself on the floor – a patch of mud streaked across my face, a clump of grass between my neck and chin. I turned sharply after hearing a sound behind me. Felix stood about fifty metres away, looking directly at me. He turned and began walking. I glanced back at Kate before setting off after him. He paused at a lane I hadn't noticed before with a signpost spelling out NEARHOPE.

I reached Felix. 'What happened?'

'Kate should be here with me, not you.'

'I don't understand. Am I dead?'

Felix placed his hand on my arm. 'Kate was to accompany Reece and me. He must have his reasons for sending you.'

'But—'

He smiled. 'I know how confusing this can seem. I've experienced it myself, but we must hurry. Reece has already passed through into ...' He smiled again and held out his hand. 'Please, Mary. You must come now.'

I took hold of his hand as if it was the most natural thing to do. My vision darkened as if I'd closed my eyes, then brightened again. At the top of a hill, we looked down a road that meandered towards a village.

He turned to face me. 'Welcome to Nearhope,' he said.

I looked into his eyes and then towards the village. 'It truly exists,' I said.

'It does.'

'But what about Kate?'

'The poison Reece took was supposed to poison Kate when she gave CPR.' I frowned. 'It allows a person to cross through the threshold.' Felix squeezed my hand. 'Kate has been chosen to assist with freeing James.'

'What about me?'

'The Nazarian willed it. You and he have a connection that stretches back centuries. Your name is not just a coincidence.'

I furrowed my brow and slowly shook my head. 'Mary from the bible?'

'Indeed. We must hurry.' Felix set off down the slope at a pace that surprised me for one so old.

'Where?' I said. Struggling to keep up with him. 'Where are we going?'

'We're meeting Reece and some of James's allies, and hopefully, we can free him.'

I grabbed hold of Felix's arm and pulled him to a halt. 'The citadel?'

'Yes.'

'But—'

'He will not hold out forever. He has the identities of the Apostles, and ...' Felix rubbed his chin. 'He has much more. If they find out what he knows, there will be no stopping them. Earth as we know it will become his.'

'Who? Asmodeus?'

Felix shook his head. 'There is someone far more dangerous than Asmodeus. He coverts our world and has done since the beginning of time. He wishes to destroy it and everyone in it.'

'But—?'

Felix held up a finger to his lips. 'We must go.'

Thomas entered the room and dropped to one knee in front of Asmodeus. 'It's done, my prince. They were where you said they would be.'

'Are you sure she's dead?'

'Yes, my prince.'

'I chose you, Thomas, because you are my most trusted. I do not feel anything. If she was truly dead, I would feel something.'

Thomas stepped forward. 'She could not have survived the impact. I am sure.'

Asmodeus rose from his throne and nodded. 'Very well, we will see. It is important she's dead. Without her, he cannot send forth the child.' He indicated for the man to stand. 'You have done well, Thomas. You will be handsomely rewarded.'

MARTIN AND CAIN

Martin stopped outside Asmodeus's office, knocked and waited until Cain opened the door and beckoned him inside. Asmodeus sat at the far end of the room behind his desk, talking on the telephone.

He waved Martin closer as he ended his call. 'Ah, Martin, the very man. I have a job for you.'

'Oh,' Martin said. 'I thought I would be practising with my bandmates.'

Asmodeus smiled and stood. 'Your naivety is endearing, but I'd have thought by now that you'd be aware that there are far more important things than music.'

'Y-yes, of course. I just—'

Asmodeus sauntered around to Martin's side of the desk and placed a hand on his shoulder. His eyes bore down on Martin, who lowered his head a little. 'Martin,' Asmodeus said, 'I have handpicked a group of people I require to carry out my wishes.'

'I'll do anything,' Martin said. 'You know that.' His eyes darted in Cain's direction, who curled his lip into a sneer.

Asmodeus grabbed Martin's arm and pulled up his shirt sleeve, exposing the ring mark. 'This,' Asmodeus said, lifting Martin's arm higher. 'Is a special mark. It singles you out as one of my men.' He moved his face closer. 'One of my most trusted.'

Martin nodded rapidly. 'I understand,' he said. 'I'll do anything you wish.'

Asmodeus glanced at Cain and smiled. 'Anything, Martin?'

'Yes. Anything.'

Asmodeus nodded and relinquished his grip. 'I have something for you,' he said. Moving back around the desk, he opened a drawer and pulled out a wooden box. 'This is for you.'

Martin accepted the box and stared at it before placing it on the desk and flicking up the clasp holding the lid shut. Slowly, he opened the box and looked down at the gleaming dagger inside – his face reflected in the knife's highly-polished surface, its blade seamlessly fitting into the ornately carved shaft. He wrapped his fingers around a perfectly formed handle, feeling the weapon's weight. A strange sensation crept through him, beginning in his fingers, it slowly travelled along his arm and shoulders. Finally, seeping down his back and throughout the rest of his body until the knife became weightless and part of him. Martin gasped as a potency erupted from the pit of his stomach. He felt powerful, as if there was little he couldn't do with this knife in his hand. An image appeared inside his mind's eye and looked down at him. Martin gasped again and dropped to his knees with the dagger held out at head height in front of him. 'My Lord,' he said.

'Do you feel his power?' Asmodeus asked.

Martin nodded. 'Yes.'

'*He who reigns supreme* has chosen you.' Asmodeus tilted his head to one side and smiled. 'You must make him an offering.'

'I must,' Martin said. He stood, took the knife in his right hand, and placed his left on the desk. Then, curling his hand into a fist and leaving the little finger exposed, he brought the blade down to rest on the second knuckle. Applying barely any pressure, he glanced at Asmodeus as the knife sliced through the digit, easily cutting through flesh and bone. Martin looked at Asmodeus and smiled as blood dripped from the self-inflicted wound. He groaned and tossed his head back as his eyes rolled in ecstasy. Then, closing them, he gently rolled his head around in a circular motion before they blinked open again.

'He is pleased,' Asmodeus said, 'but this is only the first step towards your destination. He will want much more from you.' Martin nodded his understanding. 'Go and get cleaned up,' Asmodeus said. 'Meet us downstairs in ten minutes.' Martin nodded again, then marched out.

Cain wandered over to the desk and looked down at the severed finger and small pool of blood next to it. He dipped his finger in the still-warm liquid and tasted it. 'There are still doubts within him,' he said.

Asmodeus picked up the finger and viewed it. 'Corruption, absolute corruption, takes time. He will do as I wish.' He dropped the digit inside his mouth and swallowed it before wiping the small smear of blood from his lips. 'Martin will do fine.'

Martin was conveyed from the club and into the countryside, eventually passing through the gates of a vast country estate and stopping outside the entrance. Cain stood on the threshold of the door as Martin climbed out. He sneered. 'Nice of you to join us,' he said to Martin.

Martin ignored his jibe and strode up to the doorway. 'I've been to get some clothes. Asmodeus said he wanted me to be smart.' He looked

Cain up and down. 'I take my orders from him, not you.'

Cain grabbed his arm as he passed and pushed him up against the wall. 'Listen,' he said. 'You're just a cripple who Asmodeus took a liking to. It won't last. I may not be his favoured one yet, but I will be. Don't you forget that.'

Martin wrestled free from his grip and pushed Cain away. 'We'll see,' he said.

'Boys,' Asmodeus said.

The two men turned to face their employer, who moved further along the corridor. 'Let's not have any falling out. We have more important things to think about.'

Cain glared at Martin and then joined Asmodeus. 'I'm sorry, my prince.'

Asmodeus patted his arm. 'I have news from Braxas. Sicarius is weakening. Braxas thinks it won't be long before we know who they are and where they're heading.'

Martin joined the other two. 'Who is Braxas?'

Asmodeus smiled. 'My deputy. My dextral.'

'And Sicarius?' Martin said.

'A traitor,' Cain said and spat on the floor. 'An ingrate.'

'You may know him as Judas,' Asmodeus said.

'From the bible?'

Asmodeus laughed. 'That worthless piece of shit,' he said. 'It's not an accurate account of what happened. Judas was instructed to betray the Nazarian.'

Martin frowned. 'By whom?'

Asmodeus turned and strolled along the corridor and into a large room, closely followed by the other two. 'What do you think?' Asmodeus said as he performed a slow pirouette.

Martin drank in the opulence. 'Very impressive.'

'The owner didn't want to part with it,' he said, 'but Cain and I persuaded him it was in his best interests.'

'Won't people suspect?' Martin said. 'His family and friends?'

Asmodeus glanced at Cain. 'Cain chose well. Mr Chiltern was quite the recluse. He only employs a handful of people, and they were easily manipulated. As for Mr Chiltern himself.' Asmodeus smiled. 'I thought we might have him for dinner.'

Martin stepped closer. 'Can I despatch him?'

'You promised me,' Cain said.

Asmodeus waved a dismissive hand. 'We'll see.' He strolled over to the fireplace and looked into the dancing flames. 'We have to increase our numbers.' He turned to face them and pulled two small bottles from his jacket pocket. 'This will make them more amenable. A drop or two will suffice.'

'Where will we find them?' Cain said.

Asmodeus laughed. 'Look for the degenerates, the dissolute and debauched. The journey to pure corruption will be much shorter then.'

The two men joined Asmodeus, and each took a bottle.

'They are out there,' he said. 'I expect you to find them. The hierarchy in your world is intriguing.' Asmodeus wandered across to a large bookcase in the corner, replete with books. He plucked a volume from a shelf. 'I have been reading about your history. It's absorbing. We must infiltrate those people at the top. Those that run this realm.'

'The government?' Martin said.

'Yes. We must implant some of our own people. When we have swelled our numbers sufficiently, we will insert them where they can most help us.'

Martin smiled. 'I understand.'

Martin and Cain quickly put on the police uniforms and climbed into the vehicle. Cain started the engine and screeched away from the two semi-naked bodies of the dead officers. Within minutes they'd reached their destination at the back of the Old Bailey. A security guard stepped from his hut and across to them.

'Morning, gents,' he said. 'Have you got your IDs, please?'

Cain and Martin held up their badges. 'Do you know how long it's going to be?' Cain said.

'They've just phoned down,' the guard said. 'The case has been adjourned. Waste of time bringing him from the nick if you ask me.'

'Yes,' Cain said. 'I suppose it was.'

The guard pointed to a bay. 'If you want to park over there. They shouldn't be too long.'

Cain nodded and manoeuvred the police car into the spot. He turned off the engine. 'So far, so good,' he said.

'I'll go and see where the security van is, shall I?' Martin said.

Cain gripped his arm. 'Don't get spotted.' He looked over at the security hut. 'I'll deal with the guard.'

Martin climbed from the car and crossed the car park, holding his gun by his side.

Sicarius hung like a marionette from the ceiling of the dungeon. His body weight supported by large hooks, which pierced the skin and muscle on either side of his chest, and large wires connected to anchor points where the walls and ceiling met. His skin was covered in blood that ran the length of his body, which, even now, dripped from his feet to form a pool of viscous liquid below. Death would be welcome, but this was beyond him. His soul, no longer his to possess, was held by another, without which he could not move beyond this torment. The torture and pain from his wounds were bearable, but the emptiness and desolation he felt inside outstripped mere pain and suffering. The prized possessions he held within him were greatly coveted by his torturers. He'd seen visions of Christ, which still gave him succour, but he knew he could not hold out forever. The faces of those he guarded needed to remain a secret for as long as possible. But their constant searching of his mind and the bottomless isolation he continued to endure would be his undoing.

The door in the ceiling of the oubliette dropped down, and slowly, painfully slowly, he was hoisted towards the opening. Large hands grasped him, roughly removing the hooks that held him in mid-air. More hands took hold of his feet, pulled him across the rough stone flooring, and lifted and deposited him onto a chair. A bucket of ice-cold water doused him back from his failing consciousness, and he slowly opened his eyes.

'Sicarius,' Braxas said. 'How Asmodeus so wanted to be here. He sends his best wishes. He is enjoying inhabiting your body by all accounts. However, I'm the one he has chosen to search your mind.'

Sicarius's eyes followed Braxas as far as possible as he continued circumambulating him. 'It would be much easier if you gave up your secrets and let me pass through the mental doors you have erected.'

'You know I can't do that,' he said quietly.

Braxas took hold of Sicarius's hair and gripped it tightly. 'Have it your way.' He released his grip and stood in front of his prisoner. Then, closing his eyes, he began to utter an incantation. Sicarius stiffened in his chair, preparing himself for the battle ahead.

Braxas stopped as his eyes, now glowing red, bore down on his captive. Braxas coughed, then gagged as if being sick. He gagged again and spat something onto the palm of his hand. Sicarius stared down at the worm-like creature, about one centimetre in length, as it was thrust beneath his nose. It moved slowly as Braxas pushed his palm closer. Sicarius did not fight. There was no point, he thought. He would have to battle with Braxas, and struggling would only delay the inevitable. The writhing creature, now directly below his nose, slithered its way inside his right nostril and disappeared from sight, leaving only a tiny trickle of blood that dripped from Sicarius's nose over his lip and dropped to the floor.

Cain threw open the door to the security van as the two surprised guards looked at him. Their huge prisoner, handcuffed between them, lifted his head.

Martin lowered his gun. 'Unfasten him.' The two guards complied.

'Would you like to come with us, Mick,' Cain said.

The prisoner looked at Cain. 'Who the hell are you?' he said.

'Your salvation,' Martin said.

Mick shrugged off the handcuffs and climbed free of the van.

Cain strolled across to the police car, closely followed by Mick. 'Did Billy send you?' he said. 'I haven't told them anything.'

'Forget about your former employer. Your new employer has need of your talents.' Cain opened the doors to the police car, and both men climbed inside. he picked up a hipflask and handed it to Mick. 'A drink to seal the deal.'

Mick unscrewed the top and sniffed at its contents. 'What is it?'

'Whisky.'

He grinned and greedily drank from the vessel. Cain started the engine and drove to the back of the security van with Martin still standing outside.

'Ready?' Cain said.

Martin smiled. 'One minute,' he said, laying down his weapon, taking out his dagger, and climbing into the back. Screams were heard from inside, and Mick looked at Cain. 'What the fuck's going on?'

'Martin is getting us some dinner. I'm sure you're hungry.'

Mick glanced at the van and then back at Cain. A feeling grew inside him, mushrooming and spreading throughout his body. 'Yes,' he said, grinning. 'Ravenous.'

Cain and Martin led Mick into the great hall where Asmodeus stood. 'Mick here …' Cain pointed to the huge man. 'Is the latest addition to your army, my prince.'

Ignoring Mick, Asmodeus looked at the other two. 'I'm growing tedious of my human form. It's about time you two saw the true me. This is a perfect opportunity with our new arrival.'

Cain and Martin watched in awe as Asmodeus stood tall. His eyes glowed red as two small nubs appeared on his temples. They began to grow, twisting and turning as they grew ever upwards. His skin, almost as red as his eyes, glowed slightly.

Cain and Martin dropped to their knees. 'My Lord,' they both said in unison.

Mick stepped backwards. The sight of the Demon in front of him was terrifying. 'What the …,' he said as he looked at Cain and Martin.

Martin stood and spun around to face Mick. 'Kneel before your prince and master.'

Mick knelt with his eyes fixed on the Demon as he neared. Asmodeus slowly began to change back, and within seconds the transformation was complete, except for two small nubs which remained protruding about an inch from either temple. He indicated for Mick to stand, and the huge man did as instructed.

Asmodeus ambled closer to the giant. 'It's important that you know who you serve.' Mick nodded as he continued. 'In my world,' he said, 'you would have been a sentinel. Only the most physically impressive are chosen.'

Cain nodded at Mick, who dropped to one knee lowering his head. 'My prince,' Mick said.

Asmodeus waved him upwards again. 'Cain and Martin will show you to your room. I expect much from you.' He leant in closer and looked down at Mick's huge hands. 'With those hands, you can inflict great pain?'

Mick nodded. 'I was an enforcer for—'

Asmodeus put a finger to his lips. 'I know all about your previous employer.' He clicked his fingers. Cain and Martin left the room and returned with another man. His face puffy and swollen from the beating he'd received. 'You remember Billy, Mick?'

Mick glanced at his former employer and nodded. 'Yeah.'

'Mick,' Billy said. 'Help me.'

'Well?' Asmodeus said. 'What are you waiting for? Finish what the lads have started.'

Mick strode across to Billy, who looked up at him. 'I could have had you killed inside,' Billy said.

Mick sneered. 'Maybe you should have,' he said as he punched Billy in the stomach. He doubled up in pain but remained upright, held firmly by Cain and Martin. Mick hit him again and again. The blows from the giant's hands rained down relentlessly as Billy's already bloodied face was smashed into a pulp. Mick paused to gather his breath. His relentless assault exhausting him.

'Enough,' Asmodeus said. 'I don't want you to damage those hands of yours anymore.' He picked up a large brass candlestick. 'Use this.'

Mick plucked it from Asmodeus's grasp and continued his assault as Cain and Martin relinquished their grip, allowing Billy to fall to the floor. Mick carried on regardless. His assault became more frenzied as blow after blow from the heavy object smashed onto his poor victim's head, turning what once was a face and head into a mass of bone and gore. At last, Mick stopped and viewed his handiwork, his own face blood-splattered from the relentless beating of his victim.

Asmodeus placed a hand on his shoulder. 'Do you still recognise him?'

Mick shook his head. 'No.'

'Good. You have done well.' Asmodeus walked over to the fireplace. 'We will have his head here,' he said, 'as a reminder of who you answer to.' Asmodeus handed him a knife and smiled. 'Finish the job.'

MARSHALL AND BANKOLE

KATE – I slowly opened my eyes and looked up at the nurse. 'How do you feel, Kate?' she asked.

I stared at her for a couple of moments, trying to fathom my surroundings. I was in hospital but without any idea how I'd got here. Then I remembered the accident. 'Mary?' I managed to say.

The nurse forced a smile. 'Your friend is stable.' She opened the curtains. 'She's still gravely ill but stable at present.'

'Can I see her?' I said, shuffling myself into an upright position.

She smiled again and poured me some water from the plastic jug beside my bed. 'Perhaps tomorrow. You've been here all night. The doctors have given you a good examination, and you appear fine, but you must go home and rest. You've had a bit of a shock.' The nurse checked her watch. 'Is there anyone we could phone for you?'

I shook my head. 'I feel fine.' I climbed from the bed and searched for my clothes.

'Can you wait for the doctor, Kate? He's on his round now. I'm sure he'd like to speak to you before you leave.'

'What about Mary?'

'The hospital will phone if there's any change. As I said, you may be able to visit tomorrow.'

'The two men?' I said. 'What happened …?'

'I'm sorry,' the nurse said. 'They both died.'

I lowered my head and picked up my handbag. 'Thanks. I'm going home.'

'The police would like to speak with you. There's someone here now.'

'I'll have a quick word with them when I'm dressed.'

I closed the door to my house, dropped my bag onto the hall table and mounted the stairs. Quickly undressing, I crawled, bone-weary, into bed, and within minutes I fell asleep. But this was different from my normal sleep. It was filled with vivid images and voices that appeared real.

My dreams were rudely interrupted by someone knocking on the door of my house. I rubbed my hands over my face, climbed out of bed, pulled on a pair of jogging bottoms and a sweatshirt, and padded downstairs to answer it. Two men stood outside.

'Kate Carver?' the older of the two men asked.

'Yes,' I replied.

He held out his card. 'I'm Detective Sergeant Ken Marshall.' He nodded at his young companion. 'And this is Detective Sergeant Adisa Bankole. Can we come in and have a chat?'

'Yes. Of course,' I mumbled. I turned and headed into the lounge, closely followed by the two officers. Dropping onto an armchair, I motioned for them to sit. Stifling a yawn, I rubbed my eyes. 'Sorry,' I said. 'I've only just got up. Can I get you a drink?'

Marshall looked at his companion, who shook his head. 'We're fine, Mrs Carver.'

I stood. 'It's Miss, but please, call me Kate. I'm going to make myself one. I can't function without coffee in the morning.' I needed the opportunity to gather my thoughts before the inevitable interrogation. I felt inside my pocket for my phone and held it up. 'I also need to ring the hospital and find out how Mary is.'

'We've just been there,' Marshall said. 'Your friend is stable. She's still unconscious but had a comfortable night.'

'Good,' I said, pointing towards the kitchen. 'I'll just …'

Marshall smiled pleasantly and nodded. 'No rush, Kate.'

Five minutes later, I sat opposite the officers with a steaming mug of coffee in my hand. 'So,' I said, 'you want to ask me something?'

'I have some notes from the constable you spoke to at the hospital. He said you were still groggy, so I'd like to go over some of the details.' Marshall pulled out his notebook and opened it. 'Apparently, you knew the two deceased gentlemen?'

I nodded and took a sip of my drink. 'Reece was one of my patients, and Felix is a friend of my parents.'

Marshall turned the page. 'The constable mentioned you work at a hospital. In the mental health department.'

'Yes,' I said.

'And your friend, Mary Croft?'

'We've been good friends for years, and I've recently moved back to England from Australia, so I looked her up a few days ago.'

Marshall rubbed his chin as he read his notes, then looked up again.

'Do you know why these men were on the Leyburn road?'

I sipped my coffee again and then sighed. 'It's quite complicated.'

'We can do complicated.' He briefly glanced at his colleague. 'Why don't you start at the beginning.'

I explained the events leading up to the accident but left out the part about the Nazarian.

Marshall glanced at his colleague again, then back to me. 'Clearly, Reece was having some sort of delusion,' he said, 'and you say Felix had similar delusions years ago?'

'That's what he told us.'

'Your friend Mary?' Bankole said.

'Yes.'

'What's her involvement?'

'Mary's a journalist. She was considering writing a book on peoples' visions. I suggested we speak with Felix.'

'But not Reece?' Marshall said.

'No. I relayed what Reece told me to Mary.'

'So,' Bankole said, consulting his own notes. 'Reece and Felix knew each other?'

I shook my head. 'No. Or at least that's what Felix told us.'

Marshall rubbed his chin again. 'This all seems a little strange. You say they didn't know each other, but according to what you've just told us ...' He consulted his notebook again. 'Felix rang Reece at the hospital.'

'That's right,' I said. 'Like I told your lot, the hospital where I work telephoned me to say Felix rang Reece, and Reece left the hospital.'

'There's no security?' Marshall said.

'Reece was there by choice. They couldn't stop him from leaving.' My head was beginning to ache from their tedious questions. I sighed and continued. 'He didn't give any indication that he would harm himself if that's what you're implying.'

'I'm not implying anything, Kate,' Marshall said. 'We're just trying to get to the bottom of this.' Marshall drummed his notepad with his pen. 'We've had the toxicology reports back,' he said, 'and it appears Felix Halshaw injected insulin into himself. There's no sign of foul play. Two needles were found with only Reece's and Felix's fingerprints. It looks as if they intended to kill themselves.'

'Reece,' I said, getting the impression Marshall hadn't told me everything, 'he injected insulin as well?'

Marshall glanced at his colleague. 'No. There was a different substance in Reece Sadler's bloodstream. But, unfortunately, the lab hasn't determined what it is.'

'I see.'

Marshall narrowed his eyes. 'Do you?'

I shrugged. His questions irritated me, and I pondered this for a moment. Why get annoyed, I thought. They were only doing their job. I drained my coffee and forced a smile at the pair. 'Reece was dead when we found them, but Felix was alive. Albeit barely.'

Marshall looked at his pad again. 'And you say Felix phoned you and Mary to tell you where he was going?' I nodded, and Marshall continued. 'Why would he do that?'

I shrugged again. 'I don't know.' I said, certain this wasn't what they wanted to hear.

'In your professional opinion?' Marshall said.

I considered his question for a moment. 'Felix knew about Reece. We explained to Felix that Reece and he had similar visions. This may have awakened some latent memory. Felix took it upon himself to ring Reece, and they must have agreed to meet.'

'But why would two strangers arrange to meet and then kill themselves? The insulin and needles indicate it was planned.'

'I don't know why they would do that,' I said.

'And then ring you,' Bankole said.

'I don't know that either.'

Marshall turned over the page of his notebook and read from it. 'You say a car struck Mary while you were attending to Felix?'

'Yes,' I said. Should I tell him that the driver appeared to drive at Mary deliberately? I considered this but reasoned it would only encourage him to ask more questions. 'Just an accident. It was dark, and we were parked off the road. Mary stepped out in front of the car and got hit.'

'And the driver drove off?' Bankole said.

'Yes. I guess he panicked.'

'You didn't manage to get a make?' Bankole said. I shook my head. 'License number? Or colour?' he continued.

'Detective sergeant,' I said, not even attempting to hide my irritation. 'My friend had been injured. I deemed that a little more pressing than taking down the details of a car.' The two officers stared at me as if they wanted me to continue, so I did. 'I ran to assist Mary, and before I realised what was happening, the car took off. It was over in seconds.'

Marshall nodded. 'I see. And Mr Statham ... The driver who stopped?'

'I flagged him down and asked him to call an ambulance.'

'Why didn't you or Mary phone for an ambulance,' Marshall said, 'when you found Reece Sadler and Felix Halshaw?'

'Neither of our phones worked.'

'But Mr Statham's did?' Marshall said.

'Yes.' I glared at him. 'Mobile networks are funny like that.'

Marshall glanced at his colleague again. 'Why do I get the impression you're not telling us everything?'

I folded my arms. 'I've told you the truth. And I have told you everything. When Mary recovers, she'll tell you the same.'

Marshall and Bankole stood. 'Ok, Kate,' Marshall said. 'We'll leave it there for now. But we may need to talk again.'

I stood. 'Of course. I'm only too willing to help.' My fake smile was priceless.

'What do you think, Ken?' Bankole said to Marshall once back in their car.

'She's not telling us everything. Felix and Reece must have known each other. Check into their backgrounds.'

Bankole's phone rang. 'DS Bankole … Yeah. Ok.' He hung up and turned to Marshall. 'The insulin belonged to Reece's dead wife. She had diabetes.'

Marshall nodded. 'Right. So, we know where they got the insulin from but the other substance?' He glanced back at the house. 'Check into Mary Croft's background. See if anything shows up there.' He rubbed his chin. 'Something is definitely amiss, Adi.'

Bankole nodded while studying his phone. 'Have you seen this?' he said.

'Seen what?'

Bankole held the phone up. 'Two men escaped from Broadmoor. Extremely dangerous by all accounts. That's on top of the prisoner that escaped from The Old Bailey.'

Marshall blew out. 'A mate of mine works for the Met. He reckons the men guarding him were mutilated.'

'Christ,' Bankole said. 'What with covid and that, the world's a mess.'

Marshall glanced back at the house. 'You're not wrong,' he said as Bankole started the engine and pulled away

KATE - I watched through the window as the two officers climbed into their car and waited until they drove off. Only then did I head back into the kitchen and make myself another cup of coffee. I leant against the worktop. You didn't have to be a psychiatrist to know they hadn't believed me, but the police were the least of my problems. The dream from the previous night had been so vivid. The Nazarian had been in it, and he'd told me that some people would come, and I must keep them away from others who would harm them until I could bring them to him. That's what he told me. That's what I had to do. It was so strange, yet my dream had been so lucid that I didn't doubt his words. As a psychiatrist, I found this most unsettling.

THE APOSTLES

Simon had woken the previous morning with a thought inside his head that quickly grew into a quest. He had to go somewhere, somewhere in England. It initially seemed preposterous, but gradually, the uncertainty he felt was chipped away until no trace remained. He had lied to his family and told them he was visiting an old college friend from the Midwest. In truth, he'd booked himself a ticket on the first plane available to Heathrow and hurried to O'Hare International airport.

After arriving in London, he booked a flight to Newcastle, which appeared to be the nearest airport to where he needed to be. As he got closer, the draw grew stronger and once outside Newcastle airport, he jumped into a taxi to Darlington. An address burnt brightly in his mind. He conveyed this to the driver and sat back as the vehicle sped off.

Simon exited the taxi and watched it drive away before turning to face the house that had drawn him there like a moth to a flame. Inside, someone he needed to talk to, someone who could answer his burning question. Why had he been summoned? What on earth was he doing here? Feeling foolish, he strode up the path and knocked on the door.

KATE – Most of my morning consisted of answering the door to various men who appeared to be as confused as me. I looked at the visitors in my living room and was about to offer them refreshments when I heard another knock on the door. I offered my apologies and went to open it. 'Hello,' I said. 'I've been expecting you.'

He held out his hand. 'Simon,' he said. 'Simon Zeller.'

'You're Jewish?'

He tapped the small skullcap on the top of his head. 'Did this give it away?'

'Yeah.' I beckoned him inside. 'You're not the first.'

Simon followed me into the front room, where two other young men sat. 'This is Juan and Piotr,' I said.

'Hi,' Simon said. They nodded at him.

I pointed towards the kitchen door. 'I'm about to make them a drink. Can I get you one, Simon?'

'I'm a little confused,' he said. 'I hoped you could answer some questions.'

'Such as?'

'Well,' he glanced at the other two, 'why was I …' he paused for a moment, 'why was I compelled to come here?'

I folded my arms as all three men looked at me. 'I've no idea,' I said, and I honestly didn't.

Simon edged closer. 'But, Miss …'

'Kate,' I said.

'Kate.' He smiled. 'I've travelled from Chicago. I'm worn out. I'm—'

I rolled my eyes. 'My friend is seriously ill in hospital. A few days ago, I was getting on with my life when all this …' I threw my hands out, '… all this madness happened. I know as much as you three.' I didn't divulge anything about my dreams and how I knew their appearance was imminent.

Simon held up his hands. 'I'm sorry, Kate. I apologise. I didn't mean any offence.'

I rubbed my eyes with the heels of my palms. It was pointless taking it out on them. 'No, it's me who should apologise. I'll make us some drinks, and then we'll see if we can make sense of this.'

As the kettle boiled, I leant on the worktop and closed my eyes as a lightning bolt of pain shot across my temple. I'm going mad, I thought. What do I do with these three? And Mary? Is she even in the hospital? Had she passed through into Nearhope with Reece and Felix? But they are dead. I placed my hands over my eyes as tears pooled there.

'Are you ok?' Simon said.

I turned to face him and quickly rubbed my eyes with the sleeve of my sweater. So wrapped up in my own mind, his approach had gone unnoticed. 'I'm tired, that's all.' I said without a hint of sincerity. Although, to be honest, I didn't care what he thought.

'Can I help you with the drinks?'

He smiled at me as if he understood my inner turmoil. I nodded. 'Yes please.'

Sat in an armchair, I cradled my empty coffee cup. 'That's everything I know,' I said, spilling the beans on the previous day's bizarre events.

'I had a vision,' Juan said in his barely Spanish accent. 'At the church yesterday, I saw Christ.' He blushed. 'Well, that's who it appeared to be.'

'What did he say?' Piotr said.

'He didn't say anything,' Juan said, then shrugged. 'I had a feeling, an impression. Then this thought appeared, and I knew that I must come here. I was drawn to this place. Like a ...' He paused and considered his words, '... like a mental pathway.'

'You both speak good English,' I said. And they did. Their accents barely had a trace of their country of origin.

Piotr frowned. 'Yesterday,' he said. 'I could hardly speak a word. Strange, don't you think?'

I shrugged. No stranger than anything else. 'Not after what has happened to me lately. Can I ask if you two have seen the Nazarian on YouTube?'

Piotr and Juan shook their heads. 'In the monastery,' Juan said, 'modern technology is frowned upon.'

'Where I come from,' Piotr said. 'The people are poor. I have only briefly had any dealings with TV or computers.'

'Well,' I announced, 'we have to find him.'

'How do you know that?' Simon said.

'I had a dream last night. My most vivid dream ever. In it, the Nazarian told me that you would arrive. In fact ...' I smiled, '... there will be twelve of you.'

The three men exchanged glances. 'Like the Apostles?' Simon said.

'Yes,' I said. 'Simon, you're an orthodox Jew?' He nodded. 'And Juan, you live at a monastery?' He nodded too. 'What about you, Piotr?'

'I'm training to be a priest,' he said.

'So, you are all religious men,' I said, pleased with myself. 'I'm not sure why I've been chosen, though. I've never been what you might call godly.'

'Perhaps you are,' Piotr said. 'Maybe you've been shown the path.'

Simon stood. 'According to the two men you mentioned ...'

'Felix and Reece,' I prompted.

'Yes, Felix and Reece. Asmodeus is in our world. Christ wants us to send him back to his own realm.'

I stood and clasped my hands together. 'That's about the size of it.' Simon smiled. Clearly, he understood my humour.

'And Christ's disciples are needed to achieve this?' Juan said.

'Yes,' I said. 'We can't wait here too long, though. James, or Sicarius, is being held in Asmodeus's realm. Sicarius has important information which Asmodeus needs. If he obtains this information, our world will fall. The gates of hell will be thrown open, and Satan and all his acolytes will pour forth.' I furrowed my brow. The words spoken were not my own. As if someone else uttered them. 'Erm, sorry about that. I'm not altogether sure where that came from.'

'Who is Sicarius?' Piotr said, 'and who is James?'

'They are the same person,' I said, not knowing how I knew this. 'Sicarius is James, and James is Judas. Asmodeus is using James's human form in our realm.' I gasped. The words arrived from somewhere, and although I uttered them, it was as if I was possessed. I looked at their confused faces and held up my hands. 'Don't bother asking me to explain because I can't. All I know is that we need to act quickly.'

Silence descended, and Juan spoke. 'How long have we got?'

I lowered my head. 'Hours. We can only wait a few hours more, and then we must go.'

Simon furrowed his brow. 'Go where?'

I turned to face him. 'I don't know yet. When the time is right, he will tell me.' But, again, these words were not my own.

SICARIUS – Sicarius could feel its presence moving through the corridors of his mind and steadied himself for the onslaught as the creature neared. It paused at a wall and ran its claw-like hands across the rough stonework. Something caught the creature's attention, and it leant in closer to examine the wall. Then, pressing a finger into the mortar, it scratched away a small sliver of stone. The creature grinned and continued to probe the mortar further. Another fragment fell, then another as the creature rapidly increased the intensity of its digging – clawing, scraping, it pulled at the aged stone until a gap appeared. The creature laughed. 'You are weakening,' it whispered, 'why continue the fight?'

Sicarius groaned. The pain in his head was intense. He redoubled his efforts, but this time, after many hours of this onslaught, his strength was almost spent. Then, a vision of Christ appeared. A shimmering image that smiled at him but said nothing. He groaned again as the vision faded and then disappeared. Sicarius closed his eyes as tears pushed relentlessly through his eyelids and fell to the floor.

Braxas laughed. 'What's wrong?' he taunted. 'Did your saviour forsake you again? He's making a habit of that.' Braxas took hold of his captive's head and pulled it close. 'We took you as one of our own. Asmodeus elevated you to his side, and look how you betrayed him. And your friend, The Nazarian. That abomination, that crossbreed lets you fall again. We will enjoy feasting on you. We will take everything from you. We will devour your soul.'

In summoning his last ounces of strength, Sicarius turned his face towards his torturer. 'You're just like your brother,' Sicarius said. 'He was full of hubris until I killed him. He begged for mercy, as I remember. Like a Janus would.'

Braxas howled and pushed his face closer to Sicarius. 'Let's see what secrets you possess,' he said.

The creature smashed its way through the opening, and beyond this lay a small corridor with a door at the end. Stumbling across the fallen masonry and towards the door, it turned the handle. It was locked, but the door surrendered its resistance with one mighty shove and gave way. Behind sat a man, oblivious to the creature, as it moved closer and lowered its face to a level with him. The creature drank in his features and, satisfied, roared.

Braxas pulled himself away from Sicarius and smiled. 'We have a face,' he said.

Sicarius lifted his head from his chest and viewed Braxas through bloodshot eyes.

'Asmodeus is waiting for this,' Braxas said. 'Don't get too comfortable. I'll be back.' He looked to the guards. 'Hang the traitor up again.'

THE APOSTLES CONGREGATE

Asmodeus sat on his ornate throne as Cain entered.

'You sent for me?' Cain said.

'We have one of them,' Asmodeus said, 'and a name.'

Cain grinned. 'What do you want me to do?'

'Intercept him and bring him here. We'll use him to get Braxas through the threshold.'

'Braxas is coming here? Are you unhappy with us?'

Asmodeus stood. 'Of course not, but he is my dextral.' He strolled across to Cain and gripped his shoulder. 'You have done well, Cain.' Asmodeus turned and walked to the fireplace with his hands behind his back. 'But you are not Braxas.'

'How is it possible for you to get him here?'

'The Apostle gives us the opportunity,' Asmodeus said. 'Usually, passing through the threshold is the only way, but this can only be achieved with a living person. As I'm sure you'll understand, this is difficult, and the Apostle's soul is the key. Braxas will be able to exchange places with him once the Apostle's soul is delivered into my realm.'

Cain lowered his head. 'I have tried my hardest.'

Asmodeus smiled. 'I know you have.'

Cain hurried to his side. 'I've done everything you've asked. Is there something that I've done wrong?'

Asmodeus rolled his eyes. 'You're human and no match for one of my kin.' He turned to face Cain. 'Humans are weak. They lack a certain something. They are the reason my people ended up where they are.'

Cain lowered his head again. 'I'm sorry.'

Asmodeus sneered. 'There you are. Weak.'

'When your people come, will you not need us anymore?'

'Cain,' he said, 'there will always be a place for you. But we must maintain the hierarchy. Do you understand?' Cain nodded. Asmodeus placed his hands behind his back again. 'There is another reason I want Braxas here. My people can be unreliable, treacherous even. They covert my position.'

'Then why bring him here?'

'What is that saying your people have? *Keep your friends close and your enemies closer.*'

Cain frowned deeply. 'You think he has plans to take over your realm?'

'Possibly. He is an excellent dextral, but it doesn't do to take your eye off the ball.' Asmodeus laughed. 'I do like these human sayings.'

'Why not kill him?'

Asmodeus glowered at Cain. 'You have much to learn. One does not kill one of your own brethren. It would not be tolerated. *He who reigns supreme* would disapprove. There is a place reserved for those that kill their own brethren. It is a place you would not wish to find yourself.'

'But you fight and kill others from different realms.'

'They are not my kin,' Asmodeus said and held up a hand as Cain opened his mouth to speak. 'How is our recruitment going?'

'We have two more. That makes ten.'

'Good,' Asmodeus said. 'And the scientist? Have you found a suitable one yet?'

'We think so.'

'And the laboratory?'

Cain smiled. 'It's ready.'

'Very good, Cain. I shall give you a reward. Someone from your past who did you wrong and who you would like to meet again.'

He sneered. 'My ex,' Cain said. 'She dumped me for another bloke.'

'Well,' Asmodeus said. 'We will have them brought here. You can show me what you've learned.' Cain grinned. Asmodeus put his hand into his pocket and handed him a piece of paper. 'First, though,' he said, 'you must capture the Apostle.'

Cain looked down at the drawing of a man. 'Is this him?'

'His name is Paulo. He's on a train from London to Darlington. Intercept him and bring him here.' Cain nodded, then hurried into the corridor. Halfway along it, Martin stopped him. 'What did he say?'

Cain held up the paper. 'We have a face and the name of one of the Apostles and must capture him.'

'Why?'

Cain groaned. 'Because Asmodeus said so.' He walked on, closely followed by Martin before pausing. 'He's going to use the Apostle to bring Braxas here.'

'His Dextral?'

'Yeah. We need to up our game when he comes.'

Martin took hold of Cain's arm as he turned away. 'How does Asmodeus communicate with his realm?'

Cain puffed out his cheeks. 'You ask too many questions.'

Martin lowered his eyes. 'If Braxas is coming, we must watch each other's backs.'

'Yes, I suppose, but I'm next in line when Thomas fucks up.' Cain smiled. 'And he will fuck up.'

'Fine. If you say so. I won't stand in your way. I'm curious how he knows what is happening in his realm.'

Cain leant against the wall. 'Asmodeus takes a substance.' Cain glanced up and down the corridor before continuing. 'It puts him into this trance-like sleep, and he has news from his realm when he wakes up. I secretly watched him once.'

Martin nodded. 'Did he say when Braxas is coming?'

Cain shook the paper in his hand. 'As soon as we have the Apostle. Now come on.'

Paulo stepped from the train and strode along the platform. He exited the station and glanced about.

'Are you looking for a taxi?' Martin said.

Paulo nodded. 'Yes,' he said. 'I'm sorry, my English is not great.'

'Sounds ok to me. Where to?'

Paulo fished in his pocket, pulled out a bit of paper and showed it to Martin. 'I know the address,' Martin said. 'Follow me.'

The two men crossed the road to a waiting car, and Martin opened the rear door. 'In here,' he said.

Paulo looked inside at Mick, who sat in the back seat. 'No, I think—'

Martin thrust a gun into his side. 'Get in,' he said.

'Got him?' Cain asked Martin as he climbed into the seat next to him.

'Yeah,' Martin said. 'Mick and one of the others are taking him to Asmodeus. I have the address of where the other Apostles are.'

'Good. We'll head there now.'

'Shouldn't we ask Asmodeus?'

Cain scowled at Martin. 'This is our opportunity to impress him.'

'I don't think we should do anything until Asmodeus says so.'

'Braxas is Asmodeus's main man back in his world. Once he comes here, we'll be way down the pecking order.'

'Yes, you keep saying. All the more reason to ask Asmodeus.'

Cain groaned. 'He thinks humans are weak. And it's because of people like you that he has that opinion.'

Martin sneered. 'I don't care. Asmodeus gives me the orders, not you. You don't know how many others there are, and we may be outnumbered. I'll tell you what …' Martin took out his mobile, '… I'll ring

Asmodeus now and tell him what you intend to do, shall I?'

Cain snatched the phone from him and tossed it onto the dashboard. 'Forget it. If you haven't got the balls ...' He started the car and roared off.

KATE – Dressed, I headed downstairs with the dream from the previous night still burning brightly in my mind. I pushed open the door, entered and groaned as I encountered the five men sitting in my living room.

'Did he come to you last night?' Piotr asked.

I waved a dismissive hand at him. 'Do you mind if I get a coffee first? I can't function without that first hit of caffeine.' To be honest, my head ached, and I couldn't be bothered with this first thing.

'But we need—' Piotr said

Simon lifted a hand. 'Let Kate get her coffee. A few more moments won't matter.'

Piotr nodded. 'Ok. I'm sorry, Kate.'

I carried on into the kitchen and filled the kettle as Simon followed me and stopped close by. 'I'm sorry about Piotr,' he said.

I switched on the kettle and turned. 'The Nazarian wants us to go to him.'

'Right,' Simon said. 'Where?'

'I don't know the location yet, but he implied *I would know* when the time comes. His power ...' I rubbed my face, '... I got the impression that his time on earth is limited. He is weakening.'

'Did he say that?'

'No. More of an impression. There's an urgency.'

'Then we must hurry.' He nodded towards the front room. 'Do you think the others will arrive?'

'One of them has been taken.'

'Taken? Taken where?'

I sighed. Having to explain every detail of my dreams, dreams I was not sure I fully understood, irritated me. 'Asmodeus has him. He will know that you and the others are coming here. This house isn't secure anymore.'

'Then we must go.'

'There were twelve Apostles,' I said.

'Thirteen if you count Matthias. He replaced Judas.'

I groaned. Simon's pedantry was beginning to rile me. I gulped my coffee. 'We have to wait for the others.'

'How long do we wait? Maybe the others have been taken too.'

'I'd know if they had.' I pulled my mobile from my pocket. 'I've got to phone the hospital and find out how Mary is.' I false smiled him. 'If you don't mind.'

'Yes, of course,' he said.

'Have you eaten?' I said as he turned.

Simon nodded. 'A couple of us rustled up some coffee and toast. I hope you don't mind?'

'Not at all,' I said. 'Help yourself,' I uttered under my breath. 'I'm running a bloody hotel here.' I stepped into the conservatory, went into the garden and phoned the hospital.

I'd finished my call to the hospital when my phone rang.

'Kate, it's Andy. Andy from the paper.'

I found myself smiling. It felt good to hear from someone normal. 'Hi, Andy.'

'Have you heard from Mary? She's not answering her calls.'

I brought a hand up to my mouth. 'Oh, god, sorry, Andy. I didn't think to ring you.'

'About what?'

'Mary's in hospital.'

'Hospital? What the hell—?'

'There was an accident. She's in Intensive Care but stable.'

'What kind of accident?'

'It's a long story.'

'Can I visit?'

I blew out hard. 'Close family only. Besides, she's unconscious.'

'Mary hasn't really got any close family.'

'I told them I'm her half-sister,' I said.

'I see. Are you ok?'

'I'm fine.'

'I could come around,' he said.

I glanced back at the house and rolled my eyes. 'Not today. I have to go to work, but I would like to see you.'

'Give me a ring when you're free, and we'll sort something out, but keep me informed about Mary.'

'I will do. Thanks for ringing.' I hung up, sighed loudly, and trudged back inside.

Asmodeus smiled at the man. 'You heard me right, professor,' he said.

'But you'll kill millions,' the professor said.

Asmodeus lowered himself onto his throne and laced his fingers together. 'That's the plan. Humankind has infested this place for long enough. Nature has given us an opportunity with Coronavirus, and all I want you to do is make it more virulent.'

'You're mad. I won't do it.'

Asmodeus stood and took hold of the professor by the throat, almost lifting him off the ground. The Demon's eyes blazed red as he burrowed into the professor's consciousness. His captive groaned as he relentlessly tore through his mind with images of torture and death. The professor dropped to the floor and curled up into the foetal position.

'Do you see what awaits you if you disobey?' Asmodeus squatted next to the trembling man. 'Not just you, but everyone you ...' Asmodeus sneered, '...everyone you love. Do you understand?'

The professor nodded. 'Y-e-s.'

Asmodeus stood and sat back on his chair. 'Shall we say an eighty per cent mortality rate?'

The professor lifted his head. Tears streaked his face. 'I'll try.'

Asmodeus waved his hand in an upward motion, and the professor slowly got to his feet. 'It will be the old and infirm that perish first,' Asmodeus said. 'The stronger ones will remain.'

'What will you do with those that don't die?'

'We will feast on some of them, of course. Others will be used to do our will. You and others who assist me will survive and be greatly rewarded for your efforts. I can give you anything.' Asmodeus smirked. 'I've seen inside that mind of yours. I know what you truly desire.'

The professor lowered his head. 'I-I-I don't—'

Asmodeus laughed. 'There are no secrets from me. 'Your wife,' he said, 'she's not what you truly desire. Am I right?' The professor nodded, and Asmodeus continued. 'I will give you whatever you want. An inexhaustible supply.' Asmodeus held out his hand. 'In a war, you must choose sides. Now is the time to choose yours.'

The professor dropped to his knees, took hold of Asmodeus's hand, and kissed the ornate ring. 'I will do what you want.'

'Already you feel the power. It will get stronger each day.' Asmodeus waved for him to stand. 'Whatever you need for your work, just ask.'

Paulo was dragged into the room and dumped onto the floor. He looked up at Asmodeus as he towered over him. 'Who are you?' he said, staring at the two nubs protruding from the strange-looking James/Asmodeus hybrid.

Asmodeus lowered himself to the same level as Paulo. 'Asmodeus. This ...' He gestured towards himself, '... this is only temporary.'

Paulo gasped. 'I've heard of you. You and the others.'

Asmodeus stood. 'A man of the scriptures, I see.'

Paulo looked about. 'You have no place in this world. The Almighty cast you and your sort from his kingdom. Your home is a place of darkness.'

Asmodeus sighed loudly. 'You believe the rubbish written in those books of yours. There was a time,' Asmodeus said, 'when we were favoured by him.' He wandered over to the fire and stared into the flames. 'Then you and your kind came between us.' He spun around.

'Your god is a liar. Your holy books are a fabrication. My god,' he continued, '*He who reigns supreme* will take what is rightfully his. We will raze your places of worship.' He walked back across to Paulo. 'We will cover the alters with the blood of your humankind.'

Paulo crossed himself and began to utter a prayer.

'Even now, you call to him. Even now, you believe his lies. When we have your soul, Paulo, you will truly know who the most powerful is. Your god, and your books, will be of no use.' Asmodeus waved a hand to his men. 'Ready him. Braxas is waiting.'

THE APOTHECARY

MARY – I sat at the table in the pub opposite Felix and Reece but felt distinctly at a disadvantage. They'd been here before. I hadn't.

Reece broke the silence. 'I suppose this is all very odd to you, Mary?'

That was the understatement of the year. 'You could say that. What is this place?'

'The pub?' Reece said.

'No. The whole place. I mean ...' I lowered my voice and leant in closer, '... I know you told me about Nearhope, Felix. And I read your account of it, but ...'

Felix scratched his head and shrugged. 'I haven't been here in such a long time. Yet ... It seems like yesterday.'

'James told me,' Reece said, 'that Nearhope is like a buffer zone between our world and ...' He raised his eyebrows as if he knew I would understand him.

'Hell?' I said, then winced.

'Yes,' Reece said. 'It's strange how uttering a word can be so painful.'

I rubbed my temple. 'Yes.' I regained my composure as the pain subsided. 'But even though Felix described it to Kate and me, I still didn't believe it. Even though he wrote it down on paper. Even though it seemed so real.'

Felix shrugged. 'I didn't believe it either. Not until Kate and you came to see me, then I knew. So, whether it feels weird or not, here we are.'

'Now that we're here,' I said. 'What are we going to do?'

Felix looked at Reece. 'Any ideas?' he said.

'Did you meet Celestine?' Reece said.

Felix nodded. 'And Khar.'

Reece sighed. 'I hoped those two would help us.' He sat back in his chair. 'I don't know what else to do.'

'That would involve travelling to dark Nearhope,' Felix said. 'We wouldn't have James to cloak us. The Legion could catch us.'

'Dark Nearhope?' I said. 'The one in your account?'

'Nearhope's twin,' Felix said. I nodded my understanding. Trying to remember as much of Felix's account as possible. 'It's what I call it,' he continued. 'It's not a place you would like to venture alone.'

I glanced around. 'What about the people here? Couldn't they help?'

'The people here are unaware of who they are or who they were,' Felix said, 'Except …'

'Jenny and Elizabeth,' Reece said.

'Jenny, your wife?' I said. 'But who's—?'

'My wife,' Reece said.

'They know about Nearhope and Dark Nearhope,' Felix said. 'For some reason, they have maintained a memory of that. However, they know nothing of their earthly lives.' Felix looked at me sternly. 'It must remain that way,' he said. Felix stood and looked at Reece. 'Can you organise some rooms for you and Mary, and I'll go and see Jenny and Elizabeth now?' Reece nodded and watched as Felix left.

'Hungry?' Reece said.

I was ravenous. 'Yes, I am.' I took hold of his arm as he moved to stand. 'Your wife?'

He sighed. 'Like Felix said. She remembers nothing of me.'

'Nothing?'

He shook his head. 'It's better you don't mention us.'

'I understand.'

Reece smiled. 'I'll order some food. They do a fine meal in The Slaughtered Man.'

Felix stopped outside the shop and looked up at the sign. *Apothecary*, it said. Proprietor: *J. Halshaw*. He pushed open the door and made his way across to the counter.

A woman with her back to him turned and smiled. 'Felix.'

'Hello, Jenny.'

She hurried around to the other side of the counter, and the pair embraced. 'What are you doing here? Are you—?'

'James,' he said.

'What about him? I haven't seen him in ages.'

'He's been taken. He's a prisoner at the citadel.'

She brought a hand up to her mouth and gasped. 'No!'

'I had to come back. We're going to try and get him out.'

'You know how awful that place is. We were lucky to escape last time.'

'You remember?' he said.

Jenny smiled. 'I remember a great deal. I don't know why, but I remember being at the citadel and you and James freeing me.'

'And Elizabeth?'

Jenny frowned. 'Some of it, but not as much as me. Although, she seems to remember more each passing day. Who's going to assist you in getting James out?'

'There are two people with me. Reece and Mary.'

'Do they know what they are up against?'

Felix sighed. 'James freed Reece from the citadel. Mary has never been here.'

Jenny turned away from him. 'How did you pass through the threshold?'

Felix rubbed his chin. 'You know about the threshold?'

She nodded without turning. 'James explained it to me.'

'I see.'

'Felix,' she said, 'how did you—?'

He stepped closer and placed a hand on his wife's shoulder. 'There was no alternative. No choice.'

Jenny faced him again. 'But you can never go back.'

He forced a smile. 'I was hoping my future would be here … With you.'

She placed a hand on his cheek. 'I never thought I'd see you again. But to give up your life on the outside. What about your wife … Your family?'

He smiled. 'I have no one.'

'Ok,' she said. 'I think you're mad, but—'

'Celestine and Khar? Have you heard from them?'

'Not for a long time,' she said. 'I could send someone.'

'Are they trustworthy?'

Taking hold of his hand, she squeezed it. 'Yes. I'm always careful.'

'My two friends are at The Slaughtered Man. Could you come after you close?' Felix glanced about. 'Elizabeth? Is she here?'

'She's away gathering herbs and is usually gone a couple of days.'

'Isn't that dangerous?'

Jenny smiled. 'We have contacts who assist us in obtaining them. We've been living here a long time, Felix. We know what we're doing. Besides, they are very important.'

'Why?'

Jenny raised her eyebrows. 'The reason James and the others changed.'

He frowned. 'I don't understand.'

'It's a virus. James changed from a Demon to who he is today by being infected with a virus.'

'And the others?'

'Those too,' she said. 'It's difficult to transmit, but it is possible.'

'What is it you and Elizabeth are planning?' he said.

Jenny sighed. 'We're trying to make it more virulent without much luck.'

'If they find out what you're doing,' he said, 'they will try to stop you.'

She glanced out of the shop. 'I shouldn't have told you. Keep it to yourself.'

'I will. Does James know?'

She nodded. 'He asked me to work on it. He is hoping to swell the underground numbers.'

'Let me know when you have news from Celestine.' He smiled and moved towards the door.

'Felix.' He turned back to face her. 'I'm so pleased to see you again,' she said.

Khar paused his cleaning of the bar top and listened as someone tapped on the door. He placed his cloth on a nearby table and answered it. Celestine stood outside.

He smiled. 'Celestine.'

'Aren't you going to let me in?' she said. 'It's freezing.'

'Of course.' He beckoned her inside and moved behind the bar. 'Drink?' he said, holding up a bottle.

'Large one.'

Khar half-filled two glasses. 'There's obviously a reason you're here?'

She hopped onto a stool. 'I received a message from Jenny.'

He picked up his glass and took a sip. 'Jenny? Ah, the woman who runs the apothecary. Felix's wife?'

'Yes. She assists in our quest with helping the Janus.'

He nodded. 'I remember James telling me. And this message?'

'James has been taken.'

Khar drained his glass and poured himself another. 'When?'

She shook her head. 'I don't know, but he's being held in the citadel.'

Khar slumped onto his seat. 'Then all is lost. He will tell them everything.'

'It's worse than that,' she said. 'Asmodeus has crossed the threshold.'

He lowered his shoulders and slowly shook his head. 'There is no hope. He coverts their world.'

Celestine refilled her glass. 'We have some hope. I have someone in the citadel. James does not know of his existence. I thought it would be for the best if James ever got caught ... You can't give Asmodeus information you haven't got.'

'What has he told you?'

'He's been unable to get in touch with me until now. He knew that they held an important prisoner, but he didn't know who. Braxas has only a few trusted lieutenants.'

'And your plan?' Khar said.

'We have to get James out of there.'

Khar rubbed his face. 'How the hell are we going to do that? Since James freed Jenny, the place is even more of a fortress than before.'

'There are some that are prepared to make the ultimate sacrifice.'

Khar refilled his glass. 'I see. When are you planning this?'

'Soon. The longer James is held, the more information he will give up. Some of the underground have gone into hiding.'

'If you can get him out, and it's a big if,' Khar said, 'what then?'

'Felix and Reece are in Nearhope.'

'But how did they get back?'

'They too, have made the sacrifice. There is no going back to their world for them.'

Khar sighed. 'James won't be strong enough to make the journey alone.'

'They have brought a woman with them. She will help him.'

Khar stroked his beard. 'I too, have someone inside the citadel.'

'Why haven't you mentioned this before?'

'She's keen to help,' he said, 'but I did not want her to take the risk. We have a bond.'

'Ah, I see.'

'She will help, but ...' He drained his glass. 'I would rather it didn't cost her life.'

Celestine leant across and patted his arm. 'There is always risk, my friend. You know that. We will only use her if we must.'

Sicarius groaned. He looked up at the smiling Braxas. 'Well, well,' Braxas said. 'Quite the bunch of renegades you have. Asmodeus will be so pleased to acquire their names.' Braxas took hold of a piece of paper and jotted something onto it. He turned and handed it to one of the guards. 'Give this to Orius. Tell him to capture them and bring them here.'

The guard nodded, then hurried off.

'I feel you still have more to tell me,' he said to Sicarius. 'Who else are you going to give up?'

Sicarius closed his eyes and attempted to shore up his mental defences.

Braxas took hold of his hair and pulled his head back. 'It's useless trying to hold out. You're just prolonging the agony.'

Sicarius smiled. 'How do you know the information I gave you is the truth? Maybe I've given you false names. Have you considered that?'

Braxas narrowed his eyes. 'Nice try, but I think we both know what you've told me is accurate.'

'Are you sure?' Sicarius chuckled. 'Absolutely sure.'

Braxas let go of his hair and growled. 'Take him back to his cell. I have more pressing matters.' He turned away as the guards led Sicarius away, then turned back and looked at the empty space his captive once occupied and rubbed his chin thoughtfully.

THE HOUSE

Kate looked at her watch for the umpteenth time. 'We can't wait any longer,' she said. 'We must go.'

'But the others?' Simon said. 'There are only eight of us.'

'It will have to do. Lockdown comes into force tomorrow. We'll find it difficult to travel then. Piotr, have we got everything?'

He nodded. 'I think so. Where are we going?'

'I'll give you directions as we travel. Unfortunately, I don't have the complete picture yet.'

Marshall nudged Bankole's arm. 'Stop,' Marshall said. His colleague pulled the car up a hundred metres from Kate's house. 'That's her there,' he said.

Bankole followed Marshall's line of sight. 'What's she doing?'

Marshall narrowed his eyes. 'I don't know.'

The two officers watched as Kate and eight men climbed into a minibus.

'Should I follow?' Bankole said.

'No. We'll talk to her neighbours and see if they know anything.'

As the minibus disappeared out of sight, Bankole drove forward and parked outside Kate's house. The two officers headed along the footpath of the house next to Kate's, and Marshall knocked.

'There's something pinned to her door,' Bankole said.

'See what it says,' Marshall said as the door opened. He turned to face an older woman. 'Sorry to bother you,' he said and held out his badge. 'Detective Sergeant Marshall. Do you know where your neighbour is?'

'No. She left with a load of men just now.'

'Really?'

'I don't know what's going on in that house,' she said, 'but blokes have been arriving at all hours of the day and night.'

'Do you know her well?' he said as Bankole joined him.

The woman folded her arms. 'Hardly know her at all. She hasn't lived here long. She told me she moved back from abroad – Australia, I think. We keep ourselves to ourselves.'

'Ok, thanks,' he said before turning and heading back to his car, closely followed by Bankole.

'Well?' Marshall said as he reached the vehicle. 'What did it say?'

'It had her mobile number on it.' Bankole furrowed his brow. 'It said *if you are one of the chosen*, phone.'

'One of the chosen?'

'That's what it said, Ken.' Bankole took out his mobile and showed Marshall the photo he'd taken.

The officers climbed into the vehicle, and Marshall took out his phone. 'I'll give her a ring,' he said. It rang for a few seconds.

'Hi, Kate Carver.'

'Miss Carver, it's DS Marshall.'

'Oh, hello there.'

'I wondered if we could have a chat? We're outside your house.'

'I'm out at present. Could we perhaps do it tomorrow?'

Marshall raised his eyebrows at Bankole, who leant in closer. 'Are you going to be out all day?' Marshall said.

'Erm, yes.'

Marshall indicated for Bankole to start up the engine. 'Ok. Tomorrow.' He hung up and turned to face his colleague. 'There's something fishy going on.'

'What did she say?'

'She said she'll talk with us tomorrow.'

'Maybe we should have followed her?' Bankole said.

Marshall rubbed his chin. 'Maybe we should have. I don't suppose you got the license plate?'

'No, but it's from Pattersons' hire. I could give them a ring. We know her address, so they'll have details.'

'Yeah. Do that.' He stared back towards the house. 'Definitely something dodgy going on.'

'There's nothing in her past, though. What she told us checked out.'

Marshall drummed the dashboard. 'She hasn't been back here long. Who knows what she got up to in Australia. See if you can find anything about her from her family.'

Bankole nodded. 'Back to the station?'

Marshall rubbed his chin. 'No. We'll grab a coffee, then come back here.'

'In case someone else shows up?'

'Yeah. If they phone her, she might tell them where she is.' He looked at Bankole and smiled. 'We'll follow them.'

Kate pointed to a road on the left. 'Down there,' she said.

Piotr manoeuvred the van down the narrow lane and along the bumpy road. Up ahead stood a house, barely visible within the trees.

'That's it,' she said. 'Pull up there.'

Piotr brought the vehicle to a halt and looked at Kate. 'Is this it? Are you sure? It's dilapidated.'

She nodded. 'This is it. I'm sure of it.'

Simon leant forward. 'Are we just going to knock?'

Kate studied the house. 'It does look run down, but this is definitely the place.' She looked at Simon. 'You and Piotr come with me. The others stay here.'

Kate's phone rang. 'Hello,' she said. 'Have you got transport … I'll text you the postcode.' She hung up. 'Another one. He's going to join us here.' She sent a quick message and pushed the mobile back into her pocket. 'Right,' she said. 'Let's go.'

Kate, Simon and Piotr climbed from the vehicle and headed towards the house. A gate hung precariously on one hinge as they reached the path leading to the property and trod their way along the cracked and overgrown path. She stopped at the door and knocked. Nothing stirred, so she knocked again, much louder. But, again, no sound from within.

Simon took hold of the rusty handle and turned it. 'It's locked,' he said.

'What about around the back?' Piotr said.

The other two nodded, and the three of them made their way around the property to the rear.

Kate pointed to a door. 'It's slightly open.' She hurried across and waited for Piotr and Simon to join her. Simon pushed, but the door resisted his effort. 'It's stuck.'

Piotr put his shoulder against the door. 'Together,' he said. Simon positioned himself behind Piotr, and the pair pushed. The door scraped and squeaked but opened enough for a person to squeeze through.

Kate placed a hand on Simon's arm. 'I'll go first.'

Simon glanced at Piotr, then back to Kate. 'Are you sure?'

She nodded and stepped through the gap and inside. The two men followed, and they found themselves in almost darkness. Only the meagre light from the door gave them any illumination.

Kate cursed. 'We should have brought a torch or something.'

Piotr pulled his phone from his pocket and turned on the torch. 'It's better than nothing.'

The other two did the same, and they slowly crept forward. The inside of the house appeared worse than the outside. Wallpaper hung loosely from deeply fissured walls. Split and warped floorboards creaked with every footfall as the trio made their way along a corridor with two doors at the far end. Kate paused and surveyed their surroundings. 'Where are the other rooms?' she said.

Piotr and Simon traced the same journey Kate's eyes had. Piotr shrugged. 'I'm not familiar with English architecture,' he said.

Simon rubbed his chin. 'It does seem a bit odd. However ...' he said looking at Kate, 'it reduces our options.'

Kate sighed. 'It does. That door it is then.'

They reached the large wooden doors. Kate put her hand onto the wood and ran her fingers across its surface, loosening flakes of long ago applied varnish which dropped to the floor.

She once again surveyed her surroundings. 'There's something not right.'

Simon studied the two doors. 'They're huge. Yet from there ...' He nodded back the way they'd come. '... They didn't appear so.'

Piotr placed a hand on the door. 'It reminds me of my church back home, although the doors there are in a much better state.'

Kate sucked in air, reached for the round handle on one of the doors and turned. The door swung open without resistance, and the three of them gasped as they entered.

Marshall nudged Bankole. 'He turned down that track,' Marshall said.

Bankole glanced across. 'Shall I follow?'

'Yeah. But don't put the car lights on. It's getting dark, and they may see them.'

The officers' car slowed as the pair watched the other vehicle halt a few hundred metres away.

'Stop,' Marshall said. 'We'll walk from here.'

'Shall I call for backup?'

'Not yet. Let's see what's happening first.'

Kate, Simon and Piotr stood inside the church and gawped at their surroundings.

'How on earth ...' Simon said.

Kate slowly spun on the spot. 'It's huge.'

'But the house ...' Piotr said. 'The house isn't large enough to ...'

The church groaned, and the three turned in unison as a piece of plaster fell from the wall exposing the ancient brickwork beneath.

'Look,' Kate said, pointing upwards to a hole in the roof, giving a perfect view of the full moon outside.

'I didn't see that hole before,' Piotr said.

'I don't think it was there before,' Kate said. 'Nearhope.'

Piotr frowned and glanced at Simon. 'Nearhope?' Piotr said.

'The place you told us about?' Simon said.

Kate nodded. 'Don't ask me how I know, but that's Nearhope out there.'

'What's happening to this church?' Simon said.

Kate turned to face the two men. 'It's dying. Felix told us that it dies at night, only to be reborn in the morning.' She walked along the aisle with the two men following her, then stopped and stared down at the alter. Lying on the floor was a form that looked like The Nazarian, his arms stretched wide in a cruciform shape.

'It can't be him,' Piotr said. 'This man's been dead for a long time.'

Tears fell freely from Kate's eyes. 'It's him.' She dropped to her knees in front of the body. 'Look.' Kate pointed at his hands – the palms facing upwards – and a hole in the centre of each, where blood gently oozed.

'How could he make those videos if he was already dead?' Simon said.

Kate rubbed her eyes with the sleeve of her sweater. 'I don't know.'

Juan appeared in the doorway and gasped as he stared around the room. 'Come quickly,' he said as he continued to absorb the setting.

'What's up?' Piotr said.

'Just come.'

Piotr and Simon hurried along the aisle, and Simon paused at the threshold. 'Kate,' he shouted. 'Are you coming?'

She ignored him, her eyes fixed on those of The Nazarian. Simon shook his head and followed after Piotr and Juan. He burst outside and raced around to the front where the others stood next to the van looking at something, and as he joined them, he followed their gaze. Up ahead of them stood a ghostly figure. The men stood transfixed as it approached, and as it did so, they as one, dropped to their knees. The figure grew brighter into a ball of light that enveloped them, and then it disappeared into nothing.

Marshall looked at Bankole. 'I think we'd better have that backup, Adi. There's definitely something going on here.'

Bankole took out his phone. 'Did you see that light?' he said, searching for the number.

'Yeah. Bloody weird.'

'This is DS Bankole,' he said. 'We require immediate backup. DS Marshall and I are …'

Kate stood and turned before trudging along the aisle. She stopped about halfway down and slowly turned. In front of her stood something. Covering her eyes from the blinding light until the intensity lessened, she finally opened her eyes and recognised what it was. Two large, white wings spread majestically from its back, stretching sideways. Unafraid, Kate stepped closer and closed her eyes once more, allowing the angel to wrap itself around her. When she opened them again, she was alone, and the room she stood in was no longer a church. An ordinary living room replaced it, devoid of furniture and decorations except for a large painting which hung above the spot where a fireplace once stood. The depiction of Christ on the cross stared back at her. Roused from her musings by sirens, Kate hurried outside to see a fleet of police vehicles heading along the track. The men all knelt with their eyes closed and their hands clasped together in prayer. She spun around as the house she'd just exited creaked and groaned before collapsing into rubble.

Marshall and Bankole stepped forward from the darkness and over to her. 'Good evening, Miss Carver,' Marshall said. 'Would you like to explain what this is all about?'

BRAXAS

Paulo lifted his head from his chest and looked up at Asmodeus as Cain and Martin entered.

'Sorry I've kept you waiting,' Asmodeus said.

Paulo tugged at his arm restraints. 'What are you going to do with me?'

Asmodeus circled Paulo. 'I require some information,' he said. 'It would be helpful to know what your opponent intends.'

'Opponent?'

Asmodeus stopped close to him and dropped onto his haunches. 'We both know who we are talking about, perhaps …' Asmodeus held up a finger. 'Perhaps it would help if you could see me as I really am.'

Paulo said nothing as Asmodeus smiled at him. 'As I said, I borrowed this body, so I have no need for yours. However, a friend of mine would very much like to utilise it.' He clicked his fingers, and Cain handed him a book. Asmodeus held up the volume. 'I got this from an elderly gentleman. He was incredibly knowledgable about the occult.' He held it close to Paulo. 'Impressive, isn't it?'

Paulo curled his lip and looked away.

'The pages are made from human skin, flayed from the bodies of the truest believers.'

'Believers in what?' Paulo said.

Asmodeus laughed. '*He who reigns supreme*, of course.'

Paulo frowned. 'I don't …' His eyes widened as Asmodeus stared at him with blood-red eyes. A cracking sound erupted as two small nubs on Asmodeus's temples crunched their way upwards, and as Paulo continued to watch, these grew in length and girth, twisting in an ever-growing spiral. Martin glanced at Cain, who seemed entranced, then looked back towards Asmodeus. His talon-like fingers stretched outward as sharpened fingernails protruded from the ends. Asmodeus was now unrecognisable from his former self, with long canine teeth hanging from his dark-red gums.

Paulo gasped at the demonic figure before him. His mouth dropped open in wordless surprise.

'Do you see who I am,' the Demon rasped. 'Do you now see what you are up against?'

Paulo closed his eyes against the aberration and uttered a prayer under his breath.

Asmodeus placed a finger under his captive's chin and slightly lifted it. 'Look at me,' he said. His voice a deep and foreboding sound, almost a growl. 'Look at me,' he shouted.

Paulo blinked his eyes open. 'The Lord is my shepherd ...'

Asmodeus laughed. 'Even now, you call for him.' Asmodeus turned and walked a few feet away with arms outstretched before spinning around. 'I will enjoy seeing your soul ripped from you. I will enjoy hearing you cry for your god. I will laugh as, impassively, he does nothing to help you, but don't worry, your soul will be well looked after in my realm.'

Paulo closed his eyes again and continued to utter his prayers.

Asmodeus turned to Cain and Martin. 'Prepare the room,' he said.

The two men dropped onto their knees and lowered their heads. 'Yes, my prince,' they said in unison before hurrying off.

Asmodeus took hold of Paulo's hair and pulled his head backwards, and as Paulo opened his eyes again, Asmodeus lowered his face to his. 'Yes,' he hissed. 'I shall enjoy your demise.'

Kate sat at the desk across from Marshall and Bankole. Marshall picked up a sheet of paper and studied it before looking at her. 'Miss Carver,' he said and placed it down. 'Are you happy with this account?' he said, tapping the statement.

Kate sighed. 'Yes. It's as I told you.'

Marshall scoffed. 'You and the gentlemen along the corridor are part of a ghost-seeking group?'

'Yes.'

Marshall smiled and shook his head. 'I'm sorry, Miss Carver, but I've never listened to such rubbish.'

'Why did you go to that house?' Bankole said.

'I heard it was haunted.'

'From who?' Marshall said.

'On the internet. I can't exactly remember where?'

'You do realise,' Marshall said, 'that it's an offence to enter someone's property uninvited? There's a sign warning people of the dangers of entering the property. You and your friends may well have caused the house to collapse.'

'I know it's an offence, but we were invited.'

'Who invited you?' Bankole said.

'The Nazarian.'

Bankole frowned. 'The guy from the videos?'

Kate folded her arms. 'Yes.'

'Your neighbour told us that men were coming and going at all hours,' Marshall said.

'She's just a nosy cow. Anyway, when did it become an offence to have visitors?'

Marshall smiled. 'Lucky for you, it isn't.' He took a piece of paper from his pocket and slid it across the desk. 'Can you explain this?'

'I left it on my door. There are supposed to be twelve, thirteen, including me. But, some of the others were late, so I left a note.'

'It says chosen?' Marshall said.

'There were only a few places to go on the ghost hunt. I chose twelve. Hence, chosen.'

There was a knock on the door, and an officer poked her head inside. 'I've got the info, guv.'

Marshall and Bankole stood. 'If you'd like to wait here, Miss Carver,' Marshall said, 'we'll be right back.'

'I'd rather like to go home. I haven't done anything wrong.'

'Well,' Marshall said, 'you will just have to be patient until we get to the bottom of this.'

Kate sighed again as the two officers left. Marshall closed the door and looked at the constable. 'Well?'

'Nothing from Australia. She's squeaky clean.'

'The house?' Marshall said.

'The house is owned by someone who lives abroad.' She glanced at her pad. 'Phillip Worthington. I'm unable to contact him, but I managed to speak with the solicitor who deals with Mr Worthington's affairs in this country. He emailed his client, and this is his response.' She handed him a piece of paper.

Marshall read it before handing it to Bankole. 'Thanks, Jill,' he said.

'She actually did have permission,' Bankole said.

Marshall rolled his eyes. 'Apparently.'

'What do we do now?

Marshall groaned. 'Let her go, I suppose.'

'And the others?'

'Them as well.' Marshall and Bankole entered the interview room. 'You're free to go, Miss Carver.'

Kate smiled. 'I'm happy to be of help.'

Paulo hung from the ceiling. His hands were tied behind his back, the rope suspending him fastened to his wrists. Asmodeus entered with Cain and Martin and wandered across to their victim.

'This form of torture,' he said to Paulo, 'is called strappado.' Paulo groaned. 'By now,' Asmodeus said, 'your shoulders have been dislocated. I imagine the pain you are feeling is immense.'

Paulo began to utter a prayer as Asmodeus laughed. He placed his index finger on Paulo's cheek and, using the talon-like nail, drew it down. Blood trickled from the deep incision inflicted by it.

'I could do anything to you,' Asmodeus said. 'You have no idea how much pain I can inflict.' He placed his hands on Paulo's shoulders and pulled him down. Paulo screamed, the additional weight causing ever-increasing agony. 'However,' his torturer continued, 'we require your body.' He nodded towards Cain and Martin, who cut him down. Paulo fell to the floor and groaned. 'Put him on the table,' Asmodeus ordered. Cain severed the ropes binding Paulo's wrist, and with the help of Martin, they hoisted him onto a table before restraining his ankles.

Paulo watched through barely open eyes as a pentagon was drawn around the table and black candles lit at each point. Asmodeus entered the circle and strolled across to Paulo. 'Souls,' he said, 'are bound to the person. The more pious the individual, the more tightly they bind. So I needed to weaken your resolve physically to enable me to weaken your resolve mentally.' He placed his hands on Paulo's cheeks. 'This will hurt more if you resist. But I need some information from you before I can carry on. My friend, Braxas, is waiting.'

'I'll tell you nothing. I'd rather die.'

Asmodeus laughed. 'That choice is not yours to make.' He lowered his head and glared at Paulo. Paulo resisted the mental probing, but the more he did, the greater the pain. Every inch of him stung. The atoms in his body danced in a symphony of agony that he could not hold back. The blood, which now trickled from his ears and nose, dripped onto the table and the floor. Asmodeus threw his head backwards. 'Ah,' he said. 'I see everything. I see all your desires. All your secrets. I see your guilt and your shame.' He paused. 'And there it is.' Asmodeus looked at Cain. 'Fetch me the book.'

Cain hurried to the other side of the room and snatched up the huge volume, handing it to Asmodeus. The Demon opened the pages and began to recite an incantation. Paulo's body spasmed as he shook against his fetters and then screamed. His eyes were wide and staring as the thing that was his, the thing that endured for eternity, was ripped from him. His essence was now deposited into a place of unremitting darkness. A place where only bottomless loneliness existed. A place where torture and torment reigned forever.

Asmodeus looked down at Paulo's bloodied, still, and seemingly lifeless body. But then the eyes snapped open, and he smiled at Asmodeus.

'My prince,' he said. 'It's good to see you again.' Cain and Martin untied him, and he sat up.

'Your shoulders,' Martin said. 'They're dislocated.'

Paulo looked Martin up and down before wrenching his right shoulder. It crunched as he put the joint back in place, repeating the process with his other arm.

Martin gasped. 'Doesn't it hurt?'

Asmodeus laughed. 'There is a lot you do not understand about pain. Humans are different from us.' Asmodeus looked back to Paulo. 'Let me introduce you to my friends here. This is Martin and Cain. They have been most helpful in recruiting others.'

The face of Paulo sneered. 'Humans are weak.'

Asmodeus patted him on the arm. 'Nevertheless, they have been useful.'

Paulo jumped from the table, rotated his neck, and held out his arms as if getting accustomed to his new body. 'I have news of Sicarius.'

'Later,' Asmodeus said. 'I want you up to date with this world. The Nazarian is amassing his army.'

Paulo closed his eyes and appeared to be concentrating. His features slowly changing from those of Paulo to those of Paulo and someone else.

'Braxas,' Asmodeus said. 'It's good to see you again.' Asmodeus's features returned to something resembling a human, yet retaining a hint of a Demon.

'If we want to defeat him,' Braxas said, 'we need more of our brethren.'

'I am aware of this, but it's not easy.' He turned away and pondered. 'We will have to get them through the barrier somehow.' He turned to face Braxas again. 'I will give it some thought.'

Bankole entered Marshall's office and closed the door. 'You're never going to believe it, Ken.'

Marshall looked up. 'Believe what?'

'They're gone.'

'Who?'

'The nine blokes,' Bankole said.

Marshall frowned. 'What the hell are you on about? I told you to release them.'

'That's the thing. When I went to the custody cells, they'd gone.'

'Who let them go?'

Bankole shrugged. 'No one. They just disappeared.'

Marshall stood. 'Adi,' he said, 'nine men can't vanish from our cells.'

'I asked the custody sergeant if anyone had been to see them, and he said not. He was as shocked as me when we opened the doors.'

'Have you checked the CCTV?'

'Of course. Nothing. It shows them going in but doesn't show them leaving.'

Marshall raced towards the door. 'Show me.'

THE DEMON'S PLAN

Asmodeus sat behind his desk as Braxas entered and, looking up, indicated for his dextral to sit. 'Do you understand the task ahead of us?' Asmodeus said.

Braxas slid into the seat opposite. 'This is a peculiar world indeed. However, it offers us a great opportunity.'

'Yes it does. What are your thoughts?'

He stared directly into Asmodeus's eyes. 'Your plan is good, but I think we can improve.'

Asmodeus sat back in his chair and waved a hand, indicating for him to continue. 'The plague you intend to spread throughout the world …?' Braxas said.

'What of it?'

'It seems to me that delivering and infecting the whole of humankind is an arduous task. Therefore, would it not be better if they came to you looking for assistance?'

'Carry on,' Asmodeus said.

'This virus of theirs only kills a small number. The weak and infirm, mostly. These are of little use anyway. However, if we increase the death rate by only a small amount, then offer them a vaccine we have manufactured, their governments will do the job for us.'

'A vaccine. What good would that do?'

Braxas smiled. 'Within the vaccine, unbeknown to them, is a death sentence for many.'

'How so?'

'The human woman we had working for us, who escaped with Sicarius, left behind some interesting information. The phage we hoped to introduce into the Janus population works. With one small drawback.' Asmodeus nodded for him to carry on. 'It doesn't start infecting people immediately. It takes six to twelve months for the genetic variant to activate.'

Asmodeus grinned. 'By which time earth's population will be vaccinated?'

'Exactly.'

'Will the phage work on humans?'

'Our laboratories lack the expertise on human subjects to manufacture it, but earth's don't.'

Asmodeus stood and wandered across to the blazing fire. 'I already have a facility up and running. The problem we have at present is that as the virus increases in mortality rate, it appears to decrease its ability to be passed from human to human.'

'Do you think this can be overcome?'

Asmodeus nodded. 'We are not too far away from a more virulent strain with the same, or even increased, ability to infect.'

'Good.' Braxas leant forward. 'The hierarchy in this land is unusual, but I don't think it would be that difficult to infiltrate the government.'

'I already have several people in place,' Asmodeus said.

'I see. You have been busy, my prince.'

Asmodeus sat again. 'How can you get the phage through the barrier?'

'One of our men will carry it – it's harmless to us – then he would pass through the barrier conjoined with a human.'

'Conjoined?' Asmodeus said.

'It's one of the secrets Sicarius gave up. That is how he infiltrated our lands without being spotted. He has the ability to conjoin and un-conjoin at will. But the human must be alive.'

Asmodeus scoffed. 'You might as well take their soul if they have to be alive.'

'But the human could be used more than once.'

'I see,' Asmodeus said. 'Do you have a human in mind?'

'The one who gave us Sicarius.'

Asmodeus stroked his chin. 'Who from our number will you entrust with this?'

'I have someone in mind. Someone we can rely upon.'

Asmodeus stood again. 'Good. We will begin at once.'

Braxas eased himself out of the chair. 'The humans you have working for us? Can you really trust them?'

Asmodeus shrugged. 'They are useful for now. We will have no need for them in the future.' He smiled. 'Their hearts are delicious, however.'

'The two you trust the most,' Braxas said. 'Cain and Martin?'

'They have been loyal, although Cain was a little put out when he discovered my dextral was coming.' Asmodeus laughed. 'I think he had aspirations to be my right hand.'

Braxas joined in Asmodeus's laughter. 'How absurd.' But as

Asmodeus turned away from him, Braxas furrowed his brow and closely studied his master.

Kate groaned as her doorbell rang. She tramped her way into the hall and unenthusiastically pulled open the door.

DS Marshall stood outside. 'Miss Carver.'

'I thought we'd done this?' she said.

'Could I have another word? I know I'm probably not your favourite person, but—'

She waved him indoors. 'I suppose,' she said. Marshall followed her inside and stood in the living room as Kate sat and indicated for him to do the same.

Marshall slumped into the armchair. 'Have you been to see your friend?'

'I phoned earlier. There's been no change.' She rubbed her stomach and grimaced.

'Everything all right?' he said.

'Just a bit of tummy ache.' She stood. 'I'll get us some drinks. Tea or coffee?'

'Tea would be fine. Milk, no sugar.'

Kate headed into the kitchen, quickly gathered the drinks together, along with some biscuits, and returned to the lounge. 'Help yourself to biscuits,' she said as she positioned herself opposite Marshall. She lifted her coffee to her lips and took a sip. 'So,' she said, 'I'm sure you didn't come here just to drink tea?'

Marshall placed his cup back down and cupped his hands together. 'As I'm sure you'll realise,' he said, 'all of this appears ...' He rubbed his chin, 'appears strange.'

Kate sighed. 'What do you want me to say?'

'I want you to tell me everything you know.' He lowered his head slightly. 'I know you haven't been totally honest with us, with me.'

Kate brought her hands up to her face and sighed loudly. 'I wouldn't know where to start.'

'The nine men you were with at the house? They disappeared from the police station not long after you left.'

'You did say they were free to go.'

'I'm not sure you understand. They were being held in our custody cells. When one of our officers went to release them ... When he went to the cells ...' He looked directly into Kate's eyes, 'they were gone.'

Kate frowned. 'Gone?'

Marshall nodded. 'We've checked the CCTV, and there is no sign of them leaving. However, there is a three-minute gap in the tape recording.'

'Are you saying it was doctored?'

'What I'm saying, Miss Carver—'

'Kate. Call me Kate.'

'What I'm saying, Kate ...' He rubbed his chin again, 'in broad daylight, nine men somehow got out of their locked cells and made their way from the police station, and not one officer spotted them. I've been a policeman for twenty years and never seen anything like this.'

She held up a hand and stood. 'Excuse me,' she said and hurried from the room and into the downstairs toilet.

Marshall strained to listen but could clearly hear her vomiting. She returned a few moments later, her eyes red and puffy. 'Sorry about that,' she said. 'It came over me all of a sudden.'

'Are you sure you're ok?'

'Fine. It must be something I've eaten.' Kate blew out her cheeks. 'Are you a religious man?'

Marshall frowned. 'Why do you ask?'

'Indulge me.'

'I'm Catholic. I go to church most weeks. I wouldn't say I'm devout, but ... well, let's say, once you've been inculcated into Catholicism, it's difficult to shake off.'

'I'll tell you everything, but you may struggle to believe what I'm about to say.'

Marshall clasped his hands together and leant forward. 'Try me.'

Asmodeus, looking into the fire's roaring flames, turned as Braxas entered. 'I need you to go to the laboratory and check on the progress,' Asmodeus said. 'Cain will take you.'

Braxas, with his hands behind his back, nodded. 'I don't trust him,' he said. 'It would be better if we had more of our kin here.'

Asmodeus held up a hand. 'I know it would, but we have to work with what we have. We have no way of getting them across the threshold yet.'

'But you got me through.'

Asmodeus nodded. 'I know, but that's different. Using one of The Nazarian's disciples allowed us that luxury. Unless we can locate the others, we won't be able to do it again.'

'But how will we hope to take this realm without our brethren?'

Asmodeus smiled. '*He who reigns supreme* has the power, but not yet. So we must weaken and destroy the town that sits between our realm and this place. It will also allow us to get your trusted Demon and the phage.'

'Do you want me to send a message?'

Asmodeus stood. 'Not yet. There is something I am missing. A piece of this jigsaw which I cannot yet see.'

'Sicarius?'

Asmodeus shook his head. 'Sicarius is no longer a threat.' He turned away and looked into the fireplace again. 'It's important that we are not impetuous.' He turned back to face Braxas. 'This is a chess game.'

His dextral frowned. 'Chess?'

'A game the humans play. It involves different pieces, each with its own ability to move. Some pieces are more powerful than others. So we need to remove our opposition's strongest pieces before we attack. Go to the laboratory as I say.' Braxas bowed. 'Braxas,' Asmodeus said, 'make sure you use your human form. We don't want to startle the natives.'

Braxas climbed into the car next to Cain.

'How are you settling in?' Cain said.

Braxas fixed him with a stare. 'Very well. Asmodeus told me that you were not happy about my arrival.'

'I-I-wouldn't say that.'

Braxas smiled. 'Don't worry, I'm not angry. In my world,' he continued, 'making alliances is vital.'

'Asmodeus has told me.'

'Did he tell you that he doesn't trust me?'

'Well …' Cain said. 'I'm not sure—'

Braxas held up his hand. 'Don't worry. This is between you and me. There may come a time when you have to choose sides.'

'I couldn't do anything that would go against the Prince.'

'Of course not,' Braxas said, 'but sometimes the Prince needs to be pushed in the right direction for his own good. Some of his decisions in the past have been catastrophic for my kin. We must ensure that he is led along the right path. Do you understand?'

'Yes.'

'Good. And Cain …' Braxas said, taking hold of Cain's arm, 'this conversation never happened.'

'I understand. What about Martin?'

'We will keep this to ourselves. You and I have a special bond now.'

Kate sat back in her chair and looked at Marshall. 'I said you wouldn't believe it.'

Marshall slowly shook his head. 'Even you must admit,' he said, 'this is hard to believe?'

She sighed. 'Not long ago, I came back home from Australia. I got in touch with Mary, my long-time friend, and then all this madness began.'

'Let's say for a minute that this is true. This place you mentioned …'

'Nearhope,' she said.

'Yes, Nearhope. What is it?'

She cupped her hands together. 'Felix described it as a place between our world and Hell, a hinterland. Nearhope acts as a buffer between the two.'

'How can you be certain that Felix and Reece didn't concoct this story?'

'And then form a suicide pact?'

'Yes,' Marshall said.

She held out her hands. 'I can't. All I can tell you is that I've known Felix for a long time. He's good friends with my mum and dad. So I'm certain he wouldn't do something like that.'

'The Nazarian …? You didn't know him?'

'No.'

'Yet you say he compelled you to go to that house?'

Kate sighed again. 'Yes. Through my dreams.'

'Dreams are notoriously unreliable.'

'Not these dreams. They're like nothing I have ever experienced, leaving me feeling that they are real.'

Marshall nodded slowly. 'What about your friend Mary?'

'She can confirm this when she comes out of her coma.' Kate picked up her empty cup. 'Mary said that The Nazarian gave her messages after his videos, but I never saw them. Yet …' she deeply furrowed her brow, 'I believed her. I had no reason not to.'

'And you claim you met The Nazarian at his house?'

'Yes, but he was dead.'

'We didn't find anyone, though.'

She shrugged. 'I can't explain it. He appears to give us a small amount of information. He only tells us what he wants us to know. Maybe he has a reason for this.'

'Why would he have you and the men travel there when he was already dead?'

Kate shrugged again. 'I can't answer that.'

'Did anything happen while you were there?'

'No,' Kate said. 'But …'

'But?'

She narrowed her eyes in concentration. 'I remember going inside the house, yet I found myself in an empty room. I have no recollection of how I got there.'

'What about the men?'

'I didn't have time to ask them,' she said. 'I remember being in the room and then going outside to see where they were. There was this blinding light when I got outside, and your lot turned up.'

'I saw the light,' he said. 'It could have been some trick.'

'Maybe.' She looked directly into his eyes and tapped her head. 'But something inside here tells me it wasn't. Do you feel it?'

Marshall rubbed his chin. 'Yes. Yes I do. I haven't told anyone else this,' he said, 'but within the light, I caught sight of something.'

'A man?'

Marshall laced his fingers together and glanced downwards before lifting his head to look directly at Kate. 'Not just any man,' he said. 'I saw Christ.'

KATE – Marshall left soon after and appeared just as puzzled as when he came. I attempted to remember what happened in the room at the Nazarian's house, but the more I tried to, the further it distanced itself from me, like a mental piece of ice melting away under the searing sun.

I loaded the dishwasher, turned off the lights and headed to bed. Then I noticed it when I took off my jeans and sweatshirt. My stomach looked slightly distended. I slowly ran my hand across my belly and turned side-on in the mirror to confirm what I already knew. I had a bump. The sort associated with a woman in the early stages of pregnancy.

I laughed at how preposterous that was. I hadn't been sexually active for well over six months. Nine, possibly. However, the smile on my face slowly slipped away as I brought my hands upwards and gently probed my breasts. I quickly undid my bra, allowing it to fall to the floor, and stared open-mouthed at my swollen nipples. Could I be having a false pregnancy, but another thought elbowed its way into my head. A thought that seemed genuine. Could I be pregnant?

HEADRON

Celestine crept through the woods and paused outside the decrepit building before entering. Then, pulling her dagger free from its shield, she melted into one of the dark corners but didn't have to wait long as someone appeared in the doorway.

'Celestine,' he said, 'are you here?'

Stepping free from the shadows, she made her way over to him. The pair embraced and then sat. 'You have news?' she said.

Headron nodded. 'About the phage they've been working on that will exterminate the Janus.'

'Have they succeeded?'

He sighed. 'They've halted the experiments.'

'Good news indeed, but why?'

'They're trying to develop something else. It has a human element to it.'

'Human element?'

'My source is unsure why and they are guarding it closely, but he believes that the phage is being developed to kill humans.'

She stood. 'Why would they do that?'

'Sathanas is making inroads into Asmodeus's territory, and *He who reigns supreme* will not intervene. As a result, Sathanas is becoming ever more popular with him. The feeling is that Asmodeus requires something to impress the powerful one.'

'And?'

'There is talk of leading a battalion into the town.'

She scoffed. 'They can't do that. It's forbidden. History tells how destructive it was when tried long ago.'

'Some people doubt the veracity of the story.' He sighed again. 'Braxas has crossed the threshold.'

'How could he do that? He would need the soul and body of one of the twelve.'

'It appears he has it.'

Celestine turned away. 'This is terrible news.'

'What do you think they're planning?'

She turned back to face him. 'Isn't it obvious? They are planning to take the phage across the threshold and into the realm of the humans. Asmodeus is planning to conquer their lands.'

'You've been through the threshold yourself,' he said. 'Would that be possible?'

She slumped onto a rock. 'Humans are like our children. They lack the cunning of our brethren.'

'What about The Nazarian? Surely, he would resist this. They are his people.'

'It's not that easy. James told me why it's not possible. There are only certain ways he can intervene. He who once reigned over all the realms would forbid it.'

'What do you need me to do?'

'We need to release James. Only he would know the best course of action.'

'He may already have told them everything.'

She shook her head. 'He does not know everything. It was planned like that in case he got captured. Then, Asmodeus would need to claim you, Quinxious and me. We must ensure this does not happen.'

Headron nodded. 'Asmodeus would need a human to get anyone across the threshold. The townspeople cannot cross it. They have no soul.'

'He must have someone else with which to carry the phage. Somebody one of his men could conjoin with to enable them to pass through.'

'Felix or Reece?' he said.

'They made the ultimate sacrifice when they crossed.'

'Then it must be the human woman?'

Celestine pondered. 'Indeed.'

'Is she working with Asmodeus?'

'I don't know. But she must conjoin with me at some time, and I will attempt to find out then.'

Headron moved towards the door and paused. 'I have the two you need to conjoin with Felix and Reece. They are loyal.'

'Good. I'll give you a little time before I head back. Leave any messages in the usual place.' Headron nodded his understanding and left.

Marshall looked outside into the car park of the police station as Bankole entered his office.

'Did you speak with Kate Carver?' Bankole said.

'Er, yes,' he said.

'And?'

Marshall sat back in his seat. 'Nothing. She just stuck to the story she gave us.'

'Well,' Bankole said and puffed out his cheeks. 'Things just got a little weirder.'

'How?'

'Reece Sadler.'

Marshall rolled his eyes. 'In your own time, Adi.'

'His body went missing from the hospital mortuary.'

Marshall stared wide-eyed at Bankole. 'Missing?'

'Yeah. I had a phone call this morning from one of the staff. He was there last night because the attendant was preparing him for the post-mortem. When he returned, he'd gone.'

Marshall stood. 'We'd better get over there.'

'I thought you'd say that. The department head is expecting us.'

Marshall paused at the door. 'When we followed Kate Carver and the others to the house?'

'Yeah.'

Marshall rubbed his chin. 'When we saw that bright light? Did you see anything else?'

Bankole shrugged. 'Like what?'

'My eyes aren't what they were. I just thought you might have noticed something I didn't. Something within the light.'

Bankole shook his head. 'No. I think someone else was there, and Miss Carver and her friends were up to something. The light may have been a diversion. Maybe whoever shone it used it as a distraction to get away.'

'What do you think the light was?'

Bankole pondered. 'Some big floodlight. The guys have searched thoroughly and found nothing, so whatever it was must have been portable.'

Marshall nodded. 'Good.' He watched and stared at his colleague as he wandered away, then set off after him.

Marshall and Bankole were shown into the mortuary by an attendant. 'This is where Mr Sadler's body was,' the attendant said. 'I just nipped into the rear office,' he said, indicating a room over his shoulder. 'I was no more than five minutes. And when I returned …' He nodded at the empty table.

'You're sure no one could gain entry without you knowing?' Marshall said.

'No. Only a small number of people have access. You need to punch in the code to get inside.'

'What about CCTV?' Bankole said.

'We're having a little difficulty with it. Mr Grover, the mortuary supervisor, is trying to get IT to sort it out.'

'Ok,' Marshall said. 'Can you take us to him?'

'Follow me.' The attendant led the way and stopped at a door marked *private*. He knocked and waited until a voice told him to enter. 'This is DS Marshall and DS Bankole, Bill.'

'Ah, just in time,' Grover said. 'We've just managed to get this damn thing working.' He turned the screen around so that the others could view it. The men watched as the corridor to the mortuary came into view. The video continued for a few moments before the door to the morgue opened, and someone wearing a white coat and pushing a trolley exited. He made his way along the corridor and through the door at the far end.

'Do you recognise him?' Marshall said.

Grover glanced at the attendant and then back to Marshall. 'It's Gordon Jefferson, one of the porters. He brings the deceased down to the mortuary from the wards.'

'Why would he take Mr Sadler?' Bankole said.

Grover shrugged. 'I'm not sure, but surely there's an innocent explanation. Give me a minute, and I'll get him to come here.'

Grover picked up his phone and dialled. 'Can you send Gordon up here immediately ... What time did he go for his break?' He glanced across at the clock. 'Have you his mobile ...? Can you give him a ring?' Grover hung up. 'Gordon hasn't come back from his break. They're trying to ring him on his mobile, and they're going to get back to us.'

Marshall took out his mobile and called.

'Hi,' Kate said.

'I thought I'd better check in on you,' he said. 'How are you feeling?'

'Well, it's a little strange.'

'What is?'

'I think I'm pregnant?'

'I see.'

Kate sighed. 'I don't think you do. I can't be pregnant.'

'Then what makes you think you are?'

'My swollen stomach and breasts are a bit of a giveaway. Plus, my jeans are a little snug.'

Marshall frowned. 'What do you mean?'

'You saw me yesterday?'

'Yeah.'

'Can you come around here?' she said.

'I'm at the hospital at the moment.'

'Nothing serious, I hope?'

Marshall smiled. 'No. Police stuff. I'll pop in when I'm finished.'

'You do remember we're in lockdown?'

'This is police business. Maybe we could meet outside.'

'Do you know the common at the end of my road?'

'I know it.'

'It has a small car park there. Give me a ring, and I'll meet you.'

Bankole arrived, and Marshall held up a hand at him. 'Ok,' he said to Kate and hung up. 'What's happening, Adi?'

Bankole shook his head and blew out hard. 'They've found Gordon Jefferson.'

'This doesn't sound good.'

'He's been murdered. They found his body located at the rear of the building. No sign of Reece Sadler, though. It looks as if this is where whoever killed Gordon Jefferson collected Reece Sadler.'

'Show me,' Marshall said.

The pair made their way through the building and to the hospital's rear. Forensics had already arrived. Several people with blue suits milled around the body, and one leant over it.

'You got here quick,' Marshall said.

'We weren't far from here,' the man said.

Marshall surveyed the scene. 'There's a lot of blood.'

The man stood. 'He's had his throat cut. That's what probably killed him, but there's something else …'

Marshall raised his eyebrows. 'What?'

'Whoever killed him removed his heart.'

Marshall rubbed his face, then looked at Bankole. 'Have you called for backup?'

'Yes. Your phone was engaged, and it took me a while to find you.'

'No, you did right, Adi. We'll need a full sweep of the area. Any CCTV?'

'They're sorting it out now.'

'Let me know what they find.' He paused. 'I'd better inform the Chief.'

Martin stared through the glass window into the room. On the hospital bed, connected to monitoring equipment, lay Reece Sadler. Cain joined him at the window. 'He's stable,' Martin said.

'Good. Have you spoken with Asmodeus?'

'No,' Cain said. 'I thought it would be better to do it in person. I'm on my way now. You can come if you like?' He turned and headed along the corridor with Martin in pursuit.

Martin frowned. 'What's your game? You're not usually this nice.'

Cain paused. 'With Braxas here, we must show our worth to Asmodeus. Thomas let him down badly by not killing that woman, so we don't want him thinking he doesn't need us anymore.'

'Yeah. You've got a point.'

'What do you think of Braxas?'

Martin shrugged. 'I don't know what to make of him.'

'Do you get the impression that Asmodeus and Braxas don't really get on?'

'Yeah, I know what you mean.'

'Has Asmodeus said anything to you about him?'

Martin shook his head. 'No. Not a thing. You?'

'No. But if you and I are to survive all this, we must stick together.' He patted Martin on the arm and marched off. Martin smirked and then followed him.

KATE AND MARSHALL

Kate entered the car park and pulled up next to Marshall's car. He looked across at her with his mobile to his ear and mouthed *two minutes.*

She waited until he'd finished his call, then lowered her window, and Marshall did likewise. He held up his mobile. 'Work.'

'Anything interesting?'

'I was just bringing my boss up to date.' He paused and gathered his thoughts. 'I suppose I can tell you. We were called over to the hospital today. A body has been removed from the mortuary.'

'Removed? Do you mean taken?' she said. Marshall nodded. 'Who would do that?' she continued.

'It was Reece Sadler's body.'

Kate widened her eyes. 'Reece Sadler?'

'Yes.'

'Are you sure it hasn't been misplaced? I'm sure it's not—'

'It wasn't misplaced, Kate. It was taken by a porter who works at the hospital. We found his body at the back of the building. His throat was cut, and …'

'And?'

'Whoever killed him removed his heart.'

Kate stared at him, then turned away, deep in thought.

'In light of what you told me yesterday,' Marshall said. 'About your friend's story …'

She turned back to face him. 'What Felix told Mary and me?'

'Yes. It's probably just a coincidence. I mean,' he forced a laugh, 'Demons.'

Kate shrugged. 'I suppose.'

'Anyway,' he said, 'you said on the phone that you think you're pregnant?'

She opened the door and unsteadily climbed from the car. 'Well,' she said, 'what do you think?'

Marshall's jaw dropped open. 'I can't believe it. You look at least six months pregnant.'

Kate put her hand to her eyes. 'It's a little ...' Her voice trailed off as her bottom lip quivered.

Marshall leapt from his vehicle and made his way around to her, stopping a couple of metres away. 'I don't want to come much closer,' he said. 'What with covid.'

She waved a dismissive hand. 'Don't worry, it's probably just all the hormones coursing through me.'

'I'll be honest,' he said. 'I didn't believe you when you told me on the phone, but ... Have you been to see a doctor or taken a pregnancy test?'

'I took a test this morning. The look I got from the woman in the pharmacy who served me. She must have thought ... Well ...' Kate patted her belly. 'Anyway, I'm definitely pregnant. Luckily, I don't have to see my parents. They're on holiday in Italy and stuck there because of the lockdown. I've no idea how I'd explain it.'

Marshall's phone rang. 'Just a minute,' he said to her. 'DS Marshall ... Yes ... Are you sure? Ok. Have you done a DNA test ...? I'll let my boss know. Tomorrow?' He hung up and looked at Kate. 'Forensics found a piece of the heart near to the body.' He rubbed his chin.

'And?'

'It had teeth marks on one side of it. They think they're human.'

Kate opened the passenger door of her car and slumped onto the seat. 'It's real.' She fixed him with a stare. 'It's all real. What Felix and Reece told Mary and me is real.'

Marshall hurried into the police station and along to his office. Bankole joined his colleague and followed him into the room. 'Have you heard?' Bankole said.

'About the piece of heart?'

'Yeah.'

'Forensics rang me earlier.'

Bankole puffed out his cheeks. 'You'd better go and see the guv.'

'Why?' Marshall said.

'He popped down earlier and said he wanted to see you as soon as you arrived.'

'Do me a favour, Adi,' Marshall said. 'Get me a tea. I'm spitting feathers here.'

'No problem.'

Marshall waited for Bankole to return, then headed to his superior's office. He paused outside as he could hear voices, then knocked.

'Come in,' a voice shouted.

Marshall entered and glanced at the two men sitting opposite his superior, DI Stroud. He glanced again at the other two. One in uniform, the other not, before fixing his attention on Stroud. 'You wanted to see me, sir?'

'Yes, Ken. This is Detective Superintendent Fitzpatrick,' he said, nodding at the uniformed officer, 'and Detective Chief Inspector Stuart from Scotland Yard. They'll be taking over the investigation.'

'Which investigation?' Marshall said.

'The murder at the hospital,' Fitzpatrick said.

'Right. Can I ask why?'

Fitzpatrick glanced at his colleague, then indicated for DI Stroud to speak. 'The murder bears similarities to some others,' Stroud said.

'Ok. Are you saying there's a serial killer out there?'

Fitzpatrick turned to Marshall. 'We've had ten murders with the same MO as yours. Can you remember the prisoner that escaped from The Old Bailey recently? Two security guards were murdered in a similar way. And the prisoner who escaped from a secure mental hospital in Birmingham?' Fitzpatrick glanced towards Stuart before continuing. 'Two staff members were killed in a fashion not dissimilar to the guards. There have been others in Manchester, Newcastle and Glasgow. It seems unlikely that it's just one individual doing this due to the timescale of the murders and the distance they would have had to travel. So, we're putting together a task force.'

'Could it be a gang?' Marshall said. 'Acting out some form of occult fetish?'

Fitzpatrick studied him. 'What makes you say that?'

Marshall shrugged. 'With the heart being removed and eaten.'

Fitzpatrick laughed and glanced between the others. 'We don't know that they're eating the hearts.'

Stuart glared at Marshall. 'This is not a time to speculate, detective sergeant Marshall.'

'Sorry, but forensics said that a piece they found had—'

'I'm well aware of that information,' Fitzpatrick said. 'However, a piece of heart was only found in two locations. Yours and the one in Manchester.'

'So, where do I come in?' Marshall said.

'Nowhere,' Stroud said. 'You're still investigating Kate Carver and those men that went missing, aren't you?'

'I suppose.'

'Well,' Stroud said, 'that should keep you busy for now.'

Marshall moved towards the door. 'I'll get onto it now.'

'And Marshall,' Fitzpatrick said, 'this is between us four. I wouldn't want any of this spoken about outside this room. Understand?'

'Yes, sir.'

Marshall made his way back downstairs into the incident room. Bankole intercepted him as he entered. 'What did the guv want?' Bankole said.

'We're off the hospital murder.'

Bankole frowned. 'Why?'

'A Chief Super is taking over.'

'The one from the Yard?'

'Yeah. We've got to concentrate on the Carver case.'

'But I thought we'd hit a brick wall.' Bankole said.

Marshall sighed. 'We'll have to re-double our efforts. Have you checked CCTV outside the station?'

'Of course.'

'Widen the search. See if anything further afield picked something up.'

'Ok, but—'

'Adi,' Marshall said, 'just do it.'

Marshall stood and stretched his back. He gulped down the last of his tea, wandered to the window, and looked below into the car park. The two officers from Scotland Yard headed across to their car. They spoke briefly, and Fitzpatrick climbed into the driver's seat. Stuart paused and looked up at Marshall as if sensing being watched before climbing into the passenger seat. Marshall jumped as Bankole appeared next to him. 'Bloody hell, Adi, you nearly gave me a heart attack.'

'Sorry, Ken,' he said and followed Marshall's eye line. 'Wasn't keen on those two, especially that DI Stuart.'

'Yeah,' Marshall said, turning towards his desk.

'He's been asking me about Kate Carver and the men.'

Marshall halted. 'Kate Carver?'

'Yes. Seemed very interested. You'd have thought he'd enough to worry about with the murders.'

'What did you tell him?'

'I told him what happened.' Bankole frowned. 'The thing is, he didn't seem surprised when I told him the men disappeared from a locked cell.'

'What did you tell him about Kate Carver?'

'Everything. About the house and how she came up with that cock and bull story.'

'You didn't tell him where she lived?'

Bankole frowned again. 'Why would I do that? He could find that out if he ran a search.'

Marshall grabbed his coat. 'I have to be somewhere.'

'Do you want me to come?'

'No, it's personal stuff.' He glanced at the clock. 'I'll see you in the morning.'

Marshall hurried downstairs and outside. Reaching his car, he took out his phone. Kate's number rang for a few moments, then went to the answerphone. 'Shit,' he said under his breath and, climbing into his car, tossed the mobile onto the passenger seat before speeding off. Twenty minutes later, he reached her house but drove past it and parked around the corner.

His mobile rang. 'Hello,' Kate said.

'Hi, Kate, it's Ken Marshall.'

'I know. I've got your number stored on my phone.'

'Where are you?'

'I'm nearly home,' she said.

'Don't go there.'

'Why?'

'Do you remember where we met earlier?'

'Yeah,' she said.

'Meet me there, and I'll explain. Don't drive along your road, though. Instead, come in from the other end. As I said, I'll explain when I see you.'

Marshall hung up and drove off, driving the short distance to the car park. Kate arrived minutes later. He wound down his window and motioned for her to do likewise. 'What's up?' she said.

His eyes darted left and right. 'I'm not sure. Something's not right.'

'What?'

He took in a deep breath. 'Two senior officers arrived today from Scotland Yard.' He scoffed. 'Or that's where they said they were from. They're taking over Reece Sadler's disappearance and the murder at the hospital.'

'So?'

'They were asking about you.'

She raised her eyebrows. 'Me? Why?'

'I'm not sure, but they were parked outside when I drove past your house. I recognised the licence plate.'

'Couldn't they just have wanted to interview me because I know Reece?'

He rubbed his chin. 'I'm not sure. Just call it copper's intuition.'

'What do you want me to do?' She glanced towards the rear of the car. 'I've got a load of freezer stuff in the back. It's an ordeal, I can tell you. Shopping's bad enough, but when you're pregnant ...'

Marshall smiled and shook his head. 'Shopping's the least of our worries.'

'I'm sure—'

'But what happens if there is something up?' He pondered. 'Have you anywhere you can go?'

'My parents' normally, but as I said ...'

'On holiday.'

'And this, of course.' Kate pointed at her large bump.

'Anywhere else?'

'Oh,' she said and lifted her handbag. 'I've got Mary's key. I could go there, but I still think—'

'Humour me, Kate.'

'Ok. Shall I head there now?'

He held out his hand. 'Give me your phone.'

Kate fished the mobile from her bag and handed it to Marshall, who opened his glove box and pulled out another phone. He quickly entered his work's number into it. 'Take this. It's my personal phone. No one phones me on it. I've put my work number in it.' He tossed hers into the glovebox and slammed it shut. 'I'll make some enquiries, and then I'll come to see you.'

'How long?'

He checked his watch. 'About an hour. If anyone shows up, ring me.'

She nodded, put the car in gear and headed off.

Marshall pulled up outside the church and hurried along the path and inside. It was quiet and empty but for an old lady lighting a candle. He waited until she'd finished and smiled at her as she passed. Then, dropping to one knee near the altar, he genuflected and lit a candle himself.

'Ken,' a voice said behind him.

Marshall spun around. 'Hello, Father.'

'It's been a while.'

Marshall lowered his head. 'I've not been to church much since ...'

'It's good to see you again. Are you all right? You look a little—'

'I could do with a few minutes of your time, Father.'

'Of course.' He nodded towards the confessional boxes. 'Is there something—?'

'I haven't come for that,' he said. 'I just need a little information.'

'How intriguing. I'm just about to close for the night. Give me a hand, and we can have a cup of tea at the vicarage.'

Marshall sat deep in thought as Father Vernon entered, carrying a tray with tea and biscuits. 'Help yourself,' he said. The priest studied the officer as he filled his cup and picked it up.

'So,' Father Vernon said, doing likewise, 'you said you needed some information.'

Marshall closed his eyes and took a deep breath. 'What I'm about to tell you is ... well, let's just say I can hardly believe it myself.'

Father Vernon listened dispassionately as Marshall recounted the events of the previous week. Marshall finished, sat back in his seat and gulped at his tea.

Father Vernon tapped his chin with his index finger.

Marshall glanced upwards and sighed. 'I know it sounds stupid. Fanciful even.'

'This woman …'

'Kate,' Marshall said.

'Where is she now?'

'At her friend's house in Middlesbrough.'

'Will she come here?'

Marshall nodded. 'I think so.'

'Well,' Father Vernon said. 'We'd better see what she has to say.'

'Do you believe me?'

He took a sip of tea. 'Let's just say that I'm keeping an open mind. I've known you for many years, Ken, and I know you wouldn't lie to me, but …'

'But it sounds incredible?'

'It does.'

Marshall called Kate. 'Ken,' she said breathlessly. 'I was just about to ring you.'

'What's up.'

'There's a car parked outside Mary's house. Two men are inside. One of them came to the door and knocked, but I didn't answer.'

'And they're still there?'

'Yes.'

'Stay where you are. I'm on my way over.'

Father Vernon stared at Marshall. 'Is everything all right?' he said.

'Two men are outside where Kate is. I'm going over there now.'

'Would you like me to come?'

Marshall smiled. 'I'm not sure this is your area of expertise.'

The priest placed a hand on his arm. 'If what you told me is true ...' He pondered. 'Maybe I should come.'

Marshall nodded. The two men bounded from the vicarage across the gravel drive and jumped into his car.

Kate crept slowly upstairs, sure that she'd heard something outside around the back of the house. She strained to listen and put a hand to her mouth as the back door burst open. Then, hurrying along the landing and unsure what to do, she paused, listening to the voices below.

'What are we looking for?' a male voice said.

'Anything on Reece Sadler and any clues to where Kate Carver may have gone,' a second voice, tinged with a Scottish lilt, said.

'Shall I start upstairs?'

'Yeah. And be quick. We haven't got all day. We still need to get to the hospital and finish off the woman.'

Kate clutched a hand to her mouth again, this time more to stop herself from screaming than in shock. She silently made her way into the spare bedroom and looked around. The only place she could conceive of hiding was under the bed. Lowering herself slowly to the floor, she squeezed beneath it, then shimmied to the furthest point away from the door. With her heart pounding in her chest and her hand pushed tightly over her mouth, she waited.

THE VICARAGE

Marshall turned into the street and pulled up fifty metres from Mary's property.

'What do we do now?' Father Vernon said.

Marshall pulled out his badge. 'I'm a policeman just making enquiries.'

'And me?'

Marshall grabbed his jacket from the back seat. 'Put this on. It'll disguise who you are. Leave the talking to me.'

Father Vernon nodded and struggled into the jacket. Then the two men climbed from the vehicle and made their way along the road and up the path to Mary's house. Marshall paused to listen before knocking on the door.

The man stood in the spare room of Mary's house with his hand on the drawer's handle. He listened as the door downstairs was knocked again, then turned and trod his way downstairs and into the lounge. His mate stood there.

'Who's knocking?' he said.

'It's the copper. We'd better get going. He'll only ask awkward questions.'

The pair hurried into the kitchen, out into the garden, and made their way down the path before vaulting the fence and fleeing.

'Something's up,' Marshall said. 'We'll go around the back.' Father Vernon nodded his agreement, and the duo made their way down the side of the house to the rear. The door stood open, and Marshall glanced at Father Vernon before edging through the gap and inside the kitchen. Slowly, they crept further inside the property, into the lounge and then towards the stairs. Marshall put a finger to his lips and began his ascent. The stairs, annoyingly, creaked with every footfall. Finally, he reached the top and entered the front bedroom. Objects scattered about the floor, surrounded by divested drawers and other containers, lay everywhere. He turned and checked the second bedroom, its contents like the first. Marshall made his way into the spare room. The items in this room, except for an open drawer, seemingly in their usual place.

'Kate!' he shouted, more in hope than anything.

As something stirred beneath the bed, Marshall spun around, and Kate popped her head out. 'Help me out, Ken,' she said. 'You wouldn't believe the trouble a pregnant woman has squeezing under a bed.'

'Is everything all right?' Father Vernon's voice from below said.

'Yes,' Marshall said. 'You can come up.'

Kate, assisted by Marshall, stood. 'There were two of them, I think,' she said.

Father Vernon appeared in the doorway. 'I was about to call for help.' He held up his phone.

'This is Kate,' Marshall said. 'This is a friend of mine, Father Frank Vernon.'

Kate smiled at him and extended a hand. 'We've enlisted religious help, have we?' she said.

Father Vernon frowned and offered his elbow. 'It's a pleasure to meet you, Kate.'

'Of course,' Kate said. 'Covid.' Then bumped Father Vernon's elbow with her own.

'Do you know what they were after?' Marshall said.

'They were looking for information on Reece Sadler and any clue to my whereabouts.'

Marshall rubbed his chin. 'So, they can't have known you were here?'

'No.' She took hold of Marshall's arm as he turned. 'Mary,' she said.

'Mary?' he repeated.

'I think they know about her. One said they had to go to the hospital to finish off the woman. They must mean Mary.'

He took out his phone. 'If you two can secure the house, we'll meet downstairs and get away from here.'

Father Vernon and Kate nodded and descended the stairs as Marshall dialled.

'Yes, Ken,' Bankole said.

'I want you to send a couple of officers to the hospital where Mary Croft is being treated.'

'Why?'

'I have reason to believe her life may be in danger.'

'Are you going to let me in on—?'

Marshall huffed. 'Just do it, Adi. I'll explain later.' He hung up and bounded downstairs, where Father Vernon and Kate waited.

'I've sent a couple of officers over to the hospital.' He glanced through into the kitchen. 'Everything secure?'

'I think so,' Kate said.

'I'll check outside.' Marshall opened the door and glanced along the road. 'It seems clear out there. Let's go.'

The two men sat in their car up the street from Mary's house. They watched as Father Vernon, Marshall and Kate emerged into the road.

The driver looked at his mate. 'That's Kate Carver, isn't it?'

The passenger narrowed his eyes. 'No one said she is pregnant.'

'Shit,' the first said. 'We could have had her.'

'What are we going to do?'

'I'll follow them. At least we'll know where she is. It'll please Asmodeus and Braxas if we get her.'

'Yeah,' the passenger said. 'But don't lose them.'

Asmodeus sat on his throne as Braxas entered. 'How are things progressing?' he said to Braxas.

'Very well,' Braxas said. 'We have our people in place. Infiltrating the human hierarchy is proving simple. They are easily manipulated. Most of them are no better than the Janus.'

Asmodeus stood. 'My friend, you must be more tolerant. We will need their assistance until we can get more brethren across the barrier.'

'And *He who reigns supreme*?'

'I will gift this world to him. I will then be his most favoured, and the other princes will have to bend to my will.'

There was a knock on the door and the two men, who had been to Mary's house, entered. They walked towards Asmodeus and lowered their heads. 'We found nothing at the woman's house, my prince.'

Asmodeus studied the pair. 'What about Kate Carver?'

One of the men glanced at his companion. '… Nothing on her too,' he said. 'We've made enquiries, but nothing.'

Braxas edged closer. 'What aren't you telling us?'

'N-n-nothing.'

'Nothing,' Braxas said. He lifted the head of the first man. 'Tell me, and you shall go free.'

The man glanced at his partner. 'I, we, know nothing.'

The second man stepped forward. 'It's his fault. He lost them.'

The first man lunged for his companion, but Braxas grabbed him and threw him to the ground. 'Let him speak,' Braxas said.

'He's lying,' the man on the ground said. 'He searched upstairs. She must have hidden from him, and he failed to find her. It's him who let her escape.'

Asmodeus sat and glared at the man. 'Is this true?'

'She must have been hiding, my prince.'

'Where is she now?' he said.

'She left with two men. The policeman and another. I don't know who he was.'

Braxas drew his knife. 'Shall I despatch them?'

Asmodeus smiled. 'Don't be too hasty. Is there anything else you would like to tell me?'

The man on the floor struggled to his feet. 'She's pregnant.'

Asmodeus's eyes widened. He jumped from his throne, stepped across to the man and took hold of him. 'What did you say?'

'The woman, Kate Carver,' he said. 'She's pregnant.'

Asmodeus howled. 'You idiots. You allowed her to escape.' He snatched the knife from Braxas and, pulling the man's head back, cut a deep gash in his throat from under one ear to the other. Blood gushed from the gaping wound as the man brought his hand up in a futile attempt to stem the flow. Asmodeus turned to the other man. 'Find the policeman. Find him and bring him to me.'

The bleeding man continued to convulse as Asmodeus turned to face his victim, still held in his other hand. 'Where you are going,' he said, 'there will be no end to your punishment.' Then, pulling the dying man closer, he stabbed the dagger into his eye. The weapon made a sickening pop as he pulled it free and repeated it on his other eye. The man fell limp in his hand, and Asmodeus, holding him upright, severed his head from his body, allowing the remainder of him to fall to the floor. He turned to the other man, who stood shaking. His eyes locked on his friend's severed head.

'The woman in the hospital?' Asmodeus said.

'We didn't have a chance to get there, my prince ... We thought it better to tell you about Kate Carver.'

Braxas stepped forward and took hold of him. 'You idiot. You were told to despatch her.'

'I can go now if you want.'

Asmodeus held up a hand. 'I blame Thomas for her still being alive. I have sent Cain and Martin to bring him here.' Asmodeus turned to the still-shaking man and pointed at the decapitated body of his friend. 'See what will happen to you if you fail me again.' He held up the severed head. The man nodded. 'Get out,' Asmodeus screamed and threw the head at him. The man fled, and Asmodeus turned away from Braxas. 'You were right, my friend,' Asmodeus said. 'We need more of our kind.' He turned back to face his dextral. 'Did you hear what he said?'

'About the woman being pregnant?'

'Yes. It's his child. We must find her and kill it.'

'What about our brethren?'

Asmodeus slumped onto his throne. 'We must speed up our efforts to get through the threshold. Send word to your second in command to prepare an attack on the village.'

'The woman in hospital?'

Asmodeus pondered. 'I thought she would be the one to bear his child, but we have been misled. Clearly, Kate Carver is the one.'

'Is this Mary still important?'

Asmodeus rubbed his chin. 'I shall check with my source in the village. Her entity may be there.'

Braxas widened his eyes. 'You have a source in the village?'

'I have sources everywhere. I don't tell you everything, my friend.'

Braxas frowned, and Asmodeus continued. 'Don't take it to heart. You are my dextral, but some things must remain secret.'

'As you wish, my prince,' Braxas said. 'What about Thomas?'

'Assemble the men here tonight. I want them to see what will happen if they fail me. Perhaps you could think up a fitting punishment for him.'

Braxas grinned. 'I have just the thing.'

Kate accepted the tea as Father Vernon sat beside Marshall and opposite her. 'What Ken told me,' he said, glancing at Marshall. 'Is it true?'

She took a sip from her cup and nodded. 'Yes. All of it.'

'And the baby you're carrying?' he said. 'Whose is it?'

'I don't know, but …'

'You suspect?' Father Vernon said.

Kate sighed. 'The Nazarian's.'

'You should stay here for the foreseeable future,' Father Vernon said.

Kate placed a hand on her bump. 'What about when the time comes? My pregnancy is accelerated.'

Father Vernon stood. 'As you will realise,' he said, 'pregnancies are something I know little about. However, I know of somebody who will be able to help.'

'What if there are complications?' she said. 'I should really be in a hospital.'

'We can't risk that,' Marshall said. 'If they know about you, they will try to kill you.'

'My vicarage is large,' Father Vernon said. 'You will have the run of the place.'

Marshall's phone rang, and he got to his feet. 'I'll just answer this.' He made his way into the hall. 'Adi,' he said.

'Mary Croft has gone.'

'What do you mean gone?'

'I'm at the hospital now. Someone came and took her away.'

'Who?' Marshall said.

'They said they were from some private hospital. They had the correct paperwork.'

'I thought she was really ill?'

'Apparently,' Bankole said, 'she improved over the last twenty-four hours. The ambulance was equipped with the specialist equipment needed.'

'Have you been in touch with the hospital they took her to?'

Bankole sighed. 'It doesn't exist.'

Marshall glanced back towards the living room. 'What the hell are we going to tell Kate Carver?'

'I don't know.'

Marshall groaned. 'CCTV footage?'

'They're sorting it out now.'

'Good,' Marshall said. 'I'll see you back at the station.' He hung up and returned to the living room.

Kate looked at him. 'What's up?'

'Mary's been taken.'

'Your friend?' Father Vernon said.

Kate stood, ignoring Father Vernon's question. 'By whom?'

Marshall shrugged. 'We don't know. An ambulance took her.'

Kate brought a hand to her mouth. 'They'll kill her.'

Marshall held his hands out as if to placate her. 'We don't know that. The fact that they took her in an ambulance is a good sign.'

'But she was so ill.'

'One of my officers is there now. He said that she'd improved over the last day. The hospital would not have let her leave otherwise.'

Kate slumped back into the chair. 'What are we going to do?'

'My man is obtaining the footage from the CCTV. We'll see if you recognise anyone.'

Marshall turned the car into the police station car park and pulled up. He jumped from his vehicle and bounded into the station. Once inside, he went up to his office and met Bankole just outside.

'Have you got it?' he said.

Bankole handed him a memory stick. 'It's on here.'

'Do you recognise anyone?'

'No. You can only see the faces of two of them.'

Marshall fired up his laptop and inserted the stick. He watched as three uniformed men made their way along a corridor, pushing a trolley outside towards an ambulance. The camera angle changed as the men could be seen putting the trolley into the back of the vehicle and driving off.

'Is that it?' Marshall said.

'I'm afraid so. Only two of them went inside Mary's room. The other one waited in the corridor. We've got enlargements of two of their faces.'

He handed Marshall two A4-size photographs.

Marshall studied the prints. 'I don't recognise them either.'

'Should we put something out to the media? The DI's seething. He can't believe another body's gone missing. He's asking if they're linked.'

'What about the officers from Scotland Yard?'

'He hasn't told them yet,' Bankole said.

Marshall stood and pocketed the memory stick. 'I'll go and see him now.'

Marshall knocked on the door. 'Come in,' shouted a voice from inside.

'Ah, Ken,' Stroud said. 'Have a seat. What the hell is going on?'

Marshall shrugged. 'I've only just heard, sir.'

'Are these two cases linked?'

'I don't think so.'

'First, Reece Sadler's body goes missing, and then Mary Croft is spirited away in an ambulance.'

'I realise that, sir, but—'

'But nothing.' He threw up his hands. 'They knew each other and were found at the scene of a suicide and traffic accident.'

'Yes, but I can't see how they're linked.'

The DI sighed. 'I've been putting off the officers from Scotland Yard. They've been waiting to speak to Mary Croft.'

'She's still in a coma.'

'I know. They did suggest transferring her to another hospital until she came out of it, but the hospital refused. They said she was unfit to travel.'

Marshall frowned. 'Why are they bothered about her?'

'No idea.' He held up a piece of paper and shook it. 'All I know is that I have to give them unfettered access to this case.'

'But they didn't seem concerned the other day.'

'Well, they are now. So how the hell am I going to explain her disappearance?'

'I don't know. We could put out the photographs of two of the men.'

The DI groaned. 'Let me speak to them first.' He steepled his fingers. 'What about Mary Croft's friend?'

'Kate Carver, sir?'

'Yes. Does she know anything?'

'I could ring her.'

'Do that. Get in touch with her. She may have something to do with it.'

'I don't think—'

'Ken,' he said and sighed heavily. 'You're not paid to think. It's my arse on the line. See if she knows anything about it. I'll speak to the

Scotland Yard mob.'

Marshall made his way downstairs, stepped outside into the car park and took out his phone.

'Yes, Ken,' Kate said.

'There were three men on the CCTV. Have a look and see if you recognise them. Unfortunately, you can only see the faces of two of them. I've emailed you the footage.'

'Ok.'

'My boss wants me to talk with you. But, at least with covid, I don't have to bring you in.'

'How would you explain me being heavily pregnant?'

Marshall laughed. 'Thankfully, I won't have to. I'll tell him that I couldn't contact you, and when I visited your house, it was empty, and there were signs of a struggle.'

'Will he believe you?'

'He hasn't got a clue what's going on. He's more concerned about the officers from Scotland Yard, and I don't trust them.'

'You think they're ...?'

'I can't imagine anyone from there being remotely interested in some guy committing suicide, can you?'

'No, I suppose not.' Kate said.

'You stay where you are. It's the safest place for now.' Marshall hung up and hurried across to his car. He turned on hearing footsteps behind him.

'DS Marshall?' a man said.

'Yes?'

The man pulled out a gun and levelled it at him. 'We're going for a drive,' he said. 'Don't do anything stupid. I won't hesitate to use this if you do.' The man nodded towards the exit. 'We've got a ride waiting.'

They made their way outside the car park. The man walked closely behind Marshall and nudged him in the back to encourage him in the direction of a car with its engine running.

The man opened the rear door. 'Get in.'

Marshall climbed into the back. There were two other men inside. One in the driver's seat and one already in the back. Marshall found himself sitting between this man and the one carrying the gun.

'What's this all about?' he said.

'Our boss wants to know where you've taken the girl.' He grinned. 'You might as well tell us. I've seen what he does to people.'

'I haven't a clue what you're talking about,' Marshall said.

'Have it your way.' He laughed. 'We might get a piece of your heart.' He tapped the gun barrel on Marshall's chest. 'When Asmodeus has finished with you, eh, boys.' The three men laughed. He pushed his face closer to Marshall and licked his lips. 'I'll enjoy that.'

NEWS FROM THE CITADEL

Celestine, Headron, and Quinxious sat in the back of the pub. Khar placed the drinks in front of the others and joined them at the table.

'You said you have news?' Celestine said to Quinxious.

'Yes. Asmodeus is planning to attack the village. It is, however, only a diversion. He expects to lose some of his number.'

'I thought,' Celestine said, 'he was unwilling to attempt it until the remainder of the legion returned from fighting on Sathanas's border?'

'That is true, but he must be under pressure in the realm of the humans.'

'When you say diversion,' Headron said. 'Diversion for what?'

'He has chosen one of his most trusted to carry the phage across the threshold. The aim is to cause enough mayhem amongst the townsfolk to allow him through. The human woman must know about this. She will have to conjoin with him for them to get through.'

'Can we not eliminate her?' Headron said.

'Wait a minute,' Celestine said, 'we don't know for sure that it's Mary.'

'Who else can it be?' Headron said. 'Felix and Reece made the ultimate sacrifice.'

'Even so,' Celestine said, 'we need to know for sure. We can't be certain they haven't managed to get another human through.'

'Celestine is right,' Khar said. 'We have to be certain.'

'Have you asked Felix and Reece about her?' Quinxious said.

'No,' she said. 'I will consider it. However, their part is to aid in the release of James.'

'You mean Sicarius?' Quinxious said.

'Although he has lost his human corporeal form,' she said, 'he will always be James to me.'

Khar stroked his chin. 'Asmodeus must be aware that losing some of his strongest Demons will weaken him against Sathanas?'

Quinxious took a sip of his drink. 'Even if all his legion is lost, Asmodeus will still consider it a victory if he is successful. It will win him favour with *He who reigns supreme*. Asmodeus believes he will be untouchable. He may even be allowed to take Sathanas's realm.'

Celestine thought for a moment. 'The time they attack will be the best opportunity for us to free James.'

'We should really assist the townspeople,' Headron said.

Celestine shook her head. 'We can't be in two places at the same time, so they will have to make do on their own.'

'Do we know the name of the chosen one who will carry the phage?' Khar said.

'Thedious,' Quinxious said.

'Braxas's brother,' Khar said. 'Obvious when you think about it.'

Celestine gulped her drink. 'We still need an advantage,' she said, then banged down her glass and looked at the others. 'It would help us greatly if Sathanas learned what Asmodeus planned.'

Headron and Khar glanced at each other, then back to Celestine. 'You're not suggesting …?'

'Yes,' she said. 'I am.'

'With Asmodeus weakened, Sathanas's army could overrun his realm,' Headron said. 'We would be subjugated by them.'

'That's a chance we will have to take,' she said. 'Asmodeus will have to reinforce his border. That would pull his number away from the citadel.'

'If we did this,' Khar said, 'and I'm not saying I agree. How would we get word to Sathanas?'

Celestine looked at Quinxious. 'Quinxious,' she said.

The others looked at him. 'I have been passing information to his side for some time.' Quinxious said. 'Just enough to weaken Asmodeus and prevent him from mounting an attack on Sathanas's land.'

'Why am I only finding out about this now?' Headron said.

'It was considered best if we kept this information to a small number,' Celestine said. 'Even James … I mean, Sicarius does not know.'

'When is Asmodeus planning to attack the village?' Khar said.

'In three cycles,' Quinxious said.

'That doesn't give us much time,' Celestine said. 'I will talk with Felix and Reece.' She glanced around the table. 'Ready yourselves.'

Mary wandered along the street and entered the apothecary.

Jenny looked up from behind the counter. 'Hi,' she said.

'Can we talk?' Mary said.

'Of course. I'll shut the shop up, and we can have a tea out the back.' She studied Mary. 'It sounds serious.'

'It is.'

Jenny locked the door and pulled down the blind before ushering Mary into the back. Once the kettle had boiled, she poured the water over some leaves and handed Mary a cup.

Mary smiled. 'I do like your herbal tea.'

Jenny sat opposite. 'Where are Felix and Reece?'

'At the pub. I told them I was going for a walk.'

'So,' Jenny said, cradling her cup, 'you wanted to talk?'

Mary took a small sip from her cup and looked at Jenny. 'How well do you know Reece?'

'Not that well. Why?'

Mary looked down into her tea. 'It's just a feeling.'

'A feeling?'

'At first, there was nothing, but then a small feeling ...' She forced a smile. 'I can't put it into words better than that.'

'And this feeling?' Jenny said.

'I don't trust him.'

Jenny sipped at her tea. 'Has he ever done anything to you to engender this feeling?'

Mary shook her head. 'No. I'd never met him before I came to Nearhope. My friend Kate had, but I never did.'

'Maybe this feeling will fade. Nearhope is a strange place and does unusual things to people.'

Mary shook her head again. 'That's just it. I don't think it will fade.' She tapped her head. 'Something here is telling me not to trust Reece, and I'm worried because we're going to try and get James free.'

'When did you first get this feeling?'

'When I woke.' She closed her eyes and thought hard. 'Like a dream you can't remember on waking, but you still retain the vaguest memory. Do you know what I mean?'

'I think so,' Jenny said. 'Have you told Felix?'

'No. I wouldn't know what to say.'

Jenny drained her cup. 'James was taken when he freed Reece's wife from the citadel and brought her here. The last I saw of the pair was when they headed up the road towards the church.'

Mary nodded. 'I know that Reece and James freed Elizabeth and managed to escape. Yet, James was captured shortly after.'

'Ask him about that,' Jenny said.

'I already know the story. He recounted it to my friend Kate.'

'Can you remember it fully?'

'I think so.'

'Try and trip him up,' Jenny said. 'Do it subtly. If the feeling about him is genuine, he could lead you all into a trap. The underground, Celestine and the others could be in danger.' She thought for a moment. 'We need some information he should know.'

Felix and Reece sat at a table in the pub. 'When are we meeting James's allies?' Reece said.

'Later today.'

'Will we find out when we're attempting to free him?'

'Yes,' Felix said.

Mary entered and sat with the pair. 'What does a lady have to do to get a drink around here?'

Felix stood. 'Usual?'

'Please.' Mary watched as Felix made his way over to the counter.

'Felix was just saying,' Reece said, 'that we're meeting James's allies later.'

'Good. I'm getting a little bored just doing nothing.'

Felix placed a wine glass in front of Mary. 'I'll be back shortly,' he said. 'I'm nipping up the road to see Jenny.'

'See you later,' Mary said as Reece nodded, and Felix disappeared through the door.

'What's it like,' Mary said. 'The citadel.'

'Frightening.'

'The buildings, what are they like?'

Reece shrugged. 'You know, like ordinary buildings but with bright-red stonework.'

'It must have been terrifying.'

'It was.'

'Jenny told me about the serpent's image, with three heads, above the arch as you enter.'

Reece smiled. 'Four heads.'

'Yeah, sorry, four. And the castle, what's that like?'

Reece narrowed his eyes. 'You'll see soon enough. Anyway ...' He stood. 'I think I'll stretch my legs.'

'Ok,' she said. 'See you later.'

Felix followed Jenny through into the back of the shop. 'Have a seat,' she said. 'I'll make us a brew.'

He sat and looked across at his wife. 'Any news from Celestine?'

'I'm hoping to hear something today.' She poured two cups and handed one to Felix before sitting opposite him. 'Mary was here earlier.'

'She never said. I've just left her at the pub with Reece.'

Jenny frowned. 'We had an in-depth chat.'

'What about?'

'Reece.'

Felix looked at her over the top of his cup as he took a sip. 'Reece?'

'There's no easy way of saying this,' she said. 'She doesn't trust him.'

'Did she say why?'

Jenny briefly closed her eyes. 'She has this feeling that she can't put her finger on. But she's adamant.' Jenny paused after hearing a knock on the shop door. 'I'll be back in a minute.'

Jenny returned with Mary. 'He didn't fall for it, I think ... Felix,' Mary said as she spotted him, 'I hoped you'd still be here.'

'Jenny was telling me about your doubts regarding Reece.'

'Stupid, I know, but I can't shake the feeling.'

Felix took a thoughtful drink from his cup and placed it down. 'I've learned to trust my gut instincts.'

'You believe me?' she said.

'You said he was definitely dead when he crossed through?'

'Well,' she said, 'I checked for a pulse, and there wasn't one. He didn't appear to be breathing, either. However, his skin colour looked ...'

'Normal?' Jenny said.

Mary narrowed her eyes. 'Yeah. I've seen a few dead people, and he didn't look like them. He appeared as if he was sleeping.'

Jenny looked at Felix. 'Calabaster,' she said.

Mary frowned. 'Calabaster?'

'It's a plant which grows on the outskirts of the village. Its leaves, when ingested, can mimic death.'

'Right,' Mary said as she sat. 'You think he could have taken that?'

'Possibly,' Felix said.

'We can't allow him to meet Celestine and the others. He would betray them to Asmodeus. Once they have them, the whole underground would be in jeopardy.'

'What do we do?' Jenny said.

Felix furrowed his brow. 'We'll have to eliminate him.'

Reece stealthily made his way up the incline and stopped at the top. A figure approached him and held out a hand. 'Reece?' he said.

'And you are?' Reece said.

'My name is unimportant. Do you have news?'

'I'm hoping to have the names of the rebels shortly. I will be glad when this is all over. I'm tired of inhabiting this human form.'

'Asmodeus is pleased with you. He has secured the human body in their realm.'

'My family? Are they safe?'

'Asmodeus has promised they will be, and they'll be allowed to join you once we have the rebels.'

'When should we meet again?' Reece said.

'When you have news. Tomorrow?'

'The female who crossed the threshold with Felix and me?'

'What about her?'

Reece stroked his chin. 'I think she suspects me.'

'Asmodeus wants you to slay her. She's not critical to his plan, and he feels she could become a problem.'

'How can I do that?' Reece said. 'The others would know it was me.'

'I'm sure you'll think of something. After all, your family's lives depend on it.'

THE APOSTLES RETURN

Marshall peered out the car window as it sped along the country road. The vehicle slowed as it approached a corner.

'What is it?' said the man in the back, holding the gun into Marshall's side.

The driver glanced over his shoulder. 'There's a vehicle up ahead blocking the road.'

The gunman banged his weapon on the back of the driver's seat. 'Move them. Kill them if you have to.'

'There's no need for that,' Marshall said.

The gunman turned and glared at Marshall, again pushing the pistol into his side. 'You keep out of this.'

The car stopped, and the driver and the other man in the rear climbed out, leaving Marshall and the gunman.

'What's up?' the driver said to the parked motorist.

'It just died on me. Can you and your mate give me a hand pushing it off the road?'

'Yeah, ok.'

'What the hell are they doing?' the gunman said to Marshall. Both he and Marshall turned as someone tapped on the window. Another man stood outside with a gun levelled at the pair. 'Put the gun on the floor,' he said.

Marshall's captor placed the weapon down, and the man outside opened the door. 'Get out, Ken,' he said to Marshall.

As Marshall climbed from the car, the man carrying the gun shot Marshall's captor through the head. The two men, pushing the vehicle, turned after hearing the gunshot. The stranded motorist pulled a gun from his jacket and shot one of them through the head. The other bolted, leapt a fence, disappeared into some trees, and was out of sight within seconds.

'Forget about him,' the other man said as he reached his colleague. He turned and waved Marshall over. 'Come on. We need to get away from here.'

The three men jumped in the car and sped off. The man in the passenger seat turned to face Marshall and held out a hand. 'Phillip,' he said, and that's Andrew driving.' The driver looked through the rear-view mirror and winked.

'Who are you?' Marshall said.

'Two of the twelve,' Phillip said. 'We were sent to stop you from falling into the hands of Asmodeus. So we followed you when you left the police station.'

'Thanks for that.'

'It wasn't just to save you, though,' Phillip said. 'You would have given away Kate's whereabouts.'

'She's with a friend of mine.'

'Good,' Phillip said. 'You realise how important it is to protect her unborn child.'

'How do you—?'

'We know quite a lot.'

'The baby?' Marshall said. 'Who's is it?'

'I thought you would have guessed,' Andrew said.

'I'd still like you to confirm it.'

Phillip smiled. 'He's our saviour. He has come to save humanity and rid our world of Asmodeus and his acolytes.'

'Whatever happened to *turning the other cheek*?' Marshall said, nodding behind him.

'It's the twenty-first century, Ken, not Jerusalem two thousand years ago. Asmodeus would show us and you no mercy. We must be prepared to do the same.'

'You'll have to lay low for a while,' Andrew said. 'Asmodeus will try to take you again.' He slammed the car into gear and roared off.

'How can I do that?'

'Coronavirus gives you an excuse,' Phillip said. 'Tell your bosses you have symptoms and need to isolate. Then you can take us to see Kate.'

'Ok.' Marshall studied the pair. 'I didn't see you amongst the group at the police station.'

'We arrived a day late,' Phillip said. 'When we got there, we were met by Simon and Piotr. They'd been keeping themselves out of sight, hoping we would turn up.'

'Where are they now?' Marshall said.

'We have a place not far from Darlington,' Phillip said. 'We're awaiting our instructions.'

'From whom?'

Phillip crossed himself and kissed the cross hanging from his neck.

'From our saviour.' Marshall frowned. 'Kate is carrying him,' Phillip said.

Marshall scoffed. 'He hasn't even been born yet.'

'The others, who were at The Nazarian's house,' Phillip said, 'have a connection to the baby. So, the birth will be much accelerated.'

'Yes,' Marshall said, rubbing his chin. 'Her pregnancy is progressing quicker than normal.'

'The baby will be born soon. The others sense it.'

'I see.'

'Where is Kate?' Phillip said.

'She's staying with a friend of mine, as I said. He's a priest.'

'Good,' Phillip said. 'It will be harder for Asmodeus's men to attempt to take her from holy ground. However, Andrew and I have been tasked with her safety. So, we will come with you and make sure she stays out of harm's way.'

Marshall relayed the address and gave directions to Andrew as they made their way there.

Marshall, accompanied by Andrew and Phillip, tapped on the vicarage door. The door opened slightly and then was fully opened by Father Vernon. 'Come in,' he said. 'Kate has gone into labour.'

Marshall glanced at the two men with him. 'So soon?'

'Yes. Sister Anna and Sister Bernadette are in with her now.'

'This is Phillip and Andrew,' Marshall said. 'Two of the Apostles.'

'Sorry,' Father Vernon said, taking hold of Marshall's arm as he walked past him. 'Did you say ...?'

'Yes, Apostles,' he said.

Father Vernon held out his hand to the men. 'Father Frank Vernon,' he said. The two men shook his hand in turn. 'Follow me,' Father Vernon said. They were led into a sitting room, and Father Vernon motioned for them to sit. 'I'll rustle up some drinks, shall I?'

'We'd like to see Kate if we could?' Andrew said.

'We will have to wait and let this run its course.'

Andrew was about to speak, but Phillip held up his hand. 'That's fine, Father. We'll have tea.'

'Ken, anything for you?'

'Tea as well.' He took out his phone. 'I'll just have to call work.' Then, turning, he headed out of the room, followed by the priest.

'This is all very strange,' Father Vernon said as Marshall searched his contacts.

'Tell me about it, Father. Someone abducted me at gunpoint outside the police station. Those two,' he said, nodding back to the room, 'came to my rescue.'

'What have they told you?'

'I'll just make this call, and then I'll tell you everything I know.'

NEARHOPE – Jenny ushered Celestine into the rear of the shop, where Felix sat at the table.

'We have a problem,' Felix said.

Celestine slumped into the seat opposite him and sighed loudly. 'What kind of problem?'

Felix glanced at Jenny. 'We suspect Reece is not who he says he is.'

Celestine narrowed her eyes. 'Why do you think that?'

'Mary suspects him,' Jenny said. 'She can't put her finger on it, but she's sure he is not who he says.'

Celestine shook her head. 'Reece made the ultimate sacrifice. You were there, Felix.'

'I can't be certain.' He looked at Jenny, who sat with the others.

'Calabaster,' Jenny said, and Celestine frowned. 'It's a plant that grows on the outskirts of the village,' Jenny continued. 'When the leaves are ingested, it mimics death. Certainly enough to fool people from Felix's world.'

Celestine sighed. 'Some of the others suspect Mary. They are not convinced that she is who she says.'

'Why do they think that?' Felix said.

'In order to get the phage through the threshold, the Demon Asmodeus has chosen will have to conjoin with someone still alive in your realm.'

'I saw Mary get struck by the car,' Felix said. 'It looked like an accident and not planned. There is no way it could have been faked. I'm sure of it.'

'Well,' Celestine said, 'if what you say about Reece is true, he could be the one to conjoin.'

'We think we should eliminate him,' Jenny said.

Celestine considered this for a moment. 'No. I have a better plan. We can use Reece to our advantage. We will have him deliver false information to Asmodeus's men.'

'That's a bit risky,' Felix said.

'If we eliminate him,' Celestine said. 'Asmodeus will know that we have discovered his duplicity.'

'Ok,' Felix said. 'What are you planning?'

'We will let him believe that we intend to try and rescue James on a different day.'

'When?' Felix said.

Celestine sighed again. 'They are planning an attack on the town. They will use this as a diversion and try to get the one Asmodeus has chosen through the threshold. This is the time we will attempt to free James.'

Felix rubbed his chin. 'The citadel will still be on high alert.'

'We have something in place for that.' She glanced between the pair.

'It's better you do not know. The underground only gives the information needed to their operatives. This ensures our safety should they be taken.'

'I understand,' Felix said, 'but we need Reece to conjoin with one of the underground to enable us to get James out. You always said we would need two because he will be weakened.'

'I planned to conjoin with Mary and wait on the outskirts of the citadel,' Celestine said, 'but, unfortunately, it will mean Mary and I will have to travel into the citadel.'

'You will have to explain this to her,' Jenny said.

'I think we should leave that until the last minute.'

Jenny looked at Felix and shrugged. 'When is this planned for?' she said. 'And what about the townsfolk?'

Celestine lowered her head. 'There are sacrifices we all must make. We will have to hope that few perish.'

'What do I tell Reece?' Felix said.

'Tell him the rescue of James will take place in four cycles. We will go in three.'

Jenny stood and opened a nearby drawer. 'I have the fake phage.' She took out a small vial and handed it to Celestine.

'Will it fool them?' Celestine said.

'Yes. It lacks a small genetic marker, without which the phage will remain dormant.'

Celestine stood. 'Keep it safe until we need it.' The three of them hugged, and Celestine hurried off.

OUR WORLD – Martin and Cain dragged the beaten and battered man into the room and threw him to the floor. He crawled towards Asmodeus. 'Please,' he said. 'Have mercy. It wasn't my fault.'

'When we found him,' Cain said, 'he was leaving.'

Martin tossed a plane ticket onto the floor in front of the man. 'He intended to fly to America.'

Asmodeus walked across to the fire and looked deep into the flames. 'This is the second time you have failed me,' he said.

'We were ambushed,' the man said. 'They came out of nowhere.'

Asmodeus turned. 'But how will we find the woman without the policeman?'

'Let me try. I'm sure I can succeed this time.'

'Who took the policeman from you?'

'Men carrying guns.'

Asmodeus stepped closer to him. 'Yet you are here, and your friends are dead. Tell me how you managed to escape with your life?'

'A car blocked the road. Two of us got out to deal with it and kill the driver if we had to. When we investigated, an armed man shot our man guarding the policeman. The man whose car blocked our way shot my friend. I wasn't armed. I had to flee.'

'And you did so?'

'I-I-I had no choice.'

Asmodeus tapped his lip with his index finger. 'I insist on loyalty, obedience, and bravery. Sadly, you've let me down.'

'Please, my prince. How can I atone?'

'By giving yourself to me.' Asmodeus picked up a dagger from a nearby table and handed it to the man. 'Go on,' Asmodeus said. 'Show me your bravery now.'

The man put the knife to his neck and held it there, his hand trembling.

Asmodeus sneered. 'Even now, you waver, Sean.'

The man looked up tearfully and handed the knife back to Asmodeus. 'I can't. Will you do it?'

Asmodeus laughed. 'You're pitiful. I will use you as an example of what happens if you fail me to your brethren. He motioned for Cain and Martin to grab the man.

'Please,' he shouted as Cain and Martin dragged him to his feet.

'What do you want us to do with him? Cain said.

'I think he should go the way of Saint Bartholomew. Flayed alive and beheaded. Take him to the large chamber and secure him to the table. Braxas is quite adept at the procedure, and I'm sure he'll be only too pleased to have someone to practise on.'

'Please, I beg you,' the man shouted. 'Give me back the knife. I will sacrifice myself to you.'

'Take him away,' Asmodeus said. 'I can't stand listening to him a second longer.'

Asmodeus sat at the head of the vast table with Braxas to his right and Cain and Martin to his left. Around the table sat others. The headless body of Sean hung from one of the walls as blood from his skinless body still dripped blood onto the floor beneath.

Asmodeus rose and lifted his glass towards the assembled men. 'A toast to my dextral, Braxas, for the wonderful entertainment of seeing someone flayed alive.'

'Braxas!' they all choroused.

Asmodeus began to meander around the table. 'The flaying of Sean served more than one purpose,' he said. 'It is also to remind you of your loyalty and obedience.' The men thumped the table, and Asmodeus allowed the noise to subside before continuing. 'It's a privileged position you are in, gentlemen,' he said. 'When we have taken this world completely, you will have anything you desire. First, however, it must be earnt. Sean, over there,' Asmodeus pointed to the lifeless corpse, 'couldn't even offer himself to me, in sacrifice, when I gave him the opportunity.' The men booed. Asmodeus stopped at the far end of the table and picked up the skin of Sean in one hand and his skinless, severed head in the other. 'Tonight,' Asmodeus said, 'we will not only feast on his heart but on all of him. It is only through devouring the weak we become stronger.' He looked towards Cain. 'Will you do the honours?'

Cain picked up the larger blade from the table and strode across to the body. He turned to Asmodeus. 'For *He who reigns supreme*.' Taking the knife, he sliced a piece of flesh from the back of Sean's leg and tore a portion free with his mouth. He grinned through blood-covered teeth and held up the blade, and they all did likewise. When they'd finished with the meat, a glass ewer, containing their victim's blood, was passed from hand to hand around the table until all their glasses contained a small quantity of the viscous, red liquid.

Asmodeus lifted his glass. 'To *He who reigns supreme*.'

'To *He who reigns supreme*,' they all repeated.

Asmodeus puffed on a large cigar as Braxas entered. Braxas frowned as he approached his leader. 'What is that?' he said.

Asmodeus held it up for him to see. 'I found them in a box over there. They were a favourite of the previous owner.' He laughed. 'I'm getting quite a fondness for them myself. Try one.'

Braxas shook his head. 'Maybe later.'

'So, my friend, what news have you got?'

'Thedious came to me in my sleep last night. The plan to storm the town is going well.'

Asmodeus continued to puff on his cigar. 'Good. And your infiltration of the human hierarchy? That continues?'

Braxas smiled. 'They are unusual people. They are motivated mainly by greed. No matter an individual's wealth, they never seem satisfied.'

Asmodeus nodded. 'I have noticed that. They easily give in to their basest instincts too.'

'They do. This has helped us greatly. We have acquired more sites to produce the phage once we have it.'

'Good, good,' Asmodeus said. He motioned over his shoulder. 'Are you sure you don't want to try one of those?'

Braxas flicked open the box and plucked one of the cigars from it. He sniffed it and looked across at Asmodeus. 'You just put one end in your mouth, then light the other?' Braxas said, frowning.

'That's it exactly.'

Braxas lit the cigar and puffed on it. He coughed and pulled it from his mouth. 'I'm not sure—'

'You have to take it slowly, my friend,' Asmodeus said. 'Like this?' He puffed again, allowing a vast plume of smoke to surround him.

The door opened and Cain walked in. 'My prince,' he said, bowing slightly.

'Yes, Cain?'

'We have been unable to locate the policeman or the Kate woman. We suspect that she's in the hands of the Apostles.'

Asmodeus growled. 'We cannot allow the child to survive. We must find the woman and destroy her offspring.'

'We need more of our kin in this world,' Braxas said.

Asmodeus groaned and looked at his dextral. 'Without the Apostles, we can't bring more of our brethren here,' he said.

Braxas placed down the cigar and looked at Cain. 'You're not looking hard enough,' he said to Cain.

'I assure you—' Cain said.

Braxas sneered. 'Assure me? You're not trying hard enough.'

Cain turned away from Braxas and looked at Asmodeus. 'Is there no other way?' he said. 'After all, you brought him here.' He glanced at Braxas.

Asmodeus rose from his chair and placed his cigar on a nearby ashtray. 'It's not that simple,' he said. He wandered across to Cain and put an arm around his shoulder. 'There are immutable laws that must be adhered to. The Apostles and my closest are intrinsically linked and have been for aeons. I could pass through the threshold because I inhabited James's body. His soul is held in my realm. If that remains so, then I can remain here.'

'What about the Apostle we captured?' Cain said. 'Isn't he dead?'

'They and we cannot die. The Apostle is also in my realm. Or should I say his soul is.'

'It's too complex for your minuscule brain to understand,' Braxas said.

'Please, my prince,' Cain said, ignoring Braxas's jibe. 'I wish to know.'

Asmodeus picked his cigar back up and thoughtfully puffed on it. 'I shall tell you.'

'My prince,' Braxas said. 'Is that wise?'

Asmodeus laughed. 'It doesn't matter if he knows. What can he do?'

'There is another way to get someone from my realm to here. It is not easy, however. A person can cross through the threshold to a place called Nearhope.'

'Nearhope?'

Asmodeus sneered. 'A pathetic name was given to it. Nearhope ... Hope is near.' He forced a smile. 'This place stands between this world ...' He waved his cigar from left to right, 'and my realm. It acts as a barrier.'

'Why does this place exist?'

'It was decreed long ago. An agreement between *him* …' He sneered and glanced upwards, 'and *He who reigns supreme*. Other places separate the princes' various realms and here.'

'God, you mean?' Cain said.

Braxas stepped across to Cain and took hold of him. 'Do not mention that name in front of your prince.' He shook Cain. 'Do you understand?'

'Yes,' Cain said. 'I didn't mean to …'

Asmodeus waved a dismissive hand. 'He did not know that the name is forbidden, Braxas. Let him go.'

Braxas – Cain's shirt still grasped tightly – glanced at Asmodeus and then pushed Cain away from him. 'Do not mention that name again.'

Cain edged further away from his assailant and turned to Asmodeus. 'I meant no harm.'

Asmodeus nodded. 'He who you call God cannot be trusted. Long ago, we were all one. We loved and cherished him, but we were forsaken. *He who reigns supreme* tried to take his place.' Asmodeus slumped into his seat. 'It was *He who reigns supreme's* destiny. His birth-right. A battle was undertaken and lost. We were banished to our present realms.'

'It's a long time since I read the bible,' Cain said.

Asmodeus laughed. 'The bible and other religious books don't hold the truth. What is it one of your brethren said? *It is the victors that write the history*, not the vanquished.' Asmodeus looked away from Cain. 'God does not care for your people. You are nothing to him.' He turned back to face Cain. 'Why do you think he lets your people suffer? You are unimportant to him. He knows that *He who reigns supreme* would love to possess your world, which is why he keeps it from him. He only wants it because someone else desires it. He challenges *He who reigns supreme*. He sees this realm …' Asmodeus swatted his hand in front of himself, 'as a trinket to be fought over. He is only concerned with being loved and feted by his angelic coterie.' Asmodeus took out a coin and held it aloft. 'Your world is strange. Your people show an avaricious desire for this. It amuses me. We and the Angels are one and the same. Two sides of the same coin. We lost the battle, but we will win the war.'

'What about The Nazarian?'

Asmodeus frowned. 'The Nazarian is a mongrel, a half-breed. Because he was born of a human woman, he has a vested interest in humanity.' He scoffed. 'He treats you as you treat your children.'

Braxas laughed. 'He even calls you his flock because you are all like sheep.'

'He believes that his destiny is to save humanity,' Asmodeus said. 'There are half-breeds in my world. They are despised almost as much as the Janus. There is an order. A hierarchy which must be maintained.'

'But what about Martin, me and the others?'

'There will always be a place for you, my friend. We will need humans when we are victorious.' He looked at Braxas and laughed. 'Just not seven billion.' He looked back at Cain. 'When we have removed the old and infirm. We will need people like you and Martin to keep the weak and other undesirables in check. For this,' he said, 'you will have whatever you want. Whatever you desire.'

Cain smiled. 'Thank you.'

Asmodeus stood. 'Soon, we will have one of our number pass through the barrier with something important. Something that will give us the ultimate advantage in this world.'

'What?' Cain said.

'A phage that will thin out humanity to a more manageable number. But first, we must increase the virus's potency to afflict the world.' He looked at Braxas. 'Are we there yet?'

'Very close,' Braxas said. 'Within days.'

'Good,' Asmodeus said. 'Coronavirus kills a paltry amount of people it infects. However, a virus closely related to it kills around ten per cent of people who contract it.'

Cain frowned. 'But if it only kills ten per cent …?'

Asmodeus smiled. 'Don't you see? If we spread this new variant around the globe, the governments worldwide will come running to the person with a vaccine to counteract it.'

Cain smiled. 'You?'

'Exactly,' Asmodeus said. 'We will supply the world with the vaccine, and within it …'

'Will be the phage?' Cain said.

Asmodeus nodded. 'It is undetectable. Within months, the phage will activate and do away with ninety per cent of humanity.' He waved his hand from side to side again. 'There or thereabouts and their souls deposited in my realm.'

'And *He who reigns supreme*?' Cain said.

'I will present this world to him as a gift. I will become his most favoured.' He fixed Cain with a stare as his eyes glowed red. 'The other princes will be crushed beneath my feet.'

THE REAL REECE

NEARHOPE – Kate sat in bed cradling her infant as Marshall and Father Vernon entered and stopped at the foot of the bed.

Marshall smiled. 'Have you thought of a name?'

She shook her head. 'I haven't.'

'What about Emmanuel?' Father Vernon said.

'Emmanuel?' she said.

'It means God is with us,' Father Vernon said. 'It appears in the book of Isaiah.'

Kate gazed at the baby. 'How do you like Emmanuel?' The infant continued to suck on his dummy. 'Emmanuel it is.'

'The others would like to see you,' Marshall said. 'If that would be ok?'

'Yes,' she said. 'I'd like that.'

Marshall and Father Vernon left and headed downstairs.

Andrew and Phillip stood at the bottom. 'Can we see them?' Andrew said.

'Yes,' Father Vernon said. 'I'll go and make some tea.'

Marshall followed him into the kitchen. 'He was only born a couple of hours ago,' Marshall said, 'yet he looks like a six-month-old baby.'

'Yes,' Father Vernon said. 'The pregnancy and his growth are incredible. I don't know how I could explain this to the bishop.'

'No.' Marshall scratched the back of his head. 'I don't know how I would explain it to anyone either.'

NEARHOPE – Mary entered the apothecary and made her way into the rear of the shop as Jenny locked the door. Celestine sat at the table and smiled as the woman entered.

'Hi,' Mary said to her.

'Hi,' Celestine said.

Jenny put the kettle on to boil and joined the other two at the table.

'Where are Felix and Reece?' Mary said.

Celestine glanced at Jenny and then back to Mary. 'We need to tell you something,' Celestine said. 'We think Reece is an imposter.'

Mary furrowed her brow. 'I knew it.'

'We don't think he died in your world,' Jenny said. 'Asmodeus needs someone to carry something into your world.'

'What?'

'A phage,' Jenny said.

'Phage? What's a phage?'

Celestine leant in closer. 'When Jenny was held at the citadel, Asmodeus had her working on a phage. It's like a virus that can be introduced into a victim and kill them. Jenny worked on one that would kill the Janus.'

'Why the Janus?'

'They are despised by the other Demons,' Celestine said. 'Asmodeus hopes to extinguish them all.'

'Why are they so hated?' Mary said.

Celestine sighed. 'Long ago, when only one world existed, a battle ensued. *He who reigns supreme*, and ...' She paused as if searching for the right words. 'The one you call God fought for the right to rule over all the worlds. The Janus were blamed for *He who reigns supreme* losing the war.'

'And were they responsible?' Mary said.

'No. *He who reigns supreme* could not allow his followers to believe that he alone was responsible for them being cast from paradise. So he sought a scapegoat, and the Janus fitted perfectly.'

'There are stories in my world similar to yours,' Mary said.

'This is not a story,' Celestine said. 'This happened.'

Jenny held a hand up as Mary was about to speak. 'I think we have more pressing matters,' Jenny said.

'Indeed,' Celestine said.

'I delayed my completion of the phage as long as possible,' Jenny said. 'Fortunately, James, Celestine and Felix freed me before I had time to finish it.'

'However,' Celestine said, 'our sources claim that the phage is now complete.'

'He will kill the Janus then?' Mary said.

Celestine glanced at Jenny again and sighed. 'The phage's chemistry has been altered to suit human DNA.'

'He's trying to kill us?' Mary said.

Jenny nodded. 'Yes.'

'We think,' Celestine said, 'that Reece will be inhabited by a Demon, and together they will cross the threshold into your world.'

'He's trying to wipe out humanity?' Mary said.

Celestine sighed again. 'It appears so.'

Mary lowered her head. 'What can we do?'

'We are hoping to thwart his attempt,' Celestine said. 'Without Reece, we will need someone else to assist in getting James out of the citadel.'

'I'll do it,' Mary said.

Celestine smiled. 'I hoped you'd say that.'

'What will we do once we free him?' Mary said.

'We will need to get him across the threshold,' Celestine said. 'Asmodeus is inhabiting James's corporeal form. Asmodeus won't be able to hang onto it if James returns, and he will be able to recover it from Asmodeus. Without James's form, the Demon Prince will be forced to return to his realm.'

'Will Felix help James cross the threshold?' Mary said.

Jenny shook her head. 'Felix is dead in your world. So it will have to be you.'

'But how do you know I'm still alive?'

Celestine shrugged. 'We don't. But James will be able to tell. He has the gift to distinguish between those still living and those not. He told me once that he can see the mere trace of life inside someone.'

'What about Reece?' Mary said.

'We think Asmodeus is sending someone to conjoin with Reece,' Celestine said. 'We will attempt to intercept them and replace them with someone of our own.'

'And the phage?'

Jenny smiled. 'I have created a harmless one. In case we fail in our attempt to free James, at least it will buy your people some time.'

'When are we going?'

'Tomorrow,' Celestine said. 'Asmodeus is planning his assault on Nearhope the day after. We hope to free James and return before the attack.'

'Ok,' Mary said. 'Anything else I need to know?'

Celestine held out her hand, and Jenny placed a capsule on it before holding out a second for Mary. 'This is a poisonous capsule made from a plant that grows in Asmodeus's realm. It will kill instantly.'

Mary stared at the small capsule. 'If I get caught?' she said.

Celestine nodded. 'The information I have told you, and more you will learn, would be highly prized by Asmodeus. But, if he discovered what you know, it would endanger my people.'

Mary took the capsule from Jenny. 'I understand.'

Celestine stood. 'Felix knows where to meet us. You and he will set out tomorrow.'

Mary stood and offered her hand. 'I won't let you down.'

Celestine shook it. 'I know you won't.'

KATE – I stared at Emmanuel as he sat playing with his toy. He looked up and smiled at me. His rapid growth continued – the speed of it almost impossible to believe. I'd only given birth to him yesterday, yet he was almost walking. He held out the book to me. 'Mama read,' he said.

I picked him up, sat in an armchair with my son on my lap, and began. 'The Tiger that came to tea …'

I lay the sleeping Emmanuel on the couch and covered him with a blanket. Then, I turned as someone knocked on the door, and Marshall entered.

'How are you?' he said.

'Exhausted.' I slumped into the armchair. 'I can't believe how quick he's growing.'

'I know. Father Frank has some more books and toys.'

I laughed. 'The speed he's growing, he'll be riding a bike tomorrow.'

'I'm glad you've retained your sense of humour.'

It was forced, but I had. 'What about your job?'

Marshall sat opposite me. 'I left a message saying I've got covid and self-isolating. That will give me some time, as Asmodeus will be looking for me.'

'Will he be looking for me too?'

'Definitely. I had to remove my sim card in case he tried to locate me with it. We don't know how far his control stretches.'

I looked at my sleeping son. 'What about Emmanuel?'

'We've discussed him, but we're unsure how this will work. But, clearly, his arrival is important.'

I yawned as tiredness crept through my body. 'We'll have to wait and see, I suppose.'

Marshall smiled at me. 'Why don't you go and have a nap. I'll watch Emmanuel.'

I pondered. I didn't want to be away from him for too long, but I didn't have the energy to argue. 'Ok,' I said as I stood. 'But don't let me sleep too long. I don't want to miss him going through puberty.'

Marshall laughed. 'No. What parent would?'

NEARHOPE – Reece sipped his drink. 'Where's Mary?'

'At Jenny's,' Felix said. 'Drinking her fine herbal tea, I shouldn't wonder.'

Reece drained his glass. 'I think I'll have a walk.'

Felix stretched. 'I'll have a nap. I'm all in.'

Reece stood. 'I'll see you later.' He shrugged himself into his coat and exited the pub.

Mary made her way along the street towards the pub as the receding twilight headed towards darkness. She paused on a corner to pull her coat tighter around her neck as the chill night air enveloped her. Then, glancing to her right, something appeared in her peripheral vision, but before she could decipher what it was, someone grasped her around the throat. His hand – it was definitely a man – clamped across her mouth, preventing her from screaming. He dragged Mary, who purposely dragged her feet, scraping across the ground, making moving her more difficult for her attacker.

'Stop struggling,' he whispered. 'You'll only make it worse for yourself.'

She recognised the voice and bit into his hand, allowing her to partially break free as he squealed and pulled his hand away from her mouth.

'You bitch,' he said and struck her hard across the face with the back of his hand. Mary fell backwards onto the ground and shuffled on her backside away from him as he pulled a knife from his pocket.

Reece grasped her tightly around the ankle, foiling her attempt to put distance between herself and him. He dropped to the floor, pinning Mary to the ground with his knee. She gasped, momentarily winded but still held up a defensive hand as she clawed at his face. He swatted it away and gripped her throat as Mary kicked for her life, his weight fully on top of her, preventing further struggle. Mary gasped for air, his hand tightening further as she found herself drifting into unconsciousness. Her last view of the blade above his head as it plummeted towards her.

'Mary,' the voice said. 'Can you hear me?'

She opened her eyes and gazed at the giant of a man towering over her.

She groaned. Her hand moved to her throat and softly probed at her bruised and tender neck.

'Are you injured?' Khar said.

'Reece,' she said. 'He tried to kill me.'

Khar turned, and Mary followed his gaze. 'Is he dead?' she said.

'Unconscious. I got here just in time. Celestine feared that he may try something and asked me to keep a watch on you. Another minute and … Well, let's not dwell on that. Can you stand?'

Mary nodded and, assisted by Khar, climbed to her feet. She watched as he lifted Reece like a child and threw him across his shoulder. 'We'll take him to Jenny's and find out who he really is. Can you go and fetch Felix?'

Mary nodded again.

'Bring him to Jenny's shop.'

Jenny trod towards the rear door of her shop. 'Who is it?' she said.

'Khar.'

She opened the door, moved aside as Khar entered, and lowered the unconscious Reece to the floor.

'What's happened?' she said.

'He tried to kill Mary. I got there just in time.'

'Oh, my,' she said. 'What are we going to do?'

'Someone is inhabiting Reece.'

'How do you know?' she said.

'I just do. Do you have demonshood?'

Jenny frowned. 'A small amount. What for?'

'We're going to give it to Reece.'

'It'll kill him,' she said. 'It's lethal to humans.'

'We will have to take that risk. The demonshood will force whoever is conjoined with him out. If they believe their host is dying, they will leave. If they stay and the host dies, they will be lost too.'

Jenny opened a cupboard and returned, clutching a small glass jar a few moments later. 'Are you sure about this?'

The pair of them turned as Felix and Mary came in. 'What's happening?' Felix said.

'Celestine feared that Reece would try to kill Mary and asked me to watch her. I just made it in time.'

'Why would Reece do that?' he said.

'I think Reece is being inhabited by a Demon. But, unfortunately, he probably didn't have a choice.'

'What are you going to do?' Mary said.

Khar held out his hand and took the bottle from Jenny. 'Force the Demon out. Quick,' he said to Felix, 'help me.'

The two men took hold of Reece and placed him onto a chair. 'We have to restrain him,' Khar said.

The women watched on as Khar and Felix tethered Reece to the seat. He groaned and slowly lifted his head.

'Good,' Khar said. 'He's coming round.'

Reece sneered at Khar. 'He will make you pay for what you have done.'

Khar took hold of Reece's hair and pulled back his head. 'He won't find out if there isn't anyone here to tell him. Now,' Khar said, 'open your mouth.'

'What?' Reece said.

'Open your mouth.'

'I don't take orders from a half-breed.'

Khar looked at Felix. 'Assist me,' Khar said. The big man unscrewed the bottle top and pinched Reece's nose. Reece struggled but could hardly move as Felix held onto his head. Khar tilted the bottle and allowed a couple of drops of the clear liquid to fall into his mouth.

Reece gagged, but as Khar handed the bottle back to Jenny with one hand, he clamped Reece's mouth shut with the other. Reece fought vainly as the two men held on fast to his head. Finally, after a few moments, the pair backed away.

'What have you given me,' Reece said.

Khar smiled. 'Let's see who you really are.'

Reece groaned, his eyes bulging. 'You're killing us.' His head rocked backwards and sideways as he struggled against his constraints. 'You're killing your friend.'

'That's a risk we'll have to take,' Khar said.

Reece screamed. 'We're dying.' His head continued to rock back and forth. He turned to the women. 'Please help me.'

Jenny shot a glance at Khar. 'What do we do?'

Khar held out his hand again. 'Give me the bottle. Clearly, he needs a greater invitation to leave his host.'

Reece howled. 'No. You can't.'

'Khar,' Jenny said. 'Without Reece, Asmodeus will know there is something up.'

Khar fixed her with a stare and, lowering his brow, thrust out his hand. 'Give it to me.'

Jenny picked up the bottle and handed it to Khar.

Reece's eyes bulged. 'Noooo!' he said. Mary watched as a man appeared from nowhere and fell to the floor. Khar grasped hold of him and pushed him up against the wall.

'Who are you?' Khar said.

The trembling man lowered his head. 'I'm sorry. I didn't want to do any of this. Braxas made me.'

Khar grabbed hold of the man's arm and pulled up his sleeve. Beneath it, a *J* branded into the skin on his forearm.

'You're Janus,' Khar said.

The man slumped to the floor and started to cry. 'He has my family. He said he would free them if I helped him.'

'You fool. Your family will already be dead. Asmodeus detests your people.'

Jenny rushed into the cupboard again and returned with another bottle, pouring a small amount of the green liquid into Reece's mouth. He didn't move. His vacant eyes stared into the distance.

'I didn't want to do it,' the Janus continued. 'He gave me some liquid to drink, which took away my doubts.'

Khar relinquished his grip. 'Sit,' he said, pointing at a chair.

Jenny placed a hand on Felix's arm. 'Help me get Reece into bed,' she said.

'What will you do to me?' the Janus said.

Khar scowled at him. 'I haven't decided yet.'

THE ASSAULT ON NEARHOPE

NEARHOPE – Jenny held the glass to Reece's lips as he took a sip of water. 'How are you feeling?' she said.

'Not great.'

'Do you feel up to answering a few questions?'

He rubbed his eyes and nodded. 'I think so. It's important.'

Jenny waved the others inside.

Mary, Felix and Khar arranged themselves at the foot of his bed.

'What do you remember?' Khar said.

'Fragments, really. I think James and I were ambushed on our way out of Nearhope. Someone else inhabited me. But when I woke in my own world, I thought I'd dreamed it all. However, I couldn't shake the feeling that someone was inside my head.'

'Inside your head?' Felix said.

Reece nodded. 'Clearly, the Janus was observing what was happening. It was only when I recrossed the threshold that he retook control. Unfortunately, I have little memory of what happened from then until now, but things keep coming back to me.'

'Is there nothing you can tell us? It may help.' Khar said.

Reece closed his eyes and grimaced. 'I was unable to do anything because he pushed me into a dark corner of his mind. But,' Reece raised his head and looked at them, 'every now and again, when stressed or preoccupied, his guard would come down, and I could take in what he was seeing.'

'Did he meet anyone?' Khar asked.

'Yes. A Demon, I think. He never gave his name.'

Khar rubbed his chin. 'How could a Demon get into Nearhope?'

'I don't know, but he appeared as if he was a Demon.'

'What we need to do,' Felix said, 'is get you fit and well and then you may remember more.'

'Did he mention anything about an attack?' Khar said.

Reece furrowed his brow. 'Yes, I think so.' He closed his eyes and rubbed his temples. 'I think they're planning a surprise attack on Nearhope. With the confusion this will cause, they're hoping to get someone across the threshold.'

'With the phage?' Jenny said.

Reece widened his eyes. 'Yes, it's coming back to me. The person who they hope to get across will carry it.' Reece sat up in bed. 'We have to stop him.'

Khar held up a hand. 'Calm down, Reece. We have two days.'

Reece shook his head. 'They've brought it forward. It will happen tomorrow.'

Khar glanced at the others and then back to Reece. 'Tomorrow?'

'Yes. I'm sure of it.'

Khar growled. 'I must tell Celestine. We have to try and free James tonight.'

As Khar moved towards the door, Felix took hold of his arm. 'Tonight is too soon, Khar,' Felix said. 'We will barely have time to reach the citadel.'

'We must make time,' Khar said. 'One of the other Demon realms is at war with Asmodeus. We have allowed certain information to be passed to someone on their side, informing them of Asmodeus's weakness. We are hoping they attack the outskirts of his realm.'

'How will that help?' Felix said.

'Asmodeus's elite troops will be despatched to repel any incursion. With that and the others he is sending to Nearhope, the citadel will be only lightly guarded. Because it lies well within the boundaries of his realm, we are hoping he will not suspect.'

'I see,' Felix said.

Khar looked at Mary. 'You must ready yourself,' he said.

'What about me?' Reece said.

Jenny placed a hand on his arm. 'You're too weak.'

'They will suspect if I don't turn up.'

Khar rubbed his face. 'He's right.'

'But who will you have to conjoin with him?' Felix said.

'We have no choice,' Khar said. 'We will have to send the Janus.'

'But he'll betray us,' Mary said.

'As I said, we have no choice,' Khar said. 'They know what the Janus and Reece look like when conjoined. If we supplant the Janus with another, supposing we could find another in time, they will know.'

Reece planted his feet on the floor. 'Khar's right. We have no choice.'

'Come with me,' Khar said to Reece. 'We will speak with him now.'

Reece, assisted by Felix, followed Khar through the rear of the shop and into the storeroom. The Janus, fastened to a chair, looked up at them as they entered.

'Do you remember him?' Khar said and placed a hand on the shoulder of Reece.

The Janus nodded.

'The potion they gave you?' Khar said.

'It has almost lost its potency,' the Janus said. He turned to Reece and lowered his head. 'I'm sorry for what I did.'

'Will you help us?' Reece said.

The Janus frowned. 'How?'

'We want you to conjoin with me again and meet your contact.'

'But I thought—?'

'Will you do it?' Khar said.

'You told me he would kill me once I relinquished my hold on Reece.'

'That is true,' Khar said. 'But I will prevent him from harming you. If you do as we ask, we will get you a passage to a place where Asmodeus and Braxas have no reach.'

'And my family?'

'We will do what we can to release them, but as I said earlier, they're probably dead.'

The Janus turned away with tears in his eyes. 'If they are gone, there is no point in going on. However, I will help you to atone for what I've done.' He turned back to face them. 'You have my word. I will not betray you.'

Khar nodded. 'Good.' He looked at Felix. 'Untie and feed him. I will return soon.'

Celestine beckoned Khar inside. 'What is it?' she said.

Khar waved a dismissive hand as Celestine held up a bottle. 'No thanks,' he said.

She glanced at him as she filled a glass. 'You being here can't be good news.'

'Reece tried to kill Mary.' He held up a hand as Celestine was about to speak, and she allowed him to continue. 'She's fine. I got there just in time.'

'I knew he would try something.'

'A Janus inhabited Reece.'

Celestine frowned. 'Why would a Janus help them?'

'Asmodeus told him he would release his family if he did. The Janus helped Asmodeus capture James.'

'What have you done with him?'

Khar sighed. 'We have him prisoner. It appears Braxas gave him some potion to make him more amenable. I'm not sure he would have done it otherwise.'

'We will struggle to get someone to replace the Janus at such short notice.'

'It's worse than that,' Khar said. 'The attack on Nearhope has been brought forward. So you will have to leave for the citadel today.'

'What about Reece? If he does not meet his contact, they will know.'

'The Janus has agreed to help us.'

Celestine sneered. 'Are you mad?'

'We have little choice. He has sworn that he will not betray us. I have promised him that we will try to find out what happened to his family.'

'They'll be dead. You know that.'

Khar shrugged. 'I know. I will go with Reece and the Janus to meet his contact.'

'That's incredibly dangerous, Khar. If you're discovered …?'

Khar put a hand into his pocket and pulled out a capsule. 'I have this.'

'You were to lead us towards the citadel. I don't know my way through the black forest.'

'I will draw you a map. You will have to try.'

Celestine slumped onto a chair and gulped her drink. 'Is Reece all right?'

'He's weak, but he's prepared to do it.'

'And Mary?'

'Mary will be fine,' he said. 'If you manage to free James, we will need her to get you across the threshold. We can't afford to lose her.'

'Me?'

'We will have to replace the Demon Braxas intended to send across the threshold, which means it will only be you, Headron, Mary and Felix.'

'Yes, I understand that,' she said, 'but if we get James out.' Celestine looked upwards and shook her head. 'A big if. Why do you want me to cross the threshold?'

'I feel James will need some help in the human world.' Khar held out a piece of paper. 'The Janus' family names.'

She frowned. 'It will be a waste of time.'

'I know, but please try.'

She took the paper from him. 'I will pass it on.'

'Headron will meet you on the far side of the forest. Then, I will send Felix and Mary to meet you at the ruin. One more thing …' Khar said.

Celestine narrowed her eyes. 'What?'

'The contact that the Janus and Reece met.'

'What about them?' she said.

'They met him in the village.'

'That means …' Celestine stared at Khar.

'Whoever they met must be part human. Otherwise, they could not gain access to the village.'

'Yes.' She pondered this. 'Could someone amongst our group be working for Asmodeus?'

'We must hope not. But, on the other hand, if someone is, we may already have been betrayed.'

She stood. 'I suppose I'd better get ready then.'

'Yes, there is no time to waste.'

The pair embraced, and then he was gone. Celestine poured herself another drink and downed it in one.

The battalion emerged from the wood and halted on the hilltop. 'We will rest within the trees,' the commander said. He stared into the distance at the town. High in the sky, the sun beat down on the oblivious townspeople.

'When will we attack?' one of the Demons said to his commander.

'We will wait until dark. That will give us more of an advantage.'

'Our weapons?'

'We'll leave them here,' the commander said. 'They are of no use down there. We will have to use our bare hands and teeth.'

'Maximum damage?'

'Yes. But we must not forget our primary goal. I have to reach the church and meet the contact.'

'And the Janus?'

The commander sneered. 'I will enjoy ripping his heart from him.'

Mary and Felix struggled up the incline and stealthily made their way through the undergrowth towards the trees. Felix stopped and looked at the ground. 'Someone's been here,' he said.

'Celestine and Headron?'

'No. Look at the vegetation.'

Mary scanned the flattened area and put a hand to her mouth. 'Demons?'

He nodded and waved for Mary to follow him. Slowly, they padded away from the trees and further into the undergrowth. Felix took hold of Mary and pulled her to the ground. He placed a finger to his lips, and Mary nodded her understanding. About fifty metres away stood a huge man. Felix looked at Mary and mouthed, 'Demon.' They watched as the man relieved himself and then headed away from them.

Mary released the breath she held. 'He looks so normal. Although he was a giant of a man.'

'That's what they look like to us at first glance. However, in their own world, they look hideous. The elite troops are much larger than the others. I suspect that they are picked for their size.'

'What about Celestine and Headron?' she said.

He rubbed his chin. 'We will have to skirt around and hope they do not run into the Demons.'

Mary sighed and placed a hand on Felix's arm. 'I hope Jenny is ok.'

'Me too.' He stood. 'Come on, we must not waste time. I'm not as young as I once was.'

They travelled for half an hour when Felix halted and sat on a convenient rock. 'I think we're lost.'

'I thought you knew the way?'

He sighed. 'Because we had to deviate, I've lost my bearings.'

Mary sat next to him. 'What do we do now?'

'I don't know.' Felix rubbed his face. 'We can't keep walking in case we run into more Demons.'

'And we can't just sit here,' she said.

'No.'

The pair leapt to their feet and dived into the thick foliage. 'Someone's coming this way,' he whispered.

Mary reached for his hand and squeezed it as Felix squeezed hers.

'Felix,' a voice behind them said.

The pair turned sharply and leapt to their feet. 'Headron,' Felix said. 'Thank god it's you.'

'We've been trailing you for ages,' he said. 'Luckily, you left a nice path for us to follow.'

'Where's Celestine?' Mary said.

Felix glanced between Headron and Mary. 'Mary, this is Headron. Headron, meet Mary.'

The pair shook hands. 'She's just over the next hill,' Headron said.

The humans followed as Headron trod his way into the undergrowth.

'There you are,' Celestine said as she caught sight of them emerging from the dense vegetation. The other three joined her. 'We should get going,' she said, striding off.

'Did you see the Demons?' Mary said.

Celestine stopped and spun around. 'No. Where?'

'At the top of the slope leading to Nearhope,' Felix said.

'Good. We're a long way from there.' She started walking briskly again, and Headron joined her as the other two struggled to keep up.

The Demons stepped free from the trees and slowly descended the incline. The commander turned to the Demon next to him. 'Keep quiet until we reach the town, then make maximum noise. Attack anything that moves.'

'Yes, sir,' the Demon said.

The commander continued his slow descent. 'Make sure that I'm protected at all times.' He paused again. 'Whoever is left once I reach my destination should make their way back to the citadel.' He continued, increasing his pace until he reached the sign, stopping and facing the others. 'You will be greatly rewarded for your efforts today.' He held up his arm. 'Now!' he shouted.

A man exiting the pub looked to his left at the scene that greeted him. He turned and rushed back inside. 'Beasts,' he shouted. 'Beasts are coming.'

'How many?' the landlord said.

'At least twenty.'

The landlord reached under the counter and pulled out his rifle. 'Tom,' he said to a man who stood in the corner. 'Sound the bell.'

Tom nodded and hurried from the pub.

The men assembled around the landlord. 'Fetch your weapons,' he said.

Men spilt into the street, some with guns, others with makeshift weapons. Bears and wolves met them. The landlord fired, hitting one of the bears, holding the leg of one of the townspeople clamped within its jaws, in the rump. It howled and released the man, allowing him to scramble free. It turned on the landlord and bounded towards him. Lowering his weapon, he fired again, the bullet hitting the animal between the eyes. The huge beast's front legs gave way, and it came to a sliding halt a few metres from him.

He turned and surveyed the chaos. Men battled with the beasts. He recognised a regular in his pub, beyond help as two wolves tore into him, one of the animals coming away with part of his leg, the other with his arm. He lowered his weapon again and fired. The wolf slumped to the floor as the bullet found its mark. The other animal turned on him and, quickly gathering speed, leapt at the landlord. He fired but missed, and the wolf crashed into him, sending them reeling backwards into a crumpled heap. The landlord frantically searched for his gun, which had been knocked from his grasp, but as he stretched to gather it up, the wolf leapt again, pinning him on his back to the floor. The landlord punched the animal as it tried to sink its teeth into his throat. It yelped and turned its head, snarling at whoever struck it, but before the injured animal could pounce, its assailant thrust the fork into the beast. With the tangs buried deep into its side, the animal stumbled sideways. Its injury, and the weight of the tool, hampering its escape. The man pulled the fork free and, using his body weight, plunged it into the wolf's neck. The animal briefly quivered before all movement ceased.

The landlord, now on his feet, joined his friend. 'I thought I was a goner there.'

The man retrieved the fork and followed the landlord further down the street. Dead wolves, bears, and men – torn apart by the beast's savagery – lay scattered along the street. Those not injured joined the landlord and the fork-wielding man as they slowly made their way along the road, despatching any injured beasts as they went.

The landlord glanced down at Tom – the remnants of his throat grimly clinging onto his blood-soaked head.

A man came rushing towards the group of men. 'Two have got away,' he said through panting breaths.

'Where?' the landlord said.

'Up the hill.'

The landlord snarled. 'Come with me, men. There's no escape for them.'

The commander hurried up the road and, reaching the entrance to the churchyard, allowed himself a glance back down the road. A group of men were about four hundred metres from him. He scanned the area looking for somewhere to conceal himself.

'Over here,' a voice said.

The commander turned and looked into the graveyard. Reece, conjoined with the Janus, beckoned him inside, so he raced through the gate. 'We must hide,' the Commander said.

'We'll be fine here,' the Janus said. 'The townspeople can't see this place.'

The Janus and the commander watched as the men reached the churchyard. They wandered around, searching in all directions until they gave up and made their way back down the hill to the town.

The commander followed the Janus as he headed along the path and inside the church as skeletal creatures scurried away from them.

'Why can't they see the church and graveyard?' the commander said.

The Janus shrugged. 'I don't know. They just can't.' He sat on a pew. 'My family? Have you news?'

The commander strode towards him. 'Yes, yes, they will be freed. We had an agreement. Now, Janus, how do we do this?'

The Janus stood, and Reece stepped free from him. Reece glanced between the pair, trying to take stock of his surroundings.

'You just take hold of his hand and step inside,' the Janus said. 'It's that easy.'

The commander smiled. 'Good. Now, Janus. I think we can dispense with your services.'

'You're betraying me?'

The commander laughed. 'Of course. Did you really believe we would release your family? They are vermin, and so are you. I watched while my men fed your wife into the furnace. He briefly closed his eyes and tilted his head upwards. Their screams were exquisite. We feasted on your children first.' He wiped his lips. 'Their hearts were delicious.'

The Janus glared at him and then launched himself at the commander, pulling a dagger from his belt as he attacked the giant. The Commander laughed as he easily swatted aside the puny individual. Then, picking up the knife the Janus had dropped, he towered over his victim. 'I will feast on your heart too. It will invigorate me for my journey ahead,' he said and stamped on the Janus' leg. The Janus shrieked in pain as the Commander laughed again.

'Let him go,' Khar said.

The commander turned to face him and sneered. 'What are you doing here? Shouldn't you be serving drinks at that hovel of yours?'

Khar stepped closer, his stature equal to that of the commander. 'I'll take the phage too.'

The commander frowned. 'How?'

'We know what Asmodeus is planning. We will not allow it to happen.'

The commander roared and launched himself at Khar, the pair crashing into the pews and over the top of them.

Reece groaned, powerless to do anything. The weakness he felt was sapping his energy, and he watched helplessly as the two giant men grappled along the aisle. First, one gained a slight advantage, only for the other to come back stronger.

'You must help him,' Reece said to the Janus.

The Janus shook his head. 'I can't stand. I think my leg is broken.'

Reece struggled to his feet and, using the pews for support, slowly made his way along the aisle towards the battling pair. He picked up a large candlestick holder and swung it wildly at the Commander, who now sat astride Khar. Reece tumbled to the floor as the Commander, caught a glancing blow by the would-be weapon, loosened his grip on his victim. It was enough for Khar to push him off. Khar and the Commander stood and faced each other.

'You're lucky I need you,' he said to the spreadeagled Reece. 'Otherwise, I would devour you.' He then turned back to Khar. The older Demon-Hybrid, panting hard.

'You're old,' the Commander said. 'Look at you. You are all but spent.'

Both men turned sharply as the door to the church burst open, and another Demon entered and limped along the aisle.

'Quickly,' the Commander said. 'Help me dispatch this mongrel.'

The Demon pulled a knife from his belt and moved further along the aisle towards the battling pair.

'Kill him,' the Commander said, 'and I will make you my dextral.'

The Demon reached Khar, who did not move and grinned. 'Hello, Khar,' he said.

The Commander frowned as the Demon turned to face him and plunged the knife into the Commander's stomach. He groaned. His eyes wide as he stared back at the Demon. A trickle of blood dripped from the side of his mouth as the blade was withdrawn and plunged into the Commander's heart. He stayed upright as the Demon held him up, but then removing the knife, he allowed the Commander to fall onto his knees and then forward onto his face with a tremendous crash.

The Demon turned to face Khar. 'Are you all right?'

Khar breathlessly nodded. 'Yes.' He held out a hand. 'It's good to see you, Nefluous.' Khar looked down at the wound on the Demon's leg. 'You're injured,' he said.

'It's nothing.'

'Sit,' Khar said. 'I will fetch Jenny to attend to it. The Janus requires her help too.'

Nefluous nodded and slumped onto a pew.

Headron, Celestine, Felix and Mary approached the ruin.

'He said he would meet us here,' Headron said.

'You are certain he is trustworthy?' Celestine said.

Headron sighed. 'He comes with the highest guarantee.'

'Do we have a choice?' Felix said.

'Not really,' Celestine said. 'You and Mary wait here, though. I don't want to take any unnecessary risks with you.' She turned to Headron. 'You go on alone. I'll find somewhere for Mary and Felix to hide, and then I'll join you.' Headron nodded his agreement and continued on.

Felix placed a hand on Celestine's arm. 'You seem unsure,' he said.

'I don't know Headron's contact, and I'm not comfortable working with someone I don't know.'

'But you trust Headron?' Mary said.

'Absolutely,' she said. 'But Headron takes chances. He can be a little headstrong.'

Mary sighed. 'As Felix said, we don't have much choice.'

'No.' Celestine glanced around and, locating an overhanging rock covered by vegetation, motioned for Mary and Felix to hide. The pair climbed beneath and out of sight as Celestine headed after Headron.

Headron stood with another Demon and turned as Celestine entered. 'Ah, Celestine,' he said. 'Let me introduce you to Oxium.'

Oxium held out a hand for Celestine to shake, but she ignored it. 'Oxium,' she said.

He put his hand back down. 'Is there a problem?'

'Problem?' Celestine said.

'Yes. I'm here at great risk to myself. If you have a problem with me …'

Headron held up his hand. 'There's no problem, is there, Celestine?'

'You're part human,' she said.

Oxium nodded. 'What of it? So are you and Headron.'

Celestine stared at Oxium. 'Nothing. No problem at all. I prefer working with Demons I know.'

'Look what Oxium has got for us,' Headron said and held up the seals.

Celestine took hold of one and gasped. 'They're genuine.'

Oxium smiled. 'I have a contact close to Braxas.'

'But seals are always accounted for,' she said.

'They were recovered from dead Demons fighting on the border of Asmodeus's realm. By the time it is discovered that they are missing, we will have been and gone.'

ACROSS THE THRESHOLD

NEARHOPE – Jenny fastened the bandage and stood. 'That's the best I can do,' she said.

Nefluous clambered to his feet. 'It feels much better.' He pulled a small glass bottle from his pocket and handed it to her. 'The phage,' he said. 'I recovered it from the Commander's pocket.'

She secreted it inside her coat pocket. 'I will study it and attempt to make an antidote should we require one.'

Khar held out a similar bottle and handed it to Nefluous. 'Take this one and give it to Asmodeus.'

Nefluous nodded. 'I should go.' He looked at Reece. 'Are you ready, Reece?'

Reece stood. 'Yes.'

Nefluous looked at Khar. 'What did you do with the body?'

'I put it outside in the graveyard for the scavengers.'

'Good.' He looked over to the Janus, who sat at one end of the pews with his head bowed. 'And the Janus?'

'We will get him to safety,' Khar said.

Nefluous looked around the church. 'This is a strange building. It seems to—'

'Grow old?' Khar said.

'Yes. That's it exactly.' He held out a hand to Khar. 'Hopefully, we'll see each other again.'

Khar shook his hand. 'I'm sure we will.'

The Demon walked across to Reece. 'Right,' he said. 'What do we have to do?'

Reece held out a hand. 'Take my hand, and I'll step inside you. You will retain control, but I will be able to speak with you through our thoughts. It will appear strange, I'm sure, but we have to do this.'

'I understand.'

Nefluous and the conjoined Reece made their way along the path leading out of the churchyard and stopped. Nefluous looked about before stopping and waving to Khar stood in the doorway. Then they turned away and headed into the night.

'Keep walking straight ahead,' Reece said to Nefluous. The words drifted from man to Demon in thought alone.

They emerged from a side road and onto the Leyburn road. Up ahead, about fifty metres away, a car waited. *'I guess the car is for us,'* Nefluous thought.

'I expect so,' Reece replied, then stepped further into the shadows of Nefluous's mind.

The Demon walked towards the car, and, as he neared, the back door opened, and Cain stepped out. He nodded politely as Nefluous reached him. 'Commander?' Cain said.

'I am not the Commander. It did not go according to plan,' Nefluous said. 'I must speak with Asmodeus immediately.'

'Of course,' Cain said, indicating for Nefluous to get into the car.

Cain climbed in beside him and indicated for the driver to move off. 'The phage?' Cain said. 'Did you bring the phage?'

Nefluous turned to face the human. 'I have. I will deliver it to Asmodeus in person.'

The journey to the manor house took a little over an hour. Reece remained silent as Nefluous listened to Cain, bringing him up to speed on developments. Eventually, the car pulled up outside the house, allowing Cain and Nefluous to climb from the car and head inside. The Demon followed Cain along a series of corridors before stopping at a large door where Cain knocked, waited for an acknowledgement, and then entered.

Standing in front of a roaring fire, Asmodeus turned to face the duo. 'Clearly, things did not go smoothly?' he said.

Nefluous stepped closer and bowed. 'No, my prince.' Asmodeus eyed him and then indicated for him to continue. 'Braxas's brother, the Commander, fell. He fought bravely, but the humans fatally wounded him.'

Asmodeus stepped nearer. 'Who are you?'

'I am from his battalion, sir. When the Commander fell, I went to his aid. I managed to get him away from his attackers and into the church on the outskirts of the village. But, unfortunately, he died soon after.' Nefluous put a hand into his pocket and pulled out the small bottle. 'He gave me this with orders to find the human host, kill the Janus and cross the threshold. He said delivery of this ...' He held out the bottle, '... was most urgent.'

'Did you kill the Janus?'

Nefluous nodded and smiled. 'I even had time to devour his heart.'

Asmodeus laughed and snatched the bottle from the Demon. 'You have done well. With this …' He held up the bottle, '… we shall cull the humans.'

Nefluous gestured towards Cain. 'Your human told me of the plan. It is indeed ingenious.'

Asmodeus tossed the bottle towards Cain, who deftly caught it. 'Get that to the laboratory,' he said. 'We need it inserted into the vaccine as soon as possible.' Asmodeus turned back to face Nefluous. 'Was there something else?'

'I bring bad news from your realm. Sathanas's troops have made incursions into our realm.'

Asmodeus walked across to his throne and sat, lowering his head a little. 'Yes, I am aware of that. I have ordered our troops to intercept and repel them.'

'There are rumours that his army greatly outnumbers ours. Especially with the losses at Nearhope.'

'Were there no other survivors?' Asmodeus said.

'No, sir. I would have gladly given my own life for you, but I recognised the importance of helping the Commander.'

'Indeed.' Asmodeus nodded slowly. 'You must be weary after your adventure?'

Nefluous stood straight. 'I am willing to do anything you ask.'

Asmodeus waved a dismissive hand. 'We have many humans to do my bidding. Cain will show you to your room. We will meet in the hall later for a celebration dinner. I'm sure we can find someone suitable to feast on.' He looked towards Cain.

Cain smiled. 'We have a nun, sir.'

Asmodeus sneered. 'These women give their lives up in the name of faith. Yes, that will do nicely. Any news on the woman or the policeman?'

Cain shook his head. 'Martin and a couple of the others are paying a visit to where he works. They hope one of his colleagues can provide information regarding his whereabouts.'

Asmodeus fixed Cain with a glare. 'We must find her, Cain. It is vital.'

'Yes, sir.' He turned to Nefluous. 'If you would follow me.'

Nefluous lay on the bed as Reece emerged from a dark corner of his mind.

'*That went well,*' Reece thought.

'*It appeared to.*'

'*You seem unsure.*'

Nefluous pondered. '*Fooling Asmodeus was never going to be the difficult part. However, his dextral, Braxas, is a different proposition.*'

'*Why?*'

'Braxas trusts few Demons. The Commander was one of his brothers and his most trusted. He will not be happy when he hears the news.'

'Will he doubt you?' Reece thought.

'He has no reason to distrust me, but he is suspicious of everyone and anyone. For a while, it has been rumoured that he wants to supplant Asmodeus.'

'Would he dare do that?'

'He who rules supreme actively encourages in-fighting. He believes that it makes his Demon realms more powerful. He would not discourage it.'

'But surely Asmodeus must suspect?'

'Asmodeus is arrogant. He believes no one would dare to oust him. It has not happened for a long time. From what Cain told us in the car, he hopes to deliver your human world into the hands of He who reigns supreme. If he achieves that, Asmodeus will be untouchable.'

'And if Braxas ousts Asmodeus?' Reece thought.

'His place at the right hand of He who reigns supreme will be guaranteed.'

Nefluous stood and locked the door. 'I must release you. I am tiring.'

Reece stepped from Nefluous and into the room.

'I must sleep,' Nefluous said. 'We will talk later.'

Nefluous stood, leaving the sleeping Reece behind, and crept into the bathroom. He locked the door and positioned himself on the floor. Then, pulling a small vial from his pocket, he took a small drink. When he opened his eyes, he stood before a Demon wearing a uniform.

'Did everything go to plan?' the Demon said.

'Yes. I killed Braxas's brother and took his place as Sathanas instructed.'

'Good, good. Does Asmodeus suspect?'

'I'm not sure,' Nefluous said. 'He appeared satisfied.'

'Braxas will be more difficult to fool.'

'Indeed. What do you want me to do?'

The Demon stepped closer. 'Sathanas wants you to keep an eye on what Asmodeus is getting up to in the human world. For now, observe. Ingratiate yourself into Asmodeus's circle and undermine Braxas if possible. He intends to supplant Asmodeus, and the longer Asmodeus stays away from his realm, the better chance we have of taking it.'

Nefluous nodded. 'I will do as you say.'

KATE – Emmanuel and I sat at the table. His growth continued at a pace, and he could now read. Ken Marshall and Father Frank entered.

'Can we have a word?' Marshall said.

'What about?' I asked.

'A discussion about what we will do when the time arrives,' Father Vernon said. He smiled at my son, who smiled back. 'One of the sisters will keep him amused. Would you like that, Emmanuel?'

'Yes,' Emmanuel said. He jumped from the chair and headed from the room.

Marshall closed the door behind him, and the pair joined me at the table.

'Has Emmanuel mentioned anything?' Father Vernon said.

'He's just a child,' I said. 'Although he is precocious.'

'Clearly,' Father Vernon said, 'he has come to help humanity with their fight against the Demons.'

I shrugged. 'I suppose so.'

Marshall sighed. 'I can't stay away from work indefinitely, but I'm worried Asmodeus's men may be waiting for me to contact work.'

I considered his words. If they know about Emmanuel and me, and I was sure they did, they will try to get to us through Ken. 'You would be in danger?' I said. 'And that would endanger us.'

Marshall glanced at Father Vernon. 'I'm their route to you. If they capture me, they'll find out where you are.'

'We think,' Father Vernon said, 'that it's better if you go elsewhere.'

'Where?'

'The Apostles have suggested taking you somewhere safe,' Marshall said. 'I've got an old phone with several sim cards. I'm going to drive some distance from here and phone work. That way, I can discover if anyone has been asking about me.'

'Do I have a choice?' I said. I doubted I did.

The pair glanced at each other, and Father Vernon leant in close. 'We need to keep the pair of you protected until ...'

'Until we know what the plan is,' Marshall said.

Braxas sipped his drink and then placed it down. 'Nefluous brought the phage?'

Asmodeus leant back in his throne. 'Yes.' Asmodeus eyed Braxas. 'What's wrong?'

'I don't really know him, that's all.'

Asmodeus sneered. 'You're suspicious of anyone who isn't in your cabal.'

'With good cause, my prince. You know that the renegades have many spies in your realm.'

'It did. However, with the information you gathered from Sicarius, you must surely have rooted them out by now.'

Braxas shuffled in his chair. 'It isn't as easy as that. I suspect he does not know the identities of many of them. It's probably done on purpose in case one of them is taken. Also ...'

'Also?'

Braxas sneered. 'I cannot be sure that the information we obtain is genuine. Sicarius is devious.'

Asmodeus rubbed his chin. 'The renegades may try to free him. I cannot allow that to happen. Maybe we should move him.'

'Why? The citadel is deep within your lands.'

'I don't want him to escape. If he does and crosses the threshold, he will claim his corporal form, and I will no longer be able to stay here. That must not be allowed to happen.'

'Surely the castle is the securest place to house him, though?'

'Find somewhere better,' Asmodeus said. 'Somewhere only you and I know about. Then if he does escape …' Asmodeus picked up a cigar and sniffed it. '… I will know who has betrayed me.'

Braxas stood. 'My prince, I would never—'

Asmodeus waved a hand for him to sit again. 'I trust you implicitly, my friend. I was making a joke at your expense.'

'I will make provisions for him to be moved immediately,' Braxas said.

'Good.' Asmodeus lit his cigar and puffed out a plume of smoke in Braxas's direction. 'You do that.'

ESCAPE ATTEMPT

NEARHOPE – Felix pulled Mary deeper into their hiding place as the footsteps neared.

'It's all right,' Celestine said, glancing into the space. 'You can come out.'

They clambered from their refuge and brushed the bits of foliage from their clothes.

'Everything ok?' Felix said.

'Yes,' Celestine said and glanced at Headron.

'What's up?' Mary said.

Headron sighed. 'Celestine is a little troubled. She doesn't trust the Demon who's assisting us.'

'It's not that I don't trust him,' Celestine snapped, 'it's just that I don't know him. I'd rather be working with someone I know.'

'Anyway,' Headron said, 'from this point on, we must conjoin.'

'Ok,' Mary said. 'What do I have to do?'

Felix smiled. 'It's nothing. Just take Celestine's hand, and she'll do the rest.'

The Demons held out their hands, and Mary and Felix stepped inside their respective hosts.

'*Everything ok?*' Celestine said. The thought drifted effortlessly to Mary.

'*Yes. It's a little unusual.*'

'*You'll get used to it,*' she said as Headron and her strode off into the trees.

The journey to the citadel was uneventful. Mary stayed silent as they passed through the eerie land of awe and horror. Creatures never encountered before looked hideous but, somehow, in keeping with their surroundings. She would have liked to discuss them with Felix. He had, after all, been to this place before, but her questions would have to wait.

After what seemed like an hour or more, they reached what Mary assumed to be the citadel. A colossal wall stood before them, and Celestine was – Mary could sense her great unease – terrified. An admiration grew for Celestine. To be so frightened of a place but be prepared to risk everything to save a friend was courageous.

Headron and Celestine stopped outside the entrance and drank in their surroundings.

'Ready?' Headron said to Celestine.

She sucked in a deep breath. 'As ready as I'll ever be.'

The pair stepped forward and were met by a Demon guarding the gate. 'Yes?' he said, barring the way.

Headron and Celestine presented their seals. 'We come with news from the battlefront,' Headron said.

'What news?'

'That's for your superior to know.'

'I apologise,' the Demon said. 'I meant no—'

Headron waved a dismissive hand. 'Who's in charge?'

'The Prince isn't here, and his dextral is away also.'

'Where is Braxas?'

'He's rumoured to be with the Prince.'

Headron and Celestine exchanged glances. 'I see. So, who's in charge in their absence?'

'Vexious. He's the Prince's most trusted after Braxas. Do you wish to see him?'

'We have travelled a great distance,' Celestine said. 'Maybe a little later.'

'I will call for someone to show you to your accommodation.' The guard disappeared and returned moments later. 'Someone is on their way, sir.'

Within minutes Headron and Celestine were escorted inside a building and to the accommodation block. 'We've prepared two rooms,' their escort said.

'That's fine,' Headron said.

He handed the pair a key each and pointed to two doors. 'The rooms have a connecting door should you need to talk with each other. Would you like some food and drinks?'

'Not at the moment,' Celestine said.

'Just let me know if you require anything else,' he said.

They thanked him and retired to their respective rooms.

Celestine turned the lock and made her way over to the connecting door. It opened into Headron's room.

'Have you locked your door?' she said.

'I have.'

'We can release Felix and Mary then.'

Headron tapped on the interconnecting door, which was opened by a conjoined Celestine and Mary. 'Well?' Celestine said.

'It's really quiet out there,' Headron said as he released his hold on Felix.

Celestine did the same with Mary. 'The main bulk of Asmodeus's troops?'

'I spoke with a couple of the guards. Apparently, things on the border are going badly. They've sent reinforcements from here.'

'That can only help us,' she said.

'Yes. However, there is a real concern that the defences will be breached, and this realm invaded.'

'Is that bad?' Mary said.

Headron and Felix followed Celestine and Mary into their room.

Celestine sat. 'It could be.'

'Could they reach here and affect our effort to free James?' Felix said.

Celestine shook her head. 'The border is a great distance away. That's not the problem.'

Headron addressed the two humans. 'You must understand that the realms form a tenuous existence. It would not do to have one realm gain superiority over another.'

'Why?' Mary said.

Celestine sighed. 'We would be subjugated.'

'But I thought you hated Asmodeus and how he governs this realm?' Felix said.

'Humans have a quaint saying,' Celestine said. '*Better the devil you know.*' She stood. 'We would be conquered. Sathanas would show the Janus no mercy, and we would be considered inferior to his people. It would not be a good thing.'

'Wouldn't he ...' Felix paused. '... *He who reigns supreme* intervene?'

She shook her head again. 'No. He would welcome it. He encourages conflict. He thinks allowing the realms to battle with each other will make them stronger for the final war against *He who reigns in heaven.*'

'God help us all,' Mary said. 'What are you going to do?'

'There's little we can do,' Headron said. 'Asmodeus may try to enlist help from one of the other realms. The other princes would fear Sathanas if he conquered Asmodeus. However, if they assist Asmodeus and he still falls, Sathanas would not forgive that and set his sights on their realm too.'

'The politics of these lands,' Celestine said, 'are complicated.'

'I managed to contact Oxium,' Headron said.

Celestine raised her eyebrows. 'And?'

'He wants to try the rescue attempt today.'

Celestine threw up her hands. 'I thought—?'

'There's a battalion of troops on their way back from the front, and they're expected to arrive tomorrow. He feels that with the bare minimum here until then, it would be advantageous to do it tonight.'

'How are we to get into the castle?' Celestine said.

'He's confident that he has everything we need.'

Celestine rubbed at her temple. 'There's something I don't like about this. We could be walking into a trap.'

Headron looked upwards and groaned. 'Don't you think that I haven't thought about that, but we've come this far ...'

Celestine stared at Felix and Mary. She placed a hand into her pocket and took out the capsule. 'This capsule is deadly to us,' she said. 'We have brought them with us, understanding that we cannot allow ourselves to be taken.' Mary and Felix listened intently as she continued. 'Headron and I know too much about the underground to be captured. If the moment arises, we will not hesitate to sacrifice ourselves.'

Felix glanced at Mary and then back to Celestine. 'We understand.'

'Are you sure?' Headron said. 'Because when you are conjoined, there will be no escape for you if we are lost. You will be consigned to purgatory for all eternity.'

'We understand,' Mary said. 'We have discussed what may happen. We are prepared to accept our fate should the worst ...' She glanced at Felix, who nodded.

'Very well.' Celestine said. 'We will make plans.'

Asmodeus sat slumped on his throne with his head bowed as Braxas entered. 'I've just heard the news, my prince,' Braxas said. 'What are your orders?' Braxas continued.

Asmodeus stared out of the window, then turned to face his deputy. 'Sathanas has taken advantage of the opportunity while I am away.'

'Are you contemplating returning? If you are, I am well equipped to—
'

Asmodeus glowered at him. 'I'm sure you are.'

Braxas frowned. 'I'm sorry, my prince, have I displeased you?'

Asmodeus stood and strode to the window with his hands behind his back. 'I have no intention of returning.'

'But Sathanas will invade and may conquer your realm. Your presence would lift our troops and may turn the tide.'

Asmodeus spun around to face his deputy and smiled. 'I realise that, but …' He waved his hands around, '… I will have all this. I have grown to like this place. If my realm falls, so be it. But, on the other hand, if I gain this world and present it to *He who reigns supreme*, Sathanas will have to bow to me. So not only will I recover my realm, but I will take his.'

Braxas ground his teeth. 'I see. It's a cunning plan, but how will you achieve it?'

'I need some breathing space.'

'What do you mean?'

Asmodeus paced the room. 'Some of these humans have helpful beliefs. There are some who worship *He who reigns supreme*. I have an idea.'

'I'm listening.'

'I want you to find these people. There are many out there, I'm sure. I will convert them to our cause.'

'By demonising them? But that—'

Asmodeus held up a hand. 'Enough.' He glowered at Braxas. 'They will have to carry my mark so that they're delivered into my realm. It will swell our numbers substantially.'

'They would make poor fighters, my prince.'

Asmodeus dropped onto a chair and picked up a cigar. 'I realise that, however, if we create enough of them, it will slow Sathanas down. An endless supply of cannon fodder.'

Braxas shrugged. 'They would have to commit some suitable transgression in this world.'

'I know this. There are people in this world who they call terrorists. Some carry out atrocities in *His* name.' Asmodeus sneered and glanced upwards. 'We will create a cult to carry out these acts like nothing Earth has ever witnessed. We will find them, convert them, and then send them into the world to do my bidding. My plan is already unfolding.'

'I see,' Braxas said. 'And Sicarius?'

'Sicarius?' Asmodeus smiled. 'I am dealing with that. I think you have your hands full at present.' There was a knock on the door, and Martin entered. 'You may leave us,' Asmodeus said to Braxas. Braxas bowed, turned, and glared at Martin before leaving, closing the door behind him.

Martin stepped forward. 'He seems upset.'

Asmodeus waved Martin closer, placed a hand on his shoulder and smiled. 'What you don't understand, Martin,' he began, 'is the treachery that goes on in my realm. Of course, a dextral should be loyal to his prince, but, for some time, I have doubted Braxas.'

'You don't trust him?'

'Let's just say that he may have his own agenda.'

'What are you going to do?'

Asmodeus sat back on his throne. 'The task I gave you?'

'It's going as planned,' Martin said. 'My sort are easily enticed. The cult numbers are almost two thousand worldwide.'

Asmodeus slapped the arm of his throne. 'Good. Show me your arm.'

Martin pulled up his sleeve, exposing the mark branded into his skin.

'My symbol,' Asmodeus said, 'ties you to me eternally. Therefore, the people you have recruited to our cause must be given a similar mark.'

'Why?'

'I need to bolster the troops in my realm.'

'I don't follow.'

Asmodeus stood. 'Once they have the mark, they belong to me. All we have to do is deliver them to my realm. They will achieve this by performing an act of brutality in my name. This ensures that they are delivered into my realm and no other. We'll do this until we have repelled Sathanas's troops.'

Martin grinned. 'How do I get them to accept your mark?'

'I will show you how. You must persuade them that it's in my name that they do it. We will offer them paradise and untold riches.' He laughed. 'That sort of thing usually works with your kind. Then we will give them instructions.'

'I will begin at once.'

'Martin,' Asmodeus said. 'Tell no one. Not Braxas, not Cain. No one.'

Martin bowed. 'You can rely on my discretion, my prince. I will not fail you.'

Braxas turned as Cain entered. 'You sent for me,' Cain said.

'Yes. We'll have to initiate our plan.'

'Involving James?'

Braxas nodded. 'I hoped Asmodeus would return to our realm when news of the battle reached him. Unfortunately, however, he has no attention in doing so.'

'What are you going to do?'

'The renegades that are heading to the citadel. They will have to be successful.'

'But I thought you hoped to take them,' Cain said.

'I did, but Asmodeus cannot be allowed to stay here. If he achieves his aim, he will be untouchable, and I will never be prince.'

'Are you saying you're going to allow Sicarius to cross the threshold?'

'Yes.'

'Isn't that incredibly dangerous?'

'We will have to take that chance. Once he has claimed his human body, Asmodeus will be cast back into his realm. He would need another body to return. By which time we will have taken control.'

'What do you want from me?'

'I want you to be there when Sicarius comes through the threshold.'

'Ok.'

Braxas grinned. 'Once Asmodeus is gone, we'll deal with Sicarius or James as he will then be.' He fixed Cain with a stare. 'Do well, Cain, and I'll be looking for someone as my right hand. That could be you.'

NEARHOPE – Headron and Celestine, along with their conjoined partners, exited their rooms. They hurried away from the citadel and towards the castle – a huge foreboding edifice sited high on a hill. Headron glanced to his side at Celestine. 'You're sure you've got our story right?' he said.

'Yes. We're here to escort the prisoner to Asmodeus's lair.'

'Oxium is going to meet us outside the gate. He's often there, so they shouldn't suspect anything.'

Celestine looked around as they ascended the path leading up to the massive door of the castle. 'It seems quiet,' she said.

'It's because most of his troops are away fighting.'

'Even so,' she said, 'to leave this place with only a handful of guards seems odd.'

'That gives us an advantage.'

The pair stopped as they reached the door, and Oxium appeared from around one of the corners. 'Ready?' he said as he approached them.

'Ready,' Celestine said.

Oxium reached for the knocker and banged it hard against the door. Footsteps were heard from inside, and then the door swung open. A Demon stood at the threshold and appraised the three of them.

'We have orders to take the prisoner to the Prince's lair,' Headron said.

The Demon frowned. 'He's already been taken.'

Oxium pushed past Headron. 'By whom?'

'One of the Prince's personal guards.'

The three of them exchanged glances before Headron looked back at the Demon. 'Obviously, a communication breakdown,' he said.

'They had an official order from the Prince himself. They haven't been gone long.'

'Don't worry,' Oxium said. 'We'll send word to our commander that he's already left.' The Demon shrugged and closed the door as all three headed back down the slope.

'What do we do?' Celestine said.

Headron pointed away from the castle. 'We'll follow them.'

'Through the forest?' Oxium said. 'That'll be dangerous.'

'Why have they moved him?' Celestine said. 'Why now? Do you think they knew we were coming?'

'Maybe, but why haven't we been captured?' Headron rubbed his chin. 'It could just be a coincidence.'

'Anyway,' Oxium said, 'assuming it is a coincidence, what will we do if and when we catch up with them? They aren't going to give him up easily. We don't even know how many they'll be either.'

Headron sighed. 'The longer we discuss it, the further they'll be away.'

'True,' Celestine said. 'We should go.' She looked at Oxium. 'Agreed?'

Oxium nodded. 'Agreed.'

THE CHASE

Celestine, Headron and Oxium hid within the forest, and from their vantage point, they could see the Demons ahead. James sat slumped on the floor next to a tree, his arms and legs chained to the trunk. Four or five yards from him sat two guards.

'What are we going to do?' Celestine said.

Headron rubbed his chin. 'We need to pick them off one by one. We have the advantage of numbers, but they are from Asmodeus's elite. They will be formidable.'

'What if I circle around to the other side,' Oxium said. 'Then I'll make a noise to attract one of them. They won't dare leave James unguarded.'

'Good idea,' Headron said.

Oxium stood, but Headron pulled him back down. 'Someone's coming,' Headron said.

Two other Demons appeared from out of the trees. The Demons guarding James stood as the others approached.

'More guards?' Celestine whispered.

Headron shook his head and groaned. 'They're from Braxas's personal guard. I recognise their insignia.'

The three looked on as the four Demons entered into conversation, but as it appeared that the discussion had ended, Braxas's guards drew their weapons and felled the other two, plunging the sword into them and severing their heads. The two Demons then collected the heads, wrapped them in cloth, and placed them in their backpacks. Celestine gasped as one of the two Demons looked in their direction. He said something to his compatriot, and then the pair turned and walked off in the direction they'd come from, leaving their headless victims and James behind.

'What happened there?' Oxium said.

'They heard me,' Celestine said. 'Why didn't they investigate?'

Headron narrowed his eyes and scanned the trees. 'And why leave James?'

'Maybe they didn't see him,' Oxium said.

Celestine and the other two stood. 'They must have.'

'Go and check which direction they went,' Headron said to Oxium. 'We'll check James.'

Oxium nodded, then crept past James and after the two Demons.

Celestine dropped to her knees. 'James,' she said, gently shaking his arm.

He lifted his head and viewed her. 'Who are you?' he said as he studied her.

She glanced at Headron. 'He doesn't know me.'

'He'll have been through a lot. He will remember.' Headron examined the chains. 'The dead guards must have the keys.'

Celestine searched through their pockets. Then, returning to Headron and James with a set of keys, she undid the lock and removed the chains.

'Can you stand?' Headron said to James.

James stared vacantly at him. 'Stand?' he repeated.

Each taking hold of an arm, Celestine and Headron lifted him to his feet. They turned as a snapping branch behind them broke the quiet.

Oxium came into view and joined the pair. 'I followed them for some distance,' he said breathlessly. 'They're definitely not coming back.'

'This is all very strange,' Celestine said. 'It's as if they wanted us to take him. It feels like a trap.'

Headron frowned. 'I'm not sure. Why not take us when they had the chance?'

Oxium placed a hand on his arm. 'Whatever the reason,' he said, 'we can't waste this opportunity.'

'He's right,' Celestine said.

'I'll release Felix,' Headron said. 'It is tiring carrying him.'

Felix looked around at his surroundings as he was deposited from within Headron. 'Where are we?' he said.

'We're in a forest past the citadel,' Headron said.

Felix smiled and placed a hand on James's face. 'James,' he said.

James smiled back. 'Felix, my old friend,' he said, then furrowed his brow. 'Are we going to save Jenny?'

'Jenny is safe. We saved her. Don't you remember?'

James rubbed his eyes. 'My head is clouded, my friend. I don't remember much.' He placed a hand on his chest and began to weep. 'Something is missing. I am incomplete.' He looked at the others. 'I have lost it. He has taken it from me.'

'Don't worry about that,' Felix said. 'We will get it back for you.'

'Can you conjoin with him?' Celestine said to Felix.

'I'll try. James has always been in control.'

'You'll have to,' Celestine said. 'I don't think he can walk far.'

Headron placed a hand on Felix's arm. 'When you tire, Oxium and I will take turns. It will not be easy for any of us. It is energy-sapping.'

Felix turned to James and held out a hand. 'Ready?'

James nodded. 'Ready.' He stepped inside Felix, who visibly sagged and groaned a little.

'What does it feel like?' Celestine said.

'Like I'm mentally piggybacking someone.'

She frowned. 'Piggybacking?'

Felix smiled. 'It's what we call it when you carry someone on your back.'

'Ah,' she said. 'What a strange expression.'

Felix stood straighter. 'I'll be ok for now.'

'Good,' Oxium said, 'because we need to move.'

'Can you continue to carry Mary?' Headron asked Celestine.

She nodded. 'Yes. She should stay hidden until we need her. In case we run into any Demons.'

'*Felix,*' James said from the depths of Felix's mind, the words drifting into his consciousness. '*We have a betrayer amongst us.*'

'*How do you know?*' Felix responded.

'*I suspected it previously. Only now am I certain. We must tread carefully.*'

'*I understand,*' Felix said.

OUR WORLD – Cain bounded into the room and marched across to Braxas, who lay on his bed. He opened his eyes and looked at Cain. 'The plan is proceeding well,' Braxas said.

'Did they free Sicarius?'

Braxas smiled. 'Asmodeus thought he was being clever by moving him from the citadel. Two of his elite guards were taking him to Asmodeus's lair, and there would be no chance of freeing him if they reached there, but my guards intercepted them.'

'The renegades?'

'They have him,' Braxas said. 'With a little help from my guards. They killed Asmodeus's men and left him for the renegades.'

'Won't Asmodeus suspect?'

Braxas sat up and shook his head. 'The renegades will be blamed. He will send troops to look for them, hoping to recapture Sicarius.'

'Will the renegades be able to make it to the threshold?'

'I have instructed my guards to assist them in that. They will slay any of Asmodeus's elite. However, we can't be sure that they will succeed.'

'What will we do?'

'You must recruit more to our cause. If they fail to get Sicarius across the threshold, I will challenge Asmodeus. You and I must retain our enmity for each other. That way, Asmodeus will not suspect you.'

'Can you do that? Challenge him?'

Braxas stood. 'It's not unheard of in our realm, but it is dangerous.'

'Why?'

'I would no longer be welcome in our realm or any others. My place would be here for good.'

'Would that bother you?'

Braxas smiled again. 'Like Asmodeus, I have grown accustomed to your world. Eternity here would not be a bad thing. Your people are easy to manipulate, and we could rule this world easily.' He walked across to the window and stared outside. 'It may not come to that.' He turned to face Cain again. 'We will wait and see. As I say, increase your recruiting just in case.'

'What about the woman and the child?'

'Make enquiries. The policeman who helped her. See if his colleagues know anything. The child must be slayed.' Cain nodded.

'Be discreet, though,' Braxas said as Cain paused at the door. 'We don't want Asmodeus finding out.'

NEARHOPE – Felix stumbled but regained his balance as he leant on a tree for support. Celestine joined him and took hold of his other hand to assist him.

Felix turned to face her. 'I need to rest. I'm exhausted.'

She waved the others across. 'Felix is tiring, and so am I. We could do with a rest.'

'Oxium,' Headron said, 'scout the area for Demons. We'll wait here a while.'

Celestine released Mary and then slumped to the ground with the others as Mary took in her surroundings. 'Where are we?' she said as Felix released James.

'I'm not certain,' Celestine said, glancing at Headron, who appeared deep in thought. 'Headron?' she said.

'Sorry, I was miles away.'

'Where are we?' Celestine said.

'We're about an hour's walk from Dark Nearhope.'

'You're not contemplating going there?' she said.

'It's the quickest route.'

Celestine briefly closed her eyes and considered her response. 'That will be the first place they'll look for us.'

'I'm hoping,' Headron said, 'that we have enough head start on them. It may be some time before they discover that James is gone.'

Oxium came hurrying through the undergrowth. 'Demons are heading this way. They're some distance, but they're heading this way.'

'How long?' Headron said.

He shrugged. 'Less than an hour. They're moving quickly.'

Headron rubbed his face. 'They're obviously heading for Dark Nearhope. We must take a different course.'

Oxium glanced at Celestine, then back to Headron. 'Where? There's only this way or …'

Headron fixed him with a stare. 'We have no choice.'

'What are you talking about?' Felix said.

'Bergteuful mountain,' James said. The others turned to face him. 'The land of the forsaken Demons.'

'Forsaken Demons?' Mary said.

James wearily propped himself up against a tree. 'A place reserved for Demons who kill their own.'

Headron scoffed. 'That's just a story. There's probably nothing there.'

James lowered his head. 'It is no story.'

'How do you …?' Celestine said.

'I've been there,' he said. 'I have seen it.'

'This is all very interesting,' Oxium said, 'but Asmodeus's men will be here soon.'

James clambered to his feet. 'We'd better go then.'

'Wait,' Celestine said. 'Are you saying we're going to travel into this land?'

James paused. 'We don't have a choice. We can't outrun Asmodeus's men. They will hunt us down in no time.'

'But you're still weak,' she said.

'If Oxium can assist me, we can put distance between them and us. They will not expect us to head that way.'

'I'm not sure I can carry you,' Oxium said. 'I've never done it before.'

Headron sighed. 'I will do it, but you will have to do it next. We must all take our turn.'

'I could carry Felix,' Oxium said. 'He would be easier for someone as inexperienced as me.'

'He's right,' James said to Headron. 'I am a heavy load for someone not well-versed in conjoining.'

Headron sighed. 'Very well.'

'Check how near the Demons are,' James said to Headron and Oxium. 'Then we will go.'

Oxium and Headron hurried into the dense foliage as James edged closer to Felix. As Mary and Celestine watched them disappear, he briefly took hold of Felix's hand. Felix turned to face him and nodded his understanding.

The group stopped and looked up at the mountains, which appeared to stretch forever. Headron released James, then slumped to the floor and lay on his back. 'I'm exhausted,' he said. 'I need to recover.'

James sat next to him and nodded towards a massive boulder in front of them. 'That rock marks the boundary of her land.'

Mary and Felix, released from their hosts, sat next to James. '*Her* land?' Felix said.

'The sister of *He who reigns supreme*.'

Mary frowned. 'He has a sister?'

Headron sighed. 'This is folklore, James. You're not saying you've seen her?'

James clasped his hands together. 'I committed the ultimate sin. I killed Braxas's brother.'

Celestine leant in closer. 'Why have you not told me this before?'

'It's not something I am proud of.' James lowered his head. 'I would have been captured otherwise. I had no choice.'

'So,' Headron said, 'you're saying that the soul gatherer is real?'

'Wait a minute,' Oxium said. 'If this thing is real, why are we going there? According to legend, no one has escaped her.'

James smiled. 'And yet I am here.'

'She will kill us all,' Headron said.

James shook his head. 'Mary and Felix are human, and she would not hurt them. I have lost possession of my soul and therefore would be of no interest to her.'

'But we are Demons,' Celestine said. 'And we have our souls.'

'Two of you can conjoin with Felix and Mary,' he said.

'And the other?' Oxium said.

'They would have to take their chance.'

'Can they not conjoin with you?' Felix asked James.

'It would not fool her. As I've said, I am without a soul. The Demon conjoined with me would be recognised. It would not be good for either of us.'

'How did you escape?' Mary said.

'Perhaps,' James said, 'it would be better if I told you a little of the Demon folklore.' The others gathered around as he began.

'A long, long time ago, before even time existed, and after the great battle of the angelic realm, Lucifer, *He who reigns supreme*, ruled over the Demon realms. Some were displeased with the hierarchy and the truce with the Almighty that ensued. They attempted to supplant *He who reigns supreme* but were easily defeated. She, Remiel, Lucifer's sister, led the revolt and was exiled to the mountains, but not before cursing *He who reigns supreme*. Their brother, Azrael, had taken her side and been killed in the battle. She vowed revenge on *He who reigns supreme's* followers and warned him that any of his Demons who entered her land would be devoured and their souls claimed by her.'

'And the Demons she devours,' Headron said, 'what happens to them?'

'Their souls hang from a belt around her waist. Doomed to spend eternity in torment for their crimes against their own.'

'That doesn't answer how you escaped?' Oxium said.

James took in a deep breath. 'I shall start at the beginning. On one of my visits to Asmodeus's realm, a group of Demons searching for Janus spotted me. Braxas's brother recognised my face, and they gave chase. I managed to evade them for some time until I was weary. Finally, the Demons separated – to give them a better chance of catching me – and I thought I'd lost them. But as I sat by a stream to catch my breath, Braxas's brother emerged from the trees and launched an attack.' James took another deep breath, then continued. 'We battled until I gained the upper hand and held him at bay with his weapon. The two of us were exhausted, and I would have allowed him to live, but noise from the undergrowth – I thought it was another Demon – attracted my attention, and I was momentarily caught off guard. He took the opportunity to pull out a concealed knife and launch another attack, driving it deep into my thigh. I swung his weapon catching him in the neck and fatally wounding him.'

'You left him to die?' Oxium said.

James looked at Oxium. 'He was dead when I left. Despite being hampered by my injury, I managed to bury him. I dressed my wound as best as I could and staggered on. But, unfortunately, the injury festered, and I became delirious until I wandered aimlessly in a land I'd never encountered.'

Celestine leant in closer. 'Here?' she said.

'Not far from here,' James said. 'I stumbled and fell into unconsciousness.' James paused before continuing. 'I'm uncertain how long I was out, but a figure stood above me when I awoke. He called to others and, assisting me to my feet, they led me away from where I'd fallen.'

The assembled group glanced at each other before focusing their attention on James. 'Who were they?' Headron said.

'Janus. They took me to a cave where a female tended my wound and gave me food and water.'

'What were Janus doing in this land?' Celestine said.

'Remiel and her followers allow them to live here.'

'Why would this Janus save you when you are a Demon?' Headron said.

'I carried his mark.' James pulled open his shirt, revealing a small cross on his left shoulder. 'I have not always been a Demon.' The others stared at him. 'My journey to becoming a Demon happened a long time ago. I was once a follower of Christ.' James looked at the ground. 'I betrayed him, and my punishment was to be sent to the Demon realm.

However, Asmodeus heard about me and saved me from eternal torment by taking me as one of his own.'

'But you're a Demon now?' Felix said.

James sighed. 'Sort of. I am an amalgamation of a human and a Demon. I'd already lost my humanity, so my transformation to Demon was easy. However, over time I forgot that I'd ever been human. Only Asmodeus and a few others knew. Then he came to me.'

'Who?' Celestine said.

'Christ. I found myself inside the church in Nearhope, and he appeared. He said what I did to him was my destiny, and slowly I reclaimed my humanity over time.' He paused again. 'But not all of it. There is a constant battle inside me between my human and Demon self.'

'How come you have not told us this before?' Celestine said.

James smiled at her. 'I couldn't. The words were not mine to say. But, by taking me as one of him, Asmodeus left a stain on my soul. Now that I no longer possess it, the words come easily.'

'Who were you?' Mary said.

James looked at her. 'I think you know already.'

She glanced at Felix. 'From the bible?' she said.

James smiled again. 'The religious writings are not always accurate. But my human name was Judas Iscariot.'

'Well,' Headron said. 'Now we know.'

James looked past the rock and into Remiel's land. 'We should go now. If we survive this journey, our passage to Nearhope will be clear.'

Oxium scoffed. 'If we survive.'

'We must,' James said. 'Everything hinges on us surviving.'

Mary held out a hand to Celestine, who gratefully accepted it. Felix looked at Headron and Oxium. 'Who will it be?'

'We should draw lots,' Headron said, and Oxium nodded his agreement.

The conjoined Celestine and Mary trod past the stone and into the land with James by their side. Felix and Headron closely followed as Oxium, alone, padded behind them. His eyes darted left and right as they reached a slope. At the top, a dark cloud hung low in the sky, almost touching the hilltop. They carried on as the daytime brightness gave way to the darkness of night, and a bone-seeping chill pushed its way across the land.

To be continued …

NOTES ABOUT THE AUTHOR

John Regan was born in Middlesbrough in 1965. He currently lives with his wife in Redcar.

This is the author's sixth book and a follow-up to his third – **The Romanov Relic** – A comedy thriller set in and around the Teesside and North Yorkshire area.

Currently, his full-time job is as an underground telephone Engineer at Openreach. He has worked for both BT and Openreach for the past twenty years.

He's about to embark on his ninth novel and hopes to have it completed sometime next year.

August 2020.

The author would be happy to hear feedback about this book and be pleased to answer any readers' emails.

Email: johnregan1965@yahoo.co.uk.

OTHER BOOKS BY THIS AUTHOR

THE HANGING TREE – Even the darkest of secrets deserve an audience.

Sandra Stewart and her daughter are brutally murdered in 2006. Her husband disappeared on the night of Sandra's murder and is wanted in connection with their deaths.
Why has he returned eight years later? And why is he systematically slaughtering apparently unconnected people? Could it be that the original investigation was flawed?
Detective Inspector Peter Graveney is catapulted headlong into an almost unfathomable case. Thwarted at every turn by faceless individuals intent on keeping the truth buried.
Are there people close to the investigation, possibly within the force, determined to prevent him from finding out what really happened?
As he becomes more embroiled, he battles with his past as skeletons in his own closet rattle loudly. Tempted into an increasingly dangerous affair with his new Detective Sergeant, Stephanie Marne, Graveney finds that the people he can trust are rapidly diminishing.
But who's manipulating who? As he moves ever closer to the truth, he finds the person he holds most dearly threatened.
Graphically covering adult themes, 'The Hanging Tree' is a relentless edge-of-the-seat ride.
Exploring the darkest of secrets and the depths that people will plunge to keep those secrets hidden. Culminating in a horrific and visceral finale as Graveney relentlessly pursues it to the final conclusion.

'Even the darkest of secrets deserve an audience.'

PERSISTENCE OF VISION – Seeing is most definitely not believing!

Amorphous: Lindsey and Beth are separated by thirty years. Or so it seems. Their lives are about to collide, changing them both forever. Will a higher power intervene and re-write their past and future?

Legerdemain (Sleight of hand): Ten winners of a competition held by the handsome and charismatic billionaire, Christian Gainford, are invited to his remote house in the Scottish Highlands. But is he all he seems, and what does he have in store for them? There really is no such thing as a free lunch, as the ten are about to discover.

Broken: Sandi and Steve are thrown together. By accident or design? Steve is forced to fight not only for Sandi but for his own sanity. Can he trust his senses when everything he ever relied on appears suspect?

Insidious: Killers are copying the crimes of the dead psychopath, Devon Wicken. Will Jack be able to save his wife, Charlotte, from them? Or are they always one step ahead of Jack?

A series of short stories cleverly linked together in an original narrative with one common theme—Reality. But what's real and what isn't?

Exciting action mixed with humour and mystery will keep you guessing throughout. It will alter your perceptions forever.

Reality just got a little weirder! Fact or fiction…You decide!
Seeing is most definitely not believing!

THE ROMANOV RELIC – The Erimus Mysteries

Hilarious comedy thriller!

Private Detective, Bill Hockney, is murdered while searching for the fabled *Romanov Eagle*, cast for The Tsar. His three nephews inherit his business and find themselves not only attempting to discover its whereabouts but also who killed their uncle.

A side-splitting story full of northern humour, nefarious baddies, madcap characters, plot twists, real ale, multiple showers, out-of-control libido, bone-shaped chews and a dog called Baggage.

Can Sam, Phillip and Albert, assisted by Sam's best friend Tommo, outwit the long list of people intent on owning the statue? While simultaneously trying to keep a grip on their love lives?
Or will they be thwarted by the menagerie of increasingly desperate villains?

Solving crime has never been this funny!

THE SPACE BETWEEN OUR TEARS

If tears are the manifestation of our grief, what lies within the space between them?

After experiencing massive upheavals in her personal life, Emily Kirkby decides to write a novel. But as she continues writing, the border between her real life and fiction blurs.

Sometimes even the smallest of actions can have far-reaching and profound consequences. When a pebble is cast into the pool of life, there is no telling just how far the ripples will travel.

A rich and compelling story about love in all its many guises. A story about loss and bereavement. A story about guilt and redemption, regret and remorse. But mainly, chiefly, it's about love.

THE FALLING LEAVES

One of the most perplexing cases Inspector Peter Graveney has worked on. After twenty years, a car is dredged from the bottom of a deep pond. The grisly remains of two bodies locked inside. Why is Graveney certain that this discovery is linked to a dubious businessman and the murders of the men working for him? And why does a young woman's name keep surfacing within the investigation after her release from prison for murder?

As Graveney digs deeper, he finds more missing pieces to the puzzle and is faced with his biggest struggle yet – his own mind. As the body count escalates, Graveney battles with his own Demons and in his desperation to solve the case, he allows himself to be guided by an unlikely source from his past.

A gruesome and provocative sequel to the author's first novel, 'The Hanging Tree.' The Fallen Leaves takes the reader on a breathtaking journey, from the graphic opening chapter to the emotionally charged denouement.

If you bury the past, bury it deep.

THE LINDISFARNE LITURGY

The boys from The Erimus Detective Agency are back in the funniest adventure to date. The search for an ancient Celtic Cross – The Lindisfarne Liturgy – was saved from the marauding Vikings and missing for centuries. Could this cross have somehow ended up on Teesside? Sam, Phillip and Albert, assisted by their friends, attempt to discover its whereabouts while simultaneously trying to wrestle with the vicissitudes of everyday life.

A hilarious romp containing canine offspring and Pilates. Spikey auras and misaligned chakras. Orange shirts and cravats. Monogrammed flip flops, waders and fishing flies. Irate coppers, monocles and puppy pads.
A side-splitting adventure from beginning to end. Will the boys find the cross, or will they be thwarted by a collection of individuals intent on owning it?

Mystery and intrigue have never been more enjoyable

THE WHITBY WAILERS

An exciting new thriller from the author of The Hanging Tree and The Erimus Mysteries.
Six friends, each with a story of how they ended up in the seaside town, find that some secrets won't stay hidden forever.

Deep in the past lies a story of deceit and betrayal. A chance conversation opens up a can of worms which threatens to expose a long-buried crime and set in motion devastating consequences.

When history comes looking for payment, who will suffer the ultimate price?

A gripping read that will leave you hooked from the first page and carry you on a breath-taking journey to the end. Culminating in a nail-biting climax.

Printed in Poland
by Amazon Fulfillment
Poland Sp. z o.o., Wrocław

12616551R00150